PRAISE FOR THE AYALA STORME SERIES

STORM IN A TEACUP

Mears's world is creative and fast paced, her characters witty and engaging.

~ Ellie Ann, New York Times Bestselling Author ~

ANY PORT IN A STORM

My favorite new series…if I could give it more stars I would…highly recommended.

~ RabidReads.com ~

TAKEN BY STORM

The world, creatures, social, and magic systems Mears have created are very unique.

~ OneBookTwo ~

EYE OF THE STORM

Mears has a way of writing that really elicits the feels! The Storme Series has...amazing emotional depth; it's full of love and betrayal and family and sacrifice and triumph and despair.

~ OneBookTwo ~

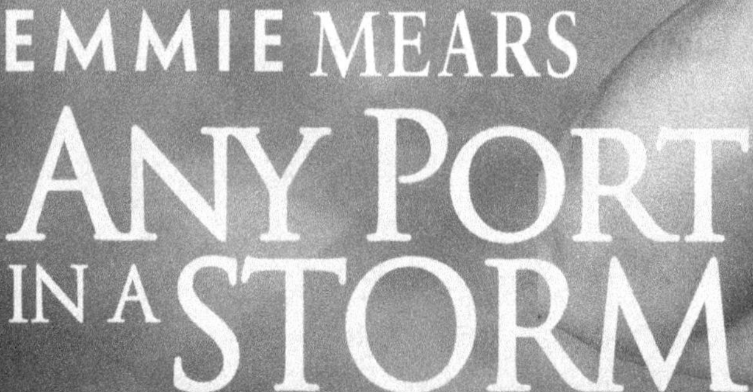

EMMIE MEARS

ANY PORT IN A STORM

AYALA STORME SERIES BOOK TWO

INDIGO
Livonia, Michigan

Cover design by Jessica Negrón

Any Port in a Storm

Published by Indigo
an imprint of BHC Press

Library of Congress Control Number:
2017936185

ISBN-13: 978-1-946006-88-2
ISBN-10: 1-946006-88-2

Visit the author at:
www.bhcpress.com

Also available in ebook & audio

ALSO BY

EMMIE MEARS

THE AYALA STORME SERIES

STORM IN A TEACUP

TAKEN BY STORM

EYE OF THE STORM

THE SHRIKE SERIES

THE MASKED SONGBIRD

RAMPANT

THE STONEBREAKER SERIES

HEARTHFIRE

STANDALONE NOVELS

A HALL OF KEYS AND NO DOORS

LOOK TO THE SUN

Available in trade paperback and ebook.
Select titles in audio.

For those who feel as though
there is no place for them,
For those who struggle to find purpose,
For those who lose their way,
May you find these things.
Always keep fighting.

AYALA STORME

BOOK TWO

ANY PORT IN A STORM

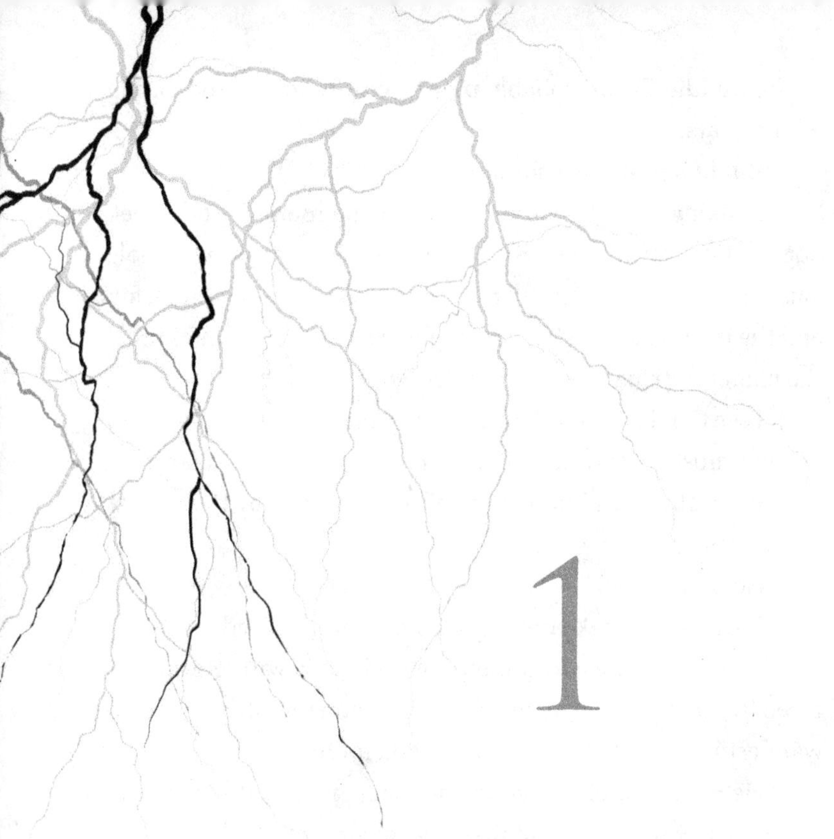

1

I DON'T KNOW IF I'll ever get used to butts all over my apartment.

They're all very nice butts—shades get the best of both hellkin and human gene pools—but that's sort of beside the point. There are butts all over my apartment yet again, and it's just another Thursday night of me having no idea where to look. The butts are bad enough, never mind the other side.

Even more annoying, it's a full moon tonight, and shades are too literal to even laugh at my jokes.

I miss Mason.

These days, I miss him the same way I miss Roger, the frog I stashed in my room for three weeks when I was a knobbly-kneed Mediator-in-Training. Roger got found out, then thrown out into the pond.

Is that awful? That I miss Mason like that? He wasn't a pet; he was a person. And he isn't really past tense at all—not in general. He's alive and well and somewhere covered in sand in the Middle East. Probably pissing off the locals and eating whole goats.

But he's past tense for me.

Looking—carefully—around my living room, my eyes seek out a tattooed shoulder. The tattoo itself is part of that whole "shades are literal" thing. It's Saturn's shoulder I'm searching for, and the ink is exactly what you might expect it to be, the rings of the planet rippling over his muscles when he moves.

I see Carrick, my roommate who I guess is pretty enough to kiss but mostly I want to kick. I see Rade and Hanu and Jax.

It's really sad I know most of these shades by their butts alone. Ugh.

No Saturn.

Frowning, I make my way through the crowded room.

Saturn said he had something to discuss with me, and at three in the morning on a work night, I don't really want to go wandering through Forest Hills to look for him.

He always sticks close to the place he first drew breath, Saturn. I saw him take that first gasp of air.

It's not as romantic as it sounds. That first breath came because his full-grown body exploded out of a woman half his size. Lena Saturn. Back when I thought she could be saved.

Jax touches my shoulder when I pass, his brown hand as callused as mine. I return the gesture. His mother was a man called Jack, and I think the *x* is Jax's way of making himself a possessive. I've yet to meet a shade whose name wasn't in some way traceable to his mother. The shades call all their hosts mothers, whether they were spawned from a male body or female body or anywhere in between. The ones who gave them life at the expense of their own.

Ain't nobody living through that.

Rade and Hanu touch my shoulders as I pass them as well, followed by the others, who stop what they're doing and reach out to me until my shoulders feel kissed by ghosts. I make sure to return each touch, meeting indigo eyes as I walk. My body never brushes their skin as I move among them. Only their fingertips make contact with me, and only mine make contact with them.

Shade culture. They're creatures of extreme violence. A gentle touch has evolved into how they say *you're safe*. That they expect the same in return from me, well. I don't know if I should be flattered or frightened.

Then again, I am also a creature of extreme violence.

Carrick finishes talking to Miles. Carrick is a white man with long hair the color of walnut wood. He's naked as a jaybird and looks even paler next to Miles, who is black with shoulder-length, delicate locks that swish when he moves. Where Carrick is a volcano with long periods of dormancy punctuated by explosions, Miles is steady like the Colorado River. Sometimes I think when the world ends, in the quiet moments when every other being is finally dead, Miles will be the only one left standing, a canyon carved away around him.

I walk among titans these days. Lordy. All except the damn one I want.

"Carrick, where's Saturn?"

I should expect Carrick's diffident little shrugs right now, but they still make my toes itch to make contact with his shins. Instead, I gesture at him, impatient.

"Is that a shrug you don't know, or a shrug you don't care, or a shrug you don't think it matters?"

"You know me too well," Carrick says. His English accent still sounds disingenuous coming from the mouth of a shade, its lilt ever-so-slightly off even to someone used to the speech of Londoners.

That's probably because his speech is held over from the seventeenth century, and no, I'm not used to that thought yet. He looks like he's in his mid-thirties. He only acts like he's twelve.

I wait, looking back and forth between Carrick and Miles. Miles, of course, is unmoved. I do see a crinkle at the corner of his eye where he's hidden away a smile, though, and the sight steels me to keep my deadpan look for Carrick. After a long pause with only the murmurs of the other shades and the clinking of Nana the Bunny in her cage in the background, Carrick scowls at me.

"He's at home."

Fuck. I just got home. I don't want to leave again.

I look at the clock over my TV. Three seventeen. If I leave now, I might catch Saturn in time to get a whopping five hours of sleep. I make a pit stop to give Nana's head a scratch and feed her a carrot, her rose-dusty fur as soft as down. When I make my way back through my living room, Hanu and Jax give me a nod goodbye. Miles watches me with indigo eyes that almost glow. His gaze falls on my shoulder, then flickers to the back of Carrick's head. It's not until I'm out the door that I understand why.

Carrick's the only one in that room who sleeps under that roof, and he's the only one who doesn't touch my shoulder in greeting.

FOREST HILLS ALWAYS MAKES me jumpy. I blame it on the fact that I took down two slummoths and a jeeling here a few months ago. By "took down," I mean I limped away from that fight with a palm sliced almost clean through, a festering, demon-poisoned bite on my shoulder, pulled muscles, and a heart that only just was still beating on the right side of my ribcage.

You know.

Memories.

By now, I know where to look for Saturn, and I tread carefully through the underbrush, the sycamores and oaks forming a cathedral in the night above, stars shining like stained glass. More important than the scenery though is the soundtrack. Even in early autumn, the crickets play their little songs, their rhythms syncopated and bright in the darkness.

Their sound is safety.

Norms ain't the only ones who hate hellkin—and fear them.

Saturn sleeps in the trees. He doesn't seem to mind gnarly bark digging into his nether bits, so I never pester him about it. Most of the other shades have some sort of shelter, but he likes it here. There's a tall oak across the clearing he tends to occupy, but even though it's dark and the yellow-orange leaves—dark grey in the night—obscure the trunk enough to hide him, the pit in my gut says he's not there.

The night is muggy and clammy in the way only southern nights can be, and the prickle that dances along the skin of my forearms has less to do with that and more to do with the way the crickets have quieted.

It's not that they've stopped—it's like someone's been gradually turning the volume knob downward until I'm not sure if it's me or my surroundings that's changed.

Except I know better.

My shoulder gives a twitch, as if it can remember that demon's teeth too well.

Slowly, I unsheathe my swords. One long and curved like Saturn's rings, one short and stabby.

I listen to the now-distant hum of the crickets, the rustle of the trees. A good stealthy person learns to move with the wind, to let the earth disguise her footsteps.

Demons, thankfully, get an F in stealth.

So why am I now surrounded by silence?

It crawls onward through the night, creeping outward, dulling my senses.

A crash of branches would be welcome.

Slowly, I swivel, turning on a full 360 degrees until I'm sure even the dim stars and sliver of setting moon have shown that I'm alone in the clearing.

A single harkast demon scampers out of a bush. Or rather, scampers about well as anything with legs that short can. Stumpy is the best word to describe these things. My blades stop the hellkin beastie before it takes three steps into the clearing, and then it's dead. A moment later, I hear a chirp of a cricket. No more demons, so why is my spider-sense still going off?

The wind shifts, and I smell them coming before I hear them.

The scent is hot and smells slightly of ash and metal and life. Shade blood. A lot of it.

I've been around them long enough, fought beside them enough to recognize it.

A moment later I hear the crash of bushes and a yell, followed by a gurgle.

I keep my sword points low, hoping the blood's not Saturn's and that the voices are friendly. My hope is misplaced. Half of it, anyway.

"Put him there!" an unfamiliar, urgent voice barks.

Then I see them, rounding Saturn's large oak.

It is Saturn. And the blood is definitely his. Mira Gonzales, another Mediator and the closest thing to a friend of mine, helps him lay back against the trunk of the tree. I don't recognize the morph with them. She moves with sharp, precise competence, pressing her hand against the side of Saturn's neck, which is the source of the blood.

My feet start moving without me, lurching me forward over the mulch-covered ground. The morph lets out a yell of alarm, but Mira sees me and waves the other woman off.

"Wane, chill. It's Ayala."

That's all Wane seems to need, because her attention snaps back to Saturn so fully that it seems she's forgotten my existence. I drop to my knees at Saturn's feet, and I finally get a good look at him in the dim clearing.

Someone sliced through almost two inches of his neck. His left side is gushing blood. It pulses out between Wane's fingers like oozing lava.

"What happened?" I've seen a lot of shit, but this makes me feel like someone's running their fingertips along the inside of my stomach lining.

Mira's violet eyes are black in the night, her brown skin turned blue grey, her hair like onyx. It's then I see the way Saturn's clutching her hand and the quick, shallow rise and fall of his chest.

His eyes are closed, but his lips form my name.

I scoot up beside Mira, feel the coolness of her presence compared with the heat of Saturn's fear. He burns like a star instead of a planet.

"He got ambushed. He was on his way home. We were supposed to meet him here and heard the fight." Mira's voice is dispassionate, but her fingers clasping Saturn's aren't.

"Did you see who did this?" I ask.

"Keen blade to the carotid. Would have finished the job if he hadn't gotten away long enough to make our presence scare them off. Whoever did this cared more about not being seen than they did about finishing the job." Wane pipes up, her voice brittle.

"Motherfuckers." Mira says.

I'm about to say something, but the morph keeps going, ignoring Mira's expletive.

"He'll live," she says. "I can feel him healing. I'm trying to help him along."

I stretch out my hand and touch it to Saturn's shoulder. His throat convulses.

Help him along. I forget that morphs can transfer energy. By nature their animal transformations are fueled by some sort of primal woo-woo creation magic—they can manipulate that when they see fit. A lot of them are in health care. From Wane's clinical choice of words, I think she probably is too.

My body relaxes a bit at her prognosis, exhales breath it had locked in my lungs.

"He said he had something to tell me," I say.

Mira shrugs. "Whatever it is, it'll have to wait."

She's not wrong about that. Saturn's not able to say anything right now.

The three of us hold watch over Saturn as the sky slowly lightens with the coming dawn. Finally, the blood flow from his neck slows to nothing, and he sleeps between us, blood drying on his naked form.

BY NINE IN THE morning, Saturn is healed enough to move him to Mira's, and I help Wane and her get him to her car and load him in, leaning the passenger seat back as far as it'll go. She covers her seats like a good little Mediator, but getting him in the car leaves crackling flakes of his dried blood dusting onto her floor mats, the seat backs, and the center console anyway.

I belt him in while Wane climbs into the back seat. I finally get a good look at her. She's of medium height and wiry, with short hair that's the color of old quarters. Her face is unlined, with a strong jaw and light brown skin. Her eyes are grey, and after being surrounded by shades and Mediators for months, the sight is welcome and a little unnerving, a reminder of the norm world I've lost track of. The reminder is like a drop of cold water falling out of the air onto my scalp. I'll have to ask Mira about this morph later.

Mira herself meets my gaze, violet to violet. Her face is unreadable for a long moment, then she gives me a cheeky smile.

"I'll take care of the invalid. Come over after work." She cranks up the radio—old school Bonnie Raitt—and waves an impatient hand at me to close the door. Before I do, Saturn reaches out and touches my shoulder with his fingertips, and for the tiniest moment, his indigo eyes flutter open and meet mine.

They drive away, and a wave of relief crests in my middle to know he'll be okay and that he's in good hands. Too much death and loss this year already. I can't bring myself to think about what I'd do if I lost him too.

I hike slowly back to my car, taking a detour to where Mira and Wane found Saturn.

It's not hard to find—his blood is still red and heavy, splashed on the trunk of a cottonwood.

After a few moments of finding exactly nothing helpful, I leave.

Whatever Saturn wanted to tell me, I have a feeling I'm not going to like it.

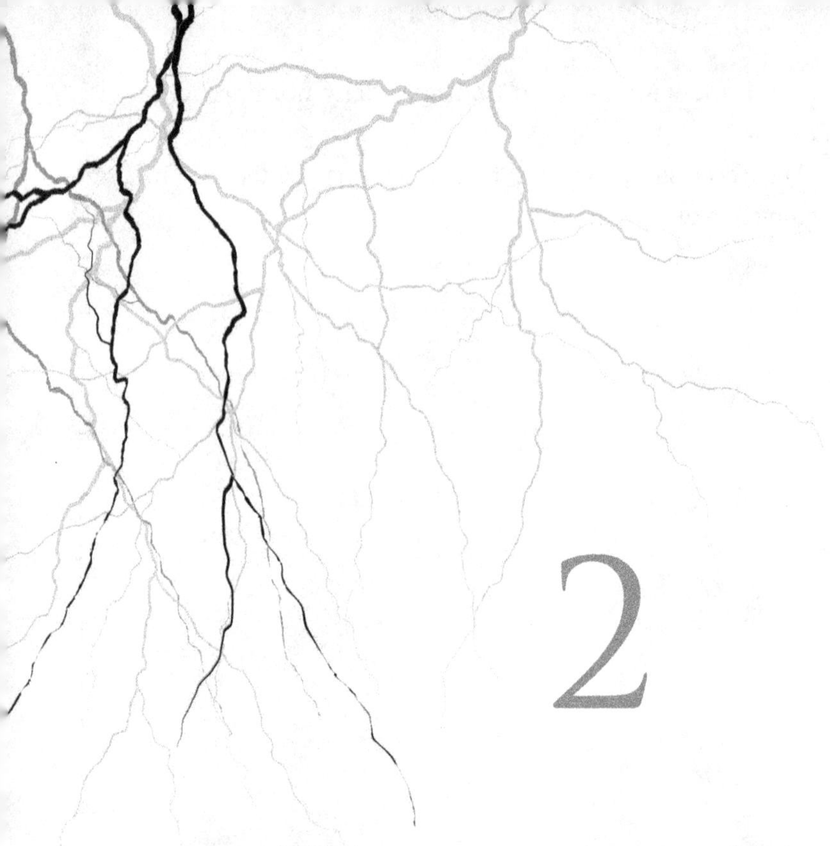

2

CARRICK'S DOOR IS CLOSED when I get home, and I'm glad for that. In my room, Nana Bunny greets me with a twitchy-nosed squeak, and I change her water and give her some hay before getting in the shower.

Flakes of Saturn's blood dissolve into the stream of water.

The hot water doesn't wash away my feeling of unease.

Three hours later, I'm bicep-deep in a pile of press releases for a new mattress store opening up in Franklin. I'm so busy compiling testimonies and blurbs that I miss my boss standing in the threshold to my office until she coughs loudly for what can't be the first time.

She's in her signature eggplant suit, and she's started dyeing her hair to cover the greys.

They started taking over right around the time she learned that the whole Mediator-killing-hellkin thing isn't as neat and tidy as it sounds.

"Sorry, Laura," I say. "I didn't see you there.

She watches me silently for a moment, her eyes the only brightness on her face.

"Have you ever thought of working for the Summit?" she asks. "I mean, do you really like putting out PR fires and puttering with press releases?"

To disguise the surprise I feel at her question, I save the layout I'm working on, push my mouse aside, and lean back in my chair. Here in my office, my painstakingly painted and designed office with its cream walls and dark blue accents, I wonder if all this time she's assumed I was just playing house.

"Well, the Summit doesn't pay for shit," I say lightly. It's true, but it's not my only reason. When Laura doesn't budge, I drum my fingers on the arm of my chair. "I like PR. I like doing something all week that doesn't involve getting blood off leather and I like not coming home smelling like rusty metal and sulfur. I like being able to solve problems with words during the day because at night, the answer's always the sharp edge of a blade."

I don't know why I tell her all that. I think of just such a clean edged blade biting into Saturn's neck, and of what might have happened if a Mediator and a morph hadn't shown up in time to stop the sword's wielder from putting it all the way through the other side.

I swallow, feeling sick.

Laura seems to sense it, because she takes three steps into my office and sits across from me.

"Did something happen?"

There's something in me that wants to just tell her about Saturn. She took it awfully well when a few months ago she found out I was being targeted by hellkin and Mediators both for working with shades.

But I don't tell her. Instead, I just nod.

There's a long pause.

"I've been thinking of making you a partner," she says finally.

What?

I stare at her blankly. Six months ago she hated my guts. Three months ago, I think she started to fear me. Now she wants me to have a stake in her business?

"I'm bringing it up because I want to know your thoughts on it," Laura goes on. "You're the reason we've been as successful as we have. I couldn't have grown this business this way without someone competent whose work I don't have to question or worry about. Meredith and Leeloo—" they're the two witches who work here too "— are great, but they're content with punching a clock, and your work shows you take pride in it."

It's one of the longest speeches I've ever heard her make, and in spite of the business with the shades and the heavy cloud of worry about Saturn, her words fill me with a bubbly sense of excitement.

The corners of my lips tug back with a twitch, a smile trying to escape. I don't know why I'm trying to suppress it. I let it curve into a grin. "Really?"

Mouth open, her surprised bemusement is contained in a pause and a blink. Then she smiles back at me. "Really."

NIGHT FINDS ME IN Belle Meade, trying to keep my mind on keeping the pointy ends of my swords ready to stick in a demon. My mind still flits around the prospect of being a partner at work.

I'm not usually one to flit in any fashion.

Being a Mediator is thankless work. Most norms greet us with fuzzy respect and apprehension. Their expressions when they see my marked eyes varies between awe and "I'm about to shit myself." If we get accolades, they come from within, from the Summit.

I have a one of those, for murdering a bunch of shades. The Mediators gave me the Silver Scale for all the blood on my hands.

Ain't that how it goes?

That was the night I met Mason. If ever there was a single day I could point to and say it forked my road good and proper, it's that one.

The norms mostly forget. And I was born into this. It was in me no matter what. Whatever I do between eleven and seven for pay is one thing. What I do from sundown until the wee hours, now, it may not put money in the bank, but it lessens the heavy weight on my chest. I do that because I have to, and because I was born to it. That's a given.

But making partner?

I earned that.

A pink glow ahead snaps me out of it.

Hellkin don't give a rat's hairy balls about what I earned. Their currency is death and teeth in the night, and I pay them back with cold steel.

I hope to all six and a half hells that this son-bitch jeeling is alone.

The pinkish light grows more pronounced as I approach, and I hear a sucking crunch.

Great. It's eating.

After coming up on a shade munching on a frat boy a few months back, a jeeling chewing on a squirrel isn't going to win any gross-out competitions, but that doesn't mean I can't feel bad for the squirrel.

Turns out, it's a cat.

From five feet away I can see the cat's tail dangling from between the jeeling's glowing fingers, and that just pisses me off. Poor kitty. I wish people would keep their critters indoors. Jeelings are big, strong, and mean as the hells they come from, but they get really into their food.

This one doesn't see me coming.

I take it off guard, hamstringing it with a flick of my sword.

The demon drops the cat and screams a grating roar into the woods, stumbling to the side. A dog starts barking in the distance, but I ignore it, darting back a couple yards until I can see what this nasty glow-worm-from-hell is going to do.

I stand on the balls of my feet, knees just bent, swords held like extensions of my arms. It's going to attack.

I wait.

Seconds tick by, and the jeeling rights itself, turning toward me.

Here it comes. I brace myself.

The jeeling runs in the other direction.

Well, sort of runs.

Its bum leg drags, but it still manages a steady clip of speed, high-tailing it away from me.

For a moment, I freeze, wondering if somehow my reputation has started inspiring fear in demonkind. Am I the thing the demon parental units warn their little spawn about? The thought is ridiculous, and a breeze from the direction the jeeling fled in knocks the thought right out of me. It also brings the smell of eau de dead cat to my nostrils.

I take off running after the jeeling. Its pink glow can't be difficult to follow at night, but even with its injury, it's fast, and after a couple hundred yards I feel like I'm chasing fog.

After a couple hundred more, I realize I lost the damn thing.

I retrace my steps, wondering if it went back for the cat, but it's not there.

More importantly, at the site of the hellkin's gruesome dinner, crickets start to chirp.

What in the hells is happening?

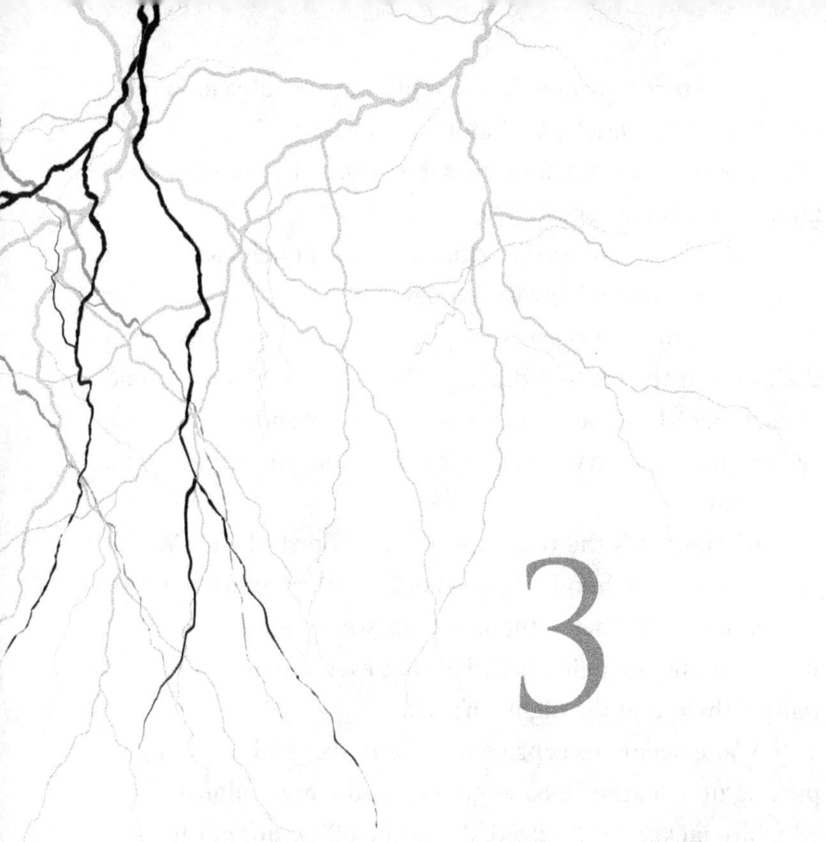

3

BELLE MEADE IS EERILY quiet after my non-encounter with the jeeling, so I go to Mira's. It's not even midnight when I arrive, and the early hour feels strange. Mira's house is a compact ranch, and she's already decorated the porch with orange and red lights for Samhain. I didn't know she celebrated that. I usually leave it to the witches, except for the annual Mediator Samhain gala, which is pretty much just an excuse for all of us to get drunk and go kill shit.

Wane meets me at the door in scrubs with sushi rolls on them, confirming my earlier suspicion. She sticks out her hand as I shut the front door of Mira's house. I grasp Wane's hand and shake. Her grip is oddly light for the firm strength in her hands.

"Wane Trujillo," she says.

"Ayala Storme."

"I know."

I nod at her scrubs. "Night shift?"

She returns my nod. "I'm an OB." She hesitates for a minute, then, "I delivered a Mediator baby yesterday."

The announcement catches me by surprise, and my heart gives a ribbit in my chest. "Oh?"

The syllable comes out with admirable nonchalance, but I hate the reminder of how we happen.

Mediators are born to happy, expectant parents. Open their eyes. If they're that dark, grayish baby blue? You're good to go. Violet? Congrats. You just spent nine months incubating and caring for and trying to name a baby you'll never see again. Mazel Tov.

Maybe that's the real reason norms don't like us. We remind them of a hundred thousand hijacked maybe-babies. We remind them that without hellkin, we could come into the world like the bouncing baby bundles everyone hopes for. We remind them that the night isn't safe.

Wane seems to sense she hit a nerve, and she coughs, picking up a leather messenger bag and a meticulously folded white jacket. "Tell Mira I should be off by noon. I'll bring by lunch."

"Are they in her room?"

"Guest room. Second door on the right."

Wane leaves, and I take off my shoes, placing them on a mat next to Mira's combat boots, wondering how an OB-GYN ended up in the middle of Forest Hills with a Mediator, saving a shade's life. I unbuckle my scabbard belts and lay them on the coffee table. Mira's home is all hardwoods and ocher walls. Small shelves make little stair-steps against the ocher paint, holding thick-based candles that give off a smell of vanilla and spice.

I make my way down the hall, my feet making the floorboards creak. Lining the corridor are framed pictures Tenochtitlan. Some are pictures of the pyramid, the Aztec ruins, nestled by lush green hills. Others depict the city as it might once have been when it was a city on a lake, thriving and organized, ringed in the deep blue of Texcoco's waters. An entire civilization there in a frame.

We Mediators all have our places we'll never visit.

I find the guest room and knock.

"Come in," Mira's voice says.

Saturn's sleeping, it seems. They got the blood cleaned off him, and he's covered to the ribcage with a white sheet. That's it—even with the hum of the air conditioner, shades run hot.

Mira stretches, twisting her back left and right. I hear a crack that sounds too loud in the quiet room. Her black angular bob shows the first hints of grease, and she has it tucked behind her ears. It makes her look weirdly vulnerable.

"Wane said she'd be back at noon tomorrow with lunch," I say, perching on the end of the bed. "How is he?"

"Better. He was able to rasp a little when he woke up." Anger lights Mira's features like a current traveling the length of a live wire. "You know what this looks like, right?"

I nod. I've been purposely avoiding the thoughts, but they're there. Keen blade to the neck screams Mediator. And whoever it was really didn't want to get caught. Which means they know of Saturn's connection to me and either know me personally or are just scared shitless of my reputation.

I mean, I'll take it. But I don't like the thought that someone whose face I've seen is trying to kill my people.

"Any ideas who?" I ask.

"No. Could have been any of those fuckers at the Summit."

I know which fuckers she means. Since what happened a few months ago, there's been some...unrest in the Summit. Even though Alamea, resident head honcho, just got a medal for having the lowest norm mortality rate in all the US Mediator territories, there are some who think all shades are plain evil. The Summit has hairline cracks through its people, and that makes me almost as nervous as what happened to Saturn.

"Do you think it could have been Ben?" Mira says after a beat.

“If it was, I’ll personally put him in bite sized chunks and feed him to Saturn.”

If my vehemence surprises Mira, she doesn’t let on. The mere mention of Ben Wheedle makes me want to shred Mira’s hardwood floors with my fingernails. A low growl escapes my throat, and I swallow it.

We’re both silent for a moment, and I watch the quiet rise and fall of Saturn’s chest.

“How was hunting tonight?” Mira asks.

I consider blowing off her question, but sitting here with her is a reminder that she is one of the only Mediators who took a stand when shit hit the demon horde a few months ago, and if I can trust any of these violet-eyed freaks, it’s her.

I tell her about the jeeling and the cat and what happened.

“It ran away?” A lock of black hair falls over her face, and she absently pushes it back. She still has blood under her fingernails, crescents of rusty color.

“Turned tail and fled.”

We’re silent again.

“Shit, Ayala. Between that and Saturn, I don’t like this. What’s changed?”

I shrug automatically, then freeze.

I know what’s changed. Same thing I’ve been dealing with since summer. This all started with the shades. We’re all adapting to this new dynamic. Humans, Mediators, witches, morphs, psychics—we all coexisted just fine, and the Mediators took care of the hell-front. Then shades happened, and no one knows what the fuck to do with them. I didn’t know what the fuck to do with them. Until Mason.

Looking at Saturn’s still form, that familiar pang twinges at my heart again.

Why do I get the feeling I’m the one who’s going to have to figure this all out?

SATURN DOESN'T WAKE UP while I'm there. As much as I will him to open his eyes and talk to me, his body must be exhausted from healing an arterial death-wound, because at three in the morning, Mira and I have covered all the finer points of our favorite Arnold Schwarzenegger movies and Saturn hasn't woken up to tell us to shut up.

I make my way home and walk through the door to find Carrick sprawled out on my sofa.

He's wearing shorts—a prerequisite of living with me—and he gives me a nod of acknowledgement.

His auburn hair is in a messy bun at the back of his head. He's taken to stealing my hair ties. He's as bad as a cat.

When I enter the living room after hanging my swords on the hook in my foyer, he moves his leg aside and pats the sofa next to him. I sit, leaning back. The day feels as though it was fifty hours long, and even though four in the morning is still pretty early for me, I feel heavy with exhaustion, my eyes sandy and my head buzzing and dizzy.

"How was your day?" he asks. His voice is deep and rich, like Bela Lugosi as Dracula. Sometimes I think Carrick wishes vampires were real so he could pretend to be one. He's the type I could imagine swishing around and sweeping swoon-prone young women into a world of lust and blood.

Have I mentioned how sexy that's not? I've been around things that look at me as lunch. No, thank you.

"My day was long," I say.

I tell him what happened to Saturn, and his laconic slouch perks up into an attentive, upright position on the couch.

"But he'll live?" To his credit, Carrick manages to sound like he cares. He and Saturn have a weird relationship. It probably has to do with the fact that Carrick just up and decided to live with me, and Saturn thinks I'm going to sleep with Carrick or something.

Again, I say no, thank you.

"He'll live. Won't be winning any reality show singing competitions any time soon most likely, but he'll live."

My apartment feels strangely chill and empty. The air conditioning is still on, but the outside air is cooler with the onset of autumn, and I can't shake the hollow feeling of my home.

Instead of dwelling on it, I change the subject.

"Have you heard from Gregor?" I ask.

Carrick nods at that. "He would like us to take them out hunting tomorrow night."

I rub my palm over my face, which carries a sheen of end-of-day grease. We've been running little hunting expeditions with the shades for a while now, taking them out to take out hellkin and learn how they move together to hone their training. Nothing new there.

It's been almost three months since Carrick moved in here, and I still don't know what to do with him. "Do you really think all this will help?" I ask.

"Help what?"

I gesture toward my balcony, feeling a pang again at the memory of how Mason used to sit out there, dangling his legs over the edge from seven stories up. "Help them. The shades. Help the Mediators or the norms or whatever."

Instead of a flippant dismissal, Carrick turns my words over in his head. I can see him considering and wonder if he really feels connected to these Tennessean shades at all. He's the only one left of his batch of shades from four hundred years ago, and while the shades we work with have formed their own circles and groups, Carrick seems like he's just punching the clock most of the time.

"I think having purpose is helpful," he says finally.

"For the shades?"

"For everyone. You have it, with the Mediators. Gregor has it."

"Fair enough."

I notice he leaves himself off that list, but I don't push.

I even think I agree with him. The shades we work with seem to want to work with us. There's a nebulous sort of relief I see in Miles and Rade and Jax and Hanu and all the others, that whatever it is we're doing is somehow legitimizing their existence so the Mediators won't just kill them.

That's a depressing thought.

I hear Nana Bunny in my room, and I get up to let her out. The leather sofa creaks under my movement. After a moment, Carrick gets up too.

Nana hops out of her corral and immediately hurries into the living room to check out the smells, ears twitching. If the scent of so many predators bothers her, she doesn't let on, only makes a frenzied circuit of the living room before coming to rest by my feet where I stand in the doorway to my room. I take a knee to scratch between her felty ears, glad for her little bunny existence.

Standing back up takes more effort than I like, and I give Carrick a wave. "Tomorrow night. Are they coming here, or are we meeting them somewhere?"

"Gregor said to meet at the Opry at midnight." Whenever Carrick says *Opry*, he gives it an ironic sort of eye roll as if it lowers his social class to even say the word.

I ignore his classier-than-thou attitude and nod. The Opry may smell like the inner sanctum of a fart from all the hot springs that have burbled up around it, but it's as good a place as any to see how the shades are doing without training wheels.

Tomorrow I plan to spend the day with a Die Hard marathon and bunny snuggles, and then I'll take a bunch of half-demons to kill full demons around a good ole country music landmark.

My life is weird.

4

I'LL NEVER GET USED to having shades simply materialize around me.

Okay, so it's not like they poof out of thin air or anything, but they move silently on their bare feet, and even the ones who are so pale their skin is incandescent somehow manage to blend into the night as well as the shades whose skin is dark.

We have seventeen of them working with us, and they surround us with Gregor, Carrick and I at the center. The sulfur smell of the Opry's hot springs isn't as bad as it is in the height of summer, but I still have to fight the urge to wrinkle my nose. Clouds hang heavy over the city, and autumn has taken to a sharp bite, the first real snap in the air I've felt this year.

Usually there are a whole gaggle of snorbits here. A snorbit is what you'd get if you bred Popeye with Andre the Giant. Seven feet tall, forearms like they do nothing but pound spinach, and they lack any endearing qualities whatsoever. They also love sulfur. They're usually a sure thing up around these parts in the middle of the night, and after the Opry burned down and the hot springs bubbled up, there's usually not a norm in Nashville who'd risk their existence to be here. Especially since the mall flooded a couple years back and never reopened. Back when it was open, the occasional skittles-blasted shopper or deeply unintelligent adolescent would be found by Mediators after they ventured too close. Nowadays, the snorbits have their run of the place.

Though with seventeen shades—eighteen counting Carrick—and two Mediators, I'm not entirely surprised that we don't have company. Even a pair of seven-foot-tall monsters will avoid a crowd like us.

Gregor is built like a stump and has a face like a monster truck himself. He's not particularly fast, but he's surprisingly agile, and he's one of the Summit leaders here in Nashville. He's also the reason I live with Carrick and deal with naked butts in my apartment on a weekly basis. This whole "train the shades into a force for good" thing was his plan.

In fact, it's mostly his fault that I'm in this mess in general. He's the one who sicced me on the mystery that turned into the shades in the first place.

Right now, I'm the last thing on his mind. Gregor surveys the parking lot, pacing back and forth. His feet trample a few sprigs of weeds growing up through the asphalt.

"I want to split up," he says. "One group with Carrick to skirt the mall, one with me to circle around the Opryland, and Ayala, you head straight to the east hot springs. If nothing's there, come back around the television joint and meet us by Dave and Busted's."

Since the mall got waterlogged, that's what everyone calls the old arcade.

Gregor barks out a few names and takes off to the north, where the Opryland sprawls out in a decayed shell of its former glory. Carrick and his group disappear to the southwest, and I'm left with Miles and Jax and three other shades. Miles nods toward the sound of traffic on Briley Parkway, and we set off to the east.

They had to build a heavy wall on the west side of the parkway because of the demon activity around the Opry. It didn't used to be this bad, but it's the only way I've known it. A little worm of thought wriggles into me as we walk, and I think about Mississippi and Alabama to the south. Mississippi is one big Hellkin Hot Springs, and Alabama's not much better. No one lives down there now. Just the demons. It makes me wonder how much Nashville has changed and if we're really keeping things at bay—or if we just think we are. Do the Mediators in Alabama know how bad they've got it? We can't travel to each other's territories, so I guess there's no real way to know. The Summit leaders talk to each other in video calls and online hangouts, but for the rest of us, it's just a guessing game.

The stench of the hot springs grows stronger as we walk, and the burr of traffic continues like a muted buzz. Jax falls into step beside me. His dark hair is a mass of curls atop his head, and though he says nothing, he turns to give me a shy smile.

Shyness was never something I expected from shades.

One of the others—Bri, I think his name is—joins us on my other side. He's white, one of those shades almost as pale as me, and his hair is that downy light blond that most kids lose as they get older. Miles and the others bring up the rear, and together we make our way to the east toward the smell of the springs.

Snorbits are large and seldom quiet, and though as we get closer to the hot springs I hear the blubbing of the bog-like spring, I don't hear the usual scuffles and mucky splashes that would indicate hellkin presence. I keep my eyes open for any sign of other demons—a couple jeelings could be a problem even with six of us. No matter how competent they are barehanded, I would feel more comfortable if the shades were open to carrying some sort of weapon. None of them will, though.

They're pretty much walking weapons as is, but going into battle with hellkin butt nekkid doesn't strike me as the wisest course of action. If they want to risk taking a rakath's projectile spines to the junkular region, I suppose that's their prerogative.

The springs appear, fetid and as appealing as week old roadkill in July. A few scraggly brown grasses grow around them, and the springs are lit peripherally by the lights on Briley Parkway that only just crest the wall that keeps cars safe from rampaging snorbits.

Occasional quiet nights used to bring me relief. Not to encounter anything too big for me to handle used to be something to celebrate with a nice glass of sake when I returned home, but this week the silence of the usually-teeming demonic presence in my city unnerves me more than if we had walked up here to find a horde.

A sudden squelch in the hot bubbling ooze of the spring makes me spin, unsheathing my swords with a muttered, "Oh, thank gods."

The snorbit rushes me like a gorilla, giant arms swinging pendulums, and I sprint toward it, the shades springing into action with me. They're faster than I, but they follow my lead, and I smell a hot rush of rotten breath along with a spray of spittle just before my swords make contact. I stab left with my short sword while swinging my saber in an arc that slices through most of the snorbit's left arm, lodging in the beast's humerus. The snorbit screams, sending another spray of spit at me. I throw myself to the side, yanking my sword from the snorbit's arm.

Its massive left appendage hangs at its side, and the right one is bleeding from where I stabbed it. Miles hits the snorbit from the side, and Jax and Beex come at it from the other. I don't see the other two shades until Miles grabs hold of the snorbit's arm and jerks. The arm detaches and lands in the spring, splashing Miles and the remaining, pissed off chunk of snorbit with rotten egg water and mud.

The other two shades seem to fall from the sky.

It takes me a second to realize they must have scaled the breakwall, and their combined weight sends the snorbit to the asphalt.

Its end comes fast. Beex and Jax take hold of its ankles, and one of the others snaps the snorbit's neck. After a moment, he thoughtfully rips off the demon's head.

I don't know what else to do, so I clean my swords and resheath them. Nothing else moves. I'll have to call for a body pickup later, but for now, I think we've found all we're going to find here.

THE SMELL ABATES AS we circle around a closed down media store, though probably not as much as I think it does. The quietness of the night unsettles me. Snorbits are almost always in pairs.

If it were just one thing, light patrols or a fleeing jeeling or a lone snorbit at one of their big watering holes—that would be okay. But all of it together makes me nervous, like I'm wearing a barbed wire thong and trying to walk.

It's almost a relief to hear screaming.

The shades and I take off toward the source of it, a patch of land between the Opry and the Opryland. The night is moonless dark, but I see well enough.

Gregor's group found the snorbit's buddies.

Eight of them.

I put two fingers in my mouth and whistle as loudly as I can. If Carrick can hear me, he'll come running. As is, thirteen of us against eight snorbits. My heart gives a thud of fear. I tighten my grip on my sword hilts, not wanting to think about what we'd have found if we'd been later.

I take off at a run, my footsteps lost in the sound of the snorbits' guttural growls and the barked snarls of the shades.

The hellkin don't really see us coming, and I stab one snorbit through the base of its spine, dropping it to the ground. Rade, the shade who'd been fighting it, gives me a grateful look and falls upon the demon, snapping its neck and crushing its skull with two quick stomps.

A screech sounds from behind me, and I spin just in time to see a trio of rakaths barreling toward me, all spines and scrabbly claws.

Fuck me.

I hear a bellow of another snorbit going down, but these rakaths will turn us all into pincushions if I don't stop them.

One of the rakaths is closer than the others, close enough now that I can see its small, slimy mouth of razor sharp teeth. The spines along its shoulders and back spring to attention, and it starts to curl forward.

Hells.

I leap forward, feinting left in a desperate attempt to keep it from balling up. My erratic movement catches it off guard just enough, and I bury my short sword in its neck, the curved saber in my right hand coming down hard to sever the rakath's clavicle. The bone snaps with a sharp sound like brittle metal, and the ridge of spines along its shoulders goes slack.

I pull back and lob off its head.

Fire explodes at the side of my neck. "Fuck!"

One movement tells me I missed one of the remaining two rakaths circling around me. It's like a sea urchin, balled up and ready to launch more spines my way. The third is busy flinging its quills at shades.

The spines in my neck—at the base of my shoulder—feel like arrows more than quills. I scream as loud as I want to, and it helps steel me enough to move. I drop my short sword and pull a knife from my belt. The nearest rakath is mostly balled up, but I've taken on these inside out knife blocks before.

I drop my other blade and throw the knife with my right hand as hard as I can.

For a moment, I think I've missed, but then the demon-ball flops over and uncurls, dead. I crouch to retrieve my swords and run at the rakath, severing its clavicle as well. If I don't, the body pickup will get a face full of spines. They reflexively spike people even in death.

The fight still rages, and I can see five snorbits still kicking. Or rather, swinging about with their enormous forearms. Sometime during my fight with the rakaths, a few slummoths arrived. And a frahlig? This far from the river?

The slummoths are dying quickly, and arcs of their slime fly through the air.

Where the fuck is Carrick?

It's as if he heard me. He descends on the battle with five shades.

I've never been happier to see his ass pointed in my direction.

The third rakath is still alive, but two shades fall on it and somehow one of them puts a fist through its collarbone. My shoulder feels like I've taken a cheese grater to it, but this fight ain't over, and I ain't stopping till we've done Loretta Lynn proud in her Opry's back yard.

I favor my right arm, keeping low and quiet. I meet Miles' eyes, and he kicks a slummoth toward me, his foot making a squelchy splat in the demon's mucus.

One heavy swipe of my blade, and the slummoth's head is on the ground. I take a step and stumble, turning to the left in time to see a snorbit's Popeye arms close around Carrick's neck, ten yards away from me.

My vision blurs, but I lurch forward, and somehow my windmilling legs propel me into a sprint. Even with the rakath venom surging through my veins, my aim doesn't suck.

My saber slips right under the snorbit's armpit, an inch from Carrick's carotid.

I fling my sword upward with as much force as I can muster. It doesn't take the arm off, but close. Carrick bursts out of the snorbit's grip like a super-powered chick from its eggshell. He snatches my short sword from my dangling left hand and stabs the demon through the chest. My knees tremble, but I take a step forward and jam my saber point-first under the demon's chin.

At seven feet tall with arms like tree trunks, I don't want this ox falling on my head. I throw my weight to the side, and it feels like I leave my head behind. My stomach clenches, turns, and bile rises in my throat.

The snorbit tumbles to the ground with a thud barely audible over the shrieks and snarls behind me.

The world looks like I'm seeing it through an oil slick. Even in the dim light of the overgrown parking lot, everything I see is mostly red.

I hear a yell, and the yell sounds wrong in my ears.

It takes four labored heartbeats to discover why.

Clothed people. Mediators. Not shades. Flashes of steel in the dark.

They're attacking the shades.

Somehow the fight got away from us. Carrick growls beside me, his nude body spattered with red blood and slummoth slime. Some of the blood is slummoth green, and Carrick'll have blisters from that.

I'm not thinking clearly. My entire left shoulder is numb, tingles twitching around its edges.

Mediators.

Here.

Where the fuck is Gregor?

Somehow, somehow, I shake off the lassitude of the rakath venom, just in time to see a shade's head detach from his body.

Rade.

No.

I scream as loud as I can. "Stop!"

My voice sounds like it's been put through a wood chipper and dipped in desperation.

And it doesn't work.

"Carrick!" I gasp.

The world presses in on me, tight like two walls shoved together with me in the middle.

I start running.

Everything slants sideways, but I manage to stay upright, racing death to save them.

I run right into the middle of the Mediators.

My shoulder's numbness is gone again, and pain washes over me in the sickly yellow light of the lamps.

"Stop," my voice rasps, sounding like it belongs to someone else.

My knees give out, and I fall forward. The leather of my loose pants saves my legs from encountering the gore and gravel.

I look up into the eyes of a Mediator I know, but whose name escapes me. Behind him, visible in my periphery, Rade's head is turned toward me.

"Friendlies," is all can say.

Gregor's angry voice intrudes, urgent and hot like molten steel, and I fall.

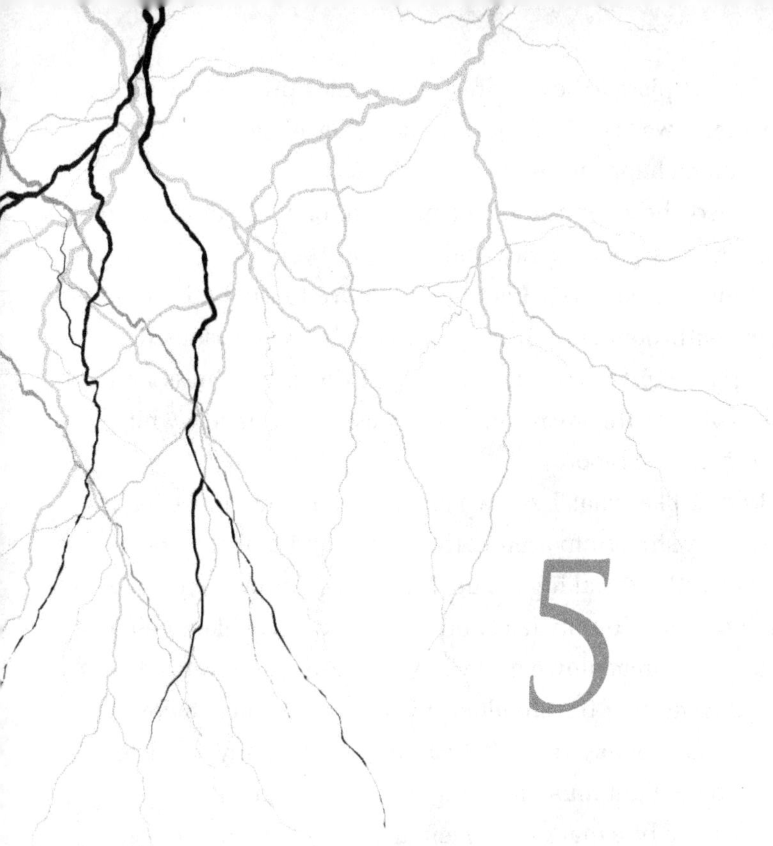

5

IT'S MILES AND JAX who catch me.

I know because Carrick tells me later.

When I come to, I'm in Gregor's living room.

It's modern and sleek and not at all like Gregor himself. The accent colors are bold jewel tones.

They laid me on my right side and haven't taken the rakath spines out yet. Thankfully, my Mediator resistance has burned off the venom.

"How long was I out?"

Gregor's house is quiet, and I can tell it's just the three of us here, even though I can't see Gregor. I don't know where the others are, but I hope they're okay. Rade isn't okay.

"An hour," Carrick says finally.

I sit up, my vision still adjusting. My bladder is full, adding one mundane discomfort to the rest of my body's aches. I look down. I'm in my bra and a pair of shorts that aren't mine. They've got happy faces on them. What the fuck, Gregor?

I'm not pissed they undressed me; they probably had to make sure I wasn't bleeding internally. I'm pissed about the gods damned happy faces.

I need these spines out of my skin, or I'll heal around them. When I say so, Carrick nods.

"I have to pee first." I get up and move to the bathroom. Gregor's bathroom is in disarray, antiseptics and various first aid supplies strewn over the counter. I do my business and avoid looking in the mirror until I've washed my hands, which itch from demon blood.

I don't like what I see when I look up. They must have cut away my shirt from around the spines, and how they managed that without waking me up, I will never know. I expected a patch of spines on my neck, but I seem to have taken half a rakath. They spread down my left shoulder almost past my deltoid and cover half the shoulder blade. I count thirty before I give up. This is going to suck. I can barely move my left arm. Continuing to fight must have dug them in deeper.

I've got a bite mark on my left arm I don't remember getting, and too many claw marks on my legs to count. They're barely scratches—thanks to my loose leathers—but they all itch like my hands.

I haven't been this beaten up in months.

Pulling out these spines is gonna be a bitch.

"Where's Gregor?" I ask when I return.

"Asleep." Carrick's cranked the lights up, and the living room is flooded with brightness. It hurts my eyes. Now that my head's cleared a bit, I can see I'm not the only one who met the pointy sides of a rakath tonight. Carrick's got a chunk of them on his side. He got off easy.

It smells like Ikea and demon blood in here.

I'd so much rather it just be Ikea. I've never been to one. I hear they're magical.

What we're about to do is less magical.

I snag supplies from the bathroom and sit back on the couch with Carrick, looking him over. His spines are what I expected mine to be, a small patch along the right side of his ribcage that's gonna hurt like a kitten in a cockfight to get out.

Either Gregor or Carrick already got out the forceps. Long and grey, they're way stronger than the average eyebrow tweezer.

Rakath spines are barbed like a porcupine full. The plus side is that the barb is semi-retractable. Grasp the spine and pinch the center, and the barb will at least partially disengage.

Still hurts like a motherfucker, though.

"You first," I say to Carrick.

He shrugs—his favorite response to anything—but I see the puffiness around his eyes and the way his arm quivers just a bit when he picks up the forceps from Gregor's faux stainless steel coffee table. Carrick's indigo eyes are bloodshot, and the thin red blood vessels look like cracks.

Gregor's got a reclining sofa, and Carrick kicks out the foot rest on his end, rolling onto his left side to give me access to the right. I gather the bottle of antiseptic, a carefully hand labelled homemade salve of witch hazel, and a stack of folded linen swatches.

I pull over an ottoman and sit. My own spines feel like they're nestling in deeper into my flesh with every movement, like they don't want to leave, and a wave of pain almost makes me want to ask Carrick to get mine out first.

But I don't.

I lay a thick black cloth on the arm of the sofa, tucking it around Carrick and the steely needles protruding from him. My fingers press the skin around the spines, gently feeling for swelling. There's some, and his skin is hot. Far hotter than the skin of his hand.

I grasp the first spine with the forceps, squeezing until I feel a pop like you get from cracking a glow stick to activate it.

The skin around the quill isn't bleeding.

"This is going to hurt like the dickens," I say. "Your skin's healing around it already."

Carrick doesn't answer, so I make sure my grip is solid and yank.

"Pah!" he spits, the muscles in his neck contorting.

"Told you. Eight to go."

I grit my teeth, my jaw locking on the knowledge that I'm next.

Gods damn it.

With three to go and a pile of spines gathering like a macabre game of pick up sticks on Gregor's table, Carrick looks up at me.

"You saved my life tonight," he says softly.

Just because I know it'll infuriate him, I shrug.

He scowls. His auburn bun is a mess, and sweat has glued flyaway to his neck. He must have really been working hard tonight—takes a lot for a shade to work up that kind of lather.

"I'm trying to give you a compliment." He grunts as I pull out another spine.

"I thought you were just stating the obvious." I grin at him then and jerk out the next spine.

He stares at me for a minute, then smiles back. It even crinkles his eyes. His smile fades as I pull the last quill. I soak a scrap of linen in antiseptic and carefully dab at the nine little punctures in his side.

Carrick grimaces. "I mean it, Ayala."

He never says my name.

"Mean what?" I switch to the salve, my fingers smearing a thick layer over his injuries. His skin ripples with goosebumps. I pat a square of fabric over it. It'll stick there for the next few hours and peel off on its own.

"You saved my life, and you fought well tonight. Better than anyone else, that's for damn sure."

I snort. "Don't tell Gregor that. He'll beat your nekkid ass bloody."

"I think he'd be proud. Is proud. He chose the right person."

I don't think I've ever seen Carrick this serious. Motioning him to get up, I take his place on the couch.

“I can handle myself all right,” I say, positioning my body so Carrick can reach me.

Three spines come out before he speaks again, and my face is buried in the black cloth so I don't yell.

“You did a lot more than simply handle yourself.”

For a time, I lose myself in the rhythm of his work, the slight crack of the spine in the forceps, the strangely cold pain of the quill leaving my flesh, the dab of antiseptic, the coolness of his breath drying over the evaporating alcohol.

“We lost three shades,” he says.

My body grows tense, and I don't even remember relaxing. How many spines has he removed so far?

“Rade and who else?” I ask, my mind begging not to hear Beex or Miles or Jax on the list.

“Thom and Sez,” he tells me.

I hate that the names relax me again, but they do. I breathe deeply, the sharp antiseptic smell glinting in my nose as Carrick pulls out two more spines.

Thom's “mother” was Thomas Derry, a man from the cesspool of Chattanooga who seems to have gone mad and turned to hells worship. Sez never mentioned his mother. Host.

As Carrick pulls out the last spine, he says, “Forty-seven. You killed at least three demons with forty-seven rakath spines in your body.”

Four total. Somehow that isn't enough. It never is.

I REMEMBER WHEN TAKING on three demons at once would have made me shit my britches. The more I think about the night's events, the more disconcerted I am.

On one hand, apparently I'll race into a fray with multiple hellkin and come out only poked full of some holes and clawed up a bit these days. On the other, is this just my life now?

Three months ago, I worked by myself, did my patrols, bagged the baddies, and trotted home to some silk and sake and Schwarzenegger.

Part of my mind whispers that I've gotten better, that I'm more formidable, but the rest of me feels the same as I ever did three months back.

Carrick and I go home before first light and sleep, and though I know we're both completely exhausted, we both wake up before eleven and pass Sunday in a daze. I curl up on the couch with him and flick on the TV to a Bruce Willis marathon until three in the afternoon.

I think Carrick thinks the movies are ridiculous, but it's a mark of our growing camaraderie that for once he doesn't make fun of me for loving the Expendables.

I'm sure a shrink would have a field day with my love of that franchise considering the color of my eyes and what it means.

When Gregor pounds on my front door at thirteen minutes after three, the sound makes my head throb. I know it's Gregor because he might as well be the giant up Jack's beanstalk for the fee-fi-fo-fum of his fists on the door.

"Coming!" I bellow.

I slide off the sofa and kick Carrick's leg out of the way. He tries to trip me.

"Asshole."

"I have one of those. So do you."

"Thanks for that anatomy lesson."

Yes, shades poop too. Everybody poops. Their farts stink just about like you'd expect from a creature that only eats raw meat.

Ew.

I open the door, and Gregor nods at me without any other greeting and stumps into the house. He's got an iced green tea blended ice frappé thing in one hand and a wrapped box of tea in the other. He kicks off his shoes—bless him—and goes straight to the living room, tossing the box of tea onto my coffee table.

"Brought you a present," he says.

My cupboards are full of tea, and he knows it. "Thanks?"

Gregor flops down in my easy chair and slurps at his drink. "You two okay today?"

I nod, disgruntled that Gregor looks far more okay than either of us do. He's got a light bruise already yellowing on the left side of his blocky face, barely visible through his tan. His short, steel-and-sand hair makes him look like a Marine. Gregor's about my height and has bricks for bones, I think.

He slurps at his green tea thing some more.

"So what's up?" I ask.

"Alamea wants to see you tomorrow."

If my facial expression could flatline, it would.

Alamea Virgili is the head of the Nashville Summit. She's a six foot tall black woman with thin locs that hang almost to her waist. She wears heels. I've seen her run in them. She also almost sliced off my arm a couple months ago when I dived in front of her blade to save a shade.

Good times.

We've had a tentative sort of truce since Mason and Saturn and the other shades pretty much saved all Mediator asses from a horde of demons, and she's got her medal from the Summit thanking her for keeping norm mortality rates so low since the big blowout.

Something niggles at my mind, but it scuttles away when Gregor opens his mouth again.

"She just wants to talk to you about the project," he says.

The project. The whole army-of-shades thing. Better on our side than that other thing, I think the Summit decided. Or at least that's what Gregor told me. Knowing that there are splinter cells within the Mediators who still think the only good shade comes with its head sold separately, I'm not entirely sure they agree on Gregor and I working with Carrick and the others to train these natural-born fighters with martial skills. I'm also not entirely sure I give a gopher's gonads what the Summit thinks. I've been locked in their underground grey beehive of doom once. That's not happening again.

Anger flickers in me like tongues of licking flame, and I douse it. I might want to parboil Gryfflet Asberry's cabbage-y face for selling me out to the Summit, but I've got my own medals and enough clout to keep them from biting at my ankles. For now.

I stare at Gregor, willing his face to give me some sort of clue of what to expect, but he just benignly sips his gods damned green tea.

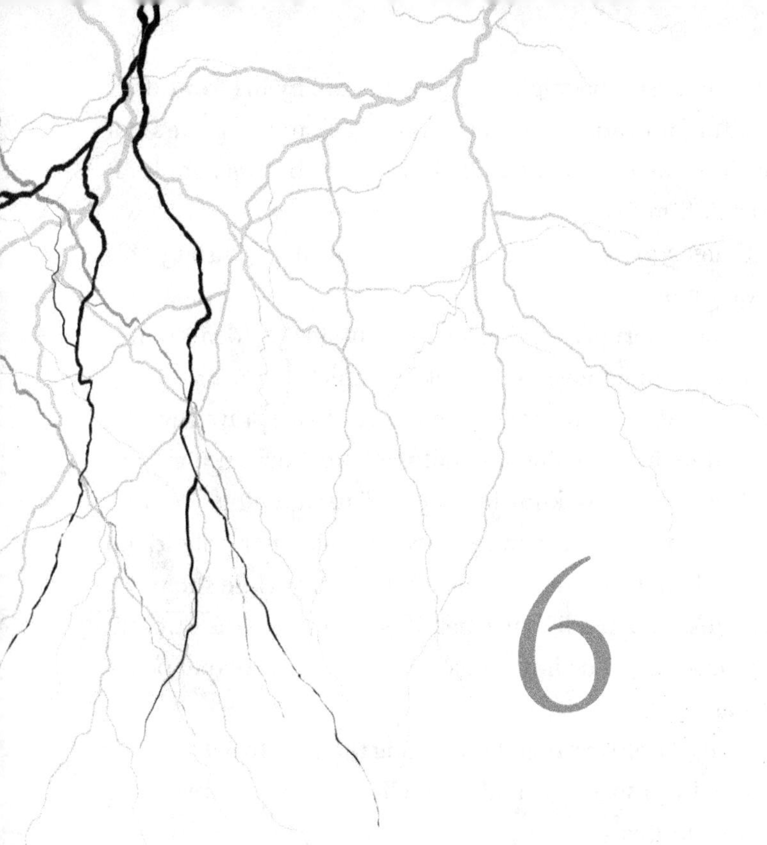

6

MONDAY ARRIVES WITH A chill in the air enough to make Laura turn off the air conditioning in the office for the first time this fall.

My shoulder is mostly healed, but it still feels tight when I lift my left arm above waist level. My sleepy shade roommate is snoring in his room when I leave, and I send Mira a text asking if I can stop by at night to see Saturn. I hope he's okay, and not just because I want to hear whatever it is he said he needed to tell me. I also hope whatever that is ends up being important, and not that he tried a new kind of wild game or ran from Nashville to Franklin and back in an hour and a half or something.

I make it to the office by quarter of eleven, and these days the wasabi-green walls actually do soothe me, along with the nearly blank clock. What I said to Laura is truer maybe than even I realized—my job really is my safe space.

Parker, the temp receptionist we hired to replace Alice, greets me with a chipper smile that makes me feel certain he spent Sunday night wagging his tail by his front door just waiting for Monday to let him go back to work. He's not a morph, so he doesn't actually have a tail, but he should. It would suit him.

"Coffee's brewed," he says, running his hand through his dark wavy hair.

He looks sort of like a Bernese mountain dog to me, if they had the excitement levels of a cocker spaniel.

I miss Alice, with her bottle blonde hair sprayed within an inch of its life. The lipstick that made its home n her front tooth. I went from not knowing her at all to watching her nearly give up her life for the mere hope of seeing her only friend again. I held her near-naked body in my arms while she wept. I hope she's enjoying life in Tibet; if nothing else, the Summit there is peaceful, and I hope Alice has found some of that peace for herself.

I think I'll always regret not taking the time to get to know her better. Even so, I can't make myself talk to Parker for longer than five minutes.

The coffee he brews is fantastic, though. He gets that artisanal, organic stuff that probably costs him an hour of pay per bag, but he shares it with everyone every day. I never said he wasn't a nice person.

On my desk when I enter my office is a stack of papers with a bright blue sticky note attached that just reads "FYI."

Laura's left company info and what my partnership would entail. It makes me almost giddy again, reading through it. The raise alone would be welcome, though I don't even know what I'd do with it. Mediators can't exactly spend money on travel. We get too far from our home territory and our innards start to liquify—or at least that's how it feels. No, thank you. I could start saving up for a house. Now there's a thought.

The excitement of paging through the packet of information helps distract me from my impending meeting with Alamea. I leave work at seven thirty and drive over to the Summit.

Sitting across from Nashville's Parthenon, the Summit is a sleek, modern juxtaposition against the Classical pillarism of the Parthenon. Well, Classical ripoff, anyway.

The parking lot is more crowded with cars than it usually is on Monday nights, and I feel a wave of relief not to see too many familiar vehicles. Namely, Ben Wheedle's. I don't think the Summit would look too fondly on me disembowling him on their doorstep. I feel like there's an internal clock in my head, like you find in factories to measure time since last safety incidents. It has been sixty-one days since I last saw Ben. I'm in no hurry to reset that counter to zero.

Inside, the yin yang on the floor feels three dimensional rather than two when I step across it. The physical depiction of the balance we seek as Mediators. Part of me expected the pull of emotion it brings me to fade when my black and white world swirled into grey this year. The first time I visited the Summit after I got out of the hospital, I stood in the center of the yin yang and stared at it, let it surround me until a Mediator-in-Training walked by and asked me for my autograph.

Mediators aren't Daoist by default—though some follow that path—but after the events of the summer, the idea that attaching judgement to the two interflowing sides of this symbol is only a perceptual projection of our own, well. Let's just say that it resonates with me a bit more than I thought it ever would.

Dark and light are two sides of the same thing, and there is no solid line between them; there are always parts of one to be found in the other, and neither is inherently good or bad.

If anything, my feet slow on the floor more now than they did before. Today there are too many people around for me to stand here and ponder, though, so I force my feet to carry me faster into the lobby.

The MIT at the front desk looks up when I approach. These days they all know who I am. Sort of like running into Nicole Kidman and Keith Urban in Green Hills. I'm a weird sort of famous in Mediator circles these days.

"What's up, Mittens?" I say lightly. "I'm here to see Alamea. She's expecting me."

The MIT gives me a nervous grin, his gawky teenage frame muscular but untrained still. He's almost as pale as I am, with a smattering of reddish freckles that clash with his violet eyes.

Mine clash too; my yellow-orange hair doesn't look too good with purple. C'est la vie of the Mediator. Stuck with the same eye color, other coloring be damned.

"Sh-she's in her office!" The MIT points upward as if I need directions, which is kind of cute.

"How old are you, Mittens?"

"Fourteen."

Lordy. I try to remember myself at fourteen and fail. "What's your name?"

"Conroy."

"Well, Conroy, keep up the good work." I feel like Uncle Sam as I walk away, or a weird amalgamate of him and Smoky the Bear. *Only you can prevent total takeover of Nashville by the teeming hordes of the hells.* Wink wink.

Alamea's office is always messy, which I respect. She never gives me shit about my car. She's got swords on her walls, gorgeous, functional swords that I can tell she cares for. They shine in the austere white light of her office, edges honed and blades bright.

Alamea herself shows signs of care. She's old money, cotton plantation owners dating back to the seventeenth century in North Carolina. The Virgili's came from Africa and took over half the South. She's one of the few Mediators who has a lineage everyone knows, though she's like the rest of us and cut off from her family. Not the first Virgili to be born a Mediator, either.

She's a titan, a legend, a walking god. Her white linen shirt is perfectly tailored; her exposed dark brown arms give the same effect. I know the strength and control in those muscles. She's over six feet tall even flat footed, and her long locs are tied in a hefty knot over her right shoulder, shots of silver winding through them like little lightning bolts. She sits with both feet up on the corner of her desk, typing away on a laptop with her desktop computer monitor angled to the side. Every so often, she looks back and forth between the screens.

My arm gives a twinge when I see her, and again I'm thankful to her reflexes that she didn't chop it off. She could have. Any slower and she would have. I'm always just a bit in awe of her, and not a little bit afraid.

I know she sees me, but she doesn't acknowledge me until I hear her hitting the return key three times with her pinky, and then she looks up, dropping her feet to the floor and moving the laptop to the surface of her desk. She straightens a stack of papers as if it'll do anything to stem the overflowing mass of them that threaten to slide off the sides of the desk, and then she gives me a tight smile.

"Thanks for coming, Ayala."

"My pleasure. I think."

Her smile widens at that.

"I hear there was a misunderstanding this weekend."

"That's one way to put it. Carson and his buddies killed one of my friends." I don't want to think about Rade, even though I know that's why I'm here. I don't want to think about Thom and Sez. I also don't want to think of all the other names of shades we would lose if the Mediators went all out against them again.

Alamea's peace medal hangs behind her in a mahogany frame, ironically bearing a sword sculpted in silver, point down. Whatever honors we win, we pay for in blood.

I don't want to think about the names of the shades I helped blow up this summer and the blood that paid for my own medal.

Alamea seems to sense my thoughts, and she sits forward in her chair. She smells like lemon cake, sweet and citrusy, and she meets my eyes, silent for a long moment. "We were wrong this summer."

Of all the words I expected to hear out of her mouth, *we were wrong* were at the bottom of the list. Somewhere around *I've decided to marry a slummoth.*

I want to say that yes, we were. And include myself in it, because before I was right I was certainly wrong. Instead my tongue sticks to the roof of my mouth, and I just wait for her to go on.

"What you're doing with Gregor is important," she says finally. "I'm glad that someone is there to give the shades purpose and direction, to show them that they can be our allies."

"Not all the Mediators agree with you. Carson was awfully quick with his sword Saturday night."

She doesn't deny it. "What do you suggest?"

My, my, but she's full of surprises today. "Have you identified the Mediators who are trying to go around your edict not to hunt shades?"

She nods, as usual taking a moment before she speaks again. "We are aware."

I notice that she doesn't say it's under control. Either she knows me well enough now to know I wouldn't believe her, or she just doesn't plan to bullshit me. Interesting.

I also notice she doesn't tell me what happened Saturday won't happen again. Then again, promises and promises you can't keep are synonymous in our business.

"Why did you want to see me?" I ask. Her office is very quiet, except for the dull ticking of a clock on her bookshelf and the ever-so-slight whooshing of the wind outside.

"How do you think it's going?"

"The shades?"

She nods.

"They work well together. They respect one another, and they don't want to die." I think of all things, their self-preservation is what motivates them at this point. Every shade I know touches my shoulder when he greets me because he needs to know he's safe with me. Well, every shade but one. They are strangers in a hostile world.

"Do you think they will turn on us again?"

“To be candid, Alamea, I don’t think they ever turned on us at all. They were born in blood and bone, spurred by instinct alone at first. They knew nothing, and why should they? We’re fortunate their memories come soon after their birth.”

A seed of irritation germinates, worming around in me like it’s seeking light. Shades begin remembering their mothers when they are new to this world. That’s where they all seem to find their names, seeking inward to understand themselves. We’re the ones who called them monsters. Some of them were, to be sure, but most of them just want what we all do—life.

“And when they fought us later, they saw us only as aggressors.” Alamea’s words come out in a soft sigh, and I look up from the floor, my forehead taut with tension.

Is she agreeing with me?

Alamea’s own face is creased and tight at once.

It’s then I understand why she called me here, why she is asking me and not Gregor about the state of our plan. She knows he can convince them, but I understand them. And she has taken a huge, huge gamble.

On me.

She’s betting on me.

I STAY A WHILE longer, talking to Alamea about tactics and letting her know about the grouping of hellkin we found at the Opry. I also tell her about the jeeling that fled, and with her peace medal hovering behind her chair, part of me wonders if fewer norms are dying because we’re better about stopping the demons—or if the demons are somehow biding their time.

The drive home takes too long—I hit the witch and morph traffic hours and end up stuck waiting for a railroad crossing a mile from home—and I run through a drive thru on the way home just because cooking is the last thing I want to do.

I should go out and hunt some hellkin, but I’m almost overcome by the strange sensation of feeling exhaustion in my bones. I'm tired. I remember this old granny Mediator when I was a Mitten; she'd come down, daggers still on her belt and dirt from her garden under her fingernails, and she'd tell us that's how she knew it was time for her to retire. Not all Mediators get to a ripe old age, but this lady had just about fallen from the tree. She told me she felt the years in her bones at the end, and it bothers me that I'm feeling something like that now.

The end is nowhere in sight for me.

My drive thru bag smells like grease and cholesterol, and I drop it on the kitchen counter, going to pour a cup of water.

Something moves on my balcony.

It's a testament to how used to shades I am that I don't spill my water everywhere from surprise. Instead, I put one hand on the hilt of my belt knife and peer out through the glass door.

Miles's face appears as he approaches.

Unlatching the sliding door, I gesture him in, my fingers finding his dark shoulder covered in a thin layer of dust. He returns the touch, and I motion at him to follow me into the kitchen.

"Aren't you supposed to be with Carrick?" I pull out my phone—sure enough, there's a text from Carrick saying that he's taking the group to the east side of the city to do some drills in an abandoned football field.

"I had to come talk to you." Miles has a voice like a lion's purr, and he speaks precisely, forming each of his words with deliberation that makes me think he'd be a good politician under other circumstances.

Though I wouldn't wish that fate on a rakath.

"What happened?" I sit down at my table and unwrap my burger, ignoring the way Miles wrinkles his nose at the smell of cooked meat.

"Jax did not meet me where he was supposed to."

My burger suddenly tastes like cardboard.

"Where was he supposed to meet you?"

"Buena Vista Park."

"Is that where he lives?"

Miles gives me a tired look and shakes his head. "He lives farther west. He was going to meet me at the park, and we were going to travel together to meet with Carrick. I waited for a long time, but he didn't come."

A long time to shades could be an hour or it could be five. Judging by the time now—half past ten—and when Carrick was supposed to gather everyone—half past six—Jax has now been missing for about four hours.

"Fuck." I finish my burger in three large bites and glug down my soda past the lump of barely-chewed sandwich. I feel like I've swallowed an egg whole, but I ignore it.

"Yes," Miles agrees.

Jax. Jax is smart, risk-averse. He keeps to himself and avoids all the areas I told him Mediators frequent.

"Can you sense him at all?"

I hate asking that question, because it reminds me of Mason. But it's useful nonetheless. Shades can sense one another. Some more than others. It's not like telepathy, per se, but it is sort of like those stories you hear about a parent knowing their child is in danger and then being right. Or feeling someone walk up behind you. When shades are close to one another like friends or family, that sense grows stronger. Sometimes I almost feel it with Miles and Jax and, to a lesser extent, Carrick. I could just be blowing smoke up my own ass.

Miles gives a slight head shake.

Even though that head shake might not mean Jax is dead, it's definitely not a good sign.

"You know where he lives?" I ask.

"Yes."

"Then let's go."

7

BEAMAN PARK IS JUST off Old Hickory Boulevard northwest of town, and on a map it looks like a diagram of a woman's reproductive system, complete with ovaries. The eastern ovary is crisscrossed with streams and hiking trails, so I'm not surprised when Miles leads me to the western chunk of the park.

The creek in this part of the park is called Little Marrowbone.

Charmingly apt.

Miles has me circle around to the north and come into the park off Little Marrowbone Road, and we leave my car parked by the side of the road. I'm always glad for my Mediator plates, which have a yin yang symbol next to the ID number. One perk of the job is that you don't get parking tickets, and you don't have to pay to register your vehicle.

There aren't any official trails on this side of the park, but Miles leads me on a deer track that I keep trying not to think of as a fallopian tube. Hey, once you see it, you can't unsee it.

The park is alive with the sounds of nature's nightlife. Good. No demons nearby.

I follow Miles, keeping a short distance behind him. He moves almost silently through the underbrush, his bare feet rolling over roots and pats of bare ground where deer hooves have worn away the grasses. I keep to his footsteps, glad for the supple leather of my boots but envious of his callouses.

A small rivulet trickles in a crease of land to our right, melding its burble with the Little Marrowbone. It's there Miles turns upstream, away from the creek's tributary. The crease of land widens into a gully. The south slope is dotted with tupelo and black oaks, and the canopy above us would be aflame with autumn foliage if the sun were up.

Miles leads me to an outcropping of land, then ducks behind it. There's a small cave, little more than a hollow. Jax must have added the crude thatching of branches; he's constructed almost a lean-to. Jax isn't there.

I crouch to enter the dwelling. He's got a burlap sack stuffed with leaves for a pillow, and a low table of bark pulled from a dead snag. On the table is a line of trinkets. A worm-carved branch of ash, swirls decorating the length. A small brass box containing 50s-style jacks that make my breath hitch. And at the end, a black plastic gadget I know all too well.

About the diameter of a quarter, it's shaped like a gumdrop. Put it on a tree trunk and press it, and it'll stick into the wood and emit a signal and a ring of light around the base. I've used them hundreds of times; they call Mediators. Usually for body pickups. Sometimes for backup. There's always a team of nearly-trained Mittens available to dispatch from the Summit if a Mediator gets too far into a fray to get out.

I pick up the beacon and turn it over. There's a dusty layer on the bottom side, like fine sawdust. I know the things are reusable, and looking closer at the beacon, I think Jax pulled it from a tree and took it home.

Recently, if I had to hazard a guess.

"Footprints," Miles says.

I duck out of the lean-to, tucking the beacon in my pocket. They have serial numbers on them, and I can find out from Alamea when this one was last used—and by whom.

I look where Miles is pointing, and I see them. Bare feet left the prints, leading across the gully. In the mud at the edge of the stream, they're deeper.

"He went up the hill instead of back down the gully," I say.

Miles looks back over his shoulder at me and nods. I can't help but glance to my left, downstream. If Jax left this way instead of going back the other way, maybe he thought someone would be waiting for him at the gully's mouth.

I'm not the best tracker in the world, but I'm no slouch either. Miles and I head up the hill, looking for the traces of displaced soil and grass and the occasional depression of the ball of a foot or a toe.

In the dark, it's slow going even with both of us having above average night vision. I don't want to light the way with my phone, especially now that it looks like Jax was running from someone.

Everything in his little shelter was very deliberate. Tidy. If he put this beacon there in plain sight, he either was trying to look like he wasn't in a hurry or he wanted someone else to find it.

Sickness sinks into my stomach like a stone.

Miles and I make it down the other side of the hill, continuing south with the tracks until we hit the Little Marrowbone again. The tracks go straight into the water.

"Jax is not stupid," Miles says. "He would travel downstream for a time before coming out."

"Or upstream." The Little Marrowbone is a healthy creek, its levels a bit lower than they would be in spring or early summer, but still deep enough in the center to come up to knee height or so. Wisps of fog have begun to form in the autumn night, and by sunup they'll have made a mist over the entire park, spreading outward from the creek.

I look at Miles. "What do you want to do?"

He thinks for a long moment.

"If Jax is okay, he will come to you or me. If he's not..."

Miles doesn't have to finish his sentence.

Fuck.

I DRIVE MILES TO the football field in East Nashville where Gregor and Carrick are still drilling the shades. Part of me hopes we'll turn up and find Jax, his skin golden brown in the floodlights, dodging and doing high knees with the rest of them.

We don't.

Instead we find the shades in formation, listening to Gregor with rapt attention, Carrick pacing off to the side in the still-healthy untrimmed grass.

The lights are dingy and only about half are functional, but the sight of the shades' naked forms under the lights gives me some small amount of comfort.

That small comfort is chased away when I do a quick headcount, wondering who's not there. Then I remember. Rade, Thom, and Sez are all dead, and Jax is now missing. And Saturn is at Mira's.

Five down. In the space of a week. I don't like it.

I don't get close enough to join in, but Gregor and Carrick each give me a wave as I walk back to my car. The beacon in my pocket presses against my leg.

I make it to Mira's in thirteen minutes. Her porch light is blazing, the Samhain lights wrapped around the railings cheery red and orange. Since my last visit, an array of squash has appeared on a table next to her porch swing.

I knock on the door.

No one answers. A moment later, I knock again, harder.

"Mira! It's Ayala!" I holler through the heavy oak door.

No way she's sleeping. I double check the texts on my phone—sure enough, she said to come on over any time after two. It's two forty.

I pound on the door with the heel of my hand, peering to the side of the door. The curtains are drawn, but light shows in the cracks. Looking closer at the door, I inspect it for any signs of forced entry. There aren't any. I kneel on the porch swing and press my ear against the cold glass of the window. Nothing.

The door's locked—any good Mediator makes sure to do that—and I know I won't find any keys under the squash on the table. I try calling Mira as I walk around the side of the house.

Inside, I hear her phone go off with the X-Files theme.

The drapes are drawn at all the windows, and I try to peek through the living room window anyway. The waves of fabric show me a patch of floor, and that's it. The phone goes to voicemail, and I hang up.

The sound seems to have been coming from the living room.

I try to convince myself that Mira's just in the bathroom, but it doesn't work.

I dial her again.

The X-Files theme comes on again. In my ear, I get three rings, four rings, five—

"Heh-oh." The voice comes through muddled and heavy, but it's Mira.

"Mira, it's Ayala. Are you okay?"

I hear a deep intake of breath sucked between clenched teeth. Inside the house, a thud reaches my ears.

"Yo! Mira!"

"I'm here." Her voice sounds like she's speaking from the bottom of a hole. "Front door."

I hurry to the door, waiting to hear movement on the other side. When the latch finally clicks and the door opens inward, I almost run through it. But the sight of Mira stops me.

She blinks at me; her left eye's pupil largely dilated while the right is a pinprick in the bright light of her foyer. Dried blood crusts her left cheek and down her neck, matting her black hair against her skin.

She sways on her feet. "Fuck me."

I catch her right before she collapses. She's almost a deadweight against me, and I loop my arm under hers, hoisting her in. I kick the door shut behind me and shuffle to it to lock it again. Mira squints in the light. I hit the dimmer with my free hand as we pass, knocking it down a few pegs to quiet the brightness.

Mira gives a tiny sigh of relief. I set her on her sofa, a puffy maroon piece that she sinks into, her head lolling back. I flick her on the nose.

"Stay awake, asshole."

Her lips give me the smallest tug of a smile, and I look around me.

Next to the rug, there's a smear of blood on the hardwood. It's close to the window. If she was lying there, that would explain how I could hear the ringtone through the glass.

I know without running down the corridor to look that Saturn isn't here. "Did Saturn do this?"

Mira's head bobs, and I can't tell if it's because of the concussion or an affirmative.

I hurry to her, sitting beside her on the sofa. "Mira. Wake up. You gotta stay awake for me. Remember how much I hated you when I got concussed and you woke me up all night? My turn. Payback's a bitch."

I get another little smile at that.

"Did Saturn do this?" I repeat the question.

This time I know it's a nod. Fuckity fuck fuck.

"Why?"

She pulls in another breath, and it whistles past her lips, which are chapped and red. A trickle of blood must have worked its way across her cheek while she was passed out on the floor, because she's got a macabre half smile like the Joker. Thankfully, it's just blood and not an actual cut.

"I tried to stop him from leaving."

Mira closes her eyes, breathing in deeply and exhaling, like it's all she can focus on doing. I don't blame her. I've had bad concussions before, and they're no fun.

"Did he say why he had to go?"

"He said he'd tell me later. But that he couldn't."

"Can I get you anything?"

"Ice pack. Kitchen."

I get up and make a beeline for the freezer, where I find a squishy blue ice pack and a dish towel and wrap the ice pack into a burrito. I also grab a cup and fill it with ice water.

Back in the living room, the only sound is Mira's ragged breathing. I press the ice pack into her hands, and her eyes flutter open again.

"Thank you."

I call Carrick and leave him a message, letting him know I'm staying at Mira's. I don't mention Jax or Saturn. After I've gotten the blood cleaned off Mira's face and her settled into bed—and alarms set on my phone so I can wake her every couple hours—I start to leave the room. Her voice stops me in the threshold.

"He's scared, Ayala."

I turn, meeting her gaze. Her eyelids droop, and she swallows the concussion nausea, blinking headily at me.

"Did he give you any idea of what?

She doesn't have to shake her head to tell me no.

I leave her door cracked and step lightly down the hallway to Saturn's recent guest room. The sheets are clean and neatly pulled up to the pillows. No blanket, as expected. I find one in a trunk at the foot of the bed and spread it out over the sheets, crawling between them after undressing to my t-shirt and underwear.

The sheets smell like mulled wine, warm and spicy, even though they're cool on my skin.

It's hard to try and sleep knowing I'll just wake up in two hours, but I try anyway. My thoughts run through the day. Alamea. Gregor. Carrick. Jax. Miles. Now Saturn.

Saturn must have been desperate to knock Mira out cold. And he could have done it with less force than he did. Sloppy.

What is Saturn so afraid of?

8

THE NEXT DAY PASSES in a blur of press releases and panicky business owners, and I've never been so grateful to put out PR fires in my entire life. Laura's out at a conference, so I spend the entirety of the workday shut in my office, guzzling water.

After work, I take a short patrol to the Cumberland, dispatching a pair of frahlig demons within the first hour. Their clusters of slimy teeth drip fish guts, and killing them quickly is just as much an incentive not to let them dribble on my leathers as it is to follow my birthright.

It's a relief also to see hellkin acting normally, and I think I go to the riverfront to hunt frahligs as much to prove to myself that they'll be there as anything else.

When I get home, Carrick is in the kitchen, chopping up flank steak into bite-sized pieces.

He looks up when I come in, and I wrinkle my nose. You'd think I'd get used to the constant smell of raw meat. Nope.

"I ordered you dinner," he says.

"What?"

"You like Thai food on Tuesdays." He points to the microwave, where I can see a rolled tight paper sack. "Summer rolls and pad Thai. Tea's in the fridge."

"Well, hell, Carrick. Look at you go."

"Just being friendly." Then he waggles his butt at me. Thankfully, he's wearing shorts.

"Cheeky is more like."

He doesn't laugh at my butt pun. I sigh and retrieve my dinner, throwing the noodles on a plate with the summer rolls. The tangy scent of my dinner finally chases away most of the bloody steak smell.

"Did Nana get fed already?"

He nods. "She's running around the apartment."

Mister Domesticity in action. "Are you okay?"

"I can't take care of some things around the place? You don't make me pay rent."

"That's because most places of business have a dress code. Like getting dressed, at the very least." I shove half a summer roll in my mouth and plunk down at the table. He's never this nice to me. "You heard about Jax then."

He pops a piece of raw beef in his mouth and nods.

"You think he's dead." I say, surprised at how evenly my words come out.

Carrick chews slowly, then swallows. His eyes frown at me, even though the rest of his face manages to stay impassive. A tendril of auburn hair curls on the side of his neck. "What we're doing—you know eventually Gregor is going to point us at an enemy."

"Yes."

"And that when enemies fight, people die."

I feign shock. "Really? Tell me more, O Agéd Wise One."

He hates when I throw his age in his face. He frowns for real now. "Some of them are going to die. You know that."

"I don't think Jax is dead."

Carrick snorts, which sounds even sillier coming from someone who's busy stuffing his face with raw meat. "Ayala, if he were alive, he would have come back by now."

I think of Saturn, and the knot the size of Little Rock on Mira's head. But I don't disagree aloud. Instead, I change the subject. "Are you going back out tonight?"

"I thought I'd stay here with you. I put Terminator on."

"Are you flirting with me?"

I want to beam at him when he blushes, but then he wrinkles his nose. "I'd sooner flirt with Nana."

"Ew."

Speaking of my bunny, she comes hopping around the corner and skids to a halt at my feet. I reach down to scratch between her ears, watching her velvety little ginger nose twitch. "Don't worry, Nana. I know you'd kick his ass."

Her foot starts thumping on the tile.

"Tomorrow night we're supposed to go up to the Tailwater. Gregor said he had some reports of slummoth activity."

"I'll go with you," I say absently. If frahlig tooth-slime is gross, the slummoths turn it up to eleven. But these days, they're among the easier hellkin for me to face.

Carrick nods, scraping his meat chunks into a bowl with the cleaver. I watch him as he cleans the cutting board and the knife. For being a four hundred year old human-demon hybrid, he's a surprisingly okay roommate sometimes.

And anyone who puts on my favorite Schwarzenegger series of their own accord gets brownie points from me.

I take my plate and Thai tea into the living room after Carrick and his meat bowl, Nana hopping behind us.

WANE OPENS THE DOOR for me when I arrive at Mira's at nine-thirty the next morning to check on her. She's wearing Star Trek themed scrubs today, and she gives me a tight smile when I come inside.

“How is she?” I ask.

“Better. Her pupils are the same size again.”

“Hey, that’s a good sign.”

Wane goes into the kitchen, and I follow her, taking a glass of orange juice when she pours it and hands it to me.

“Is she awake?”

“Damn right, she’s awake,” Mira says from behind me.

I turn around, and she rolls her eyes at me. At least the bruising on her temple is starting to fade, and she’s able to stand up without swaying. “Copy catter,” I say.

“Oh, fuck you.”

I look at Wane, who seems unfazed by Mira’s expletives. “How’d you get into all this?”

“I’ve known Mira for a while, and I saw a few shade victims this summer at the hospital.”

“In obstetrics?” The maternity ward doesn’t really seem like the place where a torn up norm would be found.

Then it hits me what she means.

“No,” I say. “You saw some of the mothers?”

“Only two. One male and one female.”

“One of the dudes who gave himself to the demons to get knocked up showed up in your ward?” I can feel the breeze from the ceiling fan on the whites of my eyes. I know hellkin worshippers are off their rockers, but a pregnant man coming to a hospital for a pre-natal exam pushes even their stupidity past the normal limits I’d assume they have.

Wane laughs, but it’s a curt, brittle sound. “He came with his partner, who was also housing a shade in her womb. Well. They weren’t actually enwombed.”

I don’t think I really want to know the anatomy and mechanics of demon-human pregnancies. I saw enough when I was there to watch Saturn explode out of his mother.

Mira and Wane exchange a glance, and Wane throws back the rest of her OJ.

“I’ve got to go. If he comes back, you’ll call me.” Wane’s pronoun usage is in no doubt, and she doesn’t make it a question.

I expect Mira to give Wane some sort of shit, but instead she just nods. Maybe Saturn hit her on the head even harder than I thought.

When the door closes behind Wane, I peer at Mira. "Are you sure you're okay?"

She motions at me to follow her, and she slumps onto the sofa in her living room. "Been better."

"Were you and Saturn..."

Mira looks at me as if I've suggested she do it with a frahlig. "Uh, no. Not into dudes."

"You and Wane?"

"Ew. She's like...family."

We're silent for a moment, and I suddenly wish I had a rewind button.

"He's my friend. After what happened this summer, I went to go find him. Got to know him." She scrubs her fingers through her hair, which falls into her face. Her eyes glow violet in the morning light. "I don't know why he'd do this to me."

I don't know either. Saturn trusts both of us, but maybe not enough. I just wish he'd told me whatever it was he'd planned to tell me.

"He didn't tell you anything, did he?" It's a futile question, and I know it. Before Mira even shakes her head no, I expect her answer.

"Look," she says. "Saturn's a scary motherfucker. When he gets scared? There's something to be scared of."

I don't know what's worse—that Mira's absolutely right, or that neither of us have a clue in all six and a half hells what it is that would get him that terrified.

9

I MEET CARRICK AND the other shades at half past midnight in the crook of the Cumberland River just before it widens into a lake at the Old Hickory Dam. The breeze off the water is cold, even though where we are, we can't even see the river.

I look at my phone where Gregor indicated the slummoths have been seen. Why no one just sent another group of Mediators to take care of it is beyond me. Even so, I draw both blades as we set off. The last thing I want is a repeat of what happened at the Opry. Gregor's not with us tonight, and if I'm the only Mediator here and another group of us shows up, I don't know if I could stop them this time, or if they'd even see me.

We walk southward. I know we're not far from Cinder Road, and not far beyond there, there are houses. Demons don't usually venture this close to human habitation, and it's a good thing, too. We're skirting the Tailwater Access Area, which is a chunk of park land that butts up against the lock and dam.

The rush of water from the dam reaches us even here, and I begin to wish the moon would hurry up and rise. It's almost full, and I wouldn't say no to a bit more light. We walk along the edge of the park, and after a few minutes, we reach Cinder Road.

Carrick is up a little ways from me, but Miles walks beside me. His presence is a small comfort, but my uneasiness grows as we turn southwest. The crickets sing loudly here, and if there are slummoths, they're not at the park.

We're heading toward a neighborhood.

I've fought hellkin in populated areas before—hell, I killed a shade in the middle of my favorite brunch spot once—but I hate it. Killing demons with norms around not only puts us on display, but it plunks their cozy little norm-butts right in the middle of danger. Not even witches and morphs stand a good chance against hellkin without proper training, and psychics are lucky if they see the damn things coming a half second before they get splatted.

The first street light appears just as the crickets go silent.

Aw, hells.

I nudge Miles with my elbow, nodding at the air and motioning to my ear. For a moment, I can almost feel something, like a pulse in the wind, but then it's gone, and every shade with us suddenly seems more alert.

I'm not stupid; I know they have their little shade ways. I think being around them as much as I am makes me think I can pick up on it.

The area around us is now silent except for the quiet padding of bare feet on asphalt and the light scuffs of my boots. Fourteen shades plus me. That's good odds, right? Even if we were pitted against eight snorbits and a bunch of slummoths and rakaths again, we might be able to do okay.

My breath comes faster, and I hate that physical representation of anxiety. I ignore it, imagining my ears like satellites, trying to pick up any sounds not made by the fifteen of us here on the road.

The river in the distance. A car honk a mile or so away. A plane overhead.

No natural sounds reach my ears.

And then I hear a scream.

Carrick points like a bloodhound, and the fifteen of us break into a run. Our feet slap the asphalt, and I try not to think about the fact that the scream sounded like the scream of a child.

The road comes to a T, and as one body, we all turn north. There aren't a ton of houses up this direction, but the scream came from here. We pass one mailbox with a chicken on it, and the scream sounds again.

"Spread out!" I bark. "Half circle that way!"

Carrick and six others break off and veer to the right, and Miles and I lead the charge north. There's a single house ahead of us, lights on downstairs and a Big Wheels in the driveway.

The screams sound so much louder against the night's backdrop of silence. I feel my own breath like wind rushing into and through my chest.

It fills me with stillness and certainty.

The first slummoth appears around the edge of the green-sided house. I erupt into motion, and my first slash with my sword adds a spray of kryptonite green to the olive of the siding.

A sound like screeching steel rises through the air. On the other side of the house, I hear the same sound doubled, tripled, quadrupled.

At least five. Great.

I've taken this beast across the chest and stomach, and a hot smell like decay and metal boils out of the slummoth with a pile of entrails. It takes a staggering step forward, and I cut its head off. The head lands on the demon's intestines.

Around me, I hear the snarls of shades and the sickening cracks and squishes where the shades' hands and feet meet slummoth slime.

My path clear, I dart around the corner of the house and stop short at the edge of their back porch.

A woman brandishes a chef's knife at a wounded slummoth. The demon drips green blood and grey ooze on the wood of the porch. Behind her is a small child, huddled next to the prone shape of a man wearing blood from shoulder blade to hips, the red his own and the green demon.

The woman's managed to sever the slummoth's clavicular tendon, and its right arm dangles at its side. Her knife—from a three hundred dollar knife block—wears a green-grey sheen.

I don't waste any more time. In one motion, I leap, rolling over the porch rail and landing on the cedar-stained wood.

I don't care that the kid is watching. I take the demon's head off.

"Call the Summit," I tell the woman.

The noises behind me make me turn. I don't wait to see if she obeys me.

I count three more dead slummoths before I round the northeast corner of the house, but I still hear snarling and the sound of dying demons.

Out of the corner of my eye, I see Miles rip off a hellkin head with his bare hands.

From the woods to the north, five more demons appear. All slummoths. Their movements are apelike, sacklike, the shimmer of their slime visible even from here.

They're not headed for this house.

Through the trees, a porch light glimmers.

"Carrick!" I bellow his name into the night. "Up five, northwest!"

Not waiting for him or any of the other shades, I make a break after the slummoths.

I think I hear someone yell behind me, but I don't care. When the house appears, its only light the one on the porch, I yell as loud as I can. "Stay inside!"

I don't know if the house's inhabitant will hear me, but it's worth a shot.

Two of the slummoths break from their formation and come my way. The other three make for the large picture window at the front of the house.

Shit, shit, shit.

I run straight at the pair of demons. They screech at me, froth bubbling from their mouths. They're close together, but if I hit one, the other will flank me.

I have the stupidest idea ever.

I let my arms relax and my swords droop, running at the demons. Ten feet. Five feet.

At the last possible second, I bring both blades up. Throwing myself at the space just between the hellkin, the points of my swords connect with slimy skin. They pierce the slummoths' chins.

Hot pain slices across my middle. I shove my blades farther into the demons' heads, then jerk back.

Gasping, I stumble to the side just as I hear the crashing tinkle that tells me the other three have busted the window.

Hells.

I can feel wetness trickle down my stomach, but I can't let this homeowner get splatted.

I give myself one deep breath, and I jump over the slummoth carcasses and race up the porch stairs, throwing my swords in and diving through the window. I'm lucky there's a couch. I hit it and roll, a crunch of broken glass against my back.

Better back than front right now.

I land a couple feet from my blades. My one recovery breath cost me, and the demons are already up the stairs.

Stairs are about the last thing I want to do right now.

I hurry up them as fast as I can, hopping over a toppled brass floor lamp on the landing, my feet cracking pieces of matte emerald glass. Somehow the bulb survived. The shadows in the stairwell are long and clawlike.

A man's scream cuts the air. The claws are coming for him.

"Lock yourself in a closet or jump out the gods damned window!" I yell, and from the slam of a door, he's listening. The door won't exactly stop the slummoths, but it'll at least slow them down a bit.

I take a minuscule pause and listen. The sound of my own breath is all I hear, and that scares me more than taking on three more demons when I'm already injured.

Slummoths are not quiet.

Demons don't do stealth.

The upper level of the house only seems to hold three rooms and a bathroom. The two guest rooms are untouched, and the slimy footprints on the wood laminate floor go straight to the master suite.

I pretend I don't see the drops of blood falling as I walk forward.

Just as I reach the threshold, something explodes though the window.

Not something.

Carrick.

ALL THREE SLUMMOTHS FALL upon him, materializing out of the clawlike shadows. Carrick screams as demon teeth sink into his shoulder. I know that feeling all too well.

I make it the remaining fifteen feet into the room and drop my short sword with a clatter. The hellkin don't look up, and I take my saber in both hands like a baseball bat.

I try to forget the wet pain in my stomach and the sound of Carrick screaming. I don't know where the others are. I hope the Summit is sending backup.

But for now, it's me.

I swing my sword like a bat. One slummoth head goes rolling across the floor, and from the closet behind me comes a surprised thud and gasp. One of the two remaining demons has his teeth sunk deep in Carrick's deltoid. The other pulls bloody claws back from Carrick's ribs and comes at me. His head joins the other on the floor.

I can't decapitate the last one without slicing into Carrick's arm, so I settle for stabbing it through the head. My sword sticks in the slummoth's skull, and his jaw stays locked on Carrick's flesh for an interminable five breaths.

Carrick is unconscious.

Already I can see the slummoth poison inflaming his shoulder, spreading like red lines of a spiderweb out over his chest, speckled with yellow pustules that turn black at the top. Pretty. I should be more worried, but he'll be okay. I think.

Now that I'm not moving, I feel the seeping blood at my stomach. It tickles, dribbling down to pool at the waistline of my pants. I'm not sure I'm okay.

The man in the closet has gone very quiet, and I realize it's probably because he thinks I'm dead.

"It's okay. You can come out now, I think."

"You think?"

I grimace, taking a couple steps to lean on the man's bedpost. It's hard to get a breath around the ball of pain at my center. "Well, these demons ain't getting any deader."

The closet door creaks open, and a bearded white man wearing only a set of black boxers with light sabers on them steps out. He promptly keels over and vomits on one of the slummoth heads. I don't really blame him, but the smell of bile threatens to make me join him in his pastime.

A thump from the broken window breaks my urge to puke.

I raise my sword again, hoping to every star in the sky that it's not another pack of slummoths coming through.

It's Miles.

"Hey," he says. "You should come down."

I nod, taking a painful three steps to retrieve my short sword. "You get Carrick."

The house's owner rises to his feet, knees shaking and a wet streak visible across the back of his hand. "You're hurt."

"Part of the job. You dead?"

"What? No."

"Then I did my job." I look at the window, watching Miles scoop up Carrick with a graceful attention to Carrick's wounds. He somehow gets out the window without adding more scrapes to the unconscious shade.

Sorry, but I ain't going out that way.

I start for the stairs, and the man follows. "Can I at least help you get downstairs?"

That makes me speed up, though it doesn't do much. I'm still moving at about the speed of a walrus in mud. He catches up, and reaches for me. To his credit, when I shake my head, he backs off.

"It's not as bad as it looks. It's just inconveniently located." Yeah, Ayala. Sure. I turn downstairs at the landing, stepping over the lamp again. Lifting my leg like that pulls at the claw wounds on my stomach, and I fight the urge to swear. Instead, I talk to light saber britches. "If you contact the Office of Norm Casualties at the Summit, they'll walk you through filing a claim."

"I don't have demon insurance."

I snort a laugh, which also pulls at the gouges in my middle. "No one does. We have an endowment for it."

I can almost hear the man blink. We reach the living room, and I can see a crowd gathered on the lawn. A mostly nude crowd, and one blocky shape that's very, very welcome.

"What's your name?" the man asks.

This isn't the first time someone I've rescued has asked me that, and it probably won't be the last unless I get myself dead in the near future. I'm not sure why I hesitate to answer. After a long pause, I say, "Ayala Storme."

I can't tell by the man's face if he recognizes the name or not, but I don't really care. I shuffle past him and out the door, where a shade named Sanj greets me with a touch on my shoulder. I move my short sword into my right hand, almost dropping it to return the gesture. A patter of footsteps sounds behind me, and I feel something soft hit my shoulder. It smells like fake grass and flowers. Turning my head to look, my cheek encounters terrycloth.

"It's raggedy, but it's clean," says the man. "You can use it to clean your swords. Or stop the bleeding."

I meet his eyes for the first time, and I give him a wry smile. He sussed out my priorities pretty well. "Thanks."

"Least I could do."

Sanj helps me get down the front steps—by which I mean he walks in front of me so if I pitch forward, my nose will hit his back instead of the slates of the footpath.

Gregor beckons me, his gaze dipping to my stomach, then returning to meet my eyes. Somehow, his backlit form exudes relief.

The not-dead inhabitant of the house calls out my name as I walk toward Gregor. "Ayala."

I turn my head to look back at him. "Yeah?"

"Thank you."

Some nights, killing things in the woods and having the Mittens Brigade pick up the pieces makes me forget the human face of what I do. For a moment, warm fuzzies threaten to well up in my chest under all the drying sweat and still-seeping blood.

Then I remember the guy's slummoth-soaked bedroom, spattered with almost every bodily fluid.

I'm just sorry this dude got a taste of my life.

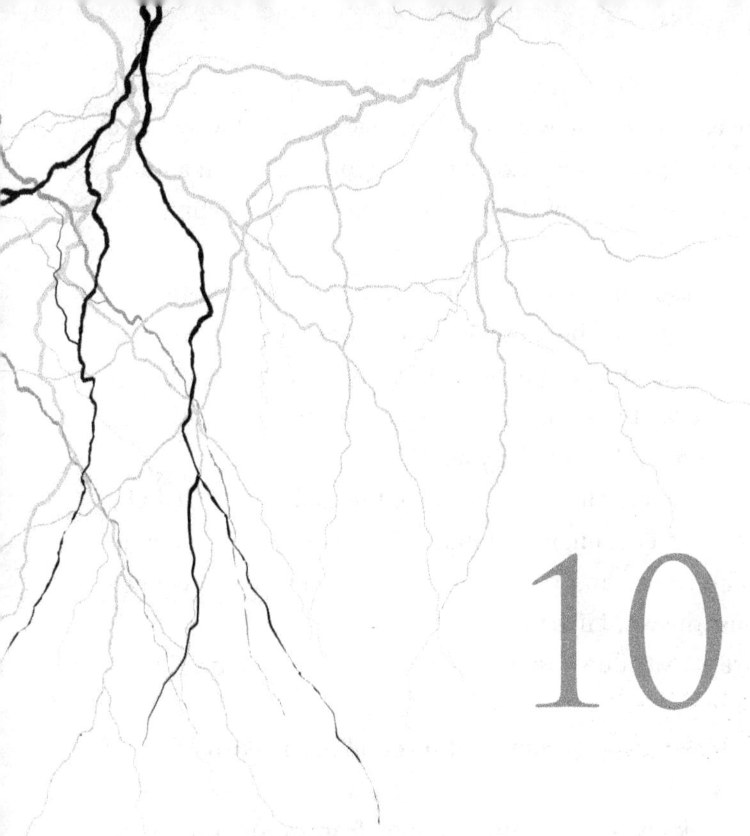

10

I'M ONE LUCKY SONOFABITCH.

The gashes across my midsection are just shallow enough not to sever much more than the skin and fat of my stomach. Fit as I am, they don't quite slice into the muscle.

Even so, I call Laura at eight in the morning to tell her I'll be taking Thursday and Friday night off. I no longer try and make up root canals and optometrist appointments to cover my injuries and hellkin-related hijinks. Instead I just tell her the truth—that a pack of demons tried to make julienne Ayala.

She asks gravely if I'm okay, and I tell her I'll live.

Laura also exudes relief about that.

For most people, living is a pretty low bar, but for me it's cause for celebration.

Carrick wakes up a couple hours after we get home, spitting mad and about ready to shred the thousand thread count sheets on my guest bed, but I lie down next to him, not touching him, just staring at the ceiling until he shuts the hell up.

I think about making a crack about his age and me saving his bare ass twice in a week, but I change my mind when I see him sleeping peacefully next to me. His long hair is an auburn tangle, and I wonder how I ended up capable of coexisting with this guy.

I manage some telework Thursday and Friday both, and by Friday night, my body itches from sternum to pelvis from the healing scratches. Carrick's back up and about, having scrubbed away the remaining scabs from the slummoth venom and thoroughly ruined my new loofah.

Gregor checks in on us at around ten, and to my delight he brings dinner. Filet mignon snippets for the recovering demonoid loofah-ruiner and pizza for me. Pizza covered in cooked meat. Just the way I like it.

Gregor sits down in my black leather easy chair. "I have a confession."

I'm never a fan of conversations that begin like that.

"Damn it."

Carrick gives me an amused look from across the room, where he's skimming titles on my bookshelf. He has a penchant for bodice rippers and kilt flippers. I subscribed him to a monthly book club. He picks one after a beat and returns to the sofa, where Nana promptly hops up beside him, curling into a little ginger ball by his leg. She falls asleep, velveteen ears twitching.

I stick my tongue out at Carrick and look back to Gregor. "Spill it, Strong Mad."

Gregor scowls at me, but he starts talking.

"I was waiting in the woods the whole time the other night," he says. He stretches, the chair squeaking as he leans back. He looks at me as if expectant of some explosive reaction.

I don't know what I was expecting, but it wasn't that.

"You and half the older Mediators in Nashville have probably done that for most of my life," I say flippantly. It's more breezy than I feel. An itch gathers between my shoulder blades.

The older Mediators always observe Mittens and the young Mediators right out of training; something about ensuring they live to get as snarky as me.

Then it hits me, what he's really saying.

"So. Did we pass?"

Gregor's thin lips become a you-got-me grin, and he nods. "You passed. Even Carrick."

Carrick doesn't budge from where he sits, book open to the blank flyleaf, but the stillness of his body betrays his agitation. By now, I speak shade.

I pretend to focus on Gregor, but I keep Carrick in my peripheral vision.

"So," I say.

"So," says Gregor.

A long pause stretches, broken only by a small thump as Nana jumps down from the couch and scurries to her litter box.

"I have a job for you."

My left hand goes involuntarily to my stomach, which is still a mass of scabs. It'll be healed to tender scar tissue by tomorrow, but I don't really feature getting all torn up again.

"What's the job?" Caution makes my question sound hesitant, and I wish I could rewind.

"Crossville. There's a trio—maybe more—of shades gnawing on the populace. I need you to go take them down."

Something seems to squiggle against my spine from the inside, and I wait a moment before responding. "Did you send anybody to talk to them?"

The flatlining of Gregor's mouth tells me no.

The squiggle grows a bit more insistent. "You want us to just go kill them."

"They're killing norms."

I don't like it, but he's right. I think. I remember the warehouse I found here in Nashville all too well. No more meat smoothies get made of the populace.

He goes over the plan then, telling me about an old barn on some farmer's property that's about to be subdivided into lots for McMansions. The shades have holed up there, and nobody will go near them.

"Have any Mediators tried?" I ask. It seems like the logical question; we're the ones who usually take care of homicidal pest control. Come to think of it, I'm not sure how I feel about classifying myself as a glorified exterminator. Then again, the Ghostbusters were exactly that. I can handle sharing their category.

Gregor shakes his head in response to my question, and behind his eyes I detect something I can't pinpoint. Summit politics. Ugh.

"When?"

"Tonight, if you're up to it."

Carrick on the sofa is still imitating a statue, but at that, he finally moves to nod. He was torn up worse than I was, but he heals faster.

The scabs on my stomach pull a bit when I stretch. I look at Carrick, thinking of a bunch of shades terrorizing Crossville. That's bad news. Then I think of Gregor, and how two days ago, us hunting packs of slummoths was seen as a test. How long did Crossville have to lose citizens before Gregor got around to asking us to do this?

I nod my assent, and Gregor leaves, but my troubled feeling doesn't.

SOMETIMES I WONDER WHAT it's like to spend Friday night at the movies. Or on a date. Or kicked back in my recliner with explosions on television, snuggled into my silk robe and sipping from a glass of sake.

Sometimes that wondering is prompted by stepping in a pile of rotting entrails. Like right now.

I bite back a curse, sidestepping the rest of the oozing offal and scraping the side of my boot on a scrubby patch of grass. The shades walking around me don't seem to care much—Harkan and Udo tread right over it—and the sight reminds me that as much time as I've spent with them, we're still very different.

The only good thing about having to clean decaying flesh off my boots is that it tells me we're on the right track.

The sky lightens above us, almost imperceptibly as the rising moon heralds the coming of the sun. If Gregor's intel is right, the shades who have been munching on Crossville's people—and leaving scraps for me to step in—should be about ready to tuck themselves in for the night. I only hope the abandoned barn they've settled isn't decorated like the warehouse by the train tracks was. That would make the pile of guts look like a paper cut.

It's hunting season, and as we walk through the underbrush and kudzu in the direction of the farmer's land, I keep my eyes peeled for any flash of orange among the trees. The last thing we need is some trigger-happy hunter alerting the shades to our presence. The news has probably spread enough to keep norms away from this place, but it only takes one clueless out of towner to spoil the surprise.

I look at the GPS tracker Gregor gave me. We're about a mile out from the barn, which I know from pictures is in an overgrown meadow the forest is trying to swallow. This time we split into three teams led by me, Carrick, and Miles. Gregor, I suspect, is sitting in a Crossville diner watching the blip of our GPS movement crawl across a screen.

Carrick leads his four shades up to the north, and Miles takes his to the east. I take my team, which consists of Carus, Udo, and Sanj, to the southwest. We linger for twenty minutes where we are, and I keep an eye on the green dots that are Miles and Carrick as they get into position. They each agreed to wear a tracker on a necklace. After all, it's not like they have any pockets you'd want to put a piece of tech into.

Not if you wanted it back, anyway.

When the others are finally in place, I motion to Udo and the others. Udo is short and lithe, like a young Jackie Chan. He moves like Spider-Man and looks like he could climb a pane of glass with only his fingertips. Sanj has a mop of black hair and brown skin and walks forward in sporadic bursts. He reminds me of a sparking live wire. Carus is white, but tanned to the point where his blond hair looks like he belongs on an eighties magazine cover. I didn't know shades could tan until I met Carus. Apparently he likes the sun.

The four of us approach the barn—or at least I think we do. All I have to go from is the little green dots converging on a green X on the GPS screen. Half a mile out, I still don't know if we're going to find the barn or a herd of deer.

A quarter mile out, I see a fluorescent orange mark on a tree, the paint still wet and dribbling down the bark like the oh-fuck feeling dribbling down the inside of my stomach.

Hunters. Nearby. They couldn't have come through here more than fifteen or twenty minutes ago.

The barn appears through the trees under the dawn-grey sky, quiet and innocuous.

I want to hope that whoever spray painted that mark on the tree was heading northwest, away from the barn and out of the range of these murderous shades. Going out to bag a deer and ending up caught between warring hellkin hybrids and a pissed off Mediator is a pretty crappy turn to the day.

I try to keep that little hope alive, but with every step toward the barn, it sputters.

A scrap of torn bright orange fabric snuffs it out entirely.

Miles' and Carrick's dots are still; with mine, they triangulate the barn. I listen for anything my ears can pick up. Sleepy crickets settling down for the night, a cold breeze rustling from the north that carries the slightest scent of woodsmoke.

We fan out until the fourteen of us form a circle around the barn. Next to me, Udo shifts his shoulders and goes still, his flaring nostrils the only movement I see him make.

After a moment, I see why. The coppery scent of blood, fresh blood, wafts through the air.

Carrick is thirty yards away, only just visible on the other side of the barn. The building is a small structure, maybe twenty feet by twenty feet. Sided in hickory, the wood in places is half-eaten by dry rot, but not quite enough to provide any visibility inside. That doesn't mean that the shades inside can't see out, though.

I can't see the door from where I stand, but pictures Gregor showed me allow me to visualize it, a large wooden panel on a rusty slide, facing east.

Turns out the shades inside don't plan to use the door.

I get one shouted warning from Carrick, and a blur coupled with the thuds of footsteps on the roof becomes a pale comet launching itself from the building at me. I whip my swords from their sheaths and dive to the side, rolling and bouncing back to my feet. Two more shapes leap from the roof of the barn in my direction. I have enough time to realize that they're using a blitz tactic before one hits me.

I'm ready, and I don't lose my footing, thrusting my sword into the hard muscles of my attacker's arm. His white skin is brushed with blood like paint, the strokes as varied as an impressionist's. My stab wound adds to it a stream down his bicep, but he doesn't stop. I jump back from him, putting steel between me and his hands that can tear my limbs off.

My saber comes down on the side of his neck, sending arterial spray arcing across my body. The shade stumbles, and I finish the job, my body flowing through the movement with grim purpose. Udo and Sanj have a second shade stretched by the arms between them, and ten feet away, Carus kneels on another. I don't watch, but I hear the snap of the enemy shades' spines as my battalion of killers takes off their heads.

Three down, and the sounds of growls tells me Gregor was wrong about it being a trio. The three shades on my team and I move east toward the barn door. Miles has wrenched it open, and from the bodies littered around it, another five shades boiled out.

There are still two alive.

One goes down as I watch, Harkan and Hux finishing him.

The last one is cornered in the barn, his eyes darting to the rafters above him as if calculating the possibility of a successful jump, and Hayn and Rex stalk toward him.

In the morning light, the final shade's eyes shine with a silvery sheen, and I can almost smell the stench of his terror over the copper blood that I can see now as well as smell. It coats the inside of the barn, seeping into the hard-packed dirt floor. I try not to look at the lump of red-spashed bright orange in the corner.

The shade backs away from Hayn and Rex until his back is against the wall.

"Help," he says.

I stop two steps inside the barn.

"Wait," I say.

Hayn and Rex slow their advance, but they don't stop. The shade goes still between them, looking back and forth with pleading eyes.

I try not to think of the carnage behind me or the twelve Crossville people Gregor told me have gone missing.

The shade closes his eyes and puts his hands in the air, and Hayn and Rex take that opportunity to pin his arms to the rough wooden wall.

"Help," the shade says again.

"He wants to surrender." The words spill from my lips, and the shade nods, sharp jerks of his head.

"Surrender." His words feel jagged around the edges, like he's not used to talking.

I feel Carrick's presence behind me before I see him pass by my right shoulder. I walk forward, toward the shade.

Urgently, I turn to Carrick. "He wants to surrender. We should help him. Teach him."

Carrick keeps walking, and suddenly I'm very aware of the other shades watching me. The one pinned to the wall still has his eyes closed.

"Carrick!"

"Help," the shade keens. "Help, help, help, surrender, help, help, surrender."

His words blur together in my mind, over and over, *helphelphelpsurrenderhelphelpsurrender.*

"Carrick!" My voice holds tinny panic, and I feel frozen in the gaze of the other shades, Udo and Harkan, Hux and Beex, Holden and Carus, Sanj and Lawlor, Boyne and Miles, Hayn and Rex. Their eyes burn me.

Carrick's hands find the shade's neck.

His pleas cut off.

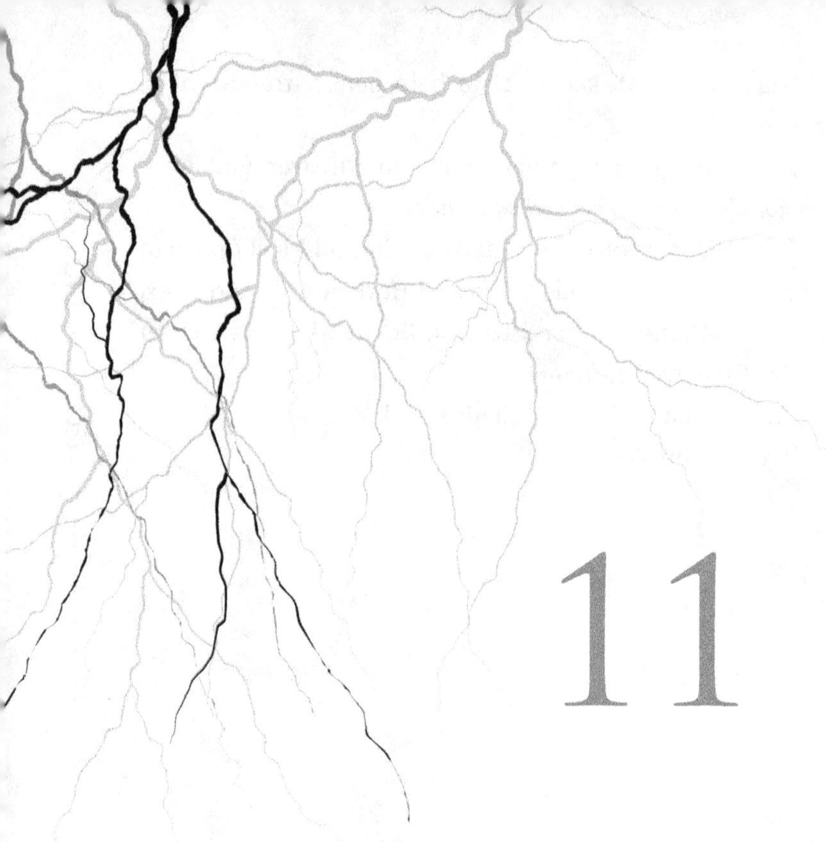

11

MIRA HANDS ME A mug with Pooh Bear on it, and the smoky heat of the whisky within reaches my nose. I take a big drink, hating that my hand is trying to shake on the mug's handle. Mira's dressed all in black, freshly showered with her sleek, asymmetrical cap of black hair so perfectly styled that she could easily waltz onto a photo shoot without anyone asking questions. Her bottom lip, though, is wedged between her top and bottom teeth, tucked into her mouth as she watches me take another sip of whisky. And another.

I don't really know why I'm here, except I didn't know where else to go.

Mira's table is shining mahogany that reflects the sunlight from the window. The top of the window is purple and red stained glass that casts glowing colors on the table. Mira sits across from me, her palms flat on the surface and her eyes tracking my every move.

The alcohol suffuses me with warmth like the early afternoon sunlight and a pleasant buzz, but it doesn't help. Not really.

In my mind, the track replays over and over again. The shade saying *helphelphelpsurrenderhelphelpsurrender* over and over until I don't know where one word starts and the other ends and I want to put my hands over my ears, even though I know that's crazy. I can't drown him out. I can't make it stop. He won't go away. He'll live in me now, this memory of a being who didn't want to die.

Gregor told me calmly that the shade was going to double cross us, that as soon as we'd turned our backs, he would have fled into the woods and eaten someone's first grader or something. I nodded along, numb and quiet, and when Gregor said he needed to talk to Carrick, I got in my car and drove straight here.

Again I remember the warehouse I blew up with more than twenty shades in it. It was my intel, my plan, my idea. Take them out. Monsters. Murderers. Demons.

And then one of them saved my life.

What would Mason think, if he were here?

Would that shade have been safe with him?

If there's anything I've learned about shades, its that they are just as much a duality of nature and nurture as norms are. In my mind, a dozen scenarios play out at once, like forks of the Cumberland, twisting through eventualities where that surrendering shade dreamed of something more, remembered his mother, wanted to be different, didn't know how.

Maybe we could have helped him. Maybe I could have helped him.

I swig down the rest of the whisky, and as soon as the mug hits the table, Mira refills it.

She knows; I told her. She watches me, waiting for me to say something.

"I could have stopped him," I blurt out. The whisky on my lips tingles, numbing the fragile skin.

She knows the *him* I'm referencing is Carrick. And it's true.

I could have stopped him. I could have gotten between them, thought faster, been cleverer. But I didn't.

"What would you have done if they'd all turned on you?" she asks carefully. Her voice is even and calm like a pond at first light. For once there's no swearing from her, just a question.

The question gives me pause. Would they? Would the shades I've spent months with simply take me down for challenging Carrick? Again my shoulders remember the touches of their fingers, the tiny touches that speak so huge. Trust. Safety. Confidence. I want to believe that those touches would translate into my immunity from their violence, but suddenly I don't know.

"I would have died." I know her question is rhetorical, but I have to say the words out loud. They don't absolve me of the surrendering shade's death, but they give me some comfort in their truth. I couldn't face all those shades on my own. I would be pulped in three seconds.

I take another drink of whisky and set the mug down again.

Mira reaches across the table and takes my hands. Her hands are so like mine. Calluses from years of wielding blades. Nails trimmed to the quick. Nicks and small scars from blades that slipped while sharpening them. They're warm and strong, and they return some of my own strength to me.

"You did the best you could," she says. Then she pulls back and stands up, going to the kitchen. She returns a minute later with a plate bearing unceremoniously dumped crackers and pre-cut squares of cheese. "Better eat something, you sad bastard, or you'll have a hangover from the hells."

I pick up a piece of cheese and nibble on it, a sharp white cheddar that's usually one of my favorites but right now I can barely taste.

"Is it always like this for you?" Mira asks suddenly.

"Like what?" I feel tired and weighed down. Maybe it's the whisky making my arms feel heavy, but I feel like it's only taking hold of an exhaustion that already exists.

"Always questioning. Wondering constantly if you're making the right decisions."

I look at her, unsure if it's only me we're talking about. Her mouth is pursed just a bit on one side, and she watches me intently.

"Yes," I say. Then after a beat, "Didn't used to be."

"Things used to be simpler."

"That they did."

Norms good, demons bad. Keep the balance. Right the scales. I was good at that.

I don't know what I'm good at anymore. Continuing to breathe? I guess that's a plus.

"What made you disobey Alamea this summer?" I ask Mira. I think back to Miller's Field that day, just as the sun set. Mason chained beside me. Mediator swords at my throat. We were the bait for Saturn and the rest of the shades. I was the only Mediator who spoke for the shades, and in the end, with the field teeming with demons, it was the shades that kept us all from getting dead. All of the Mediators were ready to kill as many hellkin hybrids as they could, never mind that I'd told them the shades have free will and that Mason had saved my life. Mira was the only one who refused. I want to know why.

I can see her face wall up at the question. Maybe disobey was the wrong word for me to use. To defect doesn't sound much better though.

For a moment I don't think she's going to answer me, but she starts to speak, haltingly.

"I've known you my whole life. You always did your job so well. When we were Mittens, you always had my back. Figuratively and most of the time literally." She gives me a sad smile, and I know she's thinking of the time we both ended up with backs full of rakath spines, pulling them out of each other.

The memory also makes me think of Carrick, and my mouthful of cheese sours on my tongue.

Mira's going on. "You always had my back," she says again. "I guess that day, seeing the way they used you and the way that gods damned witch turned you in and doped you up—well. I thought it was time someone had yours."

I meet her eyes and open my mouth to say something, but whatever words were about to materialize vanish under the sound of Mira's front door opening.

"Hey, it's me," Wane's voice comes from the entryway. "I brought lunch. Guacamole and rotisserie chicken—"

Her voice drops off, and I can actually hear the morph woman sniffing the air.

"Are you drinking?" she asks.

Wane appears around the corner, today in street clothes. Jeans and a tight royal blue t-shirt that makes her eyes pop and a black leather jacket. She stops when she sees me, frowning at the Pooh Bear mug. "Ayala. Hi."

I'm not sure if she's pissed that I'm here or just surprised, but I give her a small wave and a smile as friendly as I can muster. Which probably isn't very.

It seems to settle her anyway, and she nods at the mug. "Early start?"

"Rough night," I say.

Mira hops up and grabs a few plates from the kitchen, as well as a carafe of orange juice. Wane sits down at the head of the table, diagonally from me.

"More stuff with the shades?" She plucks a piece of cheese from the plate in front of me, peering at me.

I don't want to go into it again, but I nod. "Have you heard anything from Saturn?"

From the way Wane's gaze lingers on me, I can tell she senses that I don't want to talk about my night. She looks over her shoulder to the kitchen, where Mira's returning with lunch supplies.

Wane gets up to help her spread out the food, and I watch them move around one another. They interact seamlessly, each anticipating the other like dance partners. A little unnerved, I take a cracker. If I didn't believe Mira when she said they weren't a couple, I'd assume they were.

"Eat," Mira orders me when she sits down. She shoves a plate my way, and I salute, throwing some chicken and guacamole on it, along with some potato salad and chips.

For a little while, I can forget the weight on my chest. Mira and Wane banter back and forth, and I quietly let their easy camaraderie stitch my tattered emotions back together.

I even manage to laugh.

But when it comes time to go home, my smile fades, and not even Nana hopping forward to meet me at the door can dispel the tension I feel in my apartment. Carrick emerges from his bedroom when he hears me close and latch the front door. He smiles as if nothing's wrong, and reaches out to touch my shoulder.

I have to force myself to reach back and touch his.

12

I CAN'T LET MYSELF try to overanalyze Carrick's gesture or its timing. Instead, I sequester myself inside my room with Nana, dusting off my TV for the first time in ages. My housekeeper Clyde hasn't been by this month, and there's Nana fur everywhere. I send him an email asking him to come this week. The thought of him waltzing around the apartment and belting songs from Hair makes me happy. It restores an ounce of normalcy to my psyche.

The rest of the weekend passes in a strict routine. Saturday night I go on patrol, bag a couple hellkin in Percy Warner Park, snag some lo mein on the way home, and sleep till noon. Sunday I do the same, keeping to my room. Carrick vanishes for most of Sunday, and having my apartment to myself airs me out like an open window in spring. By the time Monday morning rolls around, I feel almost human again. I even stop and get donuts for the office on my way to work.

When I arrive at eleven, I push open the door to a startled explanation and a non-harmonious yell of "SURPRISE!"

I almost drop the donuts.

Laura beams at me, her hair pulled back in a tidy bun. She's in olive green today with a plum-colored beaded necklace. Meredith and Leeloo, the two witches who usually work three till eleven, grin from the kitchenette, and Parker claps his hands excitedly at the dumbfounded look I must be wearing.

"You guys," I say, a welter of strange emotions fizzing in my chest. I put the box of donuts on the ledge at Parker's desk, and a pair of cornflower blue eyes peeks up from the other side.

My jaw falls open. "Alice?"

Her hair, which used to be in a state of constant panic and sprayed within an inch of its life, is now a golden shade of blonde instead of peroxide platinum. It falls in gentle waves to her chest. She has crinkly crow's feet at the corners of her eyes where before her face was unnaturally smooth from whatever metaphysical face lift was the flavor of the week at the witchy beauty salon, and her face blossoms into a grin, tears filling her eyes.

She's got a smudge of pink on her right front tooth.

Some things never change.

I dart around the desk and throw my arms around her. She smells like peonies and sunshine, and she hugs me back with a firmness and confidence I don't remember her ever having before.

I probably hold onto her too long, because Laura gives a little cough that sounds suspiciously like she's trying not to cry, and I hear Leeloo grab a tissue from the box in the kitchenette. Out of the corner of my eye, I see her hand it to Parker.

Releasing Alice from the hug, I pull back to look at her again. She's wearing jeans and a light blue sweater, and she looks...happy.

Something wet drops on my boob, and I reach up to wipe my eye. "Well, hells. Surprise. You weren't kidding about that, were you?"

Alice reaches out and grabs my hand, squeezing it. "Come on! We got food."

She drags me into the conference room, where they've laid out brunch across the entire table.

Laura comes to stand beside me as I fill up my plate, tossing a raspberry jelly donut from my box onto the edge of it. "I thought it might be nice to celebrate your promotion," she says.

Fuck me, but my eyes won't stop leaking today. I put my plate on the table and hug Laura, which I think surprises her, because for a moment she goes so still I wonder if I frightened her.

"Well," she says. "Well."

I remember what I told her about this job and what it means to me, and when I pull back and plop my butt down in a chair to eat, I see her watching me and think she's probably thinking of the same thing.

Laura bustles around for a few minutes, then goes to the head of the table and raises her glass. "To Ayala, and to a long and prosperous partnership."

"To Ayala!" the rest of them echo her, and we toast with sparkling cider that I down quickly to disguise the gods damned tears that won't quit pooling in my eyes.

Alice sits down next to me, her plate overflowing. For the next hour, I listen in a happy haze as she tells me about her time at the World Summit, about learning meditation and martial arts—once she says it, I look closer and can see the new definition in her muscles through the thin cashmere sweater—and about how she has learned so much about the Mediators and what they do. She doesn't seem to care that none of the others except Laura really know why she left, and her bubbly words make me feel something I haven't felt in a long time.

Pride.

For all the frustration and pain and uncertainty of these last few months, with Alice sitting next to me, I feel like I am capable of doing good. That she is safe and happy and whole partly because of me. That she is brave and always has been, first for trying to seek out her friend in the scariest, most dangerous parts of our world, later for healing herself.

I am proud of her. When I tell her so, she gets teary again. I guess it's contagious today.

"Thank you," she says.

I know for what, and I shift in my chair, feeling uncomfortable. "You did the hardest part yourself," I say. I mean it.

She snorts, and when she looks at me, I see a clarity in her eyes that's either new or heretofore unnoticed.

"You never had to help me," she says.

I don't have time to answer, because somebody hits me with silly string, and then it's war.

But my answer sticks inside of me anyway. Yes, Alice. Yes, I did.

LAURA LETS US ALL leave work at five—not that any of us got much done—I hug Alice one more time and head back to my apartment. She's going to be joining the company again, and she's not even kicking Parker out of his job. Laura's hiring her back as an executive assistant, hands on help for the two partners.

Two partners. I'm going to be partner.

It's finally starting to feel real, this promotion.

Carrick's not home when I get there, so I throw together a box of macaroni and cheese and chop up hot dogs to go in it. I remember Ripper making fun of me when I was a Mitten, telling me that hot dogs were made up of ground harkast demon parts. He's five years older than me, and he was just out of training himself, and I was a belligerent little brat of a Mitten, so I grilled up an entire pack of hot dogs and ate them in front of him. I even managed to get back to my room before I hurled.

He felt so bad about it that he came clean right away and took my splat shifts for the next month.

Haven't seen Ripper in a while. Probably because he's BFFs with my archnemesis, Ben Wheedle.

Actually, Ben's not worthy of that title.

When I'm done eating, I leather up and prep for my night's hunt. I haven't heard anything from Gregor about training with the shades, so dial up the Mediator hotline and ask if they've got any hotspots. They point me toward Stones River Bend Park on the east side of town where they say they've had a bunch of frahlig activity.

The park is in the bend of the Stones River, as its name would suggest, and it's dotted with little lakes. Frahligs like freshwater rivers and ponds, and while they're not my favorite demons to slice and dice, they're at least pretty stupid and don't see well out of the water.

Never swim after dark.

I park at the end of a cul-de-sac on the western edge of the park, heading toward the coordinates the Summit gave me. A Great Horned Owl hoots through the trees, its quivering song rising in the night. Another owl answers, and I almost feel as though they're letting me know the way is clear.

Their calls die out when I reach the first lake—more a cluster of three ponds—and I take that as a cue to unsheathe my swords.

I skirt the lakeshore, listening for the telltale splashing and slurpy snarls that indicate the presence of a frahlig. When no such sounds come, I venture northeast into the park. Back in the trees, there is nothing but silence.

Ahead of me, a pink glow appears.

I stop in my tracks and look behind me and to the sides. Jeelings are bad enough alone, and I don't care to find out what would happen if there's more than one. The last time I had to actually fight one I almost died. Eleven feet tall, they have massive bone protrusions from their shoulders, and that's one of their finer points. They give off that pink glow for hells-knows-whatever-reason, and from the strength of the glow ahead of me, this one's either really angry or there's a jeeling party.

I can't count on this one running away from me like the one in Belle Meade did.

I type out a message on my phone to the hotline, letting them know that their frahligs are jeelings and that I'll try to get a count without dying.

The trees thin out up ahead, and I find one and get behind it. None of the trees nearby look climbable, and though I've yet to see a demon climb a tree, I don't think I want to test out any hypotheses with jeelings around.

The glow starts moving in my direction, and I suck in a breath.

Peering out around the tree, I see them now. About a hundred yards away, the pink glow materializes into three hulking shapes and illuminates the area around them enough to see that I am well and truly splatted.

The hotline was right. There are frahligs. And slummoths. And rakaths. And harkasts. And a couple snorbits. And though I've never seen one in the slimy flesh before, I think the one pawing at the ground on all fours is an aetna.

I count eighteen total. When they shift eastward, I let out my breath as slowly as I can, thanking every star above my head that they're upwind of me, even if that means I have to smell the rotten fish stink of the frahligs from here.

Texting the Summit again is probably worthless, but I do it anyway. It's another eight hours until sunup, and these monsters have the run of the land until then.

Hellkin don't gather in numbers like this, not without reason. So far the only reasons I've ever seen had to do with either making full-grown baby shades or killing the full-grown baby shades when they didn't work out as planned. Whatever they're doing is bad news.

Following them is a terrible idea, but the Summit texts back that they're sending backup and to keep an eye on the hellkin.

So I follow.

I keep my distance, staying as far back as possible while tracking the glow emitted by the jeelings. After a few minutes,

I wonder how they're planning to cross the river. The only bridge on this side of the park is to the north, and the park is only about a half mile wide. Most demons aren't particularly good swimmers.

The river is close enough for me to smell now, that scent of algae and wet rock and damp earth. I stop again behind a tree and look out.

Half the demons have vanished.

My heart suddenly seems to exist in my tonsils, and I look around me, swords ready for a rakath or slummoth to come at me. But none do.

I look again, and what I see makes me freeze.

The air around the demons seems to ripple like a parting beaded curtain. The demons are going into it, and for a moment they appear like paper going through a shredder. Then they're gone.

The jeelings are the last to go, but after a moment, they also disappear through the tear in the air. My eyes see ghosts of their pink glow when they're gone.

Eighteen demons existing peacefully, vanishing into their own dimension in front of my eyes. Alarm bells scream in my head like a tornado siren. I look at my phone. The Summit's backup is only five minutes out. I'm going to have to somehow explain this to them.

13

THE SUN'S UP BEFORE I get to leave the park.

I go to the Summit with a group of Mediators, and they call in Alamea. She arrives at half past seven looking like she meant to be up that early, her linen blouse pressed and perfect and her heels clicking too loudly on the floors of the Summit. When she hears the story, she pulls all of us into a conference room I already know is an interrogation room. I've been interrogated in it before.

Grudgingly, I have to admit that if it weren't for Jaryn the psychic, I probably wouldn't have made it home last summer.

For as much as I hate psychics for their obnoxious attitudes and I-know-what-you're-thinking smirks, if Jaryn saves my ass one more time, I'm going to have to get him a pie or something. He happens to poke his head into the room to say hello to Alamea just before one of the other Mediators closes the door. His eyes lock on mine, and his mammoth hand catches the door and holds it open.

“I think you might need me,” he says.

Ain’t nobody trying to get to the truth of something gonna say no to a psychic’s presence.

Within fifteen minutes, he’s confirmed my tale. Alamea dismisses everyone but the two of us and closes the door behind them.

“Sit,” she says.

We sit. Jaryn is as mammoth in height as his hands are, and he has to sit back an extra two feet from the table so his knees don’t bang into the divider beneath it that runs down the length of it.

She sits at the head of the table in troubled silence for three whole minutes.

“Well. This isn’t good,” she says.

“No shit,” says Jaryn.

“You don’t seem entirely surprised.” I look at her, then at Jaryn, feeling dwarfed by their presence, like a kindergartner at the big kids’ table. I’m fairly tall, but Alamea’s got six inches on me, and Jaryn’s got another six on her. I feel like my feet should be dangling from my seat. I plant them on the floor, mostly to prove to myself I can.

“Let’s just say that it’s not the only oddity going on in middle Tennessee right now.” Alamea goes silent, and I know she’s thinking. She’s always very deliberate about her words.

My mind does a quick run through the oddities I’ve seen myself. Frahligs away from water. A jeeling that fled me. Slummoths attacking the homes of norms. Two shades vanishing into thin air, at least one of them afraid enough to hurt a friend. Multiple species of demons gathering.

Yeah, I’d say a shitstorm’s a-brewin’. I sure as hells don’t want to be anywhere near the fan it’s about to hit.

Too bad I don’t have a choice.

Resigned, I meet Alamea’s eyes. “Any ideas?”

“Demons aren’t usually tactical,” she says.

“I noticed that, too.” My voice comes out more sardonic than I meant it to, and I want to swallow my tongue.

"In our history, when they start organizing, it means they're about to try something large to unbalance the scales. Tip them in their favor."

"They're always trying to do that," Jaryn says, but both Alamea and I shake our heads.

"Normally they're just trying to survive," I say. "They come here, raid for whatever food they can find at night, and go back to their snuggly hell dimensions at first light. When they start doing something other than that, things get bad fast."

"In the past, it's led to us losing entire portions of territory," Alamea says.

"Like Mississippi." I feel sick.

"Like Mississippi." Alamea seems to share my sentiment, and how could she not?

Now we've got Jaryn's attention. He knows as well as we do that when we say Mississippi, we mean Mississippi, Alabama, most of Louisiana, two strips of Tennessee—one west of Memphis and the other in the southeast near Chattanooga—and an ever-growing chunk of Arkansas all the way up to Little Rock.

I usually try not to think about that, because we're not that far from there. There used to be Mediator territories there. Not anymore. And Mediators can't retreat. We can't leave our territories. When we lose territories, well. If you're not alive, you're that other thing.

"We need to figure out what we're going to do and fast," I say. I think of the medal hanging behind Alamea's desk chair. Lowest norm mortality in the country. I have a feeling that's about to change. As if the universe is as psychic as Jaryn is, Alamea's phone goes off.

She answers it with a curt, "Talk to me."

I can't hear what the caller says, but Jaryn's face goes paper-white, and he looks at the phone in Alamea's hand as if he wants to take it from her and crush it against the marble-topped table.

When Ayala hangs up, she looks at me.

"Someone just reported two shades taking a man from his home and eating him in the middle of the street."

It is a truth universally acknowledged that if a Monday somehow manages to start out amazing, it will plummet to the depths of all the hells to make up for it.

I'm pretty sure that's what Jane Austen meant to say.

I BARELY MAKE IT home with enough time to shower, change into work clothes, and get to my office.

There's still leftover brunch food in the kitchenette, but there's not enough coffee in Tennessee to keep me from yawning through the day and into late afternoon.

Usually, I do okay on little or no sleep, but today all I want to do is crawl under my desk and nap.

My phone rings at quarter of five. Mira.

"Hey, what's up?" My computer screen blurs in front of my face. I've been staring at it for too long.

"Wane got a call from some morphs up in Franklin, Kentucky who said they have a shade hanging around town and it could be Saturn."

"Has he hurt anyone?" Alarmed, I push my chair back from my desk and bang my knee on a drawer. "Fuck."

Mira takes my swearing to mean I assume he has. "No, no, no. No one's hurt. They said he plans to move on soon, though, so we need to get up there tonight."

"I'll meet you at your house as soon as I can."

"No need. We're on our way downtown now. We can pick you up."

"Mira," I say before she hangs up. "Did they mention his tattoo?"

"They said he's wearing clothes."

Whoa.

"I'll meet you outside," I say.

"Ten minutes." She hangs up.

I duck into Laura's office before I go. "I've got to run out early," I tell her. "Mediator business."

"Be safe," is all she says.

I have spare hunting clothes in my car, and I run to the garage to grab my duffel and my spare swords from my trunk. The backseat of my car may be a disaster zone, but lately I've taken to organizing the trunk. I change in the lobby bathroom, tucking a pair of knives in my boots and slinging my sword belt over my shoulder.

There's a food truck outside that sells burritos, and I order six and several cans of Coke for the drive. I haven't eaten since I got to the office, and the combination of no sleep and no food is the difference between diplomatic me and boot-in-newly-torn-orifices me. Plus, Mira and Wane might be hungry.

They pull up just as I'm paying, and Mira leans on the horn. I give the food truck woman a ten and a twenty and tell her to keep the change, hurrying away. She looks so awed by my swords and the nearly thirty percent tip that she actually claps when I hop in the car and we drive away.

I distribute the burritos while Mira goes over what she knows.

"I think it's him. It has to be. Same build, dark hair, brown guy. Saturn's smart enough to try and blend," she says. "Though I don't like the idea of him stealing his gods damned wardrobe. Poor fool of a cop, if anybody tried to stop him, you know?"

I wince, because I know too well what can happen to cops getting in shades' way.

My mouth is full of shredded beef and cheese and tortilla, so I can't answer, but I nod at her in the rearview mirror.

By the time we get over the Kentucky border, I desperately have to pee. We pull over at a rest stop that's little more than a hole in the ground and smells like people were actively trying to avoid said hole when they used it. The sun's on its way down, and with everything going on in the hellkin world, we all try and make the stop as short as possible.

Franklin, Kentucky is just off I-65, and Mira takes the exit for the main drag, following it straight through town. It's a town of about 8,000 according to search engines, and the main street houses a few quaint brick public buildings and a few more recently boarded up storefronts.

We pass the county jail on the right, and Mira keeps on driving. Pretty soon, the town thins out, and she takes a right on a county road heading to the northwest. I have a roiling worry filling my belly, and it has nothing to do with the two taco truck burritos I ate. The last time I ventured this far to the north, I started feeling the territory sickness we face if we try to venture out of our area. At least I think I was this far north. The last thing Mira and I need is to get into it with a bunch of Kentucky morphs only to have cramps double us over and sweats soak our leathers. That'd be helpful in a fight.

I feel jittery and nervous.

We pass a small white church with a sparse, crooked cemetery, then the road curves and we pass over a creek signed as "Sinking Creek." It's little more than a stream, and Mira pulls the car over on the shoulder just past the bridge.

"They said they're along the creek," Wane says.

She's been quieter tonight than I've seen her before, but it doesn't seem to be out of any kind of antipathy. Instead, she looks...alert. Her eyes scan the wooded creek banks, and even in the falling dark I'm pretty sure she sees even better than I do in the fading light.

It occurs to me that I've never seen morphs outside the city. Most of the morphs I see around Nashville flit from hipster dive to hipster dive. I have no idea what to expect from morphs occupying Kentucky's very literal backwaters.

We make our way along the banks of the stream, which is barely a trickle. I don't know how Mira and Wane know where we're going, but I follow along behind them, keeping my ears and eyes open.

The sounds of the woods feel more resonant here, out of the city. Maybe it's that I'm used to parks, but here so far north of any large norm settlement, the insect and small wildlife noises are dense around us. The cacophony is a relief to me.

A light blooms up ahead, golden-orange instead of an alarming pink. When the wind blows in our direction, I get a whiff of woodsmoke.

Wane stands up straighter as we walk, her head high.

I've never thought to ask her what her animal form is. I'm never quite sure of morphs' social niceties, and I don't want to stumble into a faux pas with anyone whose second form has fangs.

I hear a murmur of voices around the campfire, and a single form walks toward us, silhouetted from the firelight.

Mira rushes forward with a small cry, then skids to a halt fifteen feet from the person.

I see why a moment later when she moves out of my line of sight.

It's not Saturn.

It's Jax.

"Jax," I breathe. I hurry to him, and his fingers touch my shoulder at the same time mine touch his. He's wearing a hoodie and jeans and nice hiking shoes. I've never seen him dressed before. A moment later, he pulls me into a hug. He smells like hickory smoke and night air, and the sensation of his muscles under the single layer of the hoodie is alien.

"I was worried for you," I tell him. "Miles and I tracked you as far as the creek, but that was it. I found the beacon you left in your home."

He looks from me to Mira, panic written across his face, clear to me even in the dusk.

"She's a friend, Jax. She's Saturn's friend."

He relaxes at that. Wane and Mira look over their shoulders as they pass us, heading for the morphs at the fire. I hang back with Jax.

He looks after Mira and Wane. "Saturn told me about her. He said she was different."

"She is," I say before I can stop myself. I'm not sure what I even mean by that, but it's true.

We start walking toward the fire.

"Things are bad back home," I say. "Shades are killing people."

"I know."

"Please, Jax, can you tell me why you left?"

He looks around as if he's afraid the trees are listening in. "I don't know."

"You don't know why you left, or you don't know if you can tell me?"

"Both."

"Then why did you stay here?" He had to have known we were coming.

"It's safer here," he said.

"Safer from what?" I ask gently.

"I want to be free," he says.

"What do you mean?" I feel stupid even asking. The shades working with Carrick and me, well. If they're not visibly helping, they're threatening. "Never mind."

He gives me a grateful look. "I'm sorry. You...we appreciate you."

Startled, I stop walking. From where we stand, I can see Mira and Wane talking to a group of about five morphs. One or two more pace around the perimeter of the campfire's light radius.

Jax's words slowly sink through my mind like a stone in quicksand. The shades appreciate me? "Why?"

He looks at me as if he's talking to a rock. "You're the only one who understands us."

There's a warning in those words, and I hear it ringing through in the cracks between them. "You're not coming back, are you?"

He shakes his head. "I need to go north. I hear nice things about Canada. My mother's mother was from there."

It's creepy how the shades remember the memories of their hosts. Mothers. Of their mothers. I still struggle to get it right. Maybe it's the disconnect that about half of the shades have men for mothers, but I make myself try and remember to get better at it. It makes sense. To them a mother is anyone who gives life from their body, and that's exactly what their mothers do, male or female.

"I hope you like it there," I tell him. "Do you at least have my phone number?"

I made sure to teach all the shades to use a phone, along with basic passing-for-norm skills like tying their shoes and not jay-walking.

Jax rolls up the sleeve of his hoodie. My number is tattooed on his forearm. I do my best not to cringe at the connotation of it; he has no way of knowing the history of such a thing. Unless his mother was a World War II history buff, but even so, the memories they get aren't raw footage. More of a highlight reel.

Instead, I take his arm in my hand and give it a squeeze. In many ways, the shades are innocent. Sentient beings born in blood and bone with a hunger for meat. Mix in memories of their mothers and no chance to acclimate to the world around them and multiply it by a fearful, hostile society—well.

"I'm going to go now," he says abruptly.

I drop my hand away from his arm. "Now? Right now?"

He nods. "You are good, Ayala."

In a flash, he's gone.

14

WANE IS SILENT AS we walk back to the car, and Mira walks by my side.

"I thought it was Saturn," she says.

"I know. I did too."

"Is Jax okay?"

"I hope so. I think he'll be okay." He's so childlike in some ways, more so than Mason or Saturn. I hope he really will be okay. I've seen him fight, and he does it well, but he's a gentle person. His words echo in my mind. *I want to be free.*

Don't we all.

"Things are going to go to hells, aren't they?" Mira asks suddenly.

"I think it's pretty likely." My legs feel like they're on autopilot. It's after nine, and I haven't slept in two days.

"I wanted to help Saturn."

"I think you did help him," I tell her. "He cared about you."

“Yeah, well, that Little Bunny Foo-Foo bonked me over the head like a fucking field mouse as soon as he needed to get away.” Even though Mira spits out the words, I can hear the pain in her voice.

“You’re not a field mouse. Garter snake, maybe.”

“Fuck off, I’m a gods damned copperhead.”

I grin at her, and she grins back, but after a few seconds our smiles fade. Back at the car, I grab another burrito, not caring that it’s cold, and pop open a can of Coke.

I’m not really sure what else to do.

The rest of the ride back passes quickly and quietly, all three of us lost in our thoughts. About a half hour out of Nashville, I finally ask what the morphs had to say.

At first, my only answer is the sound of the car downshifting as the speed limit drops.

“They’re migrating,” Wane says finally.

“They’re what?”

Never in my life have I heard of morphs having migration patterns. Wane and Mira exchange an unreadable look in the front seat.

“You know how animals know if a tornado is coming? Something like that.”

Well, shit.

I think of my city, the familiar skyline with the bat-eared building dominating the view. The winding squiggle of the Cumberland River. The badass hipster witches of East Nashville with their boutiques and beauty shops and bars. I don’t want Nashville to become Mississippi.

Then something strikes me. The Opry. It used to be a bustling center of country music and boasted the best of the best. Dolly Parton. Loretta Lynn. Johnny Cash. Then the hot springs bubbled up around it, and the whole thing went into the shitter.

“Mira, when’d the Opry shut down? Do you remember?”

“Ten, fifteen years back now? I’d have to look it up.”

Have we been blind this whole time? Are we already on the edge of a cliff, one mudslide away from Mississippi-status?

Suddenly the car feels too small, too hot. I roll down my window and breathe deeply, trying to dispel the sudden panic. Maybe it's my ongoing exhaustion this week, but I can't help the feeling that I'm right, that somehow we've all been missing important clues all along.

"You okay?" Mira turns around in her seat, craning her neck to look back at me.

"I don't know."

"Hey," she says. She reaches her hand back and takes mine. "It's either gonna be okay, or we'll all go overboard together."

Maybe for most people, that wouldn't make them feel better, but for me it does. The grip of her hand grounds me a little, and I take another deep breath. I've never gotten this way before, and I'm also not used to people supporting me.

Maybe it's okay sometimes.

I squeeze her hand back, and she lets go. She rolls her own window down then, and the wind gusts through the car, blowing our hair everywhere.

"Why don't you crash at my place tonight?" Mira says suddenly. "Carrick can fend for himself, right? He won't eat Nana."

Good gods. I never even thought of that possibility. I start laughing, a barking, helpless sound. "That sounds great."

WE STOP TO GET my car, and I follow them over to Mira's. It's strange getting used to having actual people to hang out with. Until the summer, I only saw other Mediators at functions and otherwise kept my presence to myself. I didn't even have the bunny. I'm surprised at how much of a relief it is to know someone else gets what's going on. I don't think any of the other Mediators does. Alamea's a tough sonofabitch, but she's my superior and not someone to confide in.

Mira pops popcorn while I change into a pair of shorts and a tank top. I steal a corner of the couch for myself and find it reclines, popping out the foot rest. Wane sets up the movie—The Expendables; I don't even care that I just watched it the other day—and Mira comes in a few minutes later with three heaping bowls of buttery popcorn. She hands one to me and plops down in the middle of the couch, propping her feet up on my foot rest.

"My section doesn't recline," she says.

"How did you know those morphs?" I ask Wane.

She's behind the entertainment center, fiddling with a wire. "One of them's a Gonzalez, like me."

I start to nod, then stop. "Wait, I thought your name was Trujillo."

Wane freezes, and beside me, Mira's foot goes still on the foot rest.

Mira's last name is Gonzalez.

Wane turns, placing her hand on the entertainment system shelf to steady herself. She looks at Mira. Mira looks at me, and I know even before the next words are spoken.

"My married name is Trujillo," Wane says.

"You're related." I look back and forth between them, more certain of this than I've been of just about anything else in the last six months. I think of them putting lunch together, the way they move together, the looks they exchange and the way Wane is here all the damn time when Mira says they're not a couple. Her reaction when I asked her. "You two are family."

Mira's chest rises and falls noticeably faster. "Cousins. Our dads were brothers."

I put my popcorn bowl down on the side table and turn in my seat to look at Mira. "Fuck, dude. Fuck. How did you—"

"Find out?" Wane asks.

I nod, again feeling helpless as if the world's spinning away from me. Mediators are taken from their families at birth. Down the water slide, snip the cord, gone. Forever. Six months ago I saw that my birth mother was missing. She ended up mother to a shade. A hells worshipper who birthed a Mediator also birthed a half-hellkin hybrid. That's what started my part in all this. Me poking around where I shouldn't have been poking. Somehow Gregor found out, put me on the scent of the missing men and women who were becoming mothers to shades, and here I am.

It's not just a no-no to go looking for your family as a Mediator. Those ties are severed. No contact. Nada. It's an edict from the World Summit. In some territories, they even change Mediator surnames, usually to some synonym or euphemism for hunter or fighter. Cazador. Jäger. Strijder. Mpiganaji.

But here's Mira with a blood-cousin, and her face is horrified when she looks at me, like she's been stripped naked in front of the Summit.

Wane stands, alarmed. She takes two steps toward us, as if she's afraid I'm going to ring a gong or page Alamea and get Mira beheaded.

Gods, I don't even know what the punishment is for this. I don't want to know. I realize both of these women are panicking. I almost trip over my words when I try to speak.

"It's okay," I say. "I'm not going to tattle on you."

Mira's breath rushes out, but Wane takes another step forward. "Mira," she says.

"She won't. She says she won't."

"But—" Wane's eyes are wide and frightened, and for the first time in the last few minutes, I consider how scary the Summit must look to an outsider. "Mira, she—"

"I trust her!" Mira almost yells it, and I jump.

Wane stops and goes still. After a moment where my breath feels stuck somewhere in my throat, Wane nods.

"Okay. Okay."

Something else strikes me. Wane is a morph. "Mira, are you a—"

She knows what I'm asking, and she shakes her head violently. "No, it doesn't work that way. Mediator genes."

"So how did you find out?"

"I deliver Mediator babies sometimes. I had to look through records for something or another, and I came across Mira's name. Gonzalez is a common enough name, but her dad's name is Ohtli. I had an Uncle Ohtli. I knew they'd lost a baby. Stillborn, we'd always been told in the family. I had to know. It's not like there's heaps of Ohtlis running around Tennessee."

"Stillborn my ass. Not so still after all," Mira snorts.

"Do your parents know?" A whole world seems to open up and spread out around me. I've never really considered what it would be like to have a family you're born into, to have parents and siblings and cousins and family reunions with red checkered picnic tablecloths and ants and more clichés than you could shake a truckload of sticks at.

But Mira shakes her head. "It would be too much," she says.

I don't ask if she means for her or for them.

"How long have you known?" I look back and forth between them again, and I see it. They have the same chin, the same slope of their brows. The same high cheekbones, the same gold-brown skin. Now that I know, I can't unsee it.

"Two years," Mira says quietly.

Two years they've kept this hidden from the Summit. Seeing them together and the way Mira has come through for me through all this makes me wonder if she's been as lonely as I've been. This life isn't easy at the best of times. Being a Mediator means a lot of sacrifices from birth until death. It's a long cycle of blood and guts and late nights, of getting a big middle finger from the majority of society. When we do our jobs well, they forget we exist. When we fail, we get to be the scapegoats. And now Mira's found someone, found a family. It may be small, but it's something.

There's a big old lump in my throat again.

"I promise that your secret is safe with me," I say, grabbing my popcorn again and throwing a handful in my mouth before I get misty.

“Thank you,” she says, then adds belatedly, “Cunt-nugget.”

“Love you too, Mira. Now can we watch these dudes blow shit up?”

15

I CONK OUT ON the couch at two in the morning, and when I wake up at ten, I find myself tucked nicely in with a blanket, my popcorn bowl gone from my side, and a note on the end table that just says, "Bagels!"

There's a text from Alamea on my phone asking for me to come by the Summit after I get off work. At least I'm rested. I can't remember the last time I had eight whole hours of sleep when I wasn't bruised, battered, or otherwise maimed.

Nothing like a good ass whooping and painkillers to make you sleep like the demons you made dead.

I find Mira's bagels in the kitchen and slather one with cream cheese for the road.

Laura seems relieved when I arrive at work with no visible injuries, but she doesn't ask about why I had to leave early. I guess she knows I'd tell her if it were important. Alice stops by my office when she gets in, and I can't help marveling again at how much she's changed. She seems at home in her own skin. She almost glows in the doorway to my office.

I spend the day working through my backlog of emails from clients, some business-related, others simply congratulatory. Laura sent out an announcement the other day, and seeing the well-wishes pour into my inbox gives me another thrill of excitement to move forward as a partner.

Alice insists on taking me out to lunch, and Parker tags along. Between the two of them, they could talk a bullfrog off his lily pad, but their happy babbling restores a bit of my good mood. There's enough to fret about. I let them talk me into eating cannoli and tiramisu after a giant bowl of ravioli, and when we go back to the office, I'm pretty sure I witnessed the bonding of best friends for life.

After work, I go straight to the Summit. Between that and the text from Gregor asking me to meet him at his house later, I have a feeling it's going to be another late night.

When I get to the front desk at the Summit, the Mitten-in-Residence informs me that she's in a meeting on the far side of the building, but that I can go up and wait for her in her office.

Even though she's on the top floor, I take the stairs to kill time. There's a kitchenette and a set of vending machines in the lobby up there, and I buy a bottle of overpriced blood orange soda and a packet of mustard pretzels and settle down in the lobby to wait. Even with permission, I feel weird hanging out in Alamea's office alone.

Also, with my track record this year, someone would probably accuse me of sedition. The Summit has seven floors aboveground, but its the bits below the surface of the Earth that I want to avoid. I've been in that prison. I don't intend to go back. It's a honeycomb of identical cells, a labyrinth of grey walls that give off a slight shimmer. You need a special light to see the directions built into the paint, so escaping your cell doesn't even do you any good. And did I mention the doors on the cells are invisible? Yeah. Good luck.

Just the thought of it makes me squirm in my seat. The chair's comfortable enough, though, and I force myself to eat a few pretzels and think about something else.

It works for approximately two minutes. When a pair of men come around the corner of the corridor, suddenly I can think of nothing else, because they're both—one directly and the other indirectly—the reason I ended up in that honeycomb hell.

Gryfflet fucking Asberry and Ben "I'll kiss you if I want" Wheedle.

For a moment they're both so absorbed in their discussion that they don't see me, and I get to spend a snippet of time thinking of exactly how many demons it would take to splat them both.

I thought I'd worked through most of my rage at them. Spent a month or so picturing every slummoth and rakath and snorbit I fought with their stupid faces projected onto the hellkin slime. But seeing them face to face for the first time since they had the gall to visit me in the hospital after me and the shades helped the Mediators of Nashville not get massacred, well. They're not nearly as on fire as I would like them to be.

It's a good thing I don't kill norms, because these two are shoulder-deep in my shit list.

When I met Gryfflet, he was a schlubby sound witch at the Hole, one of Nashville's crappier hard rock dives. In spite of his average build, he had a face like a boiled cabbage and the spine to match—at least at first. He grew a spine over the next few weeks. Then he used it to drug me, poison me, and throw me in prison. After I saved his life a couple times, no less.

And Ben—after gods know how many years of me telling him I wasn't interested, he chose to stalk me in the name of "saving me," spy on me for the Summit, and picked a moment where I was yelling at him to try and kiss me. I punched him in the stomach.

Best. Guys. Ever.

Gryfflet sees me first. Even from where I sit, I can see his eyes go cloudy as he harnesses some witch magic, and I go with the urge to laugh.

"Aren't you precious," I say. "You really think I'm going to pick a fight with you outside Alamea's office?"

It takes a moment, but his eyes go clear again, and I see his Adam's apple bob. His face has firmed up a bit, and he's nicely dressed in a grey suit and thin tie the color of a rakath spine.

I turn to Ben, who, as usual, is in jeans and a plaid flannel that makes him look like he should be a cover boy for Wrangler. He actually takes a step back when my gaze falls on him.

"What are you doing here, Ayala?" Ben asks.

"Needed a snack," I say, gesturing to my mustard pretzels. I cross my legs, leaning back in my chair to look at them. "And in case you've forgotten—" I point to my eyeballs "— still a Mediator."

Though I don't usually pay a ton of attention to them, the Summit keeps running lists of our kill counts. I've been at the top of it for the past six months, and in the last couple weeks, I got a ping for having at least ten more kills per week than the next highest person on the list. I know Ben looks at those. I smile at him as winsomely as I can.

I sort of want to shred his face.

Gryfflet's breathing fast, and I can almost see gears in his head clackity-clack-clacking through things he could say to me. "You know, if you worked with us instead of avoiding us, you could do some real good."

"Oh, ho. That's adorable. Thanks, but no thanks. Been there, done that, got the total and complete fuckover."

His face goes blotchy, with red and white patches mottling his cheeks.

"We're helping people," Ben says, and for the first time I see a spark of anger in him. "You're not the only one who gets to play the hero."

"Ends justify the means, eh, Benny-boy?" I say. I can almost feel the nerve I've struck in him twang through the air.

He licks his lips and purses them so hard I think his mouth's in danger of turning inside out. "I was trying to protect you! That's what friends do!"

I can't help it. I start laughing. It pours out of me like it's had a pressure meter slowly ticking upward for weeks and weeks and weeks. Tears squeeze themselves from my eyes and drip down my face, which is how Alamea finds me, holding my stomach and shaking while Gryfflet and Ben stand by looking as affronted as a Victorian confronted with an uncovered table leg.

She raises one eyebrow at them and says with the calm of someone who has no dog in a fight, "Don't you two have an eight o'clock meeting?"

Then she beckons me into her office. I stand, hiccuping into my half-eaten packet of pretzels.

They scurry away and don't look back.

MY EYES BURN A bit from tearing up, and I dab at them as I sit in front of Alamea's desk.

"Are those two working on some sort of project?" I ask her. "Ben seemed to be wearing his self-righteous pants today."

That gets a small smirk from Alamea, and she settles into her chair, offering me a mint, which I decline in spite of the knowledge that it's a commentary on my pretzel breath. "They've been somewhat effective at organizing teams of Mediators to work together to eliminate threats at some of the more active area hotspots."

I like her use of *somewhat*. It fills me with an inappropriate amount of spiteful glee. I'm not usually this petty, but people who get me imprisoned piss me off ever-so-slightly. Maybe I should be mad at Alamea over that too—she gave the order. But I'm not. She was working with the information she had, and between the out-of-context snippets from both Gryfflet and Ben, I'm surprised she didn't have me executed.

She looks up from shuffling papers around on her desk. "I didn't ask you here to go over Ben and Gryfflet's projects."

"I figured."

Alamea turns her computer monitor so I can see it, touching the screen to bring up a map covered in colored dots.

In the bottom corner, there's a key tying the colors to different types of demons. There's a strange symbol in several places across the map, but it's not marked on the key. One of them is over Stones River Bend Park, where I saw the herd of hellkin the other night. Alamea's long finger lands right on that spot, tapping it twice to zoom in.

"You saw an actual hotspot the other night," she says. "We've added it to our database. There are certain areas in the city where something allows the hellkin to break through into our reality. This is a new one."

"New."

I really don't like the sound of that, and it seems from the bitter set of Alamea's mouth that she really agrees.

She nods and zooms the screen out again. "Look at the map for a moment. Try to fix it in your memory."

I frown, looking. The dots are multicolored and varied, clustered around the hotspots marked by the symbol. It's like an extra-curvy question mark with a diagonal slash through it in the middle. She zooms the map out even more, beyond Nashville to the entirety of our territory, which is marked with a violet line at the edges. I've never actually seen my habitat delineated that way before. It makes me feel claustrophobic. That's my cage. I'll never be able to escape that violet line.

Alamea is oblivious to my thoughts. "Got it?"

I nod.

She moves her hands to the computer's keyboard, and with a couple strokes of the keys, the screen changes.

"This is the same map, but from five years ago at this time."

I freeze in my seat. The colors of the dots are still there, but they're mostly segregated. The slummoth greens are concentrated in Percy Warner and a few other places. Frahlig grey is dotted along the riversides, the Stones and the Cumberland. Jeeling pink is mostly to the south near Franklin, with a couple clusters up by Clarksville and a few to the east. Yellow groups of snorbits by the Opry and not many other places. Brown harkast clusters in heavily wooded areas. One cluster of aetnas on the far eastern edge of our territory at the ascent of the Smokies. There's a little smattering of overlap where green and pink and yellow and grey dots mix.

There are fewer hotspots as well.

Alamea's fingers tap her keys again. "Ten years."

Now there's almost no overlap.

"Fifteen."

The Opry has no dots over it, neither does Stones River Bend. In the crook of the Cumberland, where I fought the slummoths, there's nothing. Just a peaceful blank. No hellkin activity at all.

Alamea's fingers click on the keyboard, going forward in time again, this time year by year. I watch it flash across the screen as the demons slowly diversify in their areas, and I see something else.

The clusters fifteen years ago were sporadic, spaced out with no seeming rhyme or reason. As the years tick on, though, those clusters grow larger and branch out like veins. When she gets to three years before now, they're spaced almost equidistant from one another. When she gets to today, they blanket our territory.

"They're organizing," I breathe.

We're in a cage, and the demons are the black mold growing beneath us, sending out unnoticed spores.

"When did you notice this?"

"We've always kept data, but only in the last few years have we really had the technology to see these patterns emerge." She keeps the screen on the most recent image, her eyes lingering on it as if she can will it to spill its secrets.

“What can we do?” My stomach churns. Mediator numbers are down, I know, but then my eyes fall on Alamea’s medal again. “Alamea.”

She looks at me and follows my gaze. “What?”

“Have you included any data about our numbers in that? Or norm mortalities?”

Her eyes snap to mine, and she stares at me. “What are you saying?”

“What about the shades? Any reports on them? How do they fit into this? How do we fit into it?”

For the first time in my entire stint of working for the Summit and knowing this woman, I see something like panic in her face. “I don’t know. What are you thinking?”

“Our numbers are down. Their numbers are up. They birthed dozens of shades into our territory, but no other territory, even though Hazel Lottie said this wasn’t the end of it. They have gone from warring factions who slaughtered mindlessly to diverse groups working together. Meanwhile, they’re not killing norms.” I point at her medal, then at the map. “These things do not fit together, Alamea. I’m not saying you don’t deserve that medal, because you’re damn good at your job. But this math? This data? It doesn’t add up. There are more of them than there have ever been, and more hells-holes are opening up in our territory. We’ve lost actual ground, like the Opry. We’ve lost Mediator numbers. There are new players in town. But somehow we have the lowest norm mortality rate in the entire United States?”

She just looks at me, her mind absorbing what I’ve said, processing it. I can see it on her face.

“What if they were never bumbling, mindless killers at all? What if they were never at war with each other?” My tongue sticks in my mouth like its grown three sizes, and I take a deep swig of my blood orange soda. “What if this is what they did to Mississippi? Are we next?”

Alamea’s mouth falls open, and her gaze returns to the computer screen. For a moment, I’m sure I can feel what she does, the walls of our territory shrinking and closing in on us like the maw of a spiked trap. There are many things she knows that I will never be allowed to know. I know the Summit has its secrets and that we grunts don't get to be party to them. That's fine. I'll try to keep the world safer for the Parkers and Lauras and Alices and Merediths and Leeloos of the universe. If this trap is going to spring shut on us, I'll try to jam my swords in its mechanisms until I'm dead.

If it comes to it, I'll stand here and scream into those ragged holes of hell until it swallows me.

"Ayala," Alamea says.

"What?"

"Help me."

16

I PROMISE ALAMEA I'LL return to the Summit as soon as she's got the data compiled. We both keep our upper lips stiff through the rest of our meeting, but inside I can almost hear both our hearts ricocheting around our chests.

Alamea is the head of the Summit. She's our leader. For the first time, as I drive myself home, I wonder why she's asking me for help—and who it is at the Summit she can't trust if she's coming to me.

Carrick's not home again when I get there, and I feed Nana and settle in to eat some leftover Chinese food in my fridge. I've got a couple hours before I have to meet Gregor, so I stretch out on the couch and pretend to watch Alien.

Ripley was one of my first heroes.

I make it to Gregor's by ten, and I find him at his kitchen table with papers spread out all over it. Some of them look like expense reports. He's also got an old fashioned Rolodex on the side of the table, which I find amusing.

“Have a seat,” he says, gesturing.

I sit, waiting for him to finish scowling at papers and look up at me. He does after a minute.

“Alamea said you came to see her today.”

“She asked me to.”

“What did she want?”

I think he wants to know if she asked about the shades, and I’m not sure she wants me to talk about the data she showed me, even to Gregor, who probably already knows. So I shrug. “Nothing other than normal Mediator stuff. Nothing about Carrick and the others.”

He sits back in his chair, which looks like relief to me. I wonder why. Maybe he’s worried about the plug getting pulled on his pet project.

“Job went well the other day,” he says. “No shade deaths in Crossville since.”

“That’s good.”

Gregor grunts. “You know why I do this, right?”

I shake my head, because he’s never told me.

“They need a direction, Storme. They can’t just be left to their own devices. This way they have something to contribute to the world. It’s not like they can get a McJob and flip burgers like the rest of the millennials. They ain’t got any skills that’d make them worth the risk to an employer.”

“You don’t have to justify yourself to me, Gregor,” I say quietly. “I know them.”

He looks at me, his violet eyes sharp and canny. “I know, Storme. I know.”

There’s a pause while he stacks a bunch of papers and shoves them in a manila folder, then he gets up and walks to the fridge to grab a beer. He pops the top off with his thumb, then holds it out to me. I shake my head. He shrugs, draws deep on the bottle, and sits back down.

“There’s gonna be some jobs in the future that could be messier.”

Messier than beheading surrendering shades? I listen, wondering what he's on about. He's talking like he can predict where we'll be needed. I raise an eyebrow.

"What do you mean?"

"I mean that the work we do ain't never pretty. But it's necessary."

I think of what I said to Ben today, that the ends justify the means. I suppose that even though I meant it in snarky fashion, it might as well be the Mediator mantra. We make death with our hands because others live on if we do.

"I get that, Gregor. We've all done some messy shit in this line of work."

He nods, as if satisfied. "We're going to stay in a holding pattern for a little bit, but Carrick or I'll let you know if something comes up."

I know a dismissal when I see one. I go back to my car, feeling surly. He called me over just to say that?

HALFWAY HOME, MY PHONE rings. I pull over to the side of the road and answer—it's an unfamiliar number.

"Hello?"

"Ayala? It's Wane."

"Wane? What's up?"

I can hear a commotion in the background, and a minute later, a door shuts. "Sorry, I'm at work. Triage has gotten three patients tonight suffering from...hells. Their arms were torn off."

"What?" Oh, no.

"Three vics, all with the same issue. I usually don't hear this stuff, but one of the ER nurses was in the locker room with me, and he said he'd never seen anything like it."

"Did he say where they were found?"

"Train tracks. By the old warehouses. You know the ones." The sounds from Wane's end grow muffled, like she's put her hand over the mic.

I do know the ones. I helped blow one up. It can't be a coincidence.

"Thank you, Wane. I'm on it."

"Be safe."

She hangs up, and I get back on the road. I stop home long enough to gear up, scratch Nana behind the ears, and text Carrick, and then I head to the bridge.

Even I'm not daring enough to go waltzing into the warehouse district alone. From the bridge, I have a good view. The burned out warehouse is still a shell; even after three months, the city hasn't managed to get demolition crews over to tear down the remaining wreckage.

I pull out my scope and set it up, attaching a night vision lens to the end of it. It doesn't take long to find the scene. Even in the dark, I can see the swaths of shadow that are blood pools. How did the ambulances even get called? The only think I can think of is that one of the shades orchestrated this.

My phone buzzes, and it's Carrick. I'm still not so sure I want to talk to him, but I answer.

"Hi," I say.

"Where are you?"

"Jefferson Street Bridge, looking at the aftermath of some shade hijinks."

"Damn," says Carrick.

"Yeah, not good."

"I mean, that's why I called."

That gets my attention. "What happened? Where are you?"

"Percy Warner Park. There's a pile of bodies."

I start moving toward my car. "How big a pile?"

"Seven."

Shit. "I'll be right there."

"I'll take care of it."

"Carrick—"

"I'll take care of it! Gregor's on his way."

That should make me feel better, but it doesn't. The warehouses, Percy Warner Park. These killers are targeting places that mean something to me, specifically. I can't be crazy about this. Percy Warner is where Saturn lived. The warehouse I blew up, yes, but maybe it's something else. I met Mason there.

Could one of the shades in that warehouse have survived? The blast killed over a score of them. It troubles me to think of it, the trauma that could have caused a shade to see.

Helping set off that explosion is not on my list of things I'm proud of.

I'M HAPPY TO GO to work Thursday. Getting into the office is a relief, where I can compartmentalize away all thoughts of blood and dismembered norms that might be my fault.

On my desk is a draft of the partnership contract with a note to have it run by my lawyer.

I should probably get one.

The sight of the contract gets me through the day's appointments and meetings, and I even manage to find a lawyer during my lunch break who tells me to bring it by after work. He keeps witch hours, so he says I can bring it over after I'm off and we can go over it on his dinner break.

I pick up my cell phone at three and almost drop it. It's full of missed calls from Alamea and Gregor. When I check my work phone, it looks like they've tried calling there, too, and I missed it because I was on the other line.

Alamea gets the first callback. My skin feels shaky as the phone rings, a creepy, anxious sensation that makes me wish I could just hang up.

"I've been trying to call you for an hour," she says.

"I'm sorry. I had meetings. I just now saw my phone. What's going on?"

“There have been over twenty deaths at the hands of shades in the past day.” Her voice sounds like she’s her larynx through a ringer and is speaking with the drippings.

“Hells, *twenty?*”

“All dead. Some from trauma, a few from blood loss at the hospital. They were all called in.”

“Who called them in?” I don’t like where this is going.

“Anonymous tips.”

“Of fucking course.”

“I need you here. It’s all hands on deck.”

“I can be there at nine. I have a meeting with my lawyer at seven thirty about my partnership contract.”

The line goes quiet. “Partnership?”

“My boss is promoting me to partner.”

“That’s quite a commitment.” Alamea’s tone turns thoughtful, and I wonder why she’s not pushing me to come to the Summit earlier.

“I love my job,” I say.

“You’re a Mediator.”

“I’m a person.”

“Those two things are not mutually exclusive,” she says.

I walk back to my desk and sit down on the edge of my chair. “I know, but this is my life. I’ve earned this.”

There’s a long pause.

“I’m going to make you an offer,” Alamea says quietly.

“Excuse me?” I almost slip off my chair. What in all six and a half hells is she saying?

“I want you to work for me.”

“I can’t afford to do that,” I tell her, and I don’t just mean money.

“What is your current salary?”

I tell her, and for a moment she’s quiet again.

“I’ll double that.”

“You’ll what? Why?” Something very like terror takes hold of my guts and yanks, and I scoot back all the way in my chair. This doesn’t make any sense. I’ve turned down several job offers from the Summit, because they always lowball the salary so much it's laughable. But she's offering to pay me six figures to come work for her? What does she want me to do, torture people?

"Think about it, Ayala Storme. You saw my data. I have the rest, the figures you asked me for. We have a noose around our necks, and I don't know when it's going to jerk itself shut and break our spines. You can play house and PR queen all you want, but when those hotspots open and the hordes of all six and a half hells descend on our city, they will devour your boss, your company, and everything you love." She's quiet again for a moment. "Help me stop it."

MY BREATHS COME FASTER than my heartbeat, which sounds as sluggish and hollow as an underwater drum.

For a long moment after Alamea hangs up, I stare at the phone, wishing for it to confirm what I just heard.

From that suspended place of disbelief, I settle on three things that have to be true. One. Alamea is truly desperate. Two. She doesn't know who she can trust. Three. She trusts me.

If she doesn't know who to trust, then things at the Summit have to be worse than I thought. I think about the third thing, because if she doesn't actually trust me, then she's using me.

Why?

My phone sits on top of the draft contract from Laura, but I can't look at those pages now.

It hits me, a reason for Alamea reaching out to me.

Either she trusts me because Gregor's her second in command—or he's now one of her enemies and she's using me to keep him closer.

My mouth feels gummy and soft.

I make sure my office door is locked and dial Mira.

She answers on the third ring. "Sup?"

"What can you tell me about the splitting factions at the Summit? You're there more than I am."

She starts cursing before I'm done talking.

I know it's bad when she leads with, "You know that shit head witch Gryfflet?"

Now it's my turn to curse while she talks.

"Last I heard, he had convinced the other witches in the Summit's employ to work with him on some project, but no one knows what it is. I hear even Alamea can't get it out of him, and she's livid that he's found a way around the disclosure clause in his contract. Something about a state of emergency and leadership instability."

"Gods fucking damn it to the hells and back."

"Yep."

I pace back and forth in front of my desk. Outside my door, I hear Alice's muted giggle and an answering one from Parker.

"How do you know all this?" I ask.

"Ripper."

"Ripper?" Hells, I thought that Robert Redford wannabe had more sense than to get into this shit.

"He's one of the few people still loyal to Alamea, dude," Mira says. "Me, him, Devon. A few others I know of and probably a few I don't. Everybody's laying low right now."

"Why didn't you say something sooner?" I wonder if my being seen with Alamea at the Summit is helping or hurting her. Probably both, depending on who you ask. Ugh.

Mira's frown almost appears in the wryness of her voice. "I kind of thought you had enough on your plate."

I ask her to invite Ripper over that night, and we hang up.

I take a long drink from my water bottle, wishing to every sparkly magic in the universe that it were something stronger. It doesn't dispel the tightness in my throat. I make one more call and pick up the contract.

For a pile of paper, it feels heavier than a mountain. I feel like barfing. I've been a naïve fool to think I could make this work.

I can feel the noose around my neck loosen ever-so-slightly as I leave my office to turn down Laura's offer—but even as that noose loosens, I feel the shackles that chain me to the Summit and to this life of death.

ϟ

LAURA AND I LOOK at each other for a long time after I tell her.

I think I expect her to rage or yell or huff. Instead, she gets up from her desk, walks to me, and puts her arms around me.

I freeze, unable to hug her back.

"I don't envy your life. If you can ever come back, my offer stands," she says into my hair.

We both know it won't happen.

Alice cries when I clean out my desk. The rubber duck she left when she disappeared sit by my computer, and when she sees me pick it up, a new stream of weeping begins. I try to give the duck back to her, but her small hands close around mine, and she shakes her head.

"Keep it," she says through her tears.

Why do I feel like I'm prepping for my own funeral instead of quitting a job?

17

MY PHONE'S EXPLODING WITH texts by the time I get to my car.

> From Mira: Yo, Ripper's busy.
> From Ripper: I'm busy tonight. ♥
> Then again from Ripper: fuck
> His thumbs are as nimble as snorbit feet.
> From Gregor: ?????
> And finally, from Carrick: Come home.

I resist throwing my phone out the window.

The only person I text is the one who didn't text me in the first place. Alamea.

My text to her just says: *It's done.*

I go home, more out of a desire to snuggle my face into bunny fur than to obey Carrick.

I ignore him when I get there—he's out on the balcony, pulling a Mason and dangling his feet over the edge seven stories up—and I go looking for Nana. She's under my bed and won't come out. I put the duck from Alice on my night stand.

In the reflection on my television screen, Carrick appears in my doorway.

"How'd you find out?" I ask.

"Alamea told Gregor. Gregor told me."

Now is not the time for me to unravel the possible politics in that, and I'm still not sure I want Carrick in here, but after a minute he comes in and perches on the end of the bed. Nana hops out and lets him pick her up and put her on the bed.

"Traitor," I tell her.

"You're still cross with me."

I picture the shade again, hear his cries for help again.

"Yes."

"That was the job."

"That doesn't make it right." I remember when I knew that doing the job was doing right. Those two things were one and the same. The knowledge was like a life vest. Now I feel like I'm trying to keep my head above the surface, and the sea around me is blood.

"You're right." Carrick's words come as a surprise to me.

I look at him. His face is that of a maybe thirty-five-year-old man, but he was born in the seventeenth century. He has a few crinkles around his eyes. One or two creases in his forehead. His bare torso is mostly unmarked, though his shoulder has some fading scars still from his encounter with the slummoths, and if I look closely, I can still see the pinpricks from the rakath quills. Either his body is healing more slowly these days or he waited to get in any fights till the last few months. I never considered the possibility that shades had a natural lifespan. We learned as Mittens that hellkin do, but we're mostly encouraged to truncate that lifespan as much as possible.

The room is quiet except for Nana's snuffling around on the bed. She hops over to me, and I put her on my lap, surprised when she stays, ears and nose twitching.

Carrick looks at me. "May I?"

He raises an arm as if to tell me what he's asking permission for, and I nod. He puts his arm around me and pulls me into a bear hug.

"All right? Between us?" he asks.

I poke him in the ribs. "I guess."

But I don't pull away for another minute.

Two hugs in one day. Did someone tattoo "fragile flower" on my forehead when I wasn't looking? Fuck this.

It's already eight thirty, and I have to go meet with Alamea at the Summit. I have no idea what she'll expect my hours to be, but the idea of changing up my schedule from my eleven to seven hours I'm used to makes me nervous. Carrick goes off to meet with the other shades—they're hunting the murdering shades around Nashville, and as much as I want to be with them, I'm about to be on the clock with the Summit.

The parking lot at the Summit is fairly full, and the sight of all the cars makes me nervous. I see Ripper's truck, which has a bashed tail light to go with the rest of its dull black piece-a-shit quality. Guess this is what he meant by being busy.

I don't stop at the front desk this time. Walking over the yin yang symbol on the floor gives me a strange surge of resentment. The lines on it are so clear, the black and white clearly delineated. Reality swirls much, much more into grey. Who's even to say which of those two colors is good and which is bad?

I think of Mason, and my steps waver as I walk toward the elevator.

For as full as the parking lot is, I barely see anyone on my way to Alamea's office. If factions in the Summit really are fracturing as much as Mira thinks they are, the thought of all of them here now, under one roof, makes me wonder if I've just walked into a volcano.

She's in there when I arrive, and she immediately beckons me in. "Shut the door."

Before my butt hits the chair, she hands me a folder. I open it to find my paperwork. Job title—Chief Mediator Operative of Summit Leader NTN0047—and contract. The salary is posted on the contract as non-negotiable, and Alamea wasn't lying. It's twice what I was making working for Laura.

I read over the job description. Field work. Liaison for hybrid populations. Tracking hostile movements.

I can't help but notice she used the word "hostile" and not "hellkin."

I sign the damn thing anyway.

When I hand her the packet back after fifteen minutes of reading and trying to swallow my apprehension, she takes it, puts the whole thing through the copier behind her desk, and hands me back two copies for myself.

"Keep those somewhere safe. Make sure you look over them a bit more when you get home. I'll have your expense card to you by tomorrow."

"What are my hours?" I manage to get out, my mind stuck on the words expense card.

"You're salaried, so they may vary. But probably noon to nine."

I nod.

"You said you had the data I mentioned?" I ask. I'm not sure I really want to see it, but I have to. That's what I'm here for. I hope she asked me to do this because she does trust me, but at this point I'm not sure I can trust her. If it turns out I can't, breaching the contract I just signed will be pretty low on my list of worries, like getting taken out by an errant squirrel. It's more likely getting caught between the Summit and the shades again will pulp me.

Alamea again turns her computer so I can see it. At first the screen only displays the current map she showed me the other day. Then she hits a button, and it's overlaid with white dots that stand for Mediator deaths. There are nine for the last six months, which I know is high.

"I'm going to go back month by month this time."

I watch as the screen changes. This month only, no Mediator deaths. Month before, also none. Month before that, six.

That's the bad month, July, the month all this shit started. At least at the time, that was my perception of it.

As she goes back, most months have no deaths or one. She goes back two years and stops.

"I want you to look at demon numbers when I go forward this time. I'm also going to add in kills of norms by hellkin—" a green circle with a white center "— and kills by shades."

The latter is an indigo circle with a white center.

As the screen ticks forward in time, the weight that I usually feel on my chest, the balance we seek to right as Mediators, grows heavier and heavier.

Sometimes I hate being right.

"Hellkin numbers are way up. Mediator and norm deaths are way down. The shades are the only erratic component of this," I say.

"Gregor says your shades are working on mitigating that influence." If Alamea's voice were any more neutral, it would be taupe.

"So they tell me."

Alamea gets up from her chair and goes to the door. From a bookshelf, she pulls a small pouch that looks like the kind climbers strap to their harnesses. The dust in it isn't white though, it's black with a shimmer. She dips a finger in it and runs it along the crack in the door, top to bottom, side to side. I can see small glints of light reflecting back at me, but the moment she completes the rectangle, the whole thing flashes once, and my ears pop.

Ooh. Shiny magic.

I'd bet an even shinier nickel that she just did that so no one could eavesdrop on us. Which means she's probably about to tell me something I'm not going to like.

She sits back down at her desk. "I looked into what happened in Mississippi," she says.

I wait for her to go on.

"Most of the Summit records were destroyed. It wasn't a huge takeover, and there wasn't a final battle for the territory, at least as far as I can tell. But there was one coordinated strike against the Summit at the end, and the hellkin seemed to know right where to hit." Alamea's knee jiggles, her heel bouncing against the floor. She sees me notice and stills it. "If I had to guess, I would say that we are facing the beginning of something very similar."

"What do we do? We have warning. We have to be able to do something."

"One would think that." She gives me a wry smile, and for the first time I notice a healing cut on the corner of her lip. "We have two variables that weren't present in Mississippi, however."

"The shades," I say. Then the other dawns on me. "You're afraid your power base is crumbling."

I don't mean to blurt it out that way, but she knows, and I know, and it's stupid for either of us to keep pretending we don't know what the other knows.

I also can't shake the uncertainty of why she's brought me in, aside from the pragmatic levels I bring to the table. I'm close with the shades. I understand them. They're one of the x factors in all of this.

Alamea looks at me, but doesn't say anything for a moment. When she speaks, her words are few and deliberate. "I am no longer sure that the Summit will heed me if I bring this threat to them."

That's about what I expected. "What do you really want from me?"

"I want you to keep doing what you're doing. When you leave here, I want you to go to Carrick and his shades, and I want you to continue as you have. Help them to do some good." She looks at her watch. "We've released a short news piece about them, about how they protected the citizens of Crossville and how they are working tirelessly to hunt down those of their kind who are threatening the people of Nashville. It should be airing at ten, eleven, and midnight. Also tomorrow."

"Propaganda."

She nods grimly. "If public opinion turns fully against the shades, we'll have a lot more on our hands than simply dying at the hands of hellkin."

It's a mark of being a Mediator that that's the simple option.

"Okay," I say. "I'll do that."

I think of Mississippi and the hundreds of miles of festering swampland under near-perpetual cloud cover that infest the Gulf states.

"Did the norms get out?" I ask suddenly. "Of Mississippi. The Mediators would have all died there, but did the norms at least escape?"

I was far too young to remember anything being on the news. I don't remember Mississippi being anything other than what it is. It may have even gone down before I was born, but Alamea is in her early fifties. She would have been my age.

She shakes her head after a moment, and her eyes go distant. "I went there," she says finally. "I was just out of training when the worst of it started, and we wanted to help. We drove down, as far as we could go. We stretched ourselves to the edge of our territory. I remember the nausea."

Alamea looks at me as she says it, and I know she recalls that I am well familiar with that nausea.

"The demons must have known. We had binoculars and scopes. We could see people fleeing, in cars, on foot. It was just after sunset, and the sky was overcast, and the hellkin swarmed them. Some of the Mediators with me tried to push on, but they collapsed a hundred yards from the fighting. One of them was comatose for a month afterward. He'd been born up near the Kentucky border, and he pushed all the way out of his territory." She presses her lips together and stops.

"None of them made it?"

"Not that I saw."

I think of Laura and Alice and the others at my office. Too easily I can picture them fleeing north into the Cincinnati territory, meeting with a line of slummoths and jeelings and rakaths ready to eat them.

"Alamea," I say quietly. "If it looks like it's getting that bad, we have to evacuate the city."

"Believe me," she says, "We will try."

18

WHEN I LEAVE, I follow a text from Carrick to Percy Warner, where he and the other shades have gathered.

It's strange gathering here, in this place, without Saturn.

The canopy above us has shifted, now half-naked in the autumn.

Miles greets me first, and I'm thankful to see his face. I want to tell him about Jax, but Jax was frightened, and Jax was fleeing, and I hesitate with my mouth about to form the words, saying instead, "It's good to see you."

Carrick is talking to a few of the shades, and he doesn't seem to have seen me yet.

"Any updates on your murderous brethren?" I ask Miles.

"We caught one of them."

"Caught."

"Took care of."

I smile. "I see you're working on your euphemisms."

Miles' teeth are bright against the darkness of his skin when he grins back at me. "I've been reading."

"Anything good?"

"Carrick brought me a book."

I do my best to nod solemnly, when I'd rather laugh. Carrick's going to get them all hooked on 80s kilt flippers and bodice rippers.

"I'm going to buy you some good thrillers," I tell him, but he shakes his head at me. "Romance it is. I'll find you something good. And we'll try to get you guys library cards, but if you go in there naked, you'll get arrested."

This time Miles nods solemnly at me, and I'm not sure if it's in regards to the threat of arrest or the very serious occasion of having one's own library card.

I'll have to ask Alice and Parker if they have any ideas about making that happen. The idea of taking the shades on a field trip to the library is too precious to pass up.

The levity of the conversation makes me feel a little better, but when Gregor starts talking, the weight in my middle settles upon me again.

"Udo has told me that he discovered the number of the shades who are committing these crimes. Apart from the one we were able to find, there are three remaining," Gregor says.

His choice of words is strange to me. Crime. I suppose he's right, but for people who were born full-grown with transplanted memories and no knowledge of the legal system, the concept of criminality might be a little bit of a stretch. Even if most shades I know have their own moral code.

"Tonight, you will all spread out through the city and look for any sign of them. Any indication of their presence, any tickle behind your naked little ears. Find them." Gregor looks around, and part of me half expects him to slap somebody's bare butt as they trot off into the night, but he doesn't. I think he missed his calling as a football coach.

Carrick looks to me once before loping into the woods, and I give him a mock salute.

"Storme," Gregor says. "Pity you ain't a marathoner."

"No way I'm keeping up with them in a footrace," I agree.

We're quiet as the last of the shades vanish from sight.

"I hear you're out of a job."

"In a manner of speaking."

"I'm sorry, Storme."

I raise my eyebrows at him. "You've been trying to get me to work at the Summit for ages."

"Looks like Alamea offered you something a little more enticing."

Again I wonder what I've stumbled into. I don't like the idea of being the rope in an Alamea versus Gregor tug o' war. I shrug. "Why am I out in the woods with no one to fight?"

"Got another job coming up, and it could get rough," he says. "I just wanted to give you a bit of a warning."

To my surprise, he comes to stand beside me and places his large, square hand on my shoulder. It might be the first time in my life he's shown any affection for me whatsoever.

"Rough how?"

"Hells worshippers. Trying to pin down where exactly, but they're about to become lunch for a horde, and its our job to make sure that doesn't happen."

A horde. That sounds not fun. "I guess the norms are easier to track than the hellkin."

"They are that. As soon as we get them figured, I'll send up a flare. Should be within the next couple days."

Goody. I'm about to lose another weekend. It's a stupid thing to get plaintive about when a year from now, Nashville might all look like the Opry, but I could use a break. Even a half a day where something isn't going in the shitter.

"Just let me know," I say, turning to walk back to my car.

"Storme," he says.

"Yep." I crane my head to look at him.

"Best put on your big girl britches for this one."

"All I've got are big girl britches, boy." I flip him off as I walk away.

THERE'S SOMEONE CURLED UP in front of my door when I get home.

At the sound of my footsteps, the lump unfolds into Mira. Her eyes are red, and her usually healthy skin looks sallow and pale.

She gets to her feet as I approach, and I hurry to reach her in case she decides to fall or swoon or something else suitably un-Mira-like.

"You look like you took a stroll through the hells. Who squashed your bunny?" I cringe the moment the words leave my mouth, saying a mental apology to Nana, who I can hear scrabbling at the tile on the other side of the door.

Mira looks around and shakes her head.

I get the hint. I put my foot at the base of the door to ward off any chance of escapee rabbit, and Mira and I slide through into my apartment. Locking the door behind us, I motion to the living room. "You go sit. I'll get you something to drink."

"Just water."

"Are you sick?"

She scowls at me. "Fuck off."

"Hey, you're in my house." I bring her a cup of water, and she takes it. "What's with the paranoia? Spill."

I realize that's probably not the best command to give someone holding a full cup of liquid, but she's clearly not up to catching that foible right now.

"Carrick's not here, right?"

"He and the shades are off rescuing puppies from crazed murderers."

"Thoughtful." Mira sets the cup down half empty on the table and turns toward me, her knee almost touching mine. She reaches in her pocket and pulls out a smushed, folded piece of paper. "I found this on my gods damned pillow."

I take it from her. “Please tell me you didn’t find it when you woke up.”

“Oh hells no. I found it on my way to bed.”

I unfold the paper and recognize Saturn’s hand almost immediately. He writes more nicely than Mason did, but it still makes me a bit heartsick. Mason’s final note to me is in my bedside table. I don’t let myself look at it anymore. But this is no love note.

I’m sorry. Be careful. The shades are being used.

Then at the very bottom as if he thought it would somehow be less noticeable: *I miss you.*

“These critters read too many romance novels,” I mutter.

“He doesn’t miss me that way,” she says.

Nana scuttles around my feet, nudging a ball filled with baby carrots against the sofa. With her cheek pinned up against me, I can feel her little fuzzy mouth worrying at the stub of carrot poking out of the ball. I reach down to pet her, and she twitches until she realizes I’m not trying to steal her carrot.

“You know what this sounds like, right?” she says.

“Like he’s warning us about the shades. Or about who’s controlling the shades.” Either way, it’s not good news. “Could be he’s talking about Carrick. Or Gregor. Or Alamea. Hells, he could be talking about me.”

Both of us fall silent. Part of me hopes she’ll defend one of them, but she doesn’t say anything else for a minute.

“He’s not talking about you.”

“How do you know?”

“I just do.”

Helpful.

“You wanna hang out here for a while? We can order pizza.”

Mira starts reaching for her phone before I finish talking, and I hand her the remote.

I get up and go to my room to change, hearing the sound of gunfire on the speakers before I get to my door. I feel like I’m walking a tightrope of razor wire and there’s nothing but demons under my feet. One of these days I'm going to slip. Or lose my toes.

Normally I'd be excited for the weekend, but this time all I see in front of me is a horde of hellkin. Ain't I the lucky one.

I WISH MASON WERE here.

When Mira finally falls asleep on the couch, I bring her a blanket just like she did for me and wish I had something besides leftover pizza—of which there's not much—to offer her for breakfast.

I lie in bed for a while, staring at the ceiling. I wonder where Mason is. Egypt, maybe, or perhaps he got bored there and decided to walk the length of the Great Wall. I don't know how he managed to cross an ocean, but I know he found a way. He's nothing if not resourceful.

For a moment, I try to remember what it was like for him to be here, the heat of his body against the cool sheets. The way we slept hand in hand. I've never trusted anyone the way I trust him. Even now; his leaving wasn't any kind of breaking of that trust. He didn't leave because of me or anything I did. He left to be who he needed to be. That's fine.

But I miss him.

This is the longest I've allowed myself to dwell on Mason in a long time. I roll over on my side, eyes on the night table where Mason's note is tucked into a drawer. I hear Nana's little sigh from her bed not far from mine. She is always a reminder of Mason, since he gave her to me. He knew I had a soft spot for bunnies.

I miss having someone to trust.

Funny how I went through so much of my life relying only on myself before Mason. I miss knowing I could rely on him. He always came through. Good to know I have myself as a fallback.

19

MORNING COMES TOO SOON, and my body feels the confusion of not having to wake up at my normal time to get to work. I share a breakfast of cold pizza with Mira while Carrick looks on curiously. He's silent until she leaves, but as soon as the latches on the door are fastened in place again, he gets serious.

"Tonight's the job," he says.

I blink at him. "Tonight? Already?"

"Gregor's got them pinpointed. Got the message just now. Or rather, just when I woke. Gregor thinks we should be in place by an hour before sundown." Carrick yawns and stretches as if this news is about movie times and not going to rescue crazed, hells-worshipping norms from the murderous objects of their misplaced affection.

And this, my first official day as Alamea's own personal Mediator.

When I call her, though, she's on board with the plan. "Gregor told me about it," she says, her voice non-commital. "Just let me know how it goes."

We drive out around noon, and though I offer Carrick a seat in my car, he decides to ride with the others instead.

Gregor has been carting them around in a yellow school bus. Thanks, but no thanks. While most kids only have to deal with bullying and puking, Mediator kids get the added bonus of entrails and slummoth slime. If I never see the inside of a school bus again, it'll be too soon.

Who knows, maybe the shades get some sort of second-hand nostalgia at the school bus thing.

The day is warm for early October. The back seat of my car is loaded with gear, including my flamethrower, Lucy.

Yes, I name my flamethrower.

The front seat is littered with road food. Gummy morphs in varying stages of transformation (color-coded by animal—my favorite are the bright blue bears), pizza flavored bagel bites, and the spiciest jerky I can stomach. I also have three bottles of Coke stashed in a cooler under the front seat and a half-frozen gallon of water next to it.

According to Gregor, these hells-worshippers are gathering on the edge of an old middle Tennessee plantation that the wealthy owner just renovated in order to triple its value.

Something tells me a few scores of hell-zealots won't help the MLS listing.

The plantation is between Sale Creek and Soddy-Daisy, and the latter name made Carrick laugh so hard I thought a chunk of raw steak was going to rocket out of his nostril. It's also a two and a half hour drive from Nashville, in the south-eastern-most corner of my territory. It'll put us within only a few miles of the Chattanooga sludgepile that has overtaken nearly the entire border of southern Tennessee.

The sun shines throughout the whole trip, bathing my car in gold and making it smell like meat and feet. I don't even mind; if I try, I can pretend I'm on a real road trip like little norm teenagers take in the movies.

The only road trips we got as Mittens ended in blood and chasing each other around with hellkin entrails.

In spite of the cheery drive, snacks, and Johnny Cash's A Boy Named Sue blasting on the way down, I feel nervous. I don't know if it's my new job with Alamea or the prospect of facing a horde of hellkin with fourteen shades at my back. Or both. Saturn's note also has me pulled into its orbit, and I wish he'd been as literal and straightforward as most shades usually are.

After two hours and twenty-three minutes on the road, the sun begins its dip toward the horizon as I pull onto a road called Worley in what Mira would call "butt fuck nowhere," following the printed directions from Gregor to a single-lane paved track lined with oak trees 1800s style gas lamps, unlit.

Just west of the plantation, a dirt road branches off from the house's mile-long driveway. The kudzu and other less desirable foliage that was trimmed out of sight on the driveway creeps toward the dirt road, green tendrils finding purchase on the gravel edges. I can't see any indication that Gregor and the others have come this way—the road seems recently graded, with no dual tire marks that a heavy bus would leave behind. I have the GPS tracker he gave me, to make myself easy to find.

The woods around me feel warm and peaceful, and I can't help looking off to the south, knowing that only fifty miles away, the land turns to pockmarked pustules of sulfur and swamp.

It's hard to think of that with the calls of cardinals echoing through the trees. None are the *chip chip* of alarm; all are the birds' normal songs breaking the silence.

I text Gregor, pulling over to the side of the road where it widens briefly to allow passing cars. After fifteen minutes, he still hasn't responded. I hope we don't completely lose cell service, though the GPS tracker will work fine without it.

When he still hasn't responded in another ten minutes, I pull the car back on the road and follow its winding turns the rest of the way to the spot marked on the GPS. Parking the car about a quarter mile away, I get out and lean on the door, looking around. The sun has begun to sink toward the horizon, and with it, my mood.

Feeling antsy, I check my cell phone for any messages from Gregor, but nothing appears, even though I have three bars of signal. The area around my car is mostly wooded, but just beyond the road, there's a small clearing. Through the trees, I can see a glimpse of what looks like a guest house—which is approximately the size of Mira's regular house—that doesn't appear to be occupied.

I don't know where these hells-worshippers are, but either Gregor gave me the wrong coordinates, or they did what bipedal mammals are likely to do and moved elsewhere.

The sun inches itself into the trees, burying itself behind the still-yellow leaves of the oaks around me. The breeze bears the coolness that belies the season in the face of the warmth of the day, and I gather up my supplies from the back seat, pulling my sword belt out from underneath the gummy morph wrappers I threw back there on the drive. Lucy the Flamethrower goes on my back, her small canisters nestling between my shoulder blades. I thread the tubes out through my sleeves, shifting my weight to balance everything. In the heat of the day, my leathers immediately make me start to perspire.

I belt on my swords, stash knives where I can, and spend a few minutes limbering up. Then I let myself check my phone again. Still nothing. They said they'd be here. I pull the GPS out of my car and tuck my phone in its pocket at my waist, the GPS going in a little holster at my hip.

The dirt track encircles the entire plantation grounds, so maybe they went the other way. I start walking toward the blip on the GPS, keeping to the road at first, then veering off into the clearing after a few hundred yards.

Slowly, the darkness seeps into the sky as the sun fades, first cutting sharp yellow rays between the trunks of trees, then greying out as it falls below the line of the earth.

I see no hints of hells-worshippers, only feel the breeze through the trees that makes whispers from leaves and brings with it the faintest scent of...metal.

Turning to the south, my eyes find a ripple in the air.

I stumble backward, yanking my phone from my pocket. I dial Gregor, eyes glued to the movement.

He doesn't answer. I get his voicemail. "Gregor, you motherfucking ass, there's a hells-hole opening in front of me, and you aren't fucking here!"

I'm going to die. The last time I saw one of these things, eighteen demons poured themselves through it. If that many come out, I'll go through it with them when they return to the hells—as half-digested Mediator in their small intestines.

I should have run. I should have stayed at my car. I should have ridden with them in that gods damned yellow school bus and sang the Wheels on the Bus with those fucking hellkin hybrids and their Harlequin romances.

Saturn's message rings in my head, and I wonder why I didn't peace the fuck out of this job.

I can't run now. They'll catch me, no matter what.

This isn't supposed to be how I go. Not like this.

I call Alamea next, but she doesn't answer either. My heart spirals downward until I'm afraid it's going to land somewhere between my hips. "Alamea, there's a hells-hole opening, and I'm almost to Chattanooga. Gregor's not here. He's supposed to be—"

My phone rings. It's Gregor. My thumb hits the green circle.

"Where the fuck are you?" My voice sounds shrill and panicky.

"We're coming. Bus got a flat tire, but we're on our—"

The first demon appears, like it's reflected in shards of mirror.

I HANG UP ON Gregor and shove my phone into its pocket, unsheathing my sword.

Thank all the gods and stars it's a slummoth.

It slips through the hells-hole and comes right at me, a resonant bellow booming from its chest. For two seconds, I close my eyes and try to remember to breathe, telling my body to remember itself, remember its years of training, remember me.

I am instinct. I am a creature of extreme violence.

My body doesn't fail me.

It spins into motion, flowing through the sword forms I learned from the time I could walk. I send the slummoth's head flying the moment it steps into range just as two more materialize through the shimmering curtain of air.

My blades find their flesh and rend it from them.

I hear my breath in my ears like I imagine the sea, vast and endless and deep. Green blood spatters my leathers, but I pay it no heed.

I keep the hells-hole in front of me, catching the hellkin as they emerge, giving them no time to exist in my space. I claim the ground around me as mine and mine alone.

Darkness falls in my world; the day has fled. But I am born for the night.

Somewhere in that space of death and swords and snarls, I realize that I am going to be overwhelmed.

The burning of my muscles, I can push aside, but when the hells-hole widens and admits demons shoulder to shoulder instead of one after another, I feel my step falter.

The ground surrounding me is littered with bodies. Rakaths killed before they could shoot their quills. Slummoths, their slime coating the early-fallen leaves of autumn. A harkast.

When the pink glow begins in the air, like a floating cloud of light through this portal to nightmares, my blade slices through the neck of a slummoth—maybe the fourth, maybe the fortieth—and I step back.

Somewhere in the distance, I hear the sound of yelling, but I don't turn toward it.

There's a jeeling coming for me.

Eleven feet tall with shoulder spikes of metallic bone, the jeeling seems to tear the universe to enter my world.

It does something I've never seen one do.

It looks at me and smiles.

It's the only word I can think of for the expression on its face, its tight mouth of jagged teeth slanting upward like a sharp V.

It almost makes me turn and run. Instead I run toward it, ready to leap.

The jeeling's arm flashes out like a whip, and the ground flies up to knock the wind out of me. Dust and leaves fly into the air around me, and I gasp, scrambling to the side. More demons are coming from the hells-hole. I skitter sideways, encountering the severed neck stump of a slummoth. Chest wanting to explode, I force myself to my feet with a sound I've never heard from my mouth before.

Harkasts swarm from the hells-hole, swirling around the jeeling's knees. They don't attack me. They'll wait for it to take me down, and they will smother me with teeth and death.

Slummoths follow the harkasts, their screeching snarls turning my blood to liquid fear in my veins. Their movements are jerky, predatory. They know what I am and see what I've done around me.

I am alone.

I want Miles and Carrick and Udo and all of them to rush in from the trees, but they don't. It's just me and a horde. By myself.

Some of the slummoths lope off into the trees, but three stay. The air surrounding the hells-hole goes still again, and the sight makes me almost laugh. Too late for it to be any solace.

The jeeling seems to wait for me to move.

I run for it, straight at the giant monster and its skirt of lesser demons. I know the radius of its arms now, and I flip my short sword in my left hand, gripping it point down. At the last second, I duck, slamming my short sword into one harkast head and the saber into another. I throw my body to the right, my weight jerking both demons with me where the sharpness of my blades takes off chunks of their skulls.

I get up without thinking and run toward the jeeling again, keeping low, zig-zagging back and forth, working myself in a slow circle toward it. A slummoth comes at me, and I cut it down.

My arms feel like fire, my chest like the crater of a volcano. I take what breath I can and feint left, my saber flicking out to catch the jeeling just behind the knee.

Its a lucky hit, and though it doesn't sever anything vital, the eleven foot demon stumbles. Two more harkasts scuttle toward me. I kick one between the eyes as hard as I can, shoving it backward. The other I slice from shoulder to waist.

The jeeling bellows at me and rushes forward. I spin to the side, swinging my swords like a dervish's skirt. One catches the jeeling's shoulder bone, lopping off half a foot of the protruding appendage. I keep moving, my feet finding solid ground.

Normally, a jeeling could outrun me even with a knee injury. But with the harkasts around it, tripping it up, it struggles to track my movements.

I take out another slummoth and leave the harkasts be. Darting to the right, spinning as fast as I dare, I see my opening. The jeeling can't turn quickly. I launch myself at it, my foot finding a harkast head that I use as a springboard. I bury my downturned short sword in the jeeling's side where its kidney would be if it were human.

Even though it's not, it really doesn't like that.

I don't give it time to fuss. I thrust my saber at the center of its spine with as much force as I can muster. The jeeling pitches forward under my weight, and I yank out the sword and stamp my foot down on the wound as hard as I can.

The crack of its spine resounds in the clearing. Three harkasts and a slummoth remain. I sway on my feet, expecting them to rush me.

They stand stock still on the blood-soaked soil.

It makes them easy targets.

I kill them all.

It's only when they're all dead that I realize I never used Lucy.

20

SILENCE.

Seconds pass with nothingness cocooning me.

No crickets. No cardinals. No hellkin.

With a gasp I heave a breath and drop my swords, falling to the ground. The gibbous moon has crested the trees, and it lights the clearing with a silver sheen.

Bodies.

Everywhere.

I'm alive.

For a long time, I simply breathe. The air comes cool to my lungs, and though it brings with it the stench of metallic entrails and death, it smells of nothing but life to me. As I breathe, the crickets return. An owl hoots.

I am alive.

Somewhere in the distance, I hear a yell.

My legs are the human equivalent of Gumby, but they unfold beneath me, pushing me to a crouch. I find my sword hilts and pick them up. The blades drip slime and blood, leaves and soil caked against the steel.

I follow the sound of yelling, working my way northward through the trees, back toward my car and to the west, toward the sounds I hear. I stumble through the brush, blades as ready as my exhausted arms can make them, ears straining for the screaming I hear.

By the time I reach it, it is gone.

And I see why.

More bodies.

This time when the ground comes up to reach me, it's not because something hit me.

This time it's because I collapse.

Surrounding the guest house are bodies—but none of them belong to hellkin.

Some are nude and painted with hellish symbols. Others are clothed in rags or ripped denim.

These are hells-worshippers, and they are all dead. Their blood paints the ground. Where the demons smell of iron and sulfur, norms smell of copper and flesh. They lie in piles, haphazard and uncared for.

It's not even that that brings me to my knees.

I know what did this.

I know who did this.

When a yell once again reaches my ears, this time from the direction from which I came, I wish I could vanish into a hells-hole and never return.

My car. I need to get to my car.

I stumble again to my feet. Behind my eyes are bodies, bodies, bodies.

The woods welcome me, and I walk. And then I run. Somehow, somehow, I run. I hear the yells in the distance, but they are too far to catch me. I find my car on the road and rush to it. My blades I throw unsheathed onto the front seat, and the ignition sounds like safety. Spinning around, I floor the accelerator, the smell of dust from the road gathering through the air intake of the vents. I cough on it, but I don't slow down.

I drive down Worley Road to the state route that leads northeast. A mile passes before I remember to turn on my lights. I flip them on and drive, drive, drive.

My seatbelt presses against something, and I look down. My GPS. Two miles up the road, Chickamauga Lake butts up against the road. I roll down the passenger window and chuck the GPS as hard as I can into the waters.

It makes the most sense for me to keep driving north, to go back to the highways that will take me home, so I turn the car around with a screech of tires and go south again.

I pass Chattanooga and the I-24 detour around the lost chunk of Alabama, ditching the interstate for another state route west. I drive an hour westward before I stop the car somewhere near the ghost of a town called Winchester and nearly fall out of my seat onto the asphalt.

It's only then I let myself see it again. The bodies of hells-worshippers slaughtered, not by demons.

By shades.

We don't kill norms. We don't kill norms. We don't kill norms.

I taught them that. I did. I am the one who taught them that we don't kill norms.

It sounds like something you'd tell a two-year-old. *We don't sprinkle salt on slugs, Little Tommy, it tortures them.*

We don't pull the arms and legs off norms, little shades. It's bad. Wrong.

But they did. And Gregor knew.

Gregor must have told them to.

THE ROADSIDE IS DARK, and the crickets tell me it's safe. I peel off my leathers and stand on the shoulder in my skivvies, finding a towel in the backseat of my car to sponge off the blood with some of the water from the jug in the front seat. I rub my skin until it's almost raw, but I feel better once the corrosive demon blood is gone.

I find a rumpled t-shirt and a pair of jean shorts stuffed under the passenger seat, and I put them on. Cleaning my swords with the towel takes more time, and I do it in the headlights to make sure I get all of the blood. By the time I'm done, the towel is ruined, but some of my sanity has returned, and my brain whirs into action.

Prying my phone out of its pocket and thankful for the oversewn seam that protects it from goo, I plug it into the charger in my car and sit, doors open, to see what shitstorm of messages exists.

Gregor's name alone makes me want to hurl.

Alamea is next, with four missed calls. Then Carrick. Mira. Even Ripper.

I call Alamea back first.

The second she picks up, I almost spit words at her. "Did you know?"

"Know what, Ayala?"

"Did you know he was going to murder norms?"

She goes silent, even the soft whisper of her breath.

I don't care if I deafen her. I scream it into the phone. "DID YOU KNOW, ALAMEA? DID YOU KNOW?"

"No."

I taste salt and realize I'm crying. Two and a half decades of *don't kill norms.* I still remember the sight of Hazel Lottie's head on the bloodied grasses of Miller's Field. I never wanted to feel this way again.

I hiccup into the phone. I don't know what to say.

"I didn't know," Alamea says, "but I suspected Gregor of wrongdoing."

My hand freezes to the phone against my ear. "You what?"

"I heard...things. I didn't know I could trust you. I wanted to. Now I am sure I can."

"How?"

"You are many things, Ayala Storme, but an actor is not one of them. You could not have faked your reaction to this." Alamea sounds tired and stretched, like a string pulled taut and about to break.

Little by little, I come back to myself. Gregor. A traitor.

He has used me this whole time, since he turned up in my apartment with Carrick.

Then something hits me. No. Not since then. Before.

"Fucking motherfucker...*fuck*!" The words trip out of my mouth, and I want to scream again.

"What is it?" The low tone in Alamea's voice is urgent, but I ignore it.

"He's been blackmailing me. Or was prepared to. Fuck." I can't stop saying fuck.

"Explain."

I take a deep breath, aware that I'm about to admit to the head of the Summit that I've flirted with breaking one of our primary edicts. I think of Mira and Wane, and I will keep their secret until the worms devour my marrow, but I need to tell Alamea this.

"I tried to find my mother. This summer. I sought her out. Gregor found out somehow. That's why he brought me the case of the missing people when the shades first came into the world. He knew I'd been looking for her and that she'd gone missing just like they had." I close my eyes, and the night air is cool on my eyelids.

I open them again and see stars twinkling brightly above, shining as if they too are waiting for Alamea to speak.

"You sought out your mother?" Alamea says, her voice full of genuine surprise. "Your mother was a host to a hybrid?"

The second question drips shock, and I bark a spiteful laugh. "Yes. My mother birthed both a Mediator and a shade. Go figure. And before you ask, no, I don't know who he is. I only know he's not Mason or Saturn, and probably not any of the shades I know."

"You say Gregor knew this."

"Yes. He did. And I think he was prepared to use it to blackmail me into helping him." I remember him telling me what to do, how he kept certain things from Alamea even then. I remember him showing up in my apartment with Carrick and just dumping a strange shade into my life, certain I would go along with it. I was an easy mark; he never even had to use his leverage. And tonight...

"Gods damn it. Tonight he got me out of the way. I don't know if he was trying to kill me or just distract me. I think someone came looking for me after I escaped, but I'd already gone. I had my tracker on me. They must have tried to follow."

"They did," says Alamea grimly. "They told me they lost you. I think they thought you were dead. At least wounded."

"You spoke to them?"

"Gregor called to report," she says. "I thought at first that I had misjudged you and that you were in on it with them, but then he said he lost you."

"I'm a hard one to lose."

"That you are." If I'm not mistaken, that's a note of pride I hear in her voice.

I swallow.

"Do you know how many demons you killed tonight?"

I stay silent, because I'm not sure I want to know, but as the quiet ticks by, curiosity starts to burn.

"Fourteen," Alamea says. "You killed fourteen. You killed an entire hellkin horde."

Well. I knew that part. But...fourteen.

"Ayala?"

"I'm here."

"I'm glad you're alive."

"Me too."

I take a swig from my water jug. The ice in it dislodges and splashes water all over my chin, but I don't care. It's cold and wonderful, and I'm alive.

"So," Alamea says. "We need to get you home. But first, here's what you're going to do."

I FOLLOW ALAMEA'S DIRECTIONS to the letter. As soon as we hang up the phone, she texts me the address of a hospital in Cookeville, and I get in the car. I don't call or text anyone else. Not even Mira, to let her know I'm safe.

It takes me two hours to get to Cookeville, because I have to backtrack and go all the way north to I-40. I guzzle my Cokes and eat the remaining half bag of gummy morphs, along with a few pieces of jerky.

I only hope her plan works.

When I arrive in Cookeville, I stop at a 24-hour Wal-Mart and pick up a pair of yoga pants, a beanie, and a hoodie. Then I go through a drive thru and order the messiest burrito I can find. I make sure to drip on the hoodie, wiping off the spill with a napkin. When I'm done eating, I go to a motel at the edge of town where Alamea has already paid for a room for me. Before I check in, I tuck all my yellow-orange hair up into the beanie and pull the hoodie up over it. The motel manager doesn't look at me twice.

For the next day, I drink only water and don't change my clothes.

My phone blows up for the first day, mostly Mira. Then nothing. I let my phone die and throw my charger in the trash outside the motel room.

On the second day, I go to the hospital and call Gregor from the lobby courtesy phone.

He says he'll be right there.

While I wait, I relive the night that didn't happen, but that Gregor will soon believe did.

The jeeling almost killed me.

It gored me through the shoulder with its own shoulder spike. I killed it last, and I stumbled to my car. The venom of the jeeling spike and the slummoth blood on my leathers made me delirious. I threw my tracker in the lake, got as far as I-40, and passed out on the side of the road. When I woke up, my phone was dead. I made it to the Cookeville hospital and collapsed.

They gave me two bags of fluids and kept me all day and the next night, and released me.

My hoodie smells like my story is true. It looks like I found it in my car, and it covers my neck where even a Mediator wouldn't have healed from being gored by now. My hair is greasy and pulled back with one of those blue rubber bands you find on broccoli.

When Gregor arrives, he finds me huddled on a plastic love seat.

"Thank gods, Storme, I thought they'd done you in."

"Still kicking," I say. "No thanks to you."

Alamea's right. I'm not an actor. Which is why I'm going to be as pissed at him as I can be.

He looks around, as if searching for a nurse or someone in charge of me. Seeing no one, he plunks down next to me on the love seat. I scoot away.

"They release you officially?"

"I thought about just driving off, but I wanted to see you face to face."

"Storme, I'm sorry." Somehow Gregor manages to work his blocky face into something resembling contrition.

"Oh? Sorry you left me to fend for myself with a horde of hellkin? Or sorry they didn't finish the job?"

Anger rises in me, but not on my own behalf. I keep the bodies of the hells-worshippers firmly in my mind.

"We got held up," he says, and he pauses.

I wait for it. This is it. This is the lie he plans to tell me.

"And exactly how many shades and washed up Mediators *does* it take to change a flat tire?" That fills me with another flash of fury. He thought I'd buy that. I don't even think I bought that when he said it on the phone.

"It wasn't that, Storme," he says. He looks at me and sighs heavily.

And Alamea says I'm the one who's no actor.

“Then what the fucknuts was it?”

“The hells-zealots,” he says. “We found them and they were dead. Murdered by the hellkin. Splatted. We fanned out, because their tracks led away to the south, but by the time we got back to where you were, you were gone.”

Cute.

His speech is touchingly false, but he does tell me one important thing: he doesn’t know I saw the bodies. He has no idea I saw what he really did. His use of the word *splatted* tells me that.

I’ve seen splats. All Mediators have. Demons pulp people. Shades tear them apart and gnaw on the leftovers. Those hells-worshippers were no hellkin kills. Those were shades, even if they weren’t eaten.

At least Gregor didn’t let them go that far.

He listens to my story with his normal stoicism, which is how I know he believes me. When I’m done, he even gives me an awkward sort of hug, and I make sure to punch him in the shoulder for it.

I bicker with Gregor just enough to get him to think I’m okay to drive home, and I agree to let him follow me.

I think of Carrick at home and wonder how I’m going to face him every day now.

He better have fucking fed Nana.

21

GREGOR FOLLOWS ME ALL the way home, and I let him come up to the apartment with me. My front door, usually the gateway to peace and serenity and my neglected silk robe, now looms in front of me like a hells-hole. How am I supposed to live with Carrick after this?

I remember his touch on my shoulder, that greeting he showed me for the first time just days ago.

Nana scampers up to me as soon as my feet hit the white tile in my foyer, her little nose as busy as usual. I can see Carrick in the living room, but I don't make eye contact. Gregor latches the door behind me. The sound traps me in my own home.

My chest feels fluttery, as if Nana's nose and whiskers are in there twitching away. The walls are closer than I want them to be, and unlike Carrick, I can't shimmy down seven stories safely.

He walks toward me with a wariness I don't usually see from him. Behind me, Gregor's footsteps halt on the floor. My eyes want to keep watching my feet, but I force my gaze upward, afraid Carrick will see that I know what really happened at that plantation.

But all I see on his face is concern. "You're okay?"

I nod, not trusting my larynx to form the right sounds. Walking to the couch takes too long. Each second with Gregor at my back makes me feel more exposed. Beyond naked. Skinless.

Nana follows me all the way to the sofa. The couch feels too soft. Everything but Nana feels wrong. She doesn't notice, only settles in to nudge a ball around the floor at my feet, her little hops making muted thumps on the carpet. She looks well fed and happy. For that, at least, I can thank Carrick. I look at him, wondering how long they planned this together. And if they wanted me out of the way or dead.

Gregor clears his throat. "You did good, Storme," he says. His voice sounds even more like a bear's growl than it normally does.

The chill in my apartment is normal, but today it makes me stifle a shiver.

"Well, not dead is a good way to end the day," I say as lightly as I can.

"Can it, Storme, I'm trying to give you a compliment."

This is an interesting strategy. I give him a fake smile, knowing he'll just take it as me being a smart-ass.

If only I didn't feel like throwing up at the memory of all the bodies piled around the plantation guest house.

"What happened after I left?" I ask. Maybe if I keep them talking, I won't have to.

"I went looking for you," Carrick says. He's not looking at me though; he's looking at Gregor. Something passes between them, and my muscles tense up, but this doesn't feel like conspiracy territory to me. It feels like something else.

Gregor gives the tiniest shake of his head, and Carrick's pupils dilate, the rest of his body very still.

"I have to tell you something," Carrick says.

Gregor gets up from his chair and paces by the breakfast bar. I ignore him.

When Carrick is still silent a moment later, I poke him in the ribs. He has yellowing bruises across his torso in the shape of a baseball bat. I feel a surprising wave of respect for any hells-worshipper who would go at a shade with a bat. That takes guts and a distinct lack of smarts.

"Miles is dead," says Carrick, and any respect or amusement I felt vanishes into the air conditioned box of my apartment.

I can hear the whir of the HVAC and Gregor's raspy breathing. Nana's whiskers tickle my foot as the ball bumps into it.

My throat crawls as if worms are tracing the length of it, squiggling and writhing. I want to throw up. I can't speak.

"I'm sorry." Carrick reaches out as if he's going to take my hand, but something makes him stop.

The thoughts in my head bump into each other like bumper cars. How did this happen? Miles is—was—competent and savvy. He knew how to stay out of the way and to find his own ground, and when he found it, he was unstoppable.

How quickly the past tense comes.

Miles. Dead.

And then, a moment later, when my eyes fall on Gregor's feet, I forget to breathe.

Did he do this? Did Carrick?

I can't read Carrick well enough to know lies from truth. The other shades are terrible at lying, but he's had four hundred years of practice. When I make myself look at him, eyes burning but dry, his face is earnest, the crease in his forehead pronounced with worry.

I get up from the couch, toes sinking into the soft white carpet.

"I need to be alone," I say.

"Ayala, you're still injured," Gregor says. He makes a move toward me, and I freeze.

"I'm fine. I'm going to bed."

"It's noon."

"It's Sunday," I counter. "I can go to bed at noon on Sunday if I damn well please. I'm going to rest. For my injury."

The anger in my words is no act, and I scoop up Nana, ignoring her flails. She hates being picked up. I stalk to my room and shut the door behind me with my foot, putting Nana on her bed next to mine.

I sit down, wondering how I am going to live here with one man who might be made of lies and working for another who deserves a prize for his.

I can't even call Alamea.

I sit there, the thought of Miles dead and torn apart sapping every ounce of comfort from me.

I want to cry.

The tears don't come.

ϟ

WHEN I GET TO the Summit Monday at noon, the Mitten at the front desk—I don't know her name—stops me. Her eyes are all a-sparkle with excitement.

"Everybody's talking about it," she says. "Did you really kill all them demons yourself?"

My shoes skid on the marble floor. Sunlight filters in through the skylight above, and the floor reflects enough to cast my startled face back at me. I always forget about that damn skylight. I'm usually here at night.

"Uh," I say.

"You really did!" The Mitten actually claps her small hands together. "And Gregor—he tried so hard to protect those—"

The girl cuts off sharply with a squeak as the click of heels sounds in the lobby.

I don't have to turn to know it's Alamea. The Mitten sits back in her chair with a thump and starts furiously typing at her computer.

It'd be more believable if her fingers weren't situated between the number row and the QWERTY row.

Without a word, Alamea nods at me and pivots on her heel. I follow with a knowing wink at the Mitten, though her little outburst unsettles me. I don't have time to think about it.

Alamea isn't walking in the direction of the elevators. How she walks in those four inch spikes on the polished marble without breaking a kneecap is beyond me. I follow her down a side corridor, and when a glint of memory resurfaces with a shift of the air and a smell I can't quite place, a sheen of perspiration begins on my upper lip. She leads me to a smaller bank of elevators and presses the button. There's only one. Down.

My feet feel like rubber as the realization sinks in. The sliding doors open, and I have to walk in. Inside the elevator is a keypad. Alamea makes eye contact with me, and when she's sure I'm watching, she clearly and slowly enters the code with one long finger. 743367. She presses the button for sublevel four, and we start moving.

I've been here before. Even though I was kept blindfolded, I feel a strange hum that is at once familiar and terrifying. I know what's down here: the grey-walled honeycomb of doom. Last time I was here, it was as a prisoner in one of the cells.

No honey, either.

Also, thank the gods, no bees.

Alamea still doesn't speak as the elevator doors open with a hiss.

Stepping out into the grey corridor, all my strength goes to putting one foot in front of the other.

The walls have that faint shimmer. Around me, they turn at strange, obtuse angles. Behind me, the elevators are gone, replaced by that same identical grey, flat and seamless.

The perspiration on my lip forms beads.

Alamea starts walking. I don't know where she's going down here. It's impossible to know if even she knows; the walls bear no markings, no direction, no indicators. There are no emergency exits, no variations, no handy ball of string to guide you.

For several minutes, we just walk. My apprehension grows with every step. Even the sounds of our footfalls feel wrong. The noise ricochets in a way I instinctively feel it shouldn't, coming back to me and escaping at once like a boomerang in a dream I can't quite remember.

It's not hot down here, but I'm sweating like a hog in a hot spring.

Alamea finally stops in front of a wall. Her hand goes straight to an unmarked place at chest level—and the wall opens.

She goes right in.

I stop in the threshold.

I don't know if I can walk back into one of these cells or if I can trust Alamea not to close that seamless grey wall behind me.

743367.

She wanted me to see that code. For whatever reason, she wanted me to know it.

If this is just a trap to get me in the cell with her and she closes the door? She's going to rue the moment she had the idea to lock herself in with me.

I step through the threshold and stay there with my back to it. She's in the center of the cell.

"Ayala," she says quietly. "I need to close it."

"No." I swallow, making myself look only at her and not at the cell surrounding her.

She takes a step toward me, and I take a step back. For a flash of a moment, I regret not wearing my sword belt. I've only got my two knives stashed in my boots and one at the small of my back. I'm in jeans, not leathers, but I'm never unarmed.

Faster than I could expect in those damned heels, Alamea darts around me and hits the edge of the opening with her fist. I react without thinking, sweeping my leg under hers and knocking her to the floor.

It's too late. The wall is shut, and we are enclosed in a seamless grey honeycomb cell.

It's then I realize Alamea isn't fighting me back.

Instead, she watches me calmly from the floor, eyes wary, massaging her elbow where it hit the ground.

"We have seven minutes before the sensors pick up that there are people in here and surveillance turns on, so you need to listen to me now."

I'm stuck in a prison cell four stories below the surface; I'm not sure I have another choice.

Alamea gets to her feet and pulls something from her pocket. Two identical somethings. She hands one to me.

It's small and circular, like a lid to a bottle of Coke. It's all black, though, and the edges are curved and sleek. It reminds me a little of the beacons we use.

She points to the walls, her arm moving across the entire room. "Each one of these is a door if you know how to open it. I will show you how to get out of any one of these cells and find your way back out to the exits."

Alarmed, I look back and forth between her and the device in my hand. "Why are you telling me this?"

But I know, even before she responds.

"There is a possibility that some are seeking to have me removed as Summit leader," she says, her voice far more serene than mine would be in such a situation.

There is no stepping down for Summit leaders. If there's a coup, she won't be imprisoned. She'll be beheaded. I'll be the one they throw down here, and she's teaching me how to get out.

Fuck me.

"It may not happen, but if it does, it could happen at any moment. I thought this information could be important to you."

That's a nice way of saying, *I don't want you locked away down here forever.*

"Why me?"

She gives me a wry smile. "Lack of other options."

"Thanks awfully."

"Not only that, but your recent experience showed me that you weren't allied with Gregor. It also puts you in an excellent position to relay information about his plans to me. It's unlikely he'll let anything important slip in front of you, but even he gets sloppy now and then." Alamea points me toward the far wall opposite where we came in. "I want to trust you, Ayala. At the moment I need to trust you. Forgive me."

"For what?"

"For putting you in this cell once before."

She brought me back to the exact same cell? I wipe away the perspiration from my lip. I'll be damned. I'm not sure which news is stranger: being back in the same cell, or Alamea apologizing.

"You were doing what you thought was best," I say finally. She was, and it was mostly Ben's fault anyway.

"I shouldn't have had Wheedle spying on you. His emotions clouded his judgement and affected his relaying of information. I think also jealousy may have played a part." She quirks an amused eyebrow, and I know she's referring to Mason.

"Ben needs to fall into a pit," I mutter.

"Yes, well. I believe I'm starting to agree with you." Her tone is lighthearted, but her eyes seem to look through the wall in front of us. She pauses for a moment, and I can almost hear the buzz of her mind thinking. Alamea turns to me.

I have to look up to meet her eyes.

There's fear there, lurking like a ghost just behind her, backlighting her. It haloes her, haunts her. For that moment, I see her as I've never seen her: completely and utterly alone.

"Whatever you do, don't let them take you," she says.

Then the moment passes, and the Summit leader stands before me again. "Hold out your key."

I obey, my tongue numb with shock.

"Place your thumb and forefinger on either end of it and press."

I do, and though the device doesn't appear to have any seams or buttons, light emanates from it in a small radius.

The walls around me light up with symbols, many of them moving. They swirl around the cell, the effect after the drab grey dizzying. Some spiral, others snake across the walls.

"We don't have much time," she says. She points to the wall in front of us, where a series of circles spins slowly. Each circle is the point of a hexagon's corner, and it rotates while she gestures at it. It's about as wide as a hand. "This is the failsafe. Only the Summit leader knows it exists. And now you. If you're ever imprisoned here again, you will be able to find it. Make note of its level in comparison to your body. It's always at this level, and though it's mobile, with or without the key, you can activate it."

I nod. "Is there a pattern?"

"No. You have to press them in sequence. That's it. Once you press the first two, it stops rotating." She demonstrates, and the symbols around the cell turn static. She touches the remaining circles, and the wall opens. "Hurry."

I follow her out, still pinching the black key she gave me. The walls and floor outside the cell bear designs as well.

"Red line leads to the elevators. Blue leads to the stairs. Green is a dummy line." Each line she points to has sporadic arrows.

I turn to look at the cell we just vacated. It has a number. Cell 429.

"How did you find the cell without the light before?" I ask, hurrying to keep pace with her long strides.

"Who says I didn't have a light?" Alamea gestures at me, and I stop pressing my key. The lines on the floor and symbols on the walls vanish. Then she starts walking again.

From behind her, I see nothing. When I reach her side, I catch the faintest glimmer. It's only when I get ahead of her that the shapes blossom again.

I press my key once more and follow.

"Without the key, if you need a path, go to the center of the corridor. The same failsafe exists there as well."

I don't ask her why a failsafe would be necessary. When we get to the elevator, she waits for me to put in the code.

743367.

She gives me a grim smile as we ascend.

"I hope you'll never need to use it," she tells me as I pocket the key. "Keep it somewhere safe."

22

THERE'S A PARADE IN the lobby.

At least, that's what it looks like.

After the grey of the Summit dungeon, finding the lobby full of Mediators is a surprise. Finding them all crowded around Gregor makes it an unpleasant one. What in all six and a half hells did he tell them?

The groups of Mediators gathered around him are a mosaic of emotion. Those closest to him are beaming, clapping him on the back and looking at one another excitedly. Those on the fringes are exchanging looks that are all wariness and no excitement. A few look distressed, their eyes flitting back and forth between those grinning at Gregor and those struggling to keep their faces impassive.

It makes me afraid that I'll need what Alamea just gave me sooner rather than later.

I almost don't notice Alamea split off from me. She clicks away in her heels, a smile on her face, greeting one of the Mediators with a hand clasped on his shoulder. A few minutes later, my phone buzzes with a text from her that just says: *Come back tomorrow.*

If working for Alamea means spontaneous days off for good pay, I think I can handle that.

"Ayala!" Someone calls my name, an older Mediator named Billy Bob whose actual given name is Billy Bob. He's my height and grizzled as all get out, skin pink from too much sun, silver-grey hair kinked and frizzy and only barely tamed with an elastic at the nape of his neck. He always wears green cargo pants and matching green t-shirts from the army surplus store, and when he walks toward me I can count three blades on him that are visible, which means at least another five aren't. He also usually smells like he last wore deodorant for Y2K.

I wave at him, unsure of what to do.

A partial cheer goes up as faces turn toward me, but it sounds half-hearted and fractured, as if the people in the room don't know what to make of me. That's fine. I mostly don't like them, so I can deal with it. As long as they don't try to separate me from my head, they can think I'm the worst.

Just a couple months ago, they were all cheering and awarding me a Silver Scale, which considering I murdered a score of shades to earn it, about sums up my complex relationship with the Mediators who are the closest thing I've ever had to kin.

Gregor's saying something about me to the people in his immediate vicinity, and a couple of them give a whoop, which makes the people on the fringes of the circle scowl.

Even better, Ben Wheedle appears on the stairs.

I do my best to ignore him.

Billy Bob reaches me and smacks me hard on the back. I wince, and he apologizes.

"Sorry, kid. Forgot you got yourself gored by a jeeling." He beams at me.

I wasn't wincing out of pain, but I give him what I hope is a grateful smile, and his smile grows wider. For the name and the smell, his teeth are unstereotypically even and white.

"How're you doing, Billy Bob?" I ask him. "Haven't seen you in a while."

I ignore the crowd staring at me and focus on Billy Bob's preening.

"Been down Memphis way, chasing couple packs of markats." He pulls up the sleeve of his t-shirt to expose an inkblot-shaped mark in healing pink tissue. "Them fuckers thought they could take me down. No siree. Spit all they want, but I got 'em. Whole lot of 'em. Not as many as you did in, though. What a kill spree, kid. One for the books."

"Well, I'm just glad there weren't any markats in my bunch," I tell him. "Can't abide the spit."

Markat demons spit. A lot. And their spit is a pH of about 1.5, so if you don't get it off your skin in five minutes or so, you get souvenir Rorschach tests to show your friends, like Billy Bob's got on his arm.

Billy Bob seems tickled by my statement, and he smacks me on the back again and trundles off.

A familiar face appears through the crowd. Devon. One of the Mediators Mira said was loyal to Alamea, and one of the first to question our extermination order on the shades. I also saved his ass back when I helped blow up the warehouse and earned my Silver Scale. His face stays neutral when he sees me, but I catch a small crinkling at the corner of his eyes.

I go to him, but I don't greet him directly. Instead, I stand near him.

"Thanks for the food," he says, his voice quiet.

After his rescue, he was in a body cast for weeks. I couldn't stand him getting stuck with hospital food, so I hired a caterer to deliver his meals. Sometimes I'm a big softie. I can still beat you up.

"You're welcome," I say, just as quietly.

I look at Devon, where the scar on his face is still pink against his pale skin. It takes a lot to scar a Mediator like that. I know he's got more, too. He almost lost an arm over the summer.

"Fucking traitor," someone says behind me.

Devon and I both spin, but I can't tell who said it. Silence spreads out from us, though, and people start shifting away from Devon and me.

I check my phone, mostly hoping for something I can answer to get me out of here. There's a text from Mira.

Works for me. I bail.

SHE MEETS ME AT her front door and actually hugs me. "You shit head. Next time don't get that close to dead."

"I'll do my best."

"Clearly your best is enough."

Joan Armatrading is playing on her stereo, and she's got papers spread out all over her dining room table. I sit down, wishing I knew what to do with myself.

"Let's see it," she says when I'm settled in my seat.

"See what?"

"Your jeeling battle wound. Puncture like that's gotta leave a nice scar. Might even get to keep that one."

I consider my options. I obviously don't have a scar. I could tell her it wasn't as bad as people said, that I must have been concussed and delusional from various demon fluids getting into open wounds. But something makes me not want to lie to Mira.

Pulling back the neckline of my shirt, I show her the unblemished skin.

She looks confused for a moment, then I see her sit back. "So what the fuck happened?"

Alamea's motives I'll always second guess at least a little. Desperate people do desperate things, and she is a desperate person. But Mira didn't have to trust me with her secret about Wane, and weirdly, if Saturn trusts her, I'd be stupid to ignore that. Saturn's a good judge of character. He likes me, after all.

I tell her everything—everything except for the secrets of the honeycomb hell under the Summit. That's one thing I'll keep to myself. And Nana. I might tell Nana.

Mira's brown face looks ready to turn green when I'm done. She pushes her chair back from the table and sits with her knees splayed, elbows leaning on her legs. "Gregor."

"Yeah."

"Motherfucking Gregor."

"Yeah."

"He ordered that many norm deaths. How many?"

"I couldn't count."

"And the shades?" She looks up at me, eyes panicked. "He made them do this. And they listened. And Miles is dead?"

"Yeah." I don't know what else to say. There are so many levels of oh-fuck-no in this that I've lost track of them all.

The table smells like lemon. She must have just polished it.

"Do you think this is why Saturn left?" she asks suddenly.

That gets my attention. "It could be. His message could have been referring to Gregor."

"And Jax," she says.

"I found a Mediator beacon in Jax's house. He left it somewhere he must have know I'd find it."

"Ayala," Mira says. "Do you think it was Gregor who tried to kill Saturn?"

Fuck.

I don't have an expletive strong enough.

Mira and I look at each other, and I know we're both thinking the same thing.

"How long has Gregor been doing this?" Her voice sounds shrill and grating, like I feel.

"At least three months," I say. "I think he knew about the shades before any of this started. He must have had Carrick stashed somewhere in the area, though how he found him I have no clue. He used me to find the local shades. I think he would have blackmailed me if I hadn't have done it willingly."

"This is enough to get him executed," Mira says.

"Yeah, well. Good luck. Half the Summit was about ready to bust out the ticker tape today."

"You're joking."

"Ask Devon. He was there. I was standing by him and someone called me a fucking traitor." For a moment I allow myself to entertain the idea of Gregor deposing Alamea and taking over the Summit. The thought makes me angry enough to spit teeth.

"What are we going to do?"

That stumps me. I'm still not used to being part of a we.

"I have to keep Gregor thinking I don't know the truth. He's getting cocky. He was soaking up the cheers and ass slaps like a biscuit in gravy today." My throat feels dry again, and I feel another blip of anxiety thinking of having to go home where Carrick is.

As if reading my mind, Mira asks, "What's Carrick's role in all this?"

"I don't know. He seems on board with Gregor, and he seems to do whatever Gregor tells him to do. I'd be stupid not to assume he's keeping tabs on me. At least he fed Nana while I was gone."

It feels so strange to be sitting in Mira's dining room with the sun pouring through the windows on a Monday afternoon. I miss my job. I should be listening to Alice and Parker banter right now instead of sitting here trying to figure out exactly how deep a shithole I'm wading through.

"We need to find Saturn," Mira says.

"You're not wrong." I rub my eye. "How exactly do you propose we do that?"

Mira's smile is dry enough to leech water from a bog. "I have a really bad idea."

"ARE YOU FUCKING KIDDING me?"

I think it's the first time I've heard Wane swear, and oddly enough, it's the final puzzle piece that tells me she and Mira are definitely family.

"Come on, Wane. You know his scent. You can try to track him." Mira cajoles with the best of them.

Wane's still in her scrubs—this time a boring midnight blue set—and she looks at me as if I'm supposed to bail her out of this. I shrug and put my hands in the air. I don't even know what her animal form is, but I do know that asking a morph to change is insulting, like asking them to do a trick.

Witches hate that too.

I suppose if someone came up to me with an imp in a cage, a hopeful expression, and a request of, "Come on, Mediator! Kill! Kill!" I'd be kind of pissed too.

"It's Saturn," Mira says.

We decided not to tell Wane the whole story, but we filled her in enough, telling her that Saturn found out some dirt on a high-up Mediator who tried to kill him, and that's why he's running scared. So far that story hasn't quite been enough to get her to help, though.

Wane glares at me now, as if she's decided this is entirely my fault. Her earrings have lightning bolts on them, and they glint in the light from the now-setting sun.

I shrug at her as if to tell her this wasn't my brilliant plan.

"Please," says Mira. "If we don't find him, someone else might find him first."

I'm not so sure it's Mira's words that make Wane's gaze shift from me to her and soften, but whatever it is, Wane slowly nods.

"I just need a drink of water first," she mutters. She almost stomps into the kitchen to get one, filling a Dora the Explorer tumbler with water from the fridge filter and chugging it.

When she's finished, she tosses the tumbler into the sink with a clatter and heads toward Mira's room.

Mira shoots me a grateful look and follows, with me a little behind her.

Even though the first time I met Wane was in a triage situation, I feel apprehensive about bringing her into this. We don't know what we'll find with her sniffing out a trail, and even though she can handle a shade bleeding to death and babies popping out of vaginas, I don't know if she knows the pointy end of a sword from a handle.

Though I suppose it's possible her other form has no need of swords at all.

I've never actually seen a morph change to animal form. Morphs usually live in their human forms, and they keep to themselves. Occasionally there's a reality show about them, but they never do that well and usually get canceled after a season or two. I think a grizzly morph went a bit nuts in Seattle a couple years back and changed in front of the troll sculpture, but that's about it.

I feel strange following Mira and Wane back to Mira's bedroom, like I'm about to watch Wane strip naked.

When she actually starts stripping off her clothes, I sort of want to kick myself for that analogy.

In spite of the awkwardness of the situation, Wane strips to her skin without shame or self-consciousness. I'm so used to naked men that you'd think I wouldn't blink at a naked woman, but it's a little different when the person's default is clothes.

She even takes her earrings off and puts them on Mira's bedside table.

Her change begins so gradually that I almost don't notice at first.

The air around her shimmers like the beginnings of a hells-hole. In the films, most morphs are played by humans or witches, so the CGI departments go a little overboard. Hair growing dramatically, teeth elongating, the kind of stuff that looks shocking on a big silver screen.

But Wane's change seems to happen both slowly and all at once. One moment, there's a nude woman standing in front of me, and, like a strange trick of the light, the next moment there's a mountain lion.

She's a gods damned mountain lion.

Her whiskers go forward, and the tip of her tail twitches. She gives me a look that says, "Hope you enjoyed the show."

Wane pads over to Mira's bed on paws bigger than my palms. With a chuffing sound and a half-jump, her front paws are on the bed, and Wane sniffs at the quilt and the pillow. She gets all the way up on the bed a moment later, and Mira sighs.

"You better not tear up my quilt," she says.

Wane growls, but she hops back down on the far side of the bed and walks to the window, nudging her head at it pointedly.

Mira opens the window, and Wane leaps out.

"Come on," Mira says. We head out to the side door and meet up with Wane again on the south side of the house.

I hope none of the neighbors are trigger happy.

Standard protocol with large, non-hellkin animals is to call the SPCA hotline—yes, the morphs have a branch of the SPCA—but we're in the South, and people around here still like their guns a little too much. Few years back, some twitchy homeowner stood his ground against a wolf that turned out to be somebody's teenager. The kid lived, thank the gods, but the shooter got eighteen to life.

I like swords for more reasons than their looks. Less chance of accidental murder.

Mira lives in East Nashville, in one of the neighborhoods off Gallatin Avenue, and it's not exactly normal to see two Mediators and a mountain lion strolling down Sumner.

Wane's tail keeps flicking right and left as we walk, and Mira and I follow as close behind as we can. The sky above us is afire with pink and orange, great swaths of colors igniting the clouds. A couple bright stars appear to the north, and the rush of traffic on Gallatin meets my ears.

A cop car speeds south on Gallatin, siren wailing through the twilight. A moment later, another one. I look at Mira, who shrugs.

Wane keeps heading toward the main road, her nose low to the ground and her paws making heavy pats on the concrete of the sidewalk. When we reach the road, Wane looks up at us and gives us the dirtiest look a cat can manage. At a lull in traffic, she leaps into the street.

Mira curses and takes off after her, and I follow, my ears ringing from a third siren and the screech of tires as another cop car spins out taking the turn onto Gallatin. A few blocks down, the red and blue lights flash, illuminating a diner sign.

The Waffle Spot.

Where Lena Saturn, Saturn's mother used to work.

"Stop," I say. My chest feels tight as I look south down Gallatin at the sign.

Wane and Mira stop, looking at me. Wane jerks her head to the west, straight forward where we're heading.

"You two follow the trail. I'll catch up."

"What is it?"

"I don't know." I break into a run, breathing deep. The air smells like fast food and car exhaust.

A fourth cop car comes speeding up from the south. When I reach the block the Waffle Spot's on, the tight feeling in my chest constricts. There's blood. I can smell it from here.

I see a lump, visible just on the other side of a police car. It's draped in blood-soaked flannel.

Even though I only saw the guy once when I was looking for leads on Lena Saturn, I'm sure it's him. Flannel Crack. Dumpy white dude who sat at the bar and was friendly with Lena's friend Grace. Had a couple inches of his ass crack exposed, and that's why I gave him such a creative name. Now he's dead in front of me. And off to the side, too.

I look around, scanning the area for any sign of movement that's out of the ordinary. Some diner customers are huddled and crying. Witches on dinner break, a few hipster morphs, a smattering of distraught humans.

Then I look up, because if there's ever anything you learn as a Mediator, it's that threats don't always stay eye level.

There's a flicker on the Waffle Spot roof, and I catch a glimpse of a bare butt.

Shades.

23

I SKIRT THE COPS who are busy cordoning off the parking lot with their yellow crime scene tape. Even though it's not their jurisdiction, they'll secure the scene long enough for someone from the Summit to get here.

I ignore the thought that I could be that someone.

The parking lot is full of pot holes, and I run around the side of the diner. The stench of the dumpster blossoms in the air, and a rivulet of some unknown gods-awful substance finds its way through the cracks in the asphalt. Darting around back, there are a few beat up junker cars. And Carrick, leaning against one, nekkid as a jaybird who lost its feathers.

"What happened here?" I ask.

"What are you doing here?" He looks at his fingernail and scrapes something red out from under it.

"I asked you first." I watch him, trying to keep my face neutral.

"Tracked the shades here. One of them killed the man out front." Carrick waggles his hand at me. "I managed to claw up one of them on the way out, but the other two were long gone."

"You didn't kill him."

"The man? Of course not, Ayala. What do you take me for?"

"Not the man up front." Poor Flannel Crack. "The shade."

"Last time I checked, some scratches weren't quite enough to put one of us down."

Fair enough. "And the other two?"

"Udo and Beex were chasing them, though these shades are…slippery."

Somehow I don't think he means they're covered in butter.

A scuffing sound behind me makes me turn. "A-Ayala?"

I see a young woman stick her head around the corner of the building, and a moment later, she sees Carrick. I grab her and clap my hand over her mouth before she can scream.

"Hiya, Grace," I say. "That's Carrick. He won't hurt you. Got it?"

She nods, but I don't release her for a moment. Carrick waves at her, gives me a meaningful look, and lopes away. Grace waves back, but he's already gone. I let her go and look her over.

Grace was one of Lena Saturn's friends. Stringy brown hair, consistently frightened expression, and not really the brightest. But if she's willingly coming to talk to me, she's got something to say.

"What happened?" I ask her.

"One of those monsters came and killed Dirk."

I take it Dirk is Flannel Crack. "I saw. Carrick and a couple of his friends are trying to find the killers."

Grace shakes her head, and I don't know if she's denying what I just said about Carrick or just in shock. My phone buzzes. Probably Mira.

"He said you'd come," Grace says.

My hand stops halfway to my pocket, where my phone is still buzzing. "What?"

“The one who killed Dirk. He said you'd come.” Grace looks around, her eyes closed as if picturing everything again—or maybe trying to shut it out.

“Grace,” I say. She doesn't open her eyes. I take her by the shoulder and give her a small shake. “Grace, this is important. I need you to answer something for me.”

She doesn't open her eyes, but she nods. A tear slips out between her eyelids.

“Did the shade who did this—did he have any tattoos? Any markings you could distinguish?”

Grace shakes her head. “He was wearing a hat.”

“Excuse me?”

“They were all wearing hats. There were three of them. They came into the diner and everyone started yelling, and they grabbed Dirk. Each of them grabbed an arm, one of them grabbed Dirk's head and—” Grace shakes her head harder, faster, and her eyes scrunch closed even more, though tears seep out anyway. “They were all wearing hats, but that was all. And the one who had Dirk's head said that you would come, and they all laughed, and they pulled Dirk out into the parking lot and pulled him apart.”

I take Grace by the other shoulder and turn her toward me, this time gently. “Grace.” I say her name again. “Hey. You were really brave.”

She still doesn't open her eyes. I can somehow relate to that feeling, that knowledge that when you do, your world is going to be a little bit worse forever. Or a lot bit worse.

“I'm not brave,” Grace whispers. “I almost peed my pants.”

A grim smile spreads across my face. “Well, then you did better than me. First time I encountered that many shades at once, I did pee my pants.”

At that, her eyes open, and she peers at me. “You're full of shit.”

I raise an eyebrow at her choice of words. “Nope. I was in a warehouse, and I was surrounded, and I thought I was going to die.”

“You didn’t die.”

“Neither did you.” I give her shoulders a squeeze and drop my hands to my sides. “Come on. You need to give a statement to the police or the Summit, whoever turns up.”

“Where are you going?”

“Hunting.”

I deposit Grace in front by the crime scene tape, where a police officer is yammering on her phone to someone at the Summit, trying to explain what happened and that they’ve got the scene secured. Whoever she’s talking to doesn’t seem to be particularly helpful. When the officer sees me, she looks almost relieved. I gesture at her to give me her phone.

“Yello,” I say into it. “This is Mediator Storme. I’m on a trail and can’t stay. Send somebody capable down here, and one of the PR witches. Mediator Urquhart or someone else who won’t fuck this up.” That’s Ripper, and he’ll be pissed at me for volunteering him, but I trust him not to be a complete buffoon. The Mitten on the other end of the line starts to squawk at me, but I cut him off. “Look, you can either do your job, or I can get you put on splat duty and make sure you’re part of the cleanup crew at this scene, you hear? Can the back talk, Mittens. Get Ripper and a PR person down here, and do it now.”

I hang up.

My own phone buzzes again, and I hand the cop’s back to her. She gives me a grateful look.

“Call me if you need anything, Grace,” I say.

To my surprise, she throws her arms around my neck. “Thank you. And I think you’re brave, too.”

Well, isn’t she a precious little peach?

BY NOW, MIRA AND Wane are about ten blocks away, and I have to run to catch up with them, passing under Highway 31. I don’t like that. It gives me time to think about what happened at the Waffle Spot. I don’t know if I trust Carrick to catch these shades, but in a weird way, I trust him to try. If Gregor's intent on using them for his own ends, he doesn't need the bad publicity a few murderous hybrids will bring, so it's in his best interest to have his shades take them down.

There are too many strings tangled together, and I need to sort them all out.

Something tickles at me, and while my feet pound the pavement, I try to track it down.

It's not that the shade at the Waffle Spot mentioned me by name; that's an obvious oh-fuck fact, but it's also not necessarily that meaningful. By now everyone knows that I was behind the idea for the warehouse bombing, and though my shades have a pragmatic, philosophical sort of forgiveness for me, it's not far-fetched to think some others think I'm a bit of a menace to shade society.

I think of the places these shades have killed. The warehouse. Percy Warner. Now the Waffle Spot. They're all places connected to me. I don't like the implications of that.

It's full dark by the time I catch up to Mira and Wane down a cul-de-sac, and Mira looks about ready to tear me apart like Flannel Crack.

"Shade murder," I say by way of explanation.

That wipes the anger from her face. "How many?"

"Just one. But one's enough."

"Wane said the trail keeps going to the north from here. Off the roads."

I don't ask how Wane said it. "What do you want to do?"

"Wane can keep following and check back with us later, " says Mira. Wane gives a growl again, and I don't blame her. This could take all night, and I'm pretty sure when she turned up at Mira's tonight, she'd just gotten off a twelve hour shift.

"Well, you can probably move more quickly without us, anyway," I say to Wane. Her tail swishing is the only answer I get.

She gives us one look and springs off into the grass between two houses. Again, I hope no one decides to get trigger happy.

I tell Mira what happened and what I'm thinking about it.

"He knew you were nearby," she says.

"What?"

"The shade who killed—Dirk, was it?—He knew you were close enough to hear the sirens. Why else would he say that you'd come?"

That sends a chill through me. Has he been watching me to find out where I'm going? If Mira's right, he has.

"Fuck."

"Took the word right out of my mouth," Mira says. "I should brush up on my beheading skills in case this sonofabitch pays me a visit."

We walk back to her house with a light drizzle falling, and I spend most of the trip back hoping Wane will turn up something useful about Saturn. I don't have a lot of optimism, though. If Saturn doesn't want to be found, he won't be.

Back at Mira's, we flip on the TV. The ten o'clock news is on, and it's playing the pro-shade piece about the ones we killed outside Crossville. I'm about to turn it back off again, but a breaking story about the Waffle Spot interrupts the Summit's little bit of propaganda.

A reporter stands on the sidewalk on Gallatin, the Waffle Spot sign behind him. His white skin looks sallow, taking on the glare of the orange light from the sign. "Tonight a horrible scene unfolded at the popular East Nashville diner, the Waffle Spot. One of the demon-human hybrids currently being hunted by Summit operatives murdered one of the diner regulars in front of customers and staff. At this point, no employees or spokespeople for the diner have given this station comment, but Officer Belmont said that there was one fatality and no other casualties. It is unclear what drove the hybrids—colloquially referred to as "shades"—off the premises, but a Summit Mediator has assured us that all possible measures are being taken to ensure the safety of Nashville's residents."

At that, a little infographic pops up on the screen with a bulleted list of factoids about shades.

“Public opinion about these hybrids skews to the negative, as they can walk in sunlight, look human in appearance, and have the comparative strength of a demon. Professor Sorkin at Vanderbilt University has classified the creatures as *homo sapiens infernus*, joining the official scientific list of what are commonly called ‘norm’ species. Such classification has led to mixed response from the scientific community, some of whom argue that any being rooted in dual dimensions cannot, by definition, be classified alongside inhabitants of ours.” The infographic vanishes, and the picture returns to the reporter’s face. “One thing’s for certain: the appearance of the hybrids has brought out extremes in opinion, from activist groups who want them protected to others who believe very strongly that they ought to be Mediator targets, just like the hellkin themselves. Even within the Summit, opinions vary, though no Mediators would go on the record about their views. With a rash of recent murders by the hybrids coinciding with Mediator-hybrid special operations, this story grows more complex by the day.

“Tonight’s killing was only the most recent, and Dirk Schmidt joins the roster of eighteen other Nashville citizens to die at the hands of the hybrids.” Dirk’s face flashes onto the screen, a picture taken at Winter Solstice last year, by the look of it. He’s in a red and green flannel, and white letters at the bottom of the screen show his life bookended by the year of his birth and this one. “Schmidt was a teacher at a local junior high school, where he taught shop and life skills. He was forty-seven.”

The breaking news broadcast ends, and the screen goes back to the studio anchors. Mira mutes it.

“I have a headache,” she says.

“Me too.” But something on the muted screen catches my eye.

I snatch the remote from Mira and unmute it in time to hear another reporter say that there’s a developing story at Walden’s Puddle.

While it's not somewhere I frequent, it's where I dropped off a box of baby bunnies a few months ago after an imp killed their mother at Miller's Field.

This is too much to be a coincidence.

We sit there, me feeling helpless and Mira's face unreadable, until someone knocks on the door at midnight.

24

"WELL, I'LL BE DAMNED to all six and a half hells," Ripper says when I open the door. "And fuck you very much for having that gods damned Mitten send me off to the Waffle Spot."

"You're welcome," I say. I usher him into Mira's house, and he waves at Mira around me.

"Find anything interesting?" Mira asks. She's got a delivery menu in one hand and the remote in the other.

Ripper looks like a young Robert Redford, and his blond ponytail's mostly grown back from where an imp sliced part of it off in Miller's Field over the summer. He smacks his lips together like he's got some chaw in his gums, though I knew he doesn't chew.

"You're in a kettle, Storme," he says, taking the delivery menu from Mira and looking it over. With his free hand, he rubs his palm over his face.

"Usually am these days," I say.

I hope Mira's right, and Ripper really is loyal to Alamea, because I don't know if I can handle having to suss out someone else's motivations tonight. After a minute, he hands me the menu and tells Mira he wants a number six with no sour cream.

I pick out a burrito platter and sit down on the couch again while Mira goes off to the kitchen to order.

"How've you been, Ripper?" I ask him. It's been a while since I've seen him, but he's one of the few Mediators I like. That may be partially because he stood up for me this summer when most people didn't.

"Just dandy." He sits down in a chair and adjusts the leg of his Wranglers. "I just came over because I thought Mira'd want to know what happened at the Summit after I came back from the scene."

"I think you thought right."

Mira comes back in a moment later and lean against the archway to her kitchen. "So?"

"It's about as we thought. Wheedle's got his group of people who are on Team Gregor, and they all think Alamea's lost her marbles." Ripper looks like he swallowed a cockroach.

"Wait, Ben?" Someday I'm going to plant my boot so far up that man's ass that he'll be picking my toejam out of his teeth.

"Ye-ep." Ripper drags out the word long enough to be almost three syllables. "Here's the thing, Storme. You're never around, so you mostly exist in Mediator minds as this weird yellow-orange specter who turns up only when shit's getting sprayed through a fan. Half the Summit seems to think you're some sort of titan, and the other thinks you've just got titanic delusions of grandeur. They know you're working with Gregor and his shades, they know the shades like you, and they know you're now working for Alamea. Nobody knows what your game is, and that makes everyone suspicious of you. You're like the chips in the air, and ain't nobody got a clue where you're gonna land."

"Well, hello to you too," I mutter.

Ripper grins at me. "You're the Russia of the Summit."

"I'll take being a mystery wrapped in an enigma as long as that shit keeps me out of a jeeling's belly," I say. "I ain't trying to be wrapped in demon in any way."

"Here's to that." Mira holds up a beer and brings two more over to me and Ripper.

Six beers each and a lot of Mexican food later, we're all a little buzzed when a loud thud sounds out on Mira's porch.

"Wane," Mira says. She hops up, still steady on her feet, and hurries to the door. Sure enough, Wane comes through, smelling of musk and outdoors.

The big cat goes straight down the hall to Mira's room and emerges a few minutes later as Wane in her scrubs. "I hate putting dirty clothes back on after I change," she says. "Give me a damn beer."

Mira pops the top off a bottle and hands it to Wane, who downs half of it in one swig.

"Didn't find Saturn," she says. "But I think I found where he's been staying. Found a tree in Willow Creek Park that smelled too much like him for him to have just passed by there. He wasn't around, though."

The relief on Mira's face is contagious.

My phone rings, and it's an unfamiliar number. I pick it up. "Hello?"

"It's Carrick," comes his voice on the line. "Did you hear about the second killing?"

That gives me pause. "Killing? We heard there was a disturbance at Walden's Puddle and a developing story, but there haven't been any updates."

"The shades killed two of the late night staff."

"Where are you?" I ask.

Wane, Ripper, and Mira all go silent, listening to me.

"I'm going there now."

"I'm coming with you," I say.

I hang up before Carrick can tell me not to come.

MIRA AND RIPPER JOIN me, but Wane looks about to pass out and curls up in the guest room instead.

Together we arm ourselves and pile in Ripper's dull black truck, with me stuck in the middle between the two of them. His truck smells like beef jerky. The seats are covered with multicolored tweed, and he has a shard of smoky quartz hanging from his rearview mirror. The radio's tuned to a top 40 station that makes me raise an eyebrow, but I don't dare mention it.

His gearshift is way too close to my kneecaps to risk his wrath.

The rain's stopped, and with the windows rolled down, the scent of damp earth fills the cab.

The drive to Joelton only takes about twenty minutes, and I'm more or less sure the shades will be gone by the time we get there, but I have to go. Around me everything in my territory feels like it's spiraling out of control, and if I'm not careful, I'll be swept away with it.

Ripper's little speech on how the other Mediators see me didn't come as a surprise, not really. I've always been a loner. Until now, I haven't really had any friends. There were people I felt friendly toward, like Mira and Ripper, but before Mason I kept everyone a few steps back from arm's length.

I don't know if I can afford to do that anymore, but it scares the piss right out of me.

Ripper parks his truck a little ways from the center, and even from there we can see more police lights. None of us are surprised to see it, but still, it makes my stomach sink. The people at the center didn't deserve this. They save lives. I don't know where Carrick is going to be, but the three of us aren't bad trackers by ourselves. We may not have a morph's nose between us, but we might be able to at least figure out what direction the shades left in.

On foot, we approach the center, which is a huge building on a large plot of land. As we approach, we can hear the din of distressed animals, and it makes me think of the bunnies I dropped off here a couple months ago. I feel sick. I don't know what these shades are thinking, targeting places that I've gone, but the people they're hurting don't deserve it.

Maybe it should disturb me more, the fact that I think I'm the one who deserves their wrath, but I accept it. I wish this batch of shades would come after me instead.

There's squawking as we approach, and the lights from the police cars don't really show anything. They let us past the cordoned off area when they see our eyes, and we duck under the yellow tape and enter the building. The lights flicker when we walk in, and the fluorescents buzz unpleasantly in my ears. I hate fluorescent lighting. We Mediators never use it, and since the witch community came up with a green alternative a few years back, most businesses have switched to it. If I ever win the lottery, I'm buying them new lights here. I'm sure the animals don't appreciate the fluorescent buzz any more than Mediators do.

The lobby looks innocuous at first glance, but at the side of the desk, there's a smear of blood. When we walk up to it, the desk itself is covered in spatter.

And I recognize the head that lies alone between two wheels of a rolly chair. He's the person who took the bunnies when I brought them in. Sometimes I hate my life.

Ripper heads off down the hallway, past a door that says "Employees Only."

I make myself look at the bodies behind the desk. They're torn apart in true shade style, piled in a heap with the heads separate. I wonder if the shades do it that way so they don't feel like they're being watched by their victims.

Mira stands just beside me, her shoulder almost close enough to touch mine, but she doesn't say anything.

I start to go after Ripper, but he's already on his way back.

"Doesn't look like they so much as touched a baby skunk back there." He looks relieved at that, and I echo his relief.

That they spared the animals makes me a little confused. I know I don't want to see any dead owls or beavers or fawns, but shades usually aren't picky about who they kill. Maybe they thought the deaths of the staff members would hurt me more. I'm not sure if they're right or wrong.

I turn back to the pile of parts, trying to divorce them from their owners and look for anything helpful. Two bodies make an awfully large blood pool, and though this side of the desk doesn't have much aside from that one smear, the other side has a wide pool already growing tacky.

"They must have come straight here from the Waffle Spot," I say, and Mira nods her agreement.

She moves to the other side of the desk. "They didn't come out this way," she says. "No way they could have avoided stepping in the blood pool."

"They could have jumped over it," Ripper says, but I hold up a hand.

"Even if they'd have jumped, they'd probably leave drops of some kind." I look at the floor near my feet. It looks recently re-done in square tiles. "They were careful not to leave too many marks."

The pile of parts draws my attention again.

"Both people were killed on the other side of the desk where the blood pool is," I say. "They must have killed them, then backed up a few feet and piled up what was left."

The smell of voided bowels and blood is heavy, and though I've seen a lot worse, it still makes my stomach feel curdled, like milk with lemon juice dropped into it.

I look down at the young man's head between the chair wheels. A foot away there's a red print on the ground with what looks like the texture of human hair. "They threw the head," I say, disgusted. "Looks like they decapitated them first."

Peering around the desk, I see the other attendant's head under the desk next to a computer tower. Both heads are far enough from the blood pool to be thrown. The chair itself is black, but when I lean over to look at it, I can see an arc of blood spatter across the plastic back side, and a drying dribble across the textile-covered padded seat. Another arc leads to the one under the desk.

Footprints would make it easy, but that doesn't mean that's all the clue they left. Hard to keep your hands clean when you're pulling off heads.

There—on the edge of the desk, I see it. A finger print. A few of them, and a thumb, as if one of the shades grasped it on his way past.

There's no blood on the front door, so they must have gone somewhere else. If we can find which door they left by, we might be able to track them into the woods.

The door Ripper went through to check on the animals is clean as well, which leaves the side door out into the back enclosure. Sure enough, when we get to it, there's a drying red smudge on the handle.

"Come on," I say, pushing the door open. I'm careful to avoid the smudge; even though the Summit doesn't really have a forensic team, I don't want to destroy any evidence

The earlier rain left the ground just soft enough, and just outside the concrete pad in front of the door, there are three sets of bare footprints.

Ripper's got a flashlight in his belt—he carries a bunch of shit like some kind of Batman wannabe—and he flicks it on. Together, we follow the footprints through the enclosure. The place is fenced in chain link, but it's not topped with barbed wire or anything, so when the footprints reach the fence and reappear on the other side, the three of us alley-oop over the barrier and follow. The footprints space out, both in the stride length and the distance between the pairs.

"They started running," Mira says. "If they stay going south-ish, they'll hit Beaman Park."

"How far is it?" I ask. Beaman Park. Where Jax lived. Could these shades have been the reason he left?

"Couple miles."

I look at Ripper. "Want to meet us there in the truck?"

He nods. "I'll park off Old Hickory and wait for you at the junction of Eaton's Creek."

"We'll call you if the direction changes." I reach out and take the flashlight from him, and Mira and I set off.

The prints are even and easy to follow for now, the ground clearing as the summer grasses die away and go dormant for the winter. I keep the flashlight aimed at the trail, and Mira and I quicken our pace into a jog.

"What do we do if we find them?" she asks.

"I don't know. I'd rather take them alive than dead."

She's quiet for a moment. Our boots make a steady squishing pattern in the ground. The prints we're following shift just a bit, due south now, and I want to high five Mira for being right. We come across a narrow stream and splash across it. The prints in the mud on the other side are clear as Crystal Light and easy to follow.

"You don't want them to die, do you?" she asks. Her words are steady and unhurried, where I'm over here panting. Talking and running has never been one of my strong points.

I take a deep breath and feel it rush through me. "No. I don't."

"It's not your fault, what they're doing."

"I know."

"And the warehouse? You did what you thought you had to."

Irritated, I look over at her. She's looking at the ground, at the beam of light illuminating the trail.

"Yeah, well, I was an asshole and a fucking blockhead."

"I didn't say you weren't."

I choke and lose my breath pattern. It takes me a hundred yards to get my breathing back under control.

Mira gives me a sidelong grin and keeps running. "I think it's good that you try to help them. But even norms are sometimes beyond help."

Her words startle me, and I look at her. She couldn't mean that the hells-worshippers Gregor ordered killed had it coming?

She catches my horrified look, and she immediately shakes her head. "No, no. I know what you're thinking. I didn't mean they deserved to die if they couldn't get their shit together. Just that you can't help people who don't want help."

Wise words. We're quiet then, running along the path. Sure enough, Eaton's Creek Road appears in front of us, with the Old Hickory Boulevard junction beyond it slightly to the north. The tracks still run due south, right into the park as Mira predicted.

Ripper's truck is pulled over on the side of the road, some pop-funk track playing low on his speakers. And he's talking to Carrick through his window.

"Fuck." I pick up my pace, and Mira mirrors me.

"You think Carrick's helping them or something?" she asks.

"Nope, but if Carrick's here, it means he either found the trail and the shades, or the trail peters out somewhere."

Turns out, it's neither of those things.

Ripper flags us down as soon as he sees us—as if we'd keep running the other way—and he holds up his phone.

I stop running twenty feet from the truck and pull out my own phone. There's a text from Ripper, who's talking to Carrick about the football playoffs now.

The text says: *Need to get to Summit. Ben just called out Alamea in front of a whole committee meeting. Erase this.*

I delete the text immediately and saunter up to Carrick with as much grace as I can muster, still panting from the run. This is more running than I ever do.

"Did you find them?" I ask Carrick. "Trail keeps going south from there." I point to the road's shoulder, where even from here I can see the footprints in the soft ground.

"Harkan and Hux are on the trail. I saw Ripper pull up and though you'd be with him." Carrick nods at Ripper, who rolls up his window and turns up the music as if not caring what any of us have to say.

Mira hops in the truck.

"We followed the trail south from the refuge," I say. "But if they've picked it up here, I guess we're sort of superfluous."

“We can handle it,” Carrick says. “If you hadn’t hung up on me, I could have told you that.”

“Then handle it,” I say quietly. “If you really can, make sure they don’t kill again.”

That shuts him up.

I turn and get into Ripper’s truck before he can say anything else. By the time I look back, Carrick’s gone.

25

WE GO STRAIGHT TO the meeting hall when we arrive at the Summit, and before we even open the door, the sound of yelling reaches us. Usually the late night meetings are placid affairs, but this is anything but placid.

Something heavy thumps into the door.

"Slummoth slime on a cracker," Mira says. "What the actual fuck are they doing?"

I pull open the door, and I have to step over an unconscious Mediator to get through it. Mira's question seems like a good one.

We've walked into an all-out brawl.

Most of the fighting is going on down on the floor, though to our left three people are duking it out across two levels of terraced seats. Alamea's at the front of the room, untouched in the maelstrom, and to the side, Ben's trying to keep a woman from getting him in a chokehold. I hope she succeeds.

A young Mediator I recognize from the last elevation ceremony as being just out of training tries to snake by me, and I grab him by the ear. He twists and yells, and I have him on his knees in three seconds.

"You've got one minute to tell me exactly what started this," I say.

"Mediator Wheedle said Alamea was endangering the city by allowing shades to go unsupervised. Ow! Will you let go of my ear?"

"Nope. Keep talking."

I know this kid from the front desk over the summer. He's as green as a grass stain and clearly wasn't paying enough attention in training to fight back.

"Mediator Wheedle said that these shades are going to keep killing people and that it's going to reflect on the Summit and that Alamea's weak for not cracking down." The kid squirms, which probably makes his ear hurt worse.

Mediator Wheedle. I know Ben can't help his name, but it makes me want to punch him even more.

I'm just glad no one has the tits to try and fuck with Alamea at this point. If people were throwing fists her way, that would be even worse, though as far as silver linings go, it's pretty dingy.

I drop the kid's ear. "Go on, get." He scurries away.

Finally someone spots us, and a couple stormy faces come our way.

"Oh, hells, no," I say. It actually stops the two Mediators in their tracks. "You so much try and lay a hand on me and I will use Ben and Alamea as goal posts and punt you through them for three points."

I take two steps down the aisle toward Alamea, and one of them rushes me. I've got the higher ground and the apparent advantage of brains, and I plant a side kick on the Mediator's sternum.

He doesn't fly all the way to Alamea, but close. He lands on his back at the foot of the stairs to the dais, and his friend thinks better of coming at me and steps aside.

Ben's managed to get the woman off his back, but she's dodging every one of his punches, and if he's not careful, she's going to catch him with a round kick.

Someone takes that moment to run at Alamea, who very calmly delivers an upper cut to the Mediator's face, knocking her out cold.

"Enough!" Her voice thunders through the room with the force of a summer storm, and it distracts Ben enough that the woman he's fighting does exactly as I predicted and lands a round kick on the side of his head. His eyes glaze, and he slumps over, and I resist the urge to cheer.

"With the exception of the three newcomers who didn't realize they were walking into the pages of the Outsiders, every Mediator in this room will be subject to disciplinary action pending review by your superiors." Alamea steps to the edge of the dais and off of it, stepping over the Mediator I kicked to the floor with barely disguised disdain. "We are not schoolyard bullies, and this is not a rumble. You are grown adults and the first line of defense of this city."

Though her words are measured, when Alamea approaches me, I can see that her hands are nearly shaking with fury. Her locs swish behind her, and she looks past me without even seeming to see me. When I turn, I see Gregor at the top of the stairs, looking down at the remains of the fray with his blocky face blank. He makes eye contact with Alamea, but he doesn't say anything.

What I wouldn't give to see inside both their heads right now. I can feel Mira and Ripper's body heat behind me, and the room's sudden quiet is pierced only by the occasional groan and heavy sighs of people getting to their feet. I don't even know what to do. Never in my life would I have expected to show up to the Summit and find this.

Beneath the pierced bubble of fighting, the tension still roils and stretches, and I know it's only a matter of time before it snaps again. Alamea walks right past Gregor and out the door of the meeting chamber. After a minute of looking around and watching people stuff tissues up their nostrils to stem nosebleeds, I make for the door as well.

Gregor stops me in the threshold. "Storme, what are you doing here?"

"I stopped by to pick up some tea," I lie blandly.

He snorts and gives me a fond smile. A pang twangs through my chest. Six months ago, Gregor's fondness would have been a nice thing. Now it makes me feel like I'm his lapdog. And Alamea's lapdog. I don't want to be anybody's lapdog.

"Carrick said they lost the killers again," he says, pitching his voice low enough so that only I can hear him.

"I thought that might happen," I say. "This has to stop, Gregor."

"I know." Weirdly, I think he even means it.

"Any other jobs for us?" I ask. I don't know what I want him to say; the last thing I want is a repeat of what happened down by Chattanooga, but he has to think I'm still in his corner with my towel and my gloves, ready to fight on his team.

He shakes his head. "Catching the shades who are killing our citizens is our first priority."

Now he just sounds like a gods damned politician. I nod and start to walk by. I turn to Ripper, who's lagging behind with Mira, but Gregor reaches out and catches my arm.

"Be careful, Storme," he says, looking over my shoulder at the Mediators in the chamber. "And don't forget your tea."

The Summit supplies all of us with free tea and coffee, probably because they know most of us never get any sleep. I haven't brought any home in ages. After Gryfflet used coffee to poison me last summer, I've lost my taste for the stuff.

But when Gregor follows us into the Summit lobby, I make sure to go to the glossy, built-in cabinets in the foyer and take a few boxes.

RIPPER AND MIRA AND I talk the whole way back to Mira's house, but none of us have any good strategies for dealing with what's coming next. I leave, feeling like the whole night was an unresolved mess of upsetting happenings, one after another.

And with all the running I've been doing, I'm hungry again.

Carrick's not home when I get there, and I feed Nana, going to the fridge to see if I have anything at all. I have peach jam and some bread in the freezer, so I make four pieces of toast and start to eat them at the kitchen table.

My phone rings, and it's an unfamiliar number again. Thinking it's Carrick, I answer. "What now?"

"Was there something before?"

I almost drop the phone at the sound of the voice.

It's Mason.

My heart has to be flopping around on the floor somewhere, because I just felt it drop out of my ribcage.

"Mason?"

"Hi."

Short and to the point, as usual. Shades.

I swallow, not sure what to say. *Good for you, getting away before all hells broke loose. How's the desert? Meet any nice camels? Oh, hey, thanks for leaving me to deal with this mess?*

I don't end up saying any of it, because I can't seem to get any words out.

"Are you there?"

I force out a yes.

Again, though, I don't know what comes after it. Finally, I find some words and string them together. "Where are you?"

"Pakistan."

That seems to get my tongue working again. "Wow, could you have gone any farther away from here?"

"Physically, I think not." There's a hint of a smile in his voice, but also a hint of regret.

I will not think about that regret. I will not.

"Yeah, well. I think you had the right idea," I say.

"I heard things aren't going well there." His words are more sure of themselves now, and the difference is stark. He almost sounds like a stranger. Almost.

That makes me laugh, and the sound startles Nana, who I didn't even see come in. She makes a squeak and runs into a chair leg. I reach down and touch her back, cooing at her.

"Is that the rabbit?" Mason asks, sounding more pleased than I want him to.

"Yeah. That's Nana."

"You named her Nana."

"After the dog in Peter Pan," I say. "That poor dog never got to do anything fun."

"I don't think I know Peter Pan."

"Probably not," I agree.

"What's happening there? Saturn told me—"

It finally sinks in that if he heard things weren't going well here, someone had to tell him if he's all the way in fucking Pakistan.

"You talked to Saturn? When? Is he okay?" Now the words trip over each other to get out of my mouth, and Mason goes silent.

After a beat, he starts talking again. "He called me yesterday."

"Yesterday? That asshole knocked Mira out and took off, then he left her a cryptic note on her pillow." I remember that Mason left me an also-sort-of cryptic note under my pillow when he left, and the thought ignites my irritation all over again. "And you gave him your number? What is it with you damn shades and notes? Can't you just stick around and say what you mean?"

I think I've startled him, because he doesn't speak again for long enough that I wonder if he's lost the connection, and my heart worms back up into my chest and starts doing double time with the thought of the call ending.

"I'm sorry."

"Are you?" My head spins, and I find myself wishing I'd just wake up and find out that this whole day was a stupid dream.

"Yes." Mason's intake of breath sounds genuine enough to me. "Will you tell me what's wrong?"

"Well, everything, for a start," I snap. Then I take my own deep breath and tell my heart to stop beating so quickly. I tell him everything that's been going on, from Saturn's disappearance to Jax and Miles, who he never knew well. I tell him about Gregor and Alamea and Mira and Ripper and how some fucking shade is cutting a swath through the populace of my city and starting with places I know and care about.

"Saturn at least is okay. You don't have to worry about him."

Trust a shade to hear everything I just told him and tell me the one thing I already knew.

"He'd be a lot of help if he'd turn back up," I say. "Him running amok around Nashville and leaving notes on pillows isn't the most useful thing he could be doing."

"He has a reason."

"Which is?"

Mason hesitates. "It's not my story to tell."

"Hells, Mason."

"I'm sorry."

"Why exactly did you call?" I ask. It's not out of malice, just curiosity, but I hope he's got a reason beyond, *oh, sorry your life sucks.*

"I miss you."

Well, that's nice. I have to think a little too long before I say, "I miss you too."

"I wish I could help."

"You could, you know."

"It took me two months to get here," Mason says.

Yeah, traveling without a passport has to be a pain in the ass. Someday I'll have to ask him how he got across the Atlantic.

I don't think either one of us knows what to say after that, because for a minute or so there's just the sound of our breathing, and I remember too well those nights we spent hand in hand in my bed, learning to trust one another.

"I should go," he says.

"I'm glad you called." I think I mean it.

"Whatever happens, you can handle it." He sounds sure, and for that I'm thankful. I don't know if he's right, but I'm thankful for whatever it is that makes him believe in me.

"Have fun in Pakistan," I say.

When we hang up, I sit in my kitchen, listening to the sound of my own breathing. In the movies, true love is a thing that just is. But for me, Mason broke something when he left. I know he had to, and I'd never blame him, but love to me means you stay and fight.

My remaining piece and a half of toast is all soggy.

26

I CAN'T SLEEP AFTER that damn phone call from Mason, so I gear back up and get in my car, unsure of where to go. The Opry is my usual go-to, but after last time, I don't want to risk running into a whole horde again, even if I took out the last one singlehandedly.

I'm going to chalk that up as a fluke and make like it won't happen again. Cockiness is a good way to end up with your head on the chopping block in my line of work.

There's a park just off Charlotte Avenue where a lot of Mittens go to train, and it's a mark of how jumpy I am right now that that's the place I choose to go. It's about a fifteen minute drive from my home, in the middle of a nice, quiet neighborhood.

I wonder sometimes that any parks have visitors. I guess they're fine during the day, but there ain't a rebellious teen in middle Tennessee that'll venture into one after sunset. Even the hells-zealots know to keep their death-wish-having asses out of the parks after dark.

This one isn't a big hotspot for demonic activity, but you can usually find a few imps or a lumpy harkast or two frolicking around. Mason used to watch this ballet movie where the wise instructor would tell the hotshot new spitfire on campus to go back to the barre when times got tough, gol'darn it.

Well. This is my barre.

It feels strange being here; it's not even until I see the sign that I remember what the park's called. Richland Creek. There's a golf course along one side that I remember made the news when I was just out of training for one of the ball divers fishing a markat head out of the water hazard. Every Mitten on cleanup duty that week got called in and reprimanded for not making sure there were heads to go with each of the bodies they picked up.

I find the trailhead and walk in, and almost immediately, there are no woodland sounds. Looks like I came to the right place.

Not a quarter mile in, I hear a rustle in the bushes.

It's almost cute. A harkast stumps out of a juniper and makes a high-pitched call when it sees me. When a second follows a moment later, I almost want to use them as stepping stones again and see how many times I can hop back and forth between their dumpy, flat heads before I get bored.

I remember when these things used to scare me.

Demon or not, I decide not to play with them and dispatch both of them quickly, both swords at once through their skulls.

Coming here was supposed to be a way for me to blow off some steam, but instead it's making me more antsy. I don't want to become one of those thrill seekers who has to chase adrenaline in demon hordes of ever-increasing sizes, but a couple harkasts just won't do it for me. As they cool on the ground in front of me, I listen for the sound of the bugs coming back. A squirrel. A bird. Anything.

When I don't hear anything, I settle myself into a better state of alertness. Last time the harkast demons served as sort of electrons to the jeeling's nucleus, and even though I've taken down a few jeelings solo this year, I'm not in a hurry to try myself against the next one.

I walk deeper into the park, listening to the bushes. There's no sound but the wind. Above me, Orion's bow edges up over the treetops.

A low, murmuring burble starts in the distance, and my stomach sinks. I'm suddenly glad I only ate four pieces of toast, because I know what's around the corner.

I hear it before I see it, and part of me makes a strong case for turning around and going directly home without stopping to pass Go.

There's a loud squishing noise that sounds like a hippo falling into an Olympic-sized pool of Jell-O, and any remaining hope that I'm wrong vaporizes. The breeze brings with it a putrid smell like month-old pus.

Gods damn it. It's a golgoth demon.

This is what I get. I could have stayed home. Now I have to kill it. And I *like* these pants.

It appears on the path ahead of me. Seven feet tall and all flab, the golgoth constantly oozes. Where it's not dripping slime—which is very few places—it's covered in suppurating sores and boils. A golgoth fell on me once when I was a Mitten. I don't think I've ever gotten over it. I had to use the anti-skunk remedies for two weeks, and my bunkmate slept in the common room on a couch the whole time.

They're slow, stupid, and ungainly, but they're hungry and singleminded. I could outrun it, even with my legs sore from running miles already today.

But if I do, that means either some other poor schmuck of a Mediator would be stuck with this walking mountain of goo, and as much as the other Mediators right now probably could use this lesson in humility, I can't go running away from a demon just because it's icky.

That would just be unprofessional.

I resign myself to my ignominious future and draw my swords.

“Hey, Sir Seeps-A-Lot. Want a piece of me?” I don’t usually talk to demons, but it helps distract me from the smell. Sort of.

It grunts something in response, which might actually be a response to my question. I just don’t speak demon.

The golgoth moves slowly enough that I can try to figure out a plan of attack.

It waddles toward me with a continuous squelching sound. The thing looks like a love child of Slimer and the bubonic plague.

It’s so stupid that it takes a swing at me when I’m still ten feet away.

“See, now you’re just embarrassing yourself,” I tell it. “You should get your vision checked. Depth perception is important.”

For some reason, making fun of the golgoth makes me feel better. It takes another couple ponderous steps forward and swipes again, but I dance back. I wonder how long it would take to just run in circles around it until it gets tired.

I should probably just kill it.

Its sores drip pus in globs that fall on the footpath with audible splats. It reeks like a rotting bandage, if that bandage were seven feet tall and coming at you. Now that it’s this close, the smell is nearly overpowering. I’ve smelled some stenches in my time, but golgoth demons make me want to cut off my nose.

It takes another slime-sucking step, and I roll to the side, coming up on its right. I slash at the golgoth’s hamstring. My blade hits home, cutting through layers of flab and goo. The golgoth makes a warbling, vibrating sound like Chewbacca might make from inside Jabba the Hutt.

The gods damned thing doesn’t go down, but if anything, the smell intensifies since I’ve just sliced through half a dozen boils. My sword is covered in demon blood, slime, and pus.

I hate everything.

Trying not to heave up everything I’ve ever eaten, I get out of range of the golgoth’s swinging arms, trying to see how much damage I actually did.

One of the problems with a golgoth is that they've got so many layers of slimy flab that it takes a long sword to get the point anywhere near its heart, which is smack in the middle of its body. The head is almost as inaccessible, because the cursed mountain of goo is seven feet tall.

Now's one of those times a bow would come in handy.

I may not have a bow, but I do have knives. I drop my swords in the grass and pull my two boot knives free. The golgoth may not have been fully hamstrung, but I've hampered its movement just a bit. It turns slowly to face me, still making that warbling growl.

I take aim and throw. My knife sails through the air and lands with a thunk between the golgoth's eyes.

It screams, and my skin erupts in gooseflesh.

And it's not falling. I take the second knife and throw it too. It hits the golgoth in the nose, which is more of a slitted depression in the middle of its face. It's still coming.

I stumble backward in the grass and go for the knife I keep at the small of my back, pulling it free of its sheath and preparing to throw. The golgoth takes one more tottering step forward and falls onto its knees eight feet away.

The impact ruptures another series of pustules, and putrid pus arcs directly at me, spattering my legs from ankle to thigh.

The golgoth collapses the rest of the way forward, and I scamper out of range.

Here I thought I'd made it through without ruining my pants.

At least working for Alamea I should be able to afford new ones.

Somewhere in the bushes, a cricket chirps. It's joined a moment later by another, and another.

I think I've done enough for one night.

I turn to pick up my swords, and a dark shape blocks my path.

"Hello, Ayala Storme."

27

"WHO ARE YOU?"

My swords are still in the grass between me and the shade. I can see him more clearly now, but there's no way I can get to my swords before he does. I have one knife in my hand, and that's it. The golgoth I could nail in the head because it's huge and slow and stupid. Shades are the opposite of all three of those things.

The shade is wearing a hat.

Fuck.

The hat is a black beanie that completely covers his hair. In the dark, I can't really tell if he's white or brown skinned, and all shades have the same color eyes. None of my information besides the hat would be particularly useful in a lineup.

Carrick's been looking for this motherfucker all over Nashville. I guess I should have just wandered around alone for a while and been the bait.

“You’re the one responsible for the messes all over town, I take it?” I sound a lot braver than I feel. Behind me, the dead golgoth gurgles, its systems settling as its body realizes it’s not alive anymore.

“I helped.”

I can’t see the shade’s face clearly. He’s in the shadow of a tree, but when the wind blows the branches away, I get a glint of orange eyeshine in the moonlight.

“Who are you helping?”

“Nobody who matters to you,” the shade counters.

“What do you want?”

The shade shrugs, then stretches. Clearly he’s not worried about me being any kind of threat. Either that or he’s only here to talk. My swords in the grass are at once close and completely out of reach.

“I just came to see you.”

“Well, here I am. Sorry about the smell.”

To my surprise, the shade laughs. Disconcerted, I shift my weight.

“You’re not afraid of me.”

It’s a statement, and one I’m not sure how to respond to. I settle for honesty. “I can be afraid and function at the same time. Goes with the territory.”

“You are a fascinating person, for a murderer.”

The word chills me, not least because coming from this creature, it’s totally hypocritical. “Two’s company, right?”

The shade cocks his head in that way they do when they don’t understand an idiom or reference. After a moment, he shakes it off and goes still. “How do you choose?”

“Choose what?”

“What you kill.”

I point my thumb over my shoulder at the golgoth. “Hellkin. That’s it. I try not to kill people. Occasionally in the past it’s been hard to tell which was which.”

The shade seems to ponder that. "We'll meet again, Ayala Storme," he says. Then he gives me a strange, small bow and vanishes.

Okay, so he doesn't actually vanish, but he takes off fast enough to give me a sobering reminder of just how fast these damn creatures are. When he runs, he blurs. He's like an extra dangerous The Flash.

I retrieve my swords in a hurry, afraid he'll come back and I still won't be armed, but he doesn't return.

I feel like I just played the role of the lion at the zoo, and I don't know if he saw me roar or not.

CARRICK IS NOT AMUSED with my story when I return home.

I call in the body pick up for the golgoth and the two harkasts while Carrick paces—I forgot to do it before I left the park—and part of me hopes Alamea's put some of the brawling Mediators on cleanup duty as punishment. Probably not, though. When I get off the phone, Carrick looks so insulted I may as well have offered him a head of lettuce for dinner.

His nose twitches like Nana's at the smell emanating from my pants—even though I tried to towel them off and threw the towel in the trash can at a gas station. I quickly go change and throw the pants out on the balcony, but when I return, Carrick is still sitting on the couch and glaring.

"You could have died."

"That's an average Tuesday for me."

"That's not true, and you know it. Most things out there are no threat to you."

"Cute that you think so," I say. "I've seen better Mediators than me get killed by a lone slummoth that got lucky."

Carrick's concern is strange to me, like someone's moved me just slightly outside my own head, and I'm not sure what's happening. If the shade tonight had wanted me dead, I have every belief that I would not be standing here in a pair of aqua pajama pants and a black tank top, talking to a shade who's wearing boxers with lipstick on them.

Not lipstick marks. Little patterns of lipsticks.

"You shouldn't go out alone right now," Carrick says.

I look at him sideways, unnerved. "What on earth is your problem?"

For a moment, he just looks back at me, his face showing nothing. "I'd rather not lose you too."

Too. Oh.

I go and sit beside him, feeling like I'm walking out onto a frozen lake with no idea of how thick the ice is. I don't know if this is all just an act, with Carrick and Gregor both thinking they got through the battle at the plantation without me finding out what they did, but the apprehension in Carrick's eyes seems genuine.

"You're upset about Miles and Jax and the others," I say. Rade. Thom. Sez. I fought side by side with them for weeks. "Did you see what happened to Miles?"

Carrick shakes his head. "Immediately after the fighting calmed down, I went looking for you. But I couldn't find you, and then more hellkin turned up and Gregor said Miles got caught by a jeeling."

"I miss him too," I say, though I can't help but notice how false his story is. When I found the bodies of the hells-zealots, there were no shades nearby, no demon bodies, only earthbound flesh and blood.

But I do miss Miles. Miles was steady, kind. He always had my back. I will find out what happened to him, even if I have to pry it from Gregor with my fingernails. This story Carrick's just told—it could just be what Gregor told him, though I'm not convinced it is. Either way, Carrick seems upset.

"Before you met Gregor, what did you do?" I ask suddenly. I've asked him how he met Gregor before, but he would never answer. I don't know if I expect him to now, but I'm curious. Carrick's lived a long time, and considering the lifespans of the average norms, he's seen generations come and go. It must be a lonely life.

"Nothing of consequence," says Carrick, but his eyes turn cloudy, and his body stills, and I see sadness in every line of him.

What is it like to sum up four centuries with three pointless words? Not for the first time since Carrick showed up in my home, I realize how little I know this man, and how little I understand what he is capable of doing. Even if he seems to hate the idea of losing me, I don't think he understands quite how close he is to that—though there are different kinds of loss.

A little ember of anger in me grows. I want to know how he could do such a thing, how he could help Gregor kill that many people. I want to know why Gregor turned his back on everything we stand for as Mediators and slaughtered the very people we are born to protect. I want to know when I finally stepped over that line where I don't know who the bad guys are or even if I'm one of them.

And I want to know, sitting here on the couch with Carrick, how in the six and a half hells I'm supposed to go on like this.

I rub my hands over my face, feeling the blood rush to my skin and heat it. It feels like a sunburn for a brief moment, and I keep my palms against my skin's warmth. Carrick takes it for frustration.

"Perhaps it isn't what you want to hear," he says quietly. He turns, but doesn't look at me. His eyes find a spot across the room, a patch of blank wall, and there he fixes his gaze and does not meet mine. "I prefer not to speak of the past."

"It's your past," I say. He doesn't have to tell me. "I'm tired. I'm going to go to bed."

"Sleep well," says Carrick.

I go into my room and shut the door, climbing into bed. The cool sheets feel good against my skin, but for the next hour I toss and turn until they tangle around my legs.

My phone buzzes on the nightstand. Alamea.

She's sent a screenshot of a map where she wants me to meet her tomorrow.

For some reason, that single concrete task of *get up and meet Alamea* relaxes me enough to calm my body into sleep.

I dream of wandering through a field where the grasses bear drops of blood that shine in the dull sun. Around me are bodies. Demon, shade, witch, morph, human. There is no wind, no clouds moving across the sky. No birds or animals or insects send songs into the air. There is no breath but mine.

The grasses turn to ash and dust beneath my feet, and the earth gives under each step I take. Each movement forward sends my feet squishing deeper into the ground, and I cannot see why I sink.

I walk on through the field, each step a burden until I look down at my feet and see them rimmed in red when they bear my weight against the ground.

The bodies around me are still and silent, but as I walk through the field, every hand is outstretched toward me. In the distance I can see the tree line, and my feet keep moving toward it, but it seems to edge farther away. Each time I think the bloodied ground will take me, suck me under to join the beetles and worms, it frees my feet for one more step. I walk, and the trees come no closer. I walk, and the end of the field is as unreachable as the horizon. I walk, and the field is full of endless death.

28

THE MAP ALAMEA SENT me takes me to a strip mall Mexican restaurant on the outskirts of Murfreesboro, in a neighborhood sprinkled with trailer parks. The sky is bright blue above, and the sun shining brings with it an inherent cheeriness, especially when driving past a single wide, I see a family of four emerge, both kids running down the sidewalk with colorful pinwheels. The parents are holding hands and smiling, and even though I know the world expects you to feel pity for people who live in trailer parks, I can't help think that that family has a lot more than I ever did.

I'm just a little jealous of Wane and Mira, I think. I've never had a cousin.

I wonder what it's like.

Alamea's seated at the bar with a half empty red basket of chips and a giant margarita big enough to fit her entire face in. She's in jeans and a t-shirt, like I am, but she makes no effort to hide the dual daggers strapped to her back, nor the knives at her hips. I can see the hilts of two more poking up above the tops of her boots, as well. Wouldn't be surprised if she had some throwing stars on her somewhere as well. I've never mastered the things, but once I saw Alamea plant one in a rakath's eye from around a corner after one peek.

I sit down next to her and flag the bartender for some water and a plate of chimichangas, and Alamea raises her margarita to me. I hope she's not drunk. It's not that easy to get drunk as a Mediator, but a kiddie-pool-sized margarita'll do it.

"What'd you bring me here for? Girl's night out?" I ignore the fact that it's one in the afternoon.

Alamea raises an eyebrow, sips from her drink, and sets it back down. The blue parasol in it rolls around the rim of the glass, which looks hand-blown, little bubbles dotting the glass from base to bowl.

"I thought you might want to come with me to follow a lead on our mutual friend," she says. "I made a contact who said they had information about what he's trying to do, and they agreed to meet me today."

"Here in Murfreesboro?"

"Yes."

"How do they know him?"

"One of them said he approached them about a business arrangement, but that's all they'd say over the phone. We're supposed to meet them in about an hour, so eat fast."

Well, if anything, chimichangas should give me farts enough to impress this source of Alamea's.

By the time I'm done eating, Alamea's ordered and eaten a flan, and she's mopping up the remaining caramel with the tines of her fork.

She even picks up the check. "I'll drive," she says, jingling her keys at me.

I look at the giant—now empty—margarita.

"It was a virgin," she says drily. "I don't drink."

I follow her out to her Jeep and jump in. The back seat is littered with fast food bags and empty engine oil bottles. She catches me looking.

"You and I have a few things in common."

I don't even know what to say to that.

She heads down the pike to the first major intersection and turns left. Murfreesboro isn't a big town, and within five minutes and two more lights, we're out of it. We drive about ten miles down the state route. Alamea turns down a side road, where I can see a house at the end. Some of the homes we've passed have been old farmhouses with chipping white paint and wraparound porches. This one's just your average brown double wide on an acre or two of grass just as brown to match. There are no trees around it to speak of, but a few scraggly bushes dot the perimeter of the house, which is framed by a gnarled rail fence that wouldn't keep out even the most placid cow.

Alamea pulls into the circular driveway and parks. There's only an old white Ford pickup in the side yard, but it's got grass and weeds growing up around the wheels and doesn't look like it's budged in fifty years.

"You're sure this is the place?" I ask dubiously.

"Yep." That might be the first time I've heard her say *yep*.

I open the Jeep door with a thunk and climb out, adjusting my various swords and knives. Nothing says safety than a house in the middle of nowhere that looks like Ted Bundy ought to live here.

Approaching the house, I see a small addition on one side with a tattered screen door swinging on its hinges, and a storm cellar just visible on the back edge. Hells, it doesn't look like anyone's been here in the last decade, let alone lived here. The blinds on the front windows are down and shuttered, and when we get closer, I can tell there's curtains on the other side of them. No view in at all.

Alamea pulls open the storm door and knocks hard with a brass knocker that has a screw loose. "He's a little hard of hearing," she says.

Whoever he is doesn't answer, and we stand on the porch in the sun while she knocks two more times.

"Are you sure he's not dead?" I ask.

"He wasn't this morning."

She gives up on the brass knocker and hits the doorbell, which gives a quiet wheeze that wouldn't wake a mouse.

"Let me try," I say. I make a fist and pound on the door as hard as I can.

I still don't hear any movement behind the door, but the loose screw on the brass knocker falls out onto the porch.

I reach down and pick it back up, wondering if I can screw it back in with my utility knife or if it'll just fall out again. I've just decided to try when I hear a holler behind the door.

"Lea, that you?"

I look at Alamea. "I don't know, is it?"

"It's me!" she yells. "I told you he's hard of hearing."

A moment later, the door cracks open, and I see one giant blue eye peering out at me from behind a Coke bottle lens the size of my palm. Above it is an enormously bushy silver eyebrow and skin so pale the word *white* really does describe it.

"You ain't Lea," he says to me.

Alamea shoves me out of the way and waves at the man, who opens the door the rest of the way and grins a big toothless grin at her.

"How does he know what you look like?" I whisper to her.

"We Skyped."

All right, then.

"Come in, come in. I'll make you girls some sandwiches."

MUCH AS I WANT to get this over with, Ollie Anderson the Fourth will hear nothing of business until he has us settled in his brown linoleum kitchen with grilled cheese sandwiches and pickles he says he made himself.

"Ain't got the knees for gardenin' no more," he says, "but the neighbor girl brings me the cukes a'cause she ain't know what to do with 'em. I pickle 'em up right and proper, and she lets me keep a quarter of them."

Ollie chuckles as if it's the best thing in the world, and I start wondering just how in all six and a half hells this domestic little old man knows anything at all about Gregor or hellkin or the Summit.

"If you'll pardon me, this old bladder ain't what it used to be." Ollie gets up and tugs his tattered jeans up by the belt loops, but they immediately sag back down on his frail frame.

Alamea nods at him, and he vanishes around the corner.

I take a bite of my grilled cheese. It's surprisingly good; no gummy white bread or plastic cheese to be found, but hearty cheddar and what seems to be a homemade loaf of multigrain. On the counter, I see a bread maker. Bless this old man's little heart.

The pickles are delicious, too.

"How do you think he got his info?" I ask Alamea. "If he's left the house in the last month, I'm a badger."

Far from being in the same state of disrepair as the outside, the inside of the house is quietly and neatly out of date. Everything is paneled with dark wood, and his television is still one of the large, monstrously heavy contraptions that have now been replaced everywhere else by sleek flat screens. Few knickknacks, no dust, and crocheted afghans—blue and not brown—are scattered around the living area. A basket of yarn and crochet hooks sits under the end table, hinting that Ollie made the afghans himself.

I hear the toilet flush down the hall, and nibble at the buttery crust on my grilled cheese.

There's no sound after that but the ticking of a large cuckoo clock.

A loud *twang* sounds through the house, and I fall to the floor reflexively, landing on Alamea just in time to see something whizz above our heads and plant in the wood paneled wall with a thunk. An arrow. A motherfucking arrow.

The shooter's pant leg is visible around the corner to the corridor, and it's not the tattered denim of Ollie's too-loose jeans, but black leather.

I draw my sword and edge to my knees. Alamea makes eye contact with me and scoots back against the kitchen wall under the window.

The glass shatters, raining shards all over her. A torso leans through the window, and Alamea grabs the person by the arms and yanks them through. A pair of handguns goes sliding across the floor, and I pick them up and shove them in my waistband, checking the safety.

Screw caution.

I leap to my feet and lunge toward the corner, my left hand throwing a hook punch to the spot where I expect the shooter's kneecap.

I guess right, and the shooter swears and grabs me by the hair, but I've pulled him off balance, and he topples over. My sword point presses against the bottom of his ribcage. "Let go of my hair."

The shooter's eyes—Mediator violet—flick to the space behind me, and that's all the warning I get before something hard slams into the base of my skull.

The world flickers. Bright flashes burst in front of my eyes.

Sonofabitch pistol whipped me.

Too bad for the bowman I'm on, my sword stabs into his stomach. I can't see well, but I feel the wet glob of saliva that lands on my cheek and hear him call me my favorite insult for Carrick.

The sounds of a scuffle swirl behind me, and my vision comes back enough to see the person who hit me with the butt of his .45. He's hesitating as if he doesn't quite know what to do with me. He's wearing a mask. So's the bowman.

I scissor a kick at his shins, and he dodges—a moment too late. My kick hits his right ankle, and he stumbles.

Alamea appears from the kitchen, and he doesn't have time to dodge her kick.

At over six feet tall without heels, she has no trouble landing a front kick smack to this guy's masked face. I look at the bowman, who's clutching his bleeding stomach and groaning.

"I barely stabbed you," I tell him.

In the kitchen, the attacker who came through the window is knocked out cold, his face in Alamea's broken plate with her half-eaten pickle pressed under his cheek.

"So," I say to the groaning bowman. "Just three? Or is there more of a party? Honestly, I'm a little insulted you thought three of you could take out both of us."

He tries to spit at me again, but his abdominals are a little bit stabbed, and the gob of spit lands on his own chin, soaking into the fabric of his mask.

"You weren't supposed to be here." He's able to talk, so that's a plus.

"Alamea, look, he's being helpful." I watch the bowman and take a peek at his stab wound. He's lucky I got hit in the head, because I didn't stab him very deep. My sword could have run him through. Even so, it probably nicked something important.

Alamea goes to the basket of crocheting supplies and pulls out a ball of yarn. She kneels next to the guy who pistol whipped me and starts using the yarn to tie him up.

She's not being particularly gentle. I can see the guy's pale hands turning pink.

"This is what it's come to, has it?" She says her words carefully, as always. "Open assassination attempts?"

"You're not fit to lead the Summit," the bowman says.

I pat him on his stomach. He cries out.

"You're not being as helpful. Any more of you?" I ask. The anger in his eyes is a clear no. "Good. Now. Did you leave Ollie alive?"

If they killed that dear little old man, I might give my stabbing a second try. My head throbs where the gun made contact with my skull, but I can hit an unmoving target with the pointy end of my sword even so.

The bowman nods. "We're not the ones who kill norms, Storme."

Just Alamea, apparently. I think of Hazel Lottie, the witch who was helping magically implant fertilized demon eggs into human hosts to spawn the shades. I definitely killed her in full view of most of the Mediators in Nashville. I don't have anything to say to this guy, so I just nod. "Fair enough."

He doesn't seem to know what to say to that.

"So you don't kill norms, but you were going to assassinate the Summit leader. I'm not sure I fully understand your logic process, but indulge me," I say. "What's your beef with Alamea?"

The woman in question has finished hog-tying the first assassin and is moving on to the one in the kitchen, grimly not seeming to pay me any attention.

"She should be hunting those fucking hellkin hybrids to extinction," the bowman says. "Instead she lets you and Gregor work with them as if they're people."

"They are people," I say brightly. "Some of them have more morals than you seem to, Mr. I-Hurt-Old-Men-Who-Get-In-My-Way. Or is your reason that you were just told to?"

The bowman clams up, and Alamea's finished tying up the other guy, so I let her have him and hurry down the hall to check on Ollie.

To my profound relief, he's snoring lightly. He's got a welt and a goose egg, but he looks like he'll be okay. I dial 911 on my phone to get an ambulance anyway. For Ollie only—I imagine Alamea has other plans for the three men who wanted her dead.

29

I'M NOT WRONG.

After getting Ollie safely in the ambulance with the paramedics and helping Alamea load the three wannabe killers into her Jeep, we make the trek back to Nashville together, me following in my car close behind her.

By the time we reach the Summit, the parking lot is already filling with cars. Five Mediators meet Alamea at her parking spot while I'm still parking my own vehicle. I hurry after them, unsure what's going on. My phone buzzes as Alamea and the others disappear into the Summit building.

All call, is all the message from her says.

My stomach drops.

An all call is when every single Mediator in the territory is summoned. Sure enough, my phone also shows an alert that went out thirty minutes ago. I can't remember the last all call before my Silver Scale ceremony. And even that one was a blur, because I was still half-afraid they were going to punk me and put my head on the chopping block instead.

Treason is a big deal when it comes to the Summit. When the safety of the homo sapiens world depends on you to keep the hordes of hellkin at bay, there's sort of a zero tolerance for big fuck ups. And trying to assassinate the leader of the local Summit? Definitely qualifies as a big fuck up.

The lobby of the Summit is a-buzz with people, but I avoid everyone and go to the first floor kitchenette to get something to eat. The all call begins in an hour, and though most of the other Mediators are milling around and murmuring to one another, I don't want to answer anyone's questions. It's likely my presence at this assassination attempt will soon be common knowledge, but I want to avoid any prying eyes until I have no other choice.

The air feels heavy, and the cheesy sandwich crackers I try to shove down my throat are about as appetizing as dry dust.

When the all call's about a half hour off, I go to the convening chamber and find a seat. I'm not the only one there, but I find a spot mostly away from other people and play a game on my phone. I can't stop fidgeting. Here I helped Alamea avoid death, and the second we got back here, she took off. I feel like the ground could crack away beneath my feet at any moment, and it's not a sensation I like.

Slowly, the convening chamber fills up with Mediators. The room holds almost a thousand people, but it's only about seventy percent full, and looking around I can see at least fifty or so Mittens in here. The youngest will be at their training lodges still, but those who are close to finishing training come and live at the Summit or one of its satellites. If there's only fifty of them here during an all call, how low are our numbers?

I know Mira and Devon and Ripper are in here somewhere, but I don't see them, and I don't look for them.

Alamea takes the stage, and behind her, the three almost-assassins are prodded in to kneel at the front of the dais. Their heads are covered. Alamea wastes no time.

"Today, these three Mediators made an attempt on my life. In the process, they injured an eighty-year-old innocent, who is in the hospital in stable condition, thanks to Mediator Storme, who happened to be with me." A loud murmur ripples through the crowd, and violet eyes turn on me from around the room. Alamea gives me a nod, and I recognize it as the probable only acknowledgement she's going to give me. She goes on. "I've called you all here for two reasons. One, to decide the fate of these three Mediators. Richard Peyton, Samuel Thorpe, and Darryn Kinney.

"These three are charged with conspiracy to murder a fellow Mediator, conspiracy to assassinate a Summit leader, premeditated attempt to commit murder, and the assault of a norm." Alamea's heeled boots make dull thuds on the dais, and I can see the quickening rise and fall of each assassin's chests from where I sit. Summit justice does not hold to laws of due process in cases of treason against the Summit leader. Alamea could have executed them on the spot at Ollie's house, but she chose to come here. She wants to make a point.

They will offer no plea, and they will be heard by no jury. This is not a trial, but they may not die.

Executions are a voting process.

"It is with intent to kill that these three Mediators broke into the home of Ollie Anderson and assaulted him. They came armed and attacked me and Mediator Storme. Had they anticipated her presence, it is likely that neither of us would be here now." Alamea looks out over the crowd, her face showing no expression.

I can almost feel the hundreds of Mediators around me shift and take a collective breath. They know as well as I do that Alamea is more than a match for three Mediators unless they got very lucky. It's not my presence that caused them to fail; I only sped it along.

"There are only two possible punishments for crimes at this level of severity," she says. "Execution or imprisonment. Those who do not vote for execution will be assumed to vote for imprisonment. There can be no vote to abstain. All Mediators-in-Training who are currently present will vote as full members of the Summit."

My heart takes up a hurried beat. Her choice, as far as I can guess, is unusual. What is she playing at?

"Voting shall be by way of hands raised. There shall be no anonymous voting. Remove the traitors' hoods." Alamea stops in the dead center of the dais, and I understand.

She's not doing this to further any guise of democracy when it comes to these men.

She's doing it so she can look into the eyes of every Mediator in the Summit and see their votes.

A vote for execution will be a vote in her support.

A vote for incarceration in the prison below the Summit will imply dissent with what they know is the default consequence for attempting to kill the Summit leader.

She's doing it to size up just how deep the fractures in the Summit go.

"All in favor of execution, raise your left hand, palm forward. You have two minutes."

I can't be the first hand to go up. Thankfully, some shoot up around me, and I raise my left hand in the air. If Alamea's opponents are smart, they'll raise their hands now. Looking around, maybe thirty percent of the room has their hands raised. The seconds slip by, and more go up. Forty percent.

She needs a majority.

Her eyes on the crowd are calculating and unruffled, but I know she has to be panicking. The first minute has passed. A majority by now would have been a mandate.

Slowly, more hands raise. My arm starts to tingle from blood rushing away from my fingers, but I do my best to keep it still in the air.

I'm afraid to look around, afraid of the implications if more than half of these people don't put their hands up. The time ticks down, and someone gives a ten second warning. I don't allow myself to look.

One of the Mediators on the dais guarding the assassins is counting.

I draw in a deep breath and let it out through my nose, trying my best not to hold it.

"The Summit votes for execution," he says after a long beat. "Three hundred seventy votes in favor."

Barely half. Barely.

I feel sick as the Mediators pull the hoods from the assassins' faces.

I know these men, of course. Not well, and not enough to know much more about them than their faces or names, but they are Mediators, and they share my path.

Or they were supposed to, anyway.

I always forget why the floor in front of the dais is seamless and smooth. It's not an aesthetic choice. It's pragmatic.

We don't stay sentences in the Summit.

Alamea wields the sword.

FORTY-FIVE MINUTES LATER, I slip out of the Summit, managing to avoid most of the Mediators present. No one tries to stop me. Whatever fissures exist, whatever they think of me personally, none of us will take any joy from three of our number dying due to treason. It is a quiet exodus from the Summit's halls today.

The sun's on its way to the horizon, and a dull blanket of clouds is rolling in above me.

I reach my car, rummaging in my pocket for my keys. When I look up, there's something sitting on the roof of the car.

It's a rubber duck.

I pick it up, turning it over in my hands. It's warm, which is strange. There's not much else remarkable about it. Bright yellow, big eyes. Squeaks.

Its bill has pink lipstick.

Alice.

The duck falls from my fingers, and with neuron-quick reflexes, I catch it before it hits the ground.

The shades. They've hit Percy Warner, the Waffle Spot, the warehouses.

I've been a complete fool.

They're going for my office.

I peel out of the Summit parking lot with a screech of tires and the smell of burning rubber wafting in through the air ducts in the car. I dial Mira as I drive. She doesn't pick up.

"Gods damn it," I say, just as her voicemail answers. "My office. The shades are hitting my office. Hurry."

Me against three. I don't know if I can handle it. I don't care.

I'm lucky the one cop who pulls out behind me sees my Mediator tags and flips off the squad car's lights seconds after flipping them on. I careen in and out of traffic, thankful it's not rush hour, but not caring about any of the people who honk at me. The minutes seem to tick by on the dash clock like seconds, and no matter how far down I press my foot on the accelerator, it doesn't seem to slow them.

It takes me twelve minutes to get there, and when I leave my car parked in the fire zone outside the building, one of the security guards starts to yell at me until he sees my face and my hands on the hilts of my swords.

"Out of my way, Gary. There could be more Mediators coming. Let them past if you see them." My swords leave their sheaths with a hiss of steel and a whisper of death.

Gary backs off and fumbles for his radio. Just before the door closes behind me, I hear him telling central security to let any Mediators pass.

Good Gary.

The elevator is faster than me sprinting up the stairs, but it still takes too long. I almost smash the mirror in the elevator out of pure frustration. When the sliding doors finally open, the hallway is quiet, as if even the building knows something is wrong.

I reach the office door and throw it open. Parker leaps up from behind the receptionist's desk, and I fight the urge to kiss him.

"Ayala?" His gaze goes right to the pointy steel in my hands, and he swallows, taking a step back.

"Where's Alice and Laura?" I look around, listening for anything out of the ordinary. All I hear is the air in the vents and the percolation of the coffee maker.

"Uh, Alice is in your old office and Laura's in her office. Meredith and LeeLoo are at an event today." He looks at me, fear making his Adam's apple bob.

"Get them. Quick. Hurry."

Parker doesn't move.

"Fucking hells, Parker! Danger! There's actual danger happening, and it's not me! Go!"

He goes, almost falling over his rolling chair to get into the hall. I watch the door. There is only one other entrance to the suite, and it's got a desk in front of it, because Laura has a crush on the fire marshall and is always hoping he'll come by and punish her.

When nothing comes through the door and a breathless Laura comes up behind me, I try not to look at her. "Stay behind me."

"What's happening?" Alice asks. I notice that they all immediately follow my order, though.

"I'll explain as soon as you're all safe."

I peer out of the door to the office. The corridor is clear, and I wonder if I missed something. Maybe there's not actually a threat.

But the duck was warm when I touched it. Maybe I just got stupid lucky and picked it up moments after it had been set down.

I press the button on the elevator. Laura, Alice, and Parker all stand around me, shoulders tight and eyes searching the hallway for danger. As the ding sounds through the air, for a moment it seems like I jumped to the wrong conclusion. I herd them into the elevator, and the doors slide closed.

A bang echoes through the hall, and just before the doors close completely, three dark shapes close in on the suite we just vacated.

30

ALICE IS THE ONLY one besides me to see them, and she lets out a startled yelp as we descend. I get crap reception in here, but I grab my phone and call the front desk.

"Evacuate the building. This is Mediator Storme. You have three hybrid creatures in the building, and they are not nice. Get everyone out."

The receptionist squawks, and I hear her yell at security before she hangs up.

Mira's just bursting through the door in the lobby when we arrive on the ground floor. I point at her and just say, "Run!" Then to her, "Get them the fuck out of here!"

I hurry over to security, and Gary's barking orders into his walkie talkie, his eyes trained on the monitor for the fourth floor.

"Have they come out of the suite?" I ask.

Gary lowers the walkie, but keeps it in his hand. "Yeah. They made for the east stairwell. Will gunfire stop them?"

I shake my head. "Nothing but beheading will stop them."

"What do you want to do? Can you take them?"

"All at once? No."

I hate this. I want this over once and for all. I know where all three of these murderous bastards are, and I want them gone. But part of learning to fight is knowing when you can face a foe, and this is not that time. Not alone. Not even with Mira.

"Don't engage," I say after a long pause. "Track them until they're off premises. Can you see them on camera now?"

I look down at the monitors, and even before Gary points, I see them. They're coming out on sub level one from the east stairwell, and I know from there they can hit the streets through the garage.

Sure enough, they go straight to the garage and vanish off the CCTV.

I close my eyes and breathe, trying to concentrate on Alice, Parker, and Laura being alive. This is not a failure, because they're not dead. They are not pieces on the floor. They are not reduced to blood spatters and pools.

What would three pissed off shades do if they missed their marks?

I'm moving before I can finish the thought. "Gary, make sure someone watches the feeds. If you see them come back, you dial the Summit right away. I'll get someone on trigger response."

I don't actually know if I have that power, but if I'm Alamea's special assistant, I'm sure as hells going to try.

My car is parked terribly, but there's no ticket on the window. I call Mira as I drive.

"Yo," she says. "I've got your buddies. We're at a bar on Demonbreun. Where to next?"

"Can you get them in a Summit safe house?"

She pauses. "Yeah. You sure that's necessary?"

"I'd rather them all stay in one piece. Or three, but no more than that."

"It's done. Where are you going?"

“The Waffle Spot. If those fucking shades couldn’t get Alice and company, I’m going to make sure they don’t get Grace.” For the second time in an hour, I hit the gas hard enough to spin out.

When I pull in at the Waffle Spot, there’s no sign of any disturbance. The parking lot has been power washed since the shades last visited, and all traces of Dirk’s remains have been blasted away with high-velocity streams of water.

There are a few cars, but since it’s before the dinner rush and too late for lunch, there are plenty of spots. I hope Grace is here.

I park and hurry up to the door, thankful when she’s the first person I see. She looks like she’s just starting her shift, with her apron clean and pressed and her hair pulled back in a tight brown bun.

She doesn’t look happy to see me, but she also doesn’t throw the pot of coffee in my face, so that’s a good sign.

“What are you doing here?” She looks behind me as she asks it, and the coffee twitches in the pot like the water in the cup in *Jurassic Park*.

“I just came to check on you.”

“Oh.” She motions at me to sit at the bar. “I thought it was about the guy.”

“What guy?” Now she’s got my attention. “Was he wearing a hat?”

“What? No.” Grace walks behind the bar as a bell dings, placing the pot of coffee on the hot plate. “Hang on a sec.”

I wait while she delivers a plate of chicken fried steak—at least I think that’s what it is, considering all the gravy—to one of the only tables in the back corner. She comes back and hands me a glass of ice water and a straw.

She leans on the counter in front of me. “Want some pie?”

I blink at her. “The guy, Grace.”

“Well, have a piece of pie and I’ll tell you about him.”

Lordy.

She slides a plate of blueberry pie in front of me and hands me a rolled up fork and knife. I flick off the sticky band and take a bite, gesturing at her to talk. The pie's actually not half bad. You couldn't pay me to drink the coffee in here, but the pie's good.

"He's come in a couple times in the past week," Grace says. "He's usually underdressed for the weather."

My ears perk up at that. I take another bite. "What do you mean, underdressed?"

"Tank top. Shorts."

Tank top. "Any visible tattoos?"

"One. Saturn."

Fuck me.

"You said he's been here a couple times?"

"Yeah, he just left, actually."

"I'm sorry, what? You're feeding me pie and he just left?"

Grace looks at me, alarmed. "I didn't know he was that important! I thought he was just another Mediator. He has eyes like yours, but darker."

Sweet baby Hecate. "Which way did he go?"

I dig in my pocket and throw a twenty on the counter, not caring that the pie's probably two bucks.

Grace points to the west, away from Gallatin Avenue. Her mouth is open as if she's trying to catch a passing fly.

"Did you see anything else that could indicate where he was going?"

She starts to shake her head, but then she hesitates. "He had a realty brochure with him."

Okay, that's new. "Thanks, Grace. If you see any naked guys with hats, you lock yourself in the gods damned walk-in, you hear?"

Her eyes widen, and she nods. "I will. I'll call you."

"Good. Thanks for the pie!" I bolt out of the diner and run west along the road. Three blocks later, I feel like a complete ass, because he could have easily turned in any direction after leaving the Waffle Spot.

But then I see it. A realty sign stuck in the turf another block up on the left, with FORECLOSURE on it in big letters.

If you're going to squat in a house, why not one of those?

I approach the house cautiously—after Saturn knocked out Mira, I don't know if he'll be pleased to see me or not. When I get to the lawn, though, I'm close enough to see through the side window.

It's not Saturn I see.

It's Miles.

I'M SO STARTLED THAT I forget to duck when he looks my way, and he sees me.

A moment later, I see a flash of paler skin that has to be Saturn. Then around the corner, I hear a door open.

I stumble forward toward the door, and for a moment I don't even consider that Miles might think I'm with Gregor. I just pitch forward into his arms.

If he planned to fight me, he changes his mind right away. His arms encircle me, and I hug him as hard as I've hugged just about anyone. He's durable. He can take it.

Over the dark skin of Mile's shoulder, Saturn's looking at me, his expression unreadable. I pull away from the hug and flip him off. "You fucking broke Mira's head, asshole," I say. And after a beat, "I'm glad you're not dead."

Saturn looks around, his eyes scanning the space behind me. He's still wearing the tank top and shorts. He's even wearing flip flops, though they look like he found them in a Dumpster. He probably did.

"I think you should come inside," he says.

I oblige, following them both into the house. I notice Saturn doesn't make a move to touch my shoulder, and I'm not sure if me tackle hugging Miles counts.

Just to make sure, when we get inside, I reach out and touch my fingers to Miles's shoulder, meeting his eyes. After he stares at me for several seconds that make me want to grab my swords, he returns the touch.

Amazing how something so simple can make me relax.

Saturn keeps his distance, and I don't try to go any closer.

"What's going on, Saturn?" I ask. "Carrick and Gregor told me Miles was dead."

Miles looks at me. "They said that I was dead?"

"Yeah. Which you're clearly not. Go you."

He and Saturn exchange a glance, and again I get that little buzz of shade communication, whatever it is.

"Hey," I say to Miles. "I saw what happened. I got intercepted by a horde of demons. By the time I finished killing them, it was already done. Were you there?"

His body goes still, and he looks at the floor.

"I didn't do it," he says quietly.

"I know you didn't." I'm surprised by the forceful fire in my voice. I know Miles wouldn't do that, that he wouldn't harm a norm. "Is this why Jax left?"

Saturn takes a deep breath and walks over to me. He reaches out a hand and touches my shoulder. I return the light touch, and I let my hand linger on his arm for just a moment. The relief that fills me is potent. It washes through me, a reassuring wave of knowledge that I did not misjudge them. I do know them. They are my allies, and they mean me no harm.

"Jax left because he suspected such a thing might happen," Saturn says, his voice a little hoarse.

I'll be damned. Is he feeling something? An emotion? Saturn?

"I found him in Kentucky," I say. "Mira and Wane and I tracked him up there, thinking it was you."

Both Saturn and Miles look surprised at that.

"For someone on the lam, you stayed close to home," I tell Saturn.

"I wanted to be close enough to help if something happened."

I nod at him. "So tell me what's happening."

Miles sits on the carpet, and I follow suit. The house is empty, and there are no lights. It's full twilight now, and the house darkens with each passing minute.

"Gregor is using us," Miles says.

"Mira got your note," I say to Saturn drily, "so we kind of figured."

"He's using Carrick too," Saturn says. "I don't know how much Carrick knows."

I wonder if Carrick knows Miles is alive.

"Go on," I say. By their silence following my statement, I can't tell if they're unsure of what to say, or if it's so bad they don't know how to say it. The quiet ticks on, and my brain starts making up worst case scenarios.

It doesn't prepare me for what they say.

"The plantation owner paid Gregor," says Miles. "Half a million dollars."

"What?" For a moment, his words don't even compute. I can't make sense of them. Paid him for what?

Then I remember what Gregor said to me about the job. That a wealthy plantation owner had hells-worshippers encroaching on his land. Of course, he made it sound like the zealots were in danger, but he didn't tell me they were in danger from him.

It takes a solid half a minute for it to really sink in what they're telling me.

A Mediator took money from someone to kill norms.

Holy fucking hells.

Every hair on my body springs away from my skin, and my tongue is suddenly stuck to the roof of my mouth. This isn't what we do. We don't kill norms. We never kill norms. This isn't what we do.

I don't realize I'm saying it out loud until Miles scoots closer to me and puts his arm around my shoulder.

"Ayala," he says. "It's okay."

"It's not okay." My teeth chatter, and I clamp my mouth shut.

“It’s not okay,” Saturn agrees. In his voice I hear relief, as if my reaction erased the final lingering doubts he had about my complicity in this horror.

In the dark of the foreclosed house, I see only their silhouettes. Miles right next to me, and Saturn two feet away. I can’t see their eyes, but I feel them.

Gregor has been accepting money to kill norms. No wonder he wants to catch the murdering shades. They threaten the viability of his business model.

I want to throw up. I lean into Miles’s arm, thankful for the anchor of his too-warm skin.

There is nothing I know to say.

But I do know one thing.

I have to stop Gregor, even if it means burning the Summit to the ground.

31

IT TAKES SOME CONVINCING, but I manage to get Saturn and Miles to agree to let me tell Alamea.

She's trusted me. Now it's my turn to trust her.

From their little foreclosed squatter central, I try to figure out how to text her. I wish we had some sort of code word, like "banana hammock," or "Poughkeepsie." I settle for asking her to meet with me first thing tomorrow, and on a whim I say it's about the afghan Ollie gave her as a gift.

She'll think that's weird enough that she'll know something's up.

I say goodbye to Saturn and Miles, giving them each extra long hugs. I do smack Saturn upside the head once for Mira. He doesn't say anything. I think he understands.

When I get home, I go straight to my room and shut the door with Nana. She hops around, but eventually finds her bed and snoozes away, and I lay there, hoping Carrick won't be home when I fall asleep.

Sleep evades me for several hours, elusive and slipperier than a greased golgoth.

"First thing" when Mediators are concerned is usually around ten in the morning, and I make it to the Summit by ten on the nose. I bring donuts and coffee for Alamea, orange juice for me.

I miss coffee. I used to love the stuff. Now even carrying Alamea's latte makes me want to blow chunks.

To my surprise, she meets me at the front door to the Summit, keys in hand.

"Let's go for a drive," she says.

We get into her Jeep, and I wedge her coffee in the cup holder that to me, looks about as stable as setting it on the dashboard in front of the steering wheel. She waits until we pull out of the Summit parking lot and turns left toward the park, the Parthenon lit up gold in the morning light.

"I thought you might want to make sure we were unobserved," she says. I hand her a donut.

And I tell her what Saturn and Miles told me.

"You trust them?" Her words come out around an audible lump in her throat when I finish.

"With my life." If I'm right, that's exactly what I'm trusting them with. My life. And hers. Probably Mira's too.

A car cuts her off, and Alamea leans on the horn, slamming the heel of her hand into it. The Jeep's horn is a sort of pitiful thing, but the way Alamea beats the living tar out of her horn's button is not pitiful at all.

It kind of scares me.

"What do you want to do?" I ask her.

She laughs. She keeps driving down West End Avenue, past I-440 and farther south until we end up in Belle Meade. We're passing the Belle Meade Plantation before she finally stops, and I shove another donut in my mouth because I really don't know what to do. It tastes weird after my orange juice.

Alamea pulls into the Belle Meade Country Club's driveway and stops the car, not caring that the security people eye us askance and point at the Mediator plates as if we've rolled up with a wagon full of dead skunks.

"You know," she says, "I used to think you were the strangest damn Mediator I ever knew. You never turn up at the Summit unless you have to. You have never had friends."

I almost object there, but…she's not wrong.

"You regularly racked up the kills, though, so I figured you must've at least known what you were doing. When Gregor said he had a project for you this summer, I just thought he was trying to get you to, I don't know. Engage. Be a team player." She makes it sound like I'm a member of a varsity football team and not born into a group of demon-fighting, doomed losers.

"So glad you had such a lofty opinion of me," I say.

"I didn't," she says.

"I sort of got that."

"But let me tell you, Ayala Storme. When I saw you that day at Miller's Field, it wasn't puppy love for that shade Mason I saw on your face. It was purpose. You had something that we are supposedly born with. You found your truth and you fought for it." Alamea doesn't meet my eyes. Instead, she looks straight out the windshield of the Jeep at the traffic on Harding Pike. "It's funny. I worked my whole damn life to get where I am. I fought my way up through the ranks at the Summit even when I thought the gods damned politics of it would kill me. And I got to the head spot. I thought that'd be it. Those three men I killed in front of the whole Summit this week, they were in my MIT class. We were promoted together. And they tried to kill me. And you, this strange little Mediator half my age—you saved my life. You saved the whole Summit last summer, and now I have this feeling you're going to save it again."

Astounded, I try to keep my mouth from falling open.

"I respect you, Storme. You're a good woman, and you're a good Mediator, and I want you to help me make sure that Gregor pays for the filth he's spread across our title." Her eyes grow distant, and in them I see the same pain of betrayal that I feel.

I swallow, my mouth tasting of gritty sugar and oranges.

"I can't do it alone," I say, at a loss for any other words.

Alamea laughs. "No one's asking you to. That's not what this is about. It's not about you playing a hero, even though I know you're heroic enough. It's about salvaging what we can of this Summit, this city, this state—before it's too late."

I nod wordlessly. It takes me a few minutes to find my tongue again.

"That's what I want," I say. Then I stop. "What about the shades?"

"What about them?"

"They're people." I try to make my mouth form the words I want. All I know is that I have to try and protect them. They're caught between demons who want them dead and Mediators who don't want to try and understand them, and that will pulp them if no one looks out for them. "I want them safe too. I know there are Mediators at the Summit who want them all dead. The demons want them all dead. I want them to at least have a chance."

I watch Alamea's face, and she looks pensive; whatever thoughts are roiling beneath the surface of her skin, they are far too deep for me to see their ripples.

"They'll at least get a chance." When she looks at me now, her eyes are calculating, assessing, planning. "Be prepared, though, that if you want them protected, it could put you at risk in unexpected ways. Are you prepared for that?"

"Yes," I say. It's not even a question. I won't stand by and watch them get crushed between two warring bodies when they never asked to be here in the first place. We're quiet for a moment, then I look sideways at Alamea. "What is it you want?"

"I want a safe city, free of hellkin."

"Don't we all," I agree. "But give me a real answer, for fuck's sake."

A smile blossoms on her face, showing a row of white teeth. One of them has a tiny chip in it. "I want to get out of this alive." For a moment the fear returns, like claws almost reflected in her eyes. "I'm not finished here yet, Storme."

I understand her then, more than ever before. To stay alive, she has to keep control of the Summit. She has to fight back the encroaching hordes of all six and a half hells, and she has to do it before those hordes push the walls of our territory in and fall upon us like an avalanche.

Clarity catches me, brief and brutal.

We might all want things we can't have.

32

THAT NIGHT, I MEET with Mira, Ripper, and Devon about confronting Gregor. Wane's at the hospital all night, and I promise to brief Alamea later. She can't come; it's too risky for her to be actively involved, and I understand that.

Even though Mira's house isn't exactly a swinging hot spot of Mediators dropping by unannounced, we all travel out of town to a campsite Ripper frequents and gather around the cold fire pit. Safer where we know we won't accidentally encounter anyone we know. The woods are quiet, but not silent, most of the critters settling down for the cooler months. A few crickets still sing, and I can tell by the relaxed stances of the other Mediators that they find that as much of a comfort as I do.

I fill them in on what Saturn and Miles told me, and then I brace myself.

"You're sure?" Devon says. His face looks just as I feared it would; shocked and disbelieving.

"I know what I saw. And I trust Miles and Saturn to tell the truth. Shades aren't exactly motivated by money."

"Saturn doesn't lie," Mira says flatly, her voice about as yielding as a donkey neck deep in cement.

Ripper's the only one who doesn't say anything. He's not usually much of a talker, but he's watching one of the stones in the fire pit like he's expecting it to tell him some sort of transcendent truth.

"Yo, Ripper," Mira says. "Got something you want to share with the class?"

"You know sometimes how in training, when you were learning something new, one day your muscles would find that exact right movement that allowed you to nail a form you'd fucked up for months?" He looks at us until we nod. "Yeah. That."

Part of me wishes we'd brought marshmallows.

Ripper kicks the rock he's been staring at. "Couple months back, I was working a tracking case with Wheedle—" he spits when he says Ben's name, which surprises me, "—and we ended up down Chattanooga way. Bunch of hellkin kept poppin' their heads up, dotting up and down the countryside. It was right after all the shit hit in the summer, and it was the first good job I'd had since. Wheedle and I were at a gas station filling up my truck, and this fancy-ass Mercedes S Class pulled up. Coupe. Tinted windows, but they had 'em rolled down at first. I looked over and could've sworn I saw Gregor in that damn car, in the passenger side, laughing and grinnin' like he'd just been told the car was his for free. Big pickup drove by, cut off my view, and by the time they passed, window was rolled up, and the man I saw get out of the car sure wasn't Gregor. I wrote it off. Wheedle and I'd been up for two straight days, chasing the pack of slummoths at night and trying to triangulate a movement pattern in the day. After what you told me about this though, Storme, anybody driving that car would have had the money to pay for that much murder."

I'm not a car person, but Mira and Devon are both nodding. Mira catches my blank stare.

“Two million dollar car,” she says. “Not something you want to drip your burger juice on. Asshole driving that around’s got cash to burn on pest control.”

Pest control.

Her words sink in, and in that moment I know they’re the truth. That motherfucker at the plantation paid Gregor a half million dollars to have the conveniently monetarily-unmotivated shades murder a bunch of hells-zealots he thought were pests.

Hells worshippers are shitty human beings, but they’re still human beings.

Devon looks well enough convinced now. He sits down on a rock. “Christ on a platter,” he says. “What are we going to do?”

“It’s pretty obvious that Gregor’s managed to get himself well-connected,” I say slowly. “If we want to take him down, we need to make sure he’s isolated from the shades and publicly exposed in front of the Summit. I don’t care how much some people want Alamea gone; what Gregor’s doing is anathema.”

It’s not just cause for censure or death. It’s cause for his records to be expunged, his name stricken from Mediator record. Bound and shipped overseas to the World Summit where Alice went for safe harbor. I don’t know how they’d get him there, since we can’t leave our territory, but I do know it’s been done before.

I try to imagine what it would feel like, being put on a plane in a straitjacket in a box, your stomach churning from the first half hour of flight, each progressive minute rusting your entrails to clumps in your gut.

Just hitting the Ohio border was enough to bring it on for me. Cincinnati Mediators turned me back once upon a time. I don’t even know if a Mediator would survive a trip like that. I know an hour in, any Mediator would wish for death.

“How exactly are we going to get him in that situation?” Mira asks. She walks over and sits by Devon, pulling out one of her knives to sharpen it. The scritch-scritch-scritch of her whetstone on the blade sneaks through the air.

"We could use me." I'm dubious to how much of a plan that would be, but if Gregor thinks I've got wool blinders firmly in place as to what he's been up to, it just might work. "Lately he's been proud of me. Weirdly paternal, almost."

"He chose you in the beginning, to look into what was happening," Ripper says, thoughtful. "Do you know why?"

I do know why. He had leverage. But no one else knows that, and I can't tell them. Even so, Alamea gave me something I can say, something that makes sense. "I'm a loner. I keep to myself and don't have any friends. He probably thought that made me vulnerable to his influence."

Something flashes across Mira's face, but it's gone in an instant. I can't tell what it was, but something in my chest drops, and I'm sure I've just hurt her.

"He had to have been planning this for a while," says Devon. "I heard one of the shades he's working with is a thousand years old."

That makes me snort, but that little oh-shit feeling stays with me, nibbling at me like a baby pirhana. "Carrick's four hundred years old, and he'd bust your face into the next eon for calling him a thousand." I take a few steps back and forth, almost pacing. "But you're right. Gregor didn't just pull Carrick out of his ass. The timing was too perfect. What, we have a big blow out with the hells-hordes and all these shades and he just happens to find one from the Jacobean era?"

The sudden picture of Carrick in a frou-frou lace collar and breeches makes me want to snort again, but I resist the urge.

"It's possible the shades happened just at the right time. Maybe he was trying to figure out a way to monetize the Mediators," I say. The words taste bitter in my mouth, and I resist the urge to spit. Saliva pools, and I swallow it.

The other three also look sick at the thought. Our speculation on Gregor's past won't get us anywhere. We need to truncate his future, and fast.

"The Samhain gala next week." Mira's whetstone stops with a *snick*. "Everyone will be there. If you want to make sure everyone sees his ass when he shows it, that's when you should do it."

I don't really like the idea of massively ruining our biggest party of the year, but then again, Mediators do like gossip. It'll be unforgettable.

It'll be really nice if I live through it.

"WHAT DID YOU MEAN, you don't have any friends?" Mira catches me at the door to my car.

My feet halt in the dirt, and shame caresses my face with heat.

"Alamea said—"

"Fuck what Alamea said."

Mira's right. Hearing it out loud sounds absurd.

"Do you seriously think that?" she goes on. Her voice gets a note of gravel, and I startle. Is that tears? Mira?

Fuck.

"I don't know," I say finally.

Five dozen emotions flit across her face. Among them, frustration, anger, pity, sadness, fury.

Devon and Ripper are already in their cars, but I see Ripper's eyes on us as he pulls away. I can't bring myself to open my own car door.

"Yo," Mira says. "You gotta do better than that."

"What do you want me to say?"

"How about yeah, Mira, your trust isn't misplaced. You're not stupid for thinking growing up together and having each other's backs was sort of what friendship is about." Now she's straight pissed, and she punches me in the shoulder. Hard. "Gods damn it, Storme, you're only friendless if you want to be."

I expect her to stomp off and drive away, but she just waits.

The shades up and dip out when they feel like it, but Mira's stuck to me like a piece of gum on my shoe. She came over to help me wake up every two hours when I had a concussion. She cares about the shades. Saturn and Mira are close. She looks at them as people, just like I do. She cares about doing the right thing even if it's not what she's told is the acceptable thing.

"I'm sorry," I say, and now the gravel's in my voice. It's contagious. "You're probably the only friend I have."

She stares at me like I've just told her I fart bubbles, and for a second I think she's going to punch me again.

"Dude, knock it the fuck off. Okay, maybe, if the hells-hit shades don't count—which they do—but Alamea and Devon and Ripper will be your friends if you give them half the chance."

Mira stalks up to me, and I flinch. She throws her arms around me.

"You're not alone, Ayala. Not even a little bit."

My hands hang limp at my side for a minute before I can make myself hug her back. She smells like leaves and vanilla.

"Okay," I say.

"Okay?" She pulls back and pats my shoulder awkwardly. "Now fuck off for real. Go home. And keep an eye on that asshole Carrick."

GOING HOME IS THE plan, but it lasts about as long as it takes for me to reach view of Nashville's skyline. When I take the exit toward my apartment, the night rings with sirens.

Sirens are normal in downtown Nashville, but not this many.

Ten blocks from where I live, the air flashes red and blue. I can't see what's going on. I pull over to the side of the road, and immediately I see smashed windows, shards of glass reflecting back the flashes of color from the emergency and police vehicles. Shifting in my seat, I try to look around the ambulance that's fifty yards ahead of me, but I can't get a good angle.

The last time this happened, a single shade took down several cops before I killed him in broad daylight off Demonbreun.

A police officer is walking by, his hat slightly askew over a bright pink forehead and his body armor clearly too tight for his beer belly. He sees my Mediator tags and scowls. I roll down my window and smile brightly.

"What happened here, Officer?"

"Ain't none of your business. You people think we're some sort of glorified cleanup crew. You should be doing your damn job." He takes three steps toward my window and looks like he wants to yank me out through it.

I waggle my cell phone at him. "Want to tell that to Alamea? I can get her to show up and we can get her take on the situation, or you can just tell me what happened on this gods damned street."

I'm starting to feel like I'm in an outdoor club with all the lights strobing across the jagged glass of the downtown block. Half a mile more, and we'd be in honky tonk central, but I don't see any shredded cowboy hats or denim shirts with the broken glass. I look up at the cop, feeling like it had to be only a matter of time before I had to deal with a shitty one. The last few have been charming.

"You don't even know it's your jurisdiction," he says.

"Pretty sure I do now, or you would have just said it wasn't, Officer Walking Stereotype."

His already-pink face turns pinker.

I kind of hate that I let that come out of my mouth, but honestly, seeing him turn into a tomato is worth it.

I get out of the car and slam the door, hitting the button on my keys to lock it. "Anything happens to my Hi-Ho Silver there, and you're getting a bill from the Summit."

"You fucking Mediators think you're above the law." Spittle gathers on his lips, and he doesn't take any steps back.

I step forward and meet his eyes. I'm tall enough that his face is almost level with mine. Six inches away, I hold his eyes, making damn sure he gets a full look at the violet of mine.

"Trade you," I say. I let a smile curl across my face.

His lips close, and he gives me a look that tells me he thinks he can do my job better.

Fuck this asshole.

"Fourteen."

I let the word snap my eye contact and turn to walk away, counting my steps.

One. Two. Three. Four.

"Fourteen what, you little piss-ant?"

"Demons. At once." I grin at him over my shoulder. "Summit record. Mine. You're welcome."

I earned those gods damned bragging rights.

The scene beyond the ambulance wipes the grin right off my stupid, cocky face.

It looks like a blood volcano erupted.

At least five bodies—or what's left of them—are piled like campfire wood and surrounded by a pool that stretches almost a full ten feet from the epicenter.

There's a head on top of the pile. It's wearing a hat.

If there was any doubt that this is Mediator jurisdiction, that's gone now.

"Who's in charge right now?" I ask loudly.

A detective gives a curt wave, and I walk over. "Looks like you are now," she says.

She looks familiar, and she does a double take when she sees my face, but doesn't say anything else.

I know this woman. She was a beat cop this summer when came across the mess at Demonbreun. Glad she's gotten promoted. I don't mention our history, and she says nothing to bring up that we've met before, but she points at the pile of parts.

"Got called in twenty minutes ago. Hit and run, without the car and with more of a sense of whimsy." Her face is grim, and I want to applaud her for the coping mechanism. "Vic on top wasn't wearing a hat when they attacked. They put it on him right before they ripped off his head, witness said. Three suspects, all in the same hats as the John Doe making the cherry on that nasty sundae."

Inappropriate or not, you don't get far in this business without the ability for euphemism and making bad jokes.

"The witnesses?" I ask.

"Take your pick." She points to a small crowd of bystanders behind one of the squad cars.

I start to walk away, and she moves past me. As she does, she mutters, "Good job with Officer Ervin. Man makes calling cops pigs an insult to pigs."

She's gone before I can say anything in return.

I duck under the yellow tape to reach the gaggle of witnesses. Most are green around the gills. A couple have smears of vomit on their faces that they missed wiping all the way off. One has a splash of it on a pair of four hundred dollar shoes and a probably thousand dollar suit.

It's not the witnesses that stop me, though.

Behind them, scrawled in messy blood on the lone unbroken window on a shop front, is a large circle with a slash through it.

The slash protrudes fully outside the circle, like someone got carried away drawing a no smoking sign.

Or like they were drawing a certain ringed planet.

The sight of it makes my stomach shrivel up into a ball. They wanted me to see it. I know they did. But I have no way of knowing if they mean it as a warning. They know Saturn's close to me.

Somehow I'm certain that the pile of bodies was only meant to draw my attention to that circle of blood.

I need to catch these gods damned monsters and stop them once and for all. If they want to come after me, they should be coming after me, not after the people I care about.

Then again, there's a certain poetry in "to the pain." I guess their strategy wouldn't be as effective if I were okay with it.

I spend the next hour talking to witnesses while I wait for the coroner to come and for another Summit representative to show up and sign off. The detective wasn't kidding when she said I was in charge now; everyone from the forensics team to the crime scene photographer checks in with me while I wait.

The witnesses all say the same thing, that the shades swooped in out of nowhere and grabbed people at random, arranged them, and left. No one remembers seeing them drawing the sigil on the window, which is unsurprising considering how fast shades are and how hasty the marking looks.

Not to mention shock. Half the witnesses are shaking under emergency blankets while I talk to them. I don't blame them. Talking to them gives me almost no information at all, let alone anything new. I hear the same story five times, but each time I listen, hoping one of them will share something revelatory, something I can take to Alamea, something that might lead me to finding these shades and showing them justice.

Even as I hope for that, I don't want to kill them. I don't want that to happen. I need to think of something that can be done for them, just like I need to think of something that can be done for the shades I've worked with for months who Gregor has turned into his own personal weapons for hire. The weight at the center of my chest grows heavier and heavier, as if someone's dropping ball bearings on it one by one. It saps my energy with each witness account. They were on their way home from dinner, walking to their cars, going to meet up with a girlfriend or boyfriend. Three shades swooped in out of nowhere. People seemed to vanish in a gust of wind, reappearing in the center of the street. The shades pulled them apart one by one. Blood. More blood. They put a hat on the last one, took his head, dropped it on top of their pile.

Every single witness says the same thing. The end result is the same. More dead bodies. When the scene is finally cleaned up, each step I take feels like my feet have been dipped in hardening wax over and over.

I feel drained by the time I leave, and in spite of what Mira told me, I feel alone.

In the end, no matter how many friends you have, you're always alone.

33

I FINALLY MAKE IT home at one-thirty, just in time to see Carrick heading for the balcony door. I want to collapse on the couch, but he stops when he sees me.

"You're home," he says, his voice carrying a whiff of surprise. "I was starting to get worried."

I raise an eyebrow at that. "They killed a bunch of civilians about a mile from here."

He doesn't need to ask who *they* is.

"Where are you going?" I ask.

"I'm supposed to meet with the others," he says.

"Gregor too?" I need to be careful, but I also want to know. I want to see the others, try and get a read on them. I stoke the hope twig by twig, waiting for him to answer.

Carrick shakes his head. "Gregor's out of town. I'm just doing some training with them at the usual spot."

It's late. My feet ache, and the tips of my toes are almost numb. I just took my shoes off. I need to sleep.

"Can I come with you?"

Carrick's face goes blank, and I feel the muscles in my body tighten with tension as if I'm walking through a sheet of ice cold water.

"You just got home. You should get some rest."

"Fuck off with what I should do. Can I come?"

A small smile creeps onto his face. "You can come."

He turns away from the balcony, and we leave the apartment together.

"You smell like blood," he says when we get into my car.

"I probably stepped in some," I say shortly. "They made a mess."

"We'll catch them."

I'm beginning to doubt that. If a group of ten shades and a few hundred Mediators are having no luck finding this trio of walking blenders, they're not going to show up as big red X's on a map.

I don't say anything else for the rest of the short drive to the football field. We're the first ones there when we arrive, the lights of the field illuminating only increasingly-dormant grass in need of a voracious cutting.

The bleachers are covered in dust and rust, but I pull up a patch of bench and sit.

Slowly, in twos and threes, the rest of the shades appear from the perimeter of the field. Udo and Harkan. Rex and Carus and Hux. Hayn and Sanj. Beex and Holden and Lawlor. And Boyne, the lone straggler who approaches from the north. I haven't seen them since the incident outside Chattanooga, and anxiety tickles up from my tailbone, climbing my spine to the base of my neck. I try to suppress a shudder. Maybe this is a stupid idea, being here.

Side by side with Carrick, I walk onto the field, and we all converge on the thirty yard line.

It's Udo who comes toward me first. His face is so still and neutral that I direct all my energy to keeping my own calm.

But his hand reaches out, and his fingertips touch my shoulder, and he gives me a sad little smile that crinkles the corners of his almond-shaped indigo eyes. The others follow, two by two, touching my shoulders from both sides with fingertips that feel like butterfly wings.

I want to weep for them. They are more than weapons. I return their greetings as assertively as I can, trying to reassure them with my touch that they are safe with me, wanting to tell them with my words that I will not use them to make money.

I can't say it out loud. We're all standing on a circle of ice, and below the surface are monsters trying to break it and catch us with their teeth when we plunge through.

Carrick directs them all with a few short instructions, and I join them, flowing into the forms I've practiced since I was a child. There's peace in our movements, even though they're the basis for violence.

I'm in the center of the group, and the presence of the shades around me helps refill my near-empty reserve of strength. In martial arts, they teach you about energy and maintaining it, conserving it and harnessing it. Witches and morphs can transfer it. But here, in this moment, I almost feel like the shades are giving some of theirs to me—or as if together we are sharing in a pool we create.

A cracking sound makes us all spin around.

Rex's head falls to the ground.

There's a jeeling behind his corpse.

And behind it, a football team worth of hellkin on the twenty yard line.

Carus lets out a bellow of pain and rage.

My swords are in my hands before I even register that I'm moving. Lawlor and Boyne are on the jeeling, using its shoulder spikes to swing upward to its head. There's another jeeling farther back, surrounded by slummoths and harkasts. A trio of markats drools, their throats undulating as they ready their corrosive spit. Five and a half feet tall with bodies that look like they're made of grey industrial tubing, they flow as they move. Behind them, two snorbits sway, their giant forearms like pendulums.

The first jeeling loses its head, and chaos explodes around me.

A slummoth rushes me, and my swords make fast work of it, slicing through its gut with one hand and severing its spine with the other. Beside me, Hux and Hayn split up and flank one of the markats targeting the blows of their fists and feet to the creature's neck, pummeling it to keep it from spewing toxic spittle over the entire fight.

The twenty-five yard line becomes the line of scrimmage in a game with no ball and death the only mark of the losers. I leap over Rex's corpse and take a pair of harkasts out with two quick movements. There's a fucking hells-hole open on the five. Here. A new one. That hole wasn't on any of Alamea's maps.

I don't have much time to be flabbergasted.

The second jeeling is coming right at me.

Carrick appears at my side, and his side kick takes the jeeling in the knee. The jeeling's long arms snake out, its claws seeking Carrick's stomach. The demon misses, with Carrick circumventing the attack by almost flying to the side. I dart in and manage to slice the jeeling's side open, spilling hot blood and exposing the demon's innards.

Together, Carrick and I tag team the eleven foot monster. I feint while he flanks the beast, raining blows on its back and wrenching its left shoulder spike like a lever. The jeeling screams like tearing steel. I jam my saber up under its ribs and yank my blade to the side and out.

The demon's back breaks as Carrick puts a fist through its spine.

Around us, Harkan and Sanj have taken a splash of markat spit to the chest, both of them bearing sizzling splashes across their skin, but they take down one markat, then the other, their fingers finding space between demon muscles and pulling them apart like they're untangling unruly wires.

Out of the hells-hole, more harkasts swarm. Been and Boyne take them down, practically punting them like stumpy footballs.

One by one, the hellkin fall, and when the hells-hole finally vanishes from sight, we hunt through the bodies to find Rex's, pulling him to the side.

The shades have no funeral rites, no ceremony of mourning, but as I watch them, I think I see one incepted.

One by one, they kneel next to Rex, their hands covered in blood and slime. They touch his chest, just over his heart, and their fingers leave marks.

I'm last, and my hand shakes as it finds his chest. I can't look at the severed stump of his neck.

BEEX TAKES GUARD DUTY, watching where the hells-hole opened to make sure it doesn't start spawning more demons, and the rest of us gather down the field. I call the Summit for a body pickup, making sure to report that the hellkin came to attack the shades. The Summit needs to know that these shades are a target.

As Carrick speaks to them in low tones, I try and reconcile what I know of them with what happened at the plantation. Gregor and Carrick and I, we taught them to follow orders. We taught them to trust us. Maybe that's it. They just want to breathe freely as people, to exist as living beings who have as much of a right to be here as anyone else.

I think of Miles and Saturn, holed up in their little safe house. I think of Mason, half a world away. And I think of Alamea, sitting in her Jeep while the Belle Meade country club guards give us the stink eye, telling me that she's not done here yet. That she wants to live.

She and the shades want the same thing. I want the same thing.

I wonder if the shades will ever be able to just be part of society, to roll up to a diner off I-40 or in downtown Nashville and order a burger so rare it's mooing, have a laugh with their server, and eat raw beef with a fork. Pay for it with money they earn doing something. As security, as hunters—hell, for all the romance novels Carrick reads, maybe they could try their hands at writing some.

Until they find a way to become a part of the world, they will exist apart from it.

And while they exist apart from it, they can be exploited.

If they were Mediators, they'd probably all go to a bar and drink away their problems. Maybe get blitzed on skittles. Maybe sing bad karaoke. But instead, they sit here, ass naked in an overgrown field, spattered with markat spittle and blood and slummoth slime, which they try to rub off with handfuls of grass.

Carrick comes to sit beside me. "What are you thinking?"

I give him an ironic smile. "You really do read too many romance novels."

"They're peaceful."

"I guess they are that."

He's quiet for a moment. "It's not going to stop, you know."

"I know."

"I don't think you really do."

I look at him. "I'm a Mediator, Carrick. It never stops."

"I don't mean the hellkin in general. I mean what happened here tonight. They're not going to stop coming for us."

"The demons."

"Yes, the demons." He plucks some browning blades of grass and starts weaving them with nimble fingers. I've seen Saturn do the same thing. "I've been around for a while. I wasn't part of the first batch of shades, and they—" he gestures to the others, "—aren't part of the last. There will be more. The demons will try and breed more of them, and when they don't turn out the way the hellkin hierarchy wants, they will send the hordes to dispatch them."

I hear real pain in his voice, and I wonder about the others of his generation, how he survived. If he wishes he didn't. I wonder what he thinks he's helping, working with Gregor.

"What happened at the plantation was a nightmare," he says.

His words shock me like I've just been touched between the shoulder blades with a live current.

I go very still, choosing my words very carefully. "I wish I'd been there to help. Maybe I could have helped save some of them."

Those hells-worshippers—they may have been stupid, but they didn't deserve to be massacred. The shades don't deserve to be massacred. The only creatures who deserve a massacre are the gods damned demons who keep invading my world.

Carrick's eyes go distant, and I actually see him swallow. It's such a human stress reaction that I don't know what to do.

"Yes, well. For what it's worth, I'm very glad you weren't there to see it."

If only he knew.

"Why?" I ask. I don't mean why he wishes that, and I think he knows that.

"There are some people you cannot help," he says sadly.

The simple proclamation ricochets through the air, and the murmur of talking amongst the other shades goes silent.

In Carrick's words, a thought germinates in me. Suddenly, I'm certain he had no knowledge of the money or why they were told to kill those hells-zealots. Perhaps Carrick's just an Oscar-worthy actor, but I don't think so. He sounds like he means what he's saying, like he's stating a simple truth. That those hells-worshippers were beyond salvation.

Looking across the way at Udo's face—his arm is around Carus's shoulders, which shake softly although Carus's eyes are dry—I try to imagine myself in their place. If perhaps they saw their own mothers in those hells-worshippers. If perhaps they thought what they were doing would spare those people the misguided choice to bring more of themselves into the world. The shades come into being by killing their hosts. They are born in brutality and blood. There are no arms to hold them, no warm body to comfort them or teach them. For them, their lives are beyond kill or be killed; for them it's not either-or, but too often both.

And I understand. I understand how Gregor got them to do it. He appealed to their vulnerability, to their inborn guilt. To their desire not to see more shades born into a world that hates them, and into one where they have no place of their own.

The revelation steals my breath as I look at all their faces, full of grief and confusion. They asked for none of this. This is not their fault. Even the shades who are terrorizing the people of Nashville—they have their own story, and whatever it is, they will likely die for it. Likely at my own hands.

There is too much blood on my hands as it is.

"Would you ever kill for money?" I ask quietly, pitching my voice low enough so even the other shades can't hear me. Only Carrick hears my bare breath of voice, and he looks me in the eyes.

"Why would I need money for death? I have many skills far more valuable."

It's all the answer I need. I hear the sound of tires on gravel, and I know it's the Mittens arriving on splat duty to clean up the pile of demon bodies. The shades hear it too, and they all rise to their feet without looking in the direction of the vehicles. They disperse without a word, though they each meet my eyes before they run into the night. One of the Mediator vans is blasting hard rock loud enough to make one of the distant houses call in a noise complaint. I'm going to have to tell them to shut the heck up.

Carrick touches my shoulder gently. "I'm going to go with the others. I'll be home later."

It's already almost four in the morning. I nod at him and turn to meet the Mittens.

"You know why we like the romance novels?" Carrick says from behind me. "They have happy endings."

In the time it takes me to turn around and face him, he's already gone.

34

I SLEEP UNTIL NOON Friday and wake up because my phone has taken it upon itself to be a one-device parade. Bleary-eyed, I reach over and grab it. “Yello.”

“Storme, I need you at the Summit.”

It’s Alamea, and I’m suddenly wide awake. “I’ll be right there. I need to make a full report on last night.”

“We’ve got a lot to discuss. Double time, Storme.”

I take a three minute shower mostly because I sweat in my sleep; I washed off all the demon grime before getting into bed. Carrick is on the couch reading when I leave my room, and though I’m now sure that even he isn’t a full party to Gregor’s plans, I don’t trust him quite enough to tell him everything that’s going on. It makes me wonder how Saturn and Miles found out. And Jax.

It’s no novel Carrick’s reading, but a leather bound book the size of an atlas. It’s not mine, and I definitely don’t have time to ask about it. I can smell the dust on its pages when I walk by. Carrick gives me a smile, but doesn't speak, and I hurry out the door to get to the Summit.

In Alamea's office, she coats the edges of the door again with the same shimmery black powder, and again my ears pop with the pressure shift. I tell her everything, from the plan I hatched with Mira and the others to expose Gregor at the Summit's Samhain gala next week to the full story on the shades and how I think Gregor's managed to play them like they were strings tuned just for his fingers.

She listens, face grave, as I tell her about the hells-hole that opened on the football field, even though I reported it last night to the cleanup crew. Alamea pulls up the map on her computer again just to show me that five new hells-holes have opened in middle Tennessee since the summer. It doesn't bode well for anything.

"What do you need from me?" she asks when I finish going over the Samhain plan.

"Do you have a good idea of which Mediators will support Gregor when this happens? Or at least who will rush to defend him on principle?" If it's a large number, things will get messy, and even though the Samhain gala is pretty much the only day of the year where we put aside our leathers for fancy dress and canapés, we're always armed. Always.

Alamea nods, and she leans back, putting her feet up on the corner of her desk. Her locs are coiled atop her head today, towering like a crown. She's wearing a straight cut shirt of mottled grey linen and black trousers of the same material, and her feet on the desk are wrapped by black leather strappy wedges. Even when the world's going to shit, she's got style.

"I'll make sure the people I have know to be prepared for resistance." She drums her fingers on her desk. "You know this isn't going to be easy. It's going to cut deep and leave people raw."

"Would you prefer the alternative?" I ask. "Gregor auctioning off the shades like mercenaries, wielding them like weapons, and keeping all the profits to pad his pockets?"

I don't bring up the part where the shades are the victims in this. I think she already knows. I only hope she doesn't look at them as potential collateral damage. Mira and I might be the only two Mediators who don't think that's what they were born for.

When her alarm beeps for her two o'clock meeting, we've managed to hash out a plan for the gala. Samhain's on a Saturday this year, and that'll just about shut down the city. With so many law enforcement members at the ready and the full Summit convened for the gala, we'll have Gregor pinned down. Ironically, he's up for an award for his work with the shades. I volunteer to introduce him, and that's where we'll strike. When he's on stage. In front of the entire Summit.

And we'll end this for good.

ϟ

ALAMEA LEAVES HER OFFICE shortly before I do, and I finish up jotting down some notes before folding my notes into a tidy square and tucking them into my pocket. I don't trust them to the digital world, and I have no intention of any of Gryfflet's tech witches or any prying eyes in the Summit coming across what I've written. Paper can be burned. Ones and zeroes will never be erased.

I'm just locking the door to Alamea's office when Ben Wheedle walks around the corner.

For a split second before he sees me, I seriously consider running away. He is, as usual, the last person I want to see.

He starts when he sees me, his long eyelashes framing his violet eyes in boyish surprise. Ben's got farm boy good looks and knows it. He's one of those dudes who thinks he's a Nice Guy, but for him it just means doing what he thinks is right for other people without bothering to ask them first, then getting all in a tither when they disagree. Like say, assuming I want to be kissed when I'm yelling at him.

Yeah, that's a hint. Mixed signal. Who could blame the guy? Excuse me while I try to restrain myself from punching him again.

His eyes go from my hand on the door handle to my face and back, and he gives me a sad smile that doesn't make me want to punch him any less.

"What?" I say.

"You know she's going to turn on you," he says.

Well, that's new.

"Care to elaborate on your new super future seeing skills?"

"I don't know why you're always so mad at me." Ben squares his shoulders and adjusts the belt on his jeans.

"Then apparently your memory is about as useful as your ability to pick up on social cues."

He frowns. "I've told you over and over. This summer I was trying to protect you. I thought you needed help."

"I did need help. The kind of help that actually pays some attention instead of haring off and making assumptions. Instead, you spied on me for Alamea, didn't even try to get the actual story from me, and managed to get me imprisoned and almost killed. Yeah, thanks. And let's not forget that you seem to have a massive problem with the word *no*."

"Ayala," he tries to start talking again, but I cut him off.

"When you've asked someone out fifteen thousand times and they keep saying no? Find someone else, for cripes' sake. I'm not a fucking fantasy, Wheedle. I'm a human being. Don't you get all self-righteous on me and act like erasing my ability to speak for myself is some sort of chivalrous concept. It doesn't make you a friend, and it doesn't make you a gods damned hero. It makes you a serious asshole."

His eyes go wide, and for the first time, I see a spark of anger take root. Good. I can deal with angry Ben a lot more that sad puppy Ben.

"You want to talk about Alamea?" he says. "Let's talk about Alamea."

I don't even think he realizes it's a non-sequitur, but that fits his pattern. Selective hearing is like his superpower.

I throw up my hands. "Sure. Talk."

"She's going to turn on you, just like she turned on me," he says. "As soon as I was done being useful to her, she cut me out, tossed me aside, and moved on. To you, looks like."

Ben takes a step closer, and I cluck at him. He stops, putting his palms out as if he expects me to throw an uppercut at his chin. I still want to, but I won't unless he gives me a reason. And words, as stupid and slimy as his words might be, are never a reason.

"I don't think you know what's happening," he says in a low voice. "What's going on in the Summit. How many groups are breaking off into factions."

This ought to be good.

"Alamea's in trouble, Ayala. She's barely holding onto her hold on leadership. Nobody's happy about her executing the guys, even if they did try to kill her and that's technically her right. Most people think she's been too lenient about the shades, and now with some of them on a rampage through the city, those people are getting upset." He holds up one hand as if to say he knows what I'm going to say, because of course he thinks he knows what I'm going to say. He always, without fail, thinks he knows the inside of my head better than I do.

"So you're saying little birdies are telling you that the Summit's more bent out of shape over a couple shades than the hordes of all six and a half hells," I say. "Ain't that charming."

Surprise and frustration battle on his face. "You don't understand."

"Oh, of course I don't. What do I know? Enlighten me."

"Ayala, this is serious."

"Like a heart attack. Maybe even two whole heart attacks." I nod solemnly, and I watch as that little spark of anger bursts into a teeny tiny flame. Does he actually think I've missed all this? I was here when the Summit busted out the fisticuffs. And

Ben took one on the chin then. The memory makes this conversation a hair more bearable.

"I'm trying to save you," he hisses. "She's going to go down, and she's going to take you with her. She won't be the leader for much longer, and it's going to be your head on the chopping block without her if you keep trying to help her. Things are bad, and the second she thinks you've outlived your usefulness, she'll turn you out and feed you to the people she knows are gunning for her."

Gunning for her. Interesting choice of words. We fight with swords, but the assassins definitely brought firearms to the party.

My silence seems to work him up even more.

"You know I'm right. I know you can feel it."

"Tell me," I say, my voice even and neutral. "Just how important is it to the Summit to keep the hellkin from turning Nashville into another Mississippi?"

He blinks. "The demon kills are down, lower than ever before. They're not the danger right now."

"It's adorable that you think that."

He ignores me, and his voice turns insistent, pleading. "Let me help you, Ayala. With Gryfflet and Gregor—I know Gregor trusts you, he won't hold you working with Alamea against you—we can make sure you don't go down with her."

I've got a headache. My temples throb, punctuated by each progressively more asinine sentence he speaks. "Do you ever hear a single word I say? Ever?"

"I hear every word you say," he says softly. "I always have."

"Oh, dear gods above and below. Get a fucking grip, Wheedle." This time I take a step toward him, and he actually retreats. "We are born to fight the hordes of the hells. That is our calling and our purpose. We are the front line. We are the infantry. We are the blades that allow the norms to sleep safe. I don't give a slummoth's shit about whatever politics you think you know about. Our job starts at sundown when the demons come out, and it will continue until they are all dead or they fear us enough not to stick their noses into our world ever again. We keep the balance. The balance is not who leads the Summit, and you don't really know a gods damned thing."

He doesn't respond to anything I've said, because of course he doesn't. "Be careful. I don't want to see you die."

"Next time you see a hells-hole, Wheedle, jump through it." I turn on my heel and walk away, resisting every reflex in my body that screams at me to put my fist in his face.

If there's one thing I learned from this, it's that he seriously thinks the Summit's at breaking point.

This is going to be a gala to remember.

If only Ben would get over whatever fucked up fantasy he has in his head for me. At this point he's stuck a flag at the top of Masochism Mountain, and I'm not sure I could actually be mean enough to him to make him understand that I will never be his. I will always be my own person.

I wish he had more layers—anything beyond the dubious helpfulness level of a two-year-old with a chainsaw.

I wish that last sentence of his was a threat.

A threat I could deal with. He keeps thinking I'm his friend, and he can't grasp that he's long since made me an enemy.

35

AS SOON AS THE sun goes down, I meet Mira in Percy Warner Park, where Saturn is supposed to show up to hear our plan. Miles is laying low—one glimpse of him by any shade in Nashville, and his whole *dead* persona will scamper right out the window.

Mira's dressed in leathers seamed with stretch fabric to allow more freedom of movement. I'm going to have to ask her who her tailor is.

She approaches me where I wait under Saturn's old tree, and I can see in her face that she's still a bit pissed at me. I give her the warmest smile I can muster, and I mean it. Or at least I'm trying to mean it. I'm not used to working with other Mediators. It feels like I'm trying to wear someone else's broken-in shoes.

One look at Mira's answering smile bolsters me, though. "Hey, stud. I hear you and your shade buddies took out another bucket o' demons the other night."

"You're not wrong." I kick the tree root next to my foot. "Remember when facing one demon by itself was a lot?"

"Please. I wear demon chum and try to get them to fight me all at once, but they're too scared."

Her blustering tells me that things might just be okay. I motion at the trees beyond the clearing. "Saturn say exactly when he'd get his naked ass here?"

She pulls her phone out of a pocket and looks at the time. "Sometime in the next five or ten minutes. He should be here."

I tell her about Ben and what he said about Alamea.

"Wheedle's a dick," she says succinctly. "And of course Alamea's out for herself. She wants to keep her head attached to her neck. Doesn't mean she's going to throw you under the busload of demons."

Couldn't have said it better myself.

"Wane says hi," she says. "She and some of her witch buddies are doing a pre-Samhain shindig Friday night before the gala, and she wanted you to come. They'll be with their circles on gala night, but they always do a little get-together and play video games and drink wine all night. Last year was pretty fun if you want to join in."

"I suck at video games, but I'll come. Do I need to bring anything?"

"Nah. Nothing at all, even clothes. Everybody's sky clad."

"Wait, what?" Naked, alcohol fueled video games sounds a shit ton more like Beltane than Samhain, and after a moment of watching my face, Mira busts up laughing.

"I'm joking, asshole. Wear whatever the fuck you want."

A rustle sounds in the bushes, and I turn, expecting Saturn. Mira falls silent, following my gaze.

We've been talking like a couple half-trained losers, and we missed it. The silence isn't just the lack of our voices. It's everywhere.

"We've got company," I say.

"You think?" Her swords hiss out of their scabbards, and mine echo the sound.

"I checked. There aren't any active hells-holes in the park close to here." That doesn't mean the demons couldn't bus in, but I specifically tried to pick a place where there hadn't been any for a while. The only time one was reported here in the last five years was the day Saturn came bursting into the world.

Scanning the woods around us yields no telltale pink glow, which thankfully means no jeelings. I've had enough of them lately.

I hear a burble and a snarl, and my stomach sinks. Markats.

"You hear that?" I ask.

"Yep. I forgot my anti-spit umbrella."

"Guess we better finish them before they crank up the waterworks, hey?" I move to stand back to back with her, waiting. They'll come out. "Got eyes on it yet?"

"Not yet."

The rustling grows closer, and I'm thankful we're in a clearing. Markats travel in packs, but usually not more than three or four.

Seven materialize out of the trees.

"Gods fucking damn it," Mira says.

I know she's got a potty mouth. So do I. Sometimes they're just the best words when you spend your life facing creatures that can dissolve flesh with their spit.

"Game plan?" she asks.

"Kill the bastards."

It's bravado. Markats are faster than slummoths and more vicious, and they have the added strength of being able to dole out second degree burns by spouting their filthy spit at us. Fear and adrenaline are a steady flow in my veins. Where on earth is Saturn?

The markats lunge for us, and I dodge just in time for a stream of rank saliva to miss me. It lands with a splat on the ground where I was just standing, and I hear the chuffing gurgle that means more's coming. I'm lucky they need a minute or to to recharge, but with seven of them, a minute ain't going to be enough time.

Two more splats follow in quick succession, and a third right after that. That's four of the markats relatively disarmed. I spring at one of them, feinting right before dropping to my knee to roll and come up at is feet. I take out its left knee with my saber, completing the roll to land upright again, stabbing it through the throat with my short sword. Blood and spittle ooze over its lips and teeth, and a quick jerk of my sword leaves its neck wobbling, half cut through.

Mira's cut one down herself, its head severed clean off, but there are still five left. All five of them launch their spray at us at once, and we dive in opposite directions. Not quite fast enough. A splash of the markat spit hits my leg. The leather will keep it off my skin for about thirty minutes, but if I don't get out of these pants before then, I'll have a chemical burn.

I use Saturn's tree to springboard myself at one of the markats while they're re-pooling their next batch of projectile saliva. My saber catches it in the throat, slicing away half of it and embedding in the markat's shoulder. I land on my feet, and claws dig into my back. I scream, staggering under the weight.

Two of them are on me. I twist, but they dig their claws in deeper, puncturing my leather and worming deeper into my flesh. It burns like pure hydrochloric acid; markats lick their claws to coat them in venom, and my back feels like a forest fire.

Out of the corner of my eye, I can see Mira whirling between the other two remaining markats, dodging their streams of spit, but unable to land a blow.

Reversing my blades, I slam them behind me as hard as I can, a raw shriek tearing itself from my throat. My blades land, and one of the markats drops away. I pull forward and stab backward again, and the claws rip from my flesh just as a stream of hot liquid coats my back.

It drips through the holes in my leathers, and now I really scream. With a half-sob, I turn and almost fling my arm in a wide arc, decapitating one of the markats. The other I must have stabbed through the lung, because it stumbles to the side, a grating wheeze coming from its chest. Mira's felled one of hers as well, and I take three excruciating steps forward and send my last markat to whatever hell-beyond-hells they go to when they croak.

My back is pools of lava.

Mira slices through the final markat's throat just as I hear the gurgle.

"Mira, look out!"

Her blade opens up its throat, and a gush of fluid sprays right in her face. She rips herself away at the last second, her yell a high-pitched keen. She falls to the ground.

I take two strides and take the damn demon's head the rest of the way off, and I collapse to my knees beside her. She's face down in the dirt screaming. Her voice echoes through the trees around us, and I hope to any stars or gods that'll listen that those markats were all the demons in this park. She'll be blinded. That much markat spit to the face...

I scramble forward, reaching for her. "Mira," I say. "Mira, stay with me."

My hands find her shoulder, and I ignore the raging maelstrom of pain in my back to tug at her, trying to turn her toward me. The burning claw holes in my skin are no match for the terror that takes up residence in my ribcage.

"You're going to be okay," I tell her. "Mira, answer me."

I roll her over, expecting to see her face covered in the stuff, expecting to see her violet eyes eaten away. Her face is clear, except for a few flecks of pink in her brown skin. Her neck, though—"Fuck."

Her neck is covered in markat spit from her ear down into her leather jacket. If I don't get that off of her, it'll eat right through her skin and get into her bloodstream through her carotid artery and erode her heart from the inside out.

"I have to move you. It's gonna suck. Be the tough bitch I know you are," I tell her. I roll to my knees and bend over, air bursting from between my lips as new pain rips through my back. Grabbing hold of her arms, I wrangle her over my shoulders in a fireman's carry.

She bellows, then clenches her teeth. "Fucking hurts," she gets out.

"I know," I say.

"Your back."

"It's fine."

"Fucking fine my ass."

"Keep talking." I don't care that my swords are on the ground. I stumble for the edge of the clearing. It's a half mile walk back to my car, and every second I waste brings her closer to an agonizing death.

There's another rustle up ahead. I stop short, panic welling in my chest. Mira doesn't hear it, but she feels me stop.

"Ayala?" the voice comes through the leaves from a hundred feet away.

It's Saturn.

"Saturn!" In the space of a single breath, he's by my side. He scoops up Mira from my back.

"What do you need?"

"My car," I gasp.

"I'll take her." He vanishes into a blur, and I track him for about five seconds before he's gone.

I stagger back to where our swords dropped and gather them up, then start jogging as fast as I can manage back to the car. Saturn reappears about a minute later, and he doesn't stop to ask, only picks me up and runs. His arm against my back makes me yell, but he doesn't stop.

I can feel the markat spit on my leg working through the leather, and as soon as Saturn puts me down by the side of my car, I kick off my shoes and strip naked.

Mira's breath is coming in shallow gasps. She's slumped against the car tire, her hand working at the gravel like a stress ball. She looks up at Saturn.

"You see the woman. Get my fucking clothes off me."

My car might be messy, but I know where the important shit is. While Saturn peels off Mira's clothes, I open the door and grab my gallon of water. Under the passenger seat is my safety kit. It sticks on the seat's adjustment lever, and I yank it out.

I thrust the water at Saturn. "Pour it over her. Anywhere the venom got. Try to save a little for me."

Exposed to the air, my back sings with pain. My fingers fumble at the zipper of the safety pack, but I manage to get it open. I hear a splash, and Mira hollers like a goat in a bear trap.

There. A brand new can.

It's the size of a hairspray canister, and I can't get the lid off. My arms are going numb. I grab it by the base and smash the plastic lid against the edge of the car door. It pops off and skitters away on the gravel.

I fall to my knees beside Mira, grabbing her right hand and squeezing it. "You ready?"

"Hurry the fuck up."

She squeezes her eyes shut. My thumb just barely depresses the trigger, and the cold smell of pressurized anti-venom fills the air. It coats her neck and face before my hand fails me, and I drop the can.

Saturn snatches it up and turns her over, spraying every pink splotch on her naked body. The markat spit dribbled between her breasts, looping under her right one when she fell on her side. Her throat wobbles, twitching with the relief the anti-venom brings. It's mixed with aloe and forms a gelatinous seal over the affected areas. A breath goes out of me, and I almost pitch forward. The gravel digs into my knees.

She's going to be okay. Her hand is still clasped in mine.

I don't even realize Saturn's finished with her until I hear the slosh of water in the jug behind me.

"Hold still," he says.

The water hits my back like it's made of liquid knives.

I think I'm screamed out, because the sound that I make sounds like the shifting rocks under my knees. Saturn takes my hand from Mira's and lays me out flat, face down on the ground. If the water is liquid knives, the anti-venom is cool healing. It spreads out and coats my back, settling into the punctures from the markat claws. My breath still comes fast, but the pain slowly begins to abate.

I think. The world feels fuzzy.

"Next time don't be late," I mutter at Saturn, and then I pass out.

36

MY FRONT HALF FEELS like it's made out of gravel, and my back half feels like it's made out of glue.

When I pry myself off the ground, the first thing I see is Mira's ass, still bare naked and dangerously close to my face.

The second thing I see is Saturn's arm stretching out to help pull me to my feet. "I was beginning to worry," he says.

"Beginning?"

Mira stirs, and Saturn helps her up.

"Never have I ever been more thankful to heal quickly," she says, spitting a small pebble from her lip.

"Seven markats," I say. "I've never seen that many together before."

"Not working together, I haven't," Mira agrees. She sways on her feet, and her hand reaches up to gingerly touch the side of her neck. "Fuck me, this sucks."

"We should have run."

"Yeah, sure. And died when they caught us. Those son-bitches are fast."

She's right, but we're alive.

We get in the car, Saturn climbing over the heaps of mess in the back to sprawl half on and half off the seat. I make matters worse for him by pushing my seat all the way back so I can perch on the edge of it and not have to lean back against it.

Never in my life did I think I'd be naked in my car with another woman and a human-hellkin hybrid. Our leathers are all destroyed. It sounds like something from a bad porno movie. When I get home, I'm ordering a new wardrobe.

Mira and I fill in Saturn on the way to her house, and I drop them both off there.

"If you knock her out again, I will make you into a purse," I tell Saturn.

"She'll have to beat me to it," Mira adds, kicking him in the shins. She's barefoot, so it's about as effective as throwing a bumble bee at him.

"Never again," Saturn says, and I think he actually means it.

I find an old towel in the back of my car and wrap it around myself to get into my building, but it doesn't keep the security guard from staring. I probably look like hell. My hair's sticking to the anti-venom gel on my back, I'm wearing a towel, and I still have the depression marks from a bunch of small rocks from head to toe.

"Rough night?" the guard asks, looking more perplexed than anything.

"You could say that."

Let him think of Mediators what he will.

Carrick is properly alarmed when I come through the door, and he runs into my room and grabs my Injured Robe without me even having to ask him. The cloth will stick to the gel like crazy, but it's better than me sitting around in a towel. I tell Carrick what happened, while he fetches me a glass of water. He looks troubled, and I reassure him again that I'm fine.

But the shadow on his face tells me it's not just me he's worried about.

He rotates the sofa so it's perpendicular to the TV so I can lie on my stomach and watch, and he puts on Die Hard and orders a pizza before I even know what's happening.

"What's wrong with you?" I ask, shifting my weight so my boobs don't get too squished against the arm of the couch. Even with the ramp of pillows I built to support me, it's not very comfortable.

"Nothing," he says.

If that's how he's going to be, I'll leave him alone.

The pizza arrives, and even though I'm ravenous, I can only eat three slices because being on my stomach puts too much pressure on my abdomen. Carrick gets up every ten minutes, pacing around the room before sitting back down in the armchair, as still as a tree trunk.

After an hour of this, I pause the movie and lean forward to look at him. "Carrick. What in the hells is wrong?"

He gets up again, and for a second I think he's going to walk straight out the balcony door and over the edge.

It takes a solid five minutes before he'll look at me.

"I saw Miles," he says.

"What?" The blood has almost all rushed to my head, hanging over the edge of the couch like I am, but his words make it drain from my face.

"I know. It's mad." He gets to the balcony door, and I can see his face reflected in it. He looks tormented. "What is it?" I can feel every breath I take in a strange way, the pizza in my belly and the sensation of lying in this position making me very aware of my injured back and the fact that I'm almost immobile.

If this turns bad, if he knows I've been hiding this from him, or if he thinks I'm...I don't know. Panic wriggles through me, and I start to push myself up.

"Don't, Ayala. It's okay. It's just...this is going to sound madder still."

I freeze.

"I think Gregor lied to me. I don't know why he would. He told me that he saw Miles die. He would have had to see Miles lose his head for that to be true, and the Miles I saw tonight most certainly had his head fully attached to his body." Carrick turns back from the balcony and looks at me, his face earnest and lost. "Why would he do such a thing?"

Slowly, I push myself to a sitting position. It makes me woozy, and I reach out and grab my glass for another sip of water. Sitting pulls on the wounds on my back.

For a moment, I'm baffled that Carrick seems to trust Gregor so much. I think until this moment, I've assumed that Carrick spent the last four hundred years becoming worldly and cynical, because he acts like an ass sometimes and makes a habit of showing his, metaphorically and literally.

But what if he's just spent the last four hundred years very, very lonely?

"You really saw him?" I ask. Internally, a war stages itself over whether I should come clean or not.

He nods, and I swallow, taking another drink of water to try and chase away the lump in my throat.

I can't risk Carrick's trust.

"I know Gregor lied," I say.

I tell him everything.

I HAVE TO GO back to the Summit Saturday morning, and the first person I see when I walk through the doors at eleven is Ben Wheedle.

I almost turn on my heel and walk out.

My back is healing, the gel starting to slowly slough off, and I chose loose-fitting clothes to be safe, but at the sight of Ben, my whole body starts to itch.

He comes right over to me. "I need to talk to you."

“Not now, Wheedle. I’m busy.” I try to get past him, but he blocks my way. The Mitten at the front desk looks over with only mild interest, then turns back to his phone, texting away.

I take another step to get around Ben, and he throws out an arm and grabs mine. “You don’t understand, Storme. I need to talk to you. It’s important.”

“If you don’t take your hand off me in three seconds, I’m going to rip it off and feed it to a jeeling.”

He drops his hand, but he points toward the corridor that leads off to the left from the main lobby. I follow reluctantly. I’m going to regret this.

“Make it fast,” I say.

“I have people. They’ve been keeping an ear out for any of the unrest in the Summit. I’ve had them tracking Alamea and trying to find out what she’s up to.”

“Up to? Do you even fucking hear yourself?”

Ben’s eyes are wild, and he looks like he wants to punch the wall behind my head. “This is bad. It’s really bad, and you need to know.”

I stare at him, waiting. Last time he told me everything I already knew, just with more histrionics.

“I don’t know the details yet, but I know Alamea is trying to frame Gregor for something big. Something huge. It could get him killed.” Ben’s voice rises on the last sentence, and I just watch him.

Covert ops, not for Ben Wheedle.

“Do you remember what I said to you last time I saw you?” I ask.

He looks flustered. “What? No. Hells, Ayala, I’m trying to tell you something important.”

“And I’m trying to clue you in to what a hysterical asshole you look like right now. Last time you went plunging into something without knowing all the details, you almost got me killed.”

Stricken, he taps his index finger against the hem of his jeans. He opens his mouth.

"No, Wheedle," I say. "If something's going on—and I know tensions are high right now—and you go haring off throwing false intel at people, you're going to have Mediator blood on your hands. Take a gods damned second and listen to yourself. You're talking about accusing the leader of the Summit of what, conspiracy? And with only hearsay to back you up and no details? At best right now, you could get imprisoned. At worst, you could start an internal war."

For a second I think he might actually listen. He bites his lip and sits back on his heels. Then he shakes his head. "No. I trust my sources. I won't let anything happen to Gregor. He appreciated what I told him—"

"What did you just say?"

My voice comes out like a hollow echo in a vast cavern, and it shuts Ben up mid-sentence.

Samhain's a week from today. We had everything worked out. And now Gregor's going to know something's up.

Ben stares at me, uncomprehending. "He deserves to know someone's gunning for him."

It takes every single year of training I have to control my muscles enough not to slam Ben Wheedle into the wall. "Out of the two of them, which one of them had actual people gunning for her?"

"Yeah, but—"

"I have to go."

"Ayala, wait."

"Because of you, people are going to get killed. People. Not demons. People. Every drop of blood spilled because of what you done is on your head, Wheedle. Congratulations. You just ruined every hope of stabilizing the Summit." I shouldn't do it, but I turn and pull my hair back to show him the perimeter of gel protruding over the collar of my shirt. "See that? I got set upon by seven markats last night with Mira. We both almost died. Five years ago, you'd never see more than two or three of them at once.

"And my new little kill record? When was the last time you saw a mixed gaggle of fourteen demons, five different breeds, all at once in one place without them ripping each other to pieces?"

Ben just shakes his head.

"You've been tracking the norm death rate, and that's just dandy. But if you can't see what's happening, if you can't get it through your concrete skull that there is something much bigger going on than who's fucking King of the Summit, then you're more than stupid, Ben Wheedle. You're going to get us all killed."

I do turn on my heel then, and my sheer panic propels me out of the Summit.

I'm supposed to be in Alamea's office in two minutes, but I can't go straight there now. I head to my car at a near run and drive off, dialing Alamea as I pull out of the parking lot.

She answers on the first ring. "What's wrong?"

"Ben's gone to Gregor and told him he heard you were trying to frame him for something huge."

"That fucking troll." I think it's the first time I've heard her say fuck.

"Samhain's off. There's no way we can last a week before something happens."

"I'll call you later. Be on your guard."

She hangs up, and that's it. I speed home as fast as I can, almost tripping over my own feet to get into the apartment. Carrick better be home. I push open the door, and Nana tries to dart out. I catch her by the ears and immediately feel awful for it, scooping her up and depositing her back inside the apartment.

"Carrick!"

He doesn't answer right away, but I hear a thump and a footfall in the bedroom, and a moment later he emerges, looking haggard and tugging his shorts up as he walks. "What happened?"

"Ben tipped off Gregor that Alamea's on to him. Told him she's trying to frame him for something. He'll know she knows."

"Bloody hells."

We drive straight to the foreclosed house where Saturn and Miles are staying. I make Carrick stay in the car while I run up and rap on the back door. I hurriedly explain, and after a long, incomprehensible moment between Miles and Saturn, they motion at Carrick to come in.

I try calling Ripper and Devon, but neither of them answer at first. Nor does Mira.

"When did you leave her house?" I ask Saturn.

"At first light," he says.

"She was okay?"

"She was swearing at me."

So she was okay.

Carrick and Miles are sitting close together, and I feel like one of them needs to speak before the turn of the century, but I can't try to fix their friendship right now.

Devon picks up when I try to call him again. "Ayala?"

I explain as fast as I can and tell him to meet us at Mira's. Mira doesn't answer again, and I leave her a message to call me. Ripper doesn't answer either, and I leave him a message to meet us at Mira's too.

We all pile in my car, which doesn't work out any better with two shades in the backseat than it did with one. I try to pretend not to notice when Saturn pulls a fast food straw from between his butt cheeks.

I pull up at Mira's and I can't tell if she's home or not. I can't see her car.

My phone rings. The inside of my car smells like shades, warm skin and a slightly stale scent that lingers from the inside of the foreclosure. I answer the phone.

"It's Ripper," says Ripper. "Mira's not home. She's with me."

"Where are you?"

"I can't tell you. We'll meet you at the spot. Hurry up. Devon's on his way already."

Shades have good hearing. They all go very still.

I hit the gas and drive.

Twenty minutes later, we pull up to the campsite where we gathered before and Mira punched me for saying I didn't have any friends. Now, surrounded by shades and Mediators I trust, I think that punch was well-deserved.

Mira's fist connects with a tree trunk. Her scream of fury tears through the air, startling the few migrating birds into silence.

"What happened?" I hurry to her, but jump back when she punches the tree again. It's only then that I see tear tracks on her face. My stomach sinks like an anvil.

"Gregor fucking took Wane."

37

IT TAKES A FEW seconds for what she's said to process.

Gregor took Wane.

Mira's cousin. He took Mira's cousin. He knows they're family.

"Where did he take her?" I ask. Images of her tied to the railroad tracks like some sort of shitty cartoon damsel in distress flash through my head, and I shove them away.

"He imprisoned her at the Summit. In the basement. You know where."

Devon looks almost as incensed as Mira, and Ripper has the look of the first swell of a tsunami.

Thank you, Alamea.

"It's going to be okay," I say, forgetting how that's the absolute worst thing to say to people in almost any situation.

Mira looks murder at me, and I take a step back. I do not want to be that tree trunk. I drop to one knee and dig in my left boot.

“I mean it, Mira. It’s going to be okay.” I pull out the key Alamea gave me. “Alamea taught me how to get out of there.”

All three Mediators turn and stare at me. The shades don’t seem to have any idea what’s happening, but they listen with curiosity.

Mira’s hands fall to her sides. “Alamea did what?”

“She gave me a way to get out of the prison. She knew people were trying to get her ousted, and she was afraid they’d throw me down there again. She didn’t want me to get trapped.” It’s only saying that out loud that I realize just how much Alamea has trusted me. “I can get Wane out.”

Mira grabs my hand. “Tell me you’re serious.” Her eyes plead with me. I’ve seen her pissed and I’ve seen her hurt, I’ve seen her silly and drunk and brave, but I’ve never seen her this scared.

“I’m serious,” I tell her softly. “I can get her out. I just need to find out what cell she’s in.”

“Seven eighteen,” says Ripper.

“How in the hells did you know that?” I gape at him.

“How do you think Mira found out what happened to Wane? I’ve got a buddy who’s a psychic. He’s known Alamea since he was a kid and trusts her with everything he is. He’s her go to. I think he saved your ass once.”

Jaryn. Jaryn the Wonder Psychic. Well, I’ll be a skunk’s uncle.

“This makes three times he’s saved my ass,” I say. “Remind me to buy that guy a drink.”

“If you get Wane back, drinks are on me for the next decade,” says Mira.

“Okay.” I look around at the five of them. “Let’s do this. How’s it going to happen?”

Devon drives an SUV, so we all pile into that. He keeps it a lot cleaner than my car. I’ve got my swords and the key, but I can’t walk into the Summit lobby fully armed in broad daylight without someone raising some eyebrows. As he drives back southward toward Nashville, we try to plan the prison break.

"You should go in the side door," Mira says. "The east entrance. There aren't cameras there like there are in the lobby. Your ID will scan and log your name, but it doesn't ping anyone."

"Good call. It's closer to the elevators down, too." I won't have to get close enough to the lobby to be on camera, and if we park off-premises, no one will know we're there. This time of day, the Summit should be pretty quiet. "When I get out with her, I'll text you. Bring the car down that side alley as close as you can get to the fence. If I have to throw her over, I will."

"Do you think he's hurt her?" Carrick asks, piping up for the first time. I know him well enough by now to hear the undercurrent in his voice, a reverberating rage that a seismograph would probably pick up.

Mira swallows and looks out the window. "If he has, I'll kill him myself."

The air in the car is heavy and thick.

We arrive just after one, and Devon pulls the SUV around the side streets to come at the Summit from the east. It's a strange view, to see the early afternoon sun glinting off the facets of the glass dome, refracting into rainbows that make it look as though the Summit is capped by a giant diamond.

He drops me off at the southeastern corner of the parking lot, and I hop out. I don't see anyone in their cars, and the lot is mostly deserted. I've only got my saber belted at my waist, and I wish I had on leathers even though it would make my still-sticky back into a nightmare.

I scan my ID at the eastern door and enter the Summit, looking around for any sign of movement.

No one's there, and I say a silent thank you that the elevators to the prison below are in an out-of-the-way corridor. I hit the button for the elevator, eyes alert and ears listening for any footsteps on the floors. Though the main lobby is marble, the eastern corridors are thin carpet. When the elevator arrives with a soft *ding*, I get in and hit the door close button.

Nothing happens. Those things aren't even connected to anything. Ugh.

I can feel the prickle of early perspiration beginning on my forehead again. Just the thought of going back down here makes my body want to reject me. I punch in the code. 743367.

The doors close. I hit the button for sub level seven.

I keep my hand on my sword's grip as the elevator descends. When it eases to a halt at sub level seven, I edge over to the side as the doors open.

Peering out, I wait, looking for any sign that the floor is occupied.

The plus side of a prison like this is that you don't need guards. I've never heard of any existing. The damn thing guards itself.

Stepping out of the elevator, I turn to watch the doors close. The wall fades into that seamless, taunting grey.

Terror takes me for a moment, and images of me trying the key and having it fail dance before me. A voice whispers, *what if she trapped you*?

I pull the key out of my pocket and press it.

Symbols blossom into being on the walls, and lines appear beneath my feet. On unsteady knees, I walk forward. I don't know how the cells are numbered, and at first I can't see any pattern. 742 is directly across from 711. I turn left along the nearest wall and watch the numbers until I can work out what they're doing.

It's a spiral. I find 725 and 724, and I work from that.

The prison is dizzying, just as it's meant to be. Even with direction, I feel lost, like I could wander forever down here.

It's never occurred to me to wonder what happens to the prisoners when they die. I don't even know how they're fed. My cell didn't even have a toilet.

719.

The next cell is 718.

My throat is dry, and my hand shakes as I raise the key to the wall. The hexagon of circles spins infinitely.

If this is a trap, and if it's Gregor in there waiting for me, I don't know what I'll do.

I put my hand up to the wall and press each circle, one after the other.

The wall opens.

Huddled in the obtuse corner immediately to my left is Wane.

SHE LOOKS UP AND skitters backward in the same motion, but her movements are sluggish. She's been drugged.

"Wane," I say. "It's me, Ayala Storme."

She blinks and looks at me. "I know it's fucking you. I'm sedated, not blinded."

I don't know what to say to that.

"Come on," I say finally. "I'm going to get you out of here."

I look up. I can't see the cameras, but I know they're there. I hope I'm out of range. I don't know if they only take a picture ever ten minutes or if there's a live feed that's motion-sensitive, but I think it's the former. They might be able to turn on a live feed, but keeping seven floors of feeds going constantly would be a large expense even for the Summit.

Even so, I don't want to stick around.

"Can you make it to me without help?" I ask. I can't go in there, even with the key between my fingertips.

Wane nods and gets to her feet. She uses the wall as a brace. Even though she's moving slowly, she's fairly steady. Enough that with my help, we can get out of here.

She makes it to me and grasps my arm at the elbow. "You smell wrong," she says.

"It's the anti-venom gel," I say.

"That'd do it."

With Wane on my left side, I hold up the key in my left hand and start tapping the circles. Just as I hit the last one, she teeters off balance. The key leaps from my fingertips and hits the ground.

It bounces right into the cell as the door becomes a wall.

“No, no, no, no, no,” I say.

Wane goes ashen, and she steadies herself on the wall where the door used to be. My right hand is still at the level where the spinning circles are, but I can’t risk reopening the cell. It could take too long, and the cameras could catch up to us—and we need to get out of here.

She looks around at the honeycomb of doom, and even more color drains from her skin. “We’re never going to get out,” she says.

It’s too close to the inside of my head for me to respond. I try to hold my hand in the same position, marking the distance between the circles that I just pressed.

“Lean against the wall,” I tell Wane.

I move to the center of the corridor, trying to steady my breathing. I can feel the walls, the dizziness, the knowledge that there are six levels between me and breaking ground into the light of day again. It’s hard to get a gauge on what the exact place in the corridor is that’s equidistant between the two walls. But I have to try.

I stretch out my arms straight on either side of me, trying to guess from the amount of space between my fingertips and the wall.

When I think I’m close, I kneel. My back itches all over, and I think it’s only partially because of the gel that’s starting to peel.

My fingers touch the floor. I press once, twice. Then again, a half inch away. Once, twice. Again. Once, twice.

I want to close my eyes, and my breath races in and out of my lungs. Once, twice.

Once, twice.

Nothing.

Once, twice.

Once, twice.

Against the wall, Wane has her back pressed to it, and her eyes are closed, her lips trembling. “You can do it, Ayala,” she says.

Once, twice.

Nothing.

Once, twice.

I move my hand just a hairsbreadth to the left.

Once, twice.

Nothing.

Back to the right, slightly more.

Once, twice.

The circles light up. With a strangled cry, I press the rest of the circles. The walls and floor come alive. There it is. The line. The way out.

I don't know how long it will last. I sling Wane's arm over my shoulder and we shuffle forward as fast as we can move. I don't know if her sedative starts to wear off or if she's just desperate enough, but we start to run. We turn when the glowing red line turns, and the elevator is before us. I press the circles on its wall as fast as I can and drag Wane in.

743367. I hit the ground floor button so hard I'm afraid it'll break and trap us. The doors slide close, and we begin to ascend.

"Thank you," Wane says. "Thank you."

"Don't thank me yet," I tell her as the elevator halts.

The doors slide open.

There are voices in the lobby. Angry ones.

38

"YOU IMPRISONED A CIVILIAN woman without my consent!" Alamea's voice booms through the lobby. "You have overstepped your bounds and your authority."

Fuckles.

I press my phone into Wane's hands. "Stay behind me and text Mira that we're out and need backup."

"We need backup?"

Grimly, I consider the exit routes. We could go back down to the sub levels and take the stairs up, coming up in a different corridor closer to the building exit, but I will not risk getting trapped down there. From the lobby, there's a straight line of sight down the hall we need to take to get out, and there's no stairwell where we are. I look at Wane, but I don't need to say anything. She starts texting Mira.

"I won't let them put you back in there," I murmur.

"We might both end up back in there," she says.

She had to say that, didn't she?

"They're coming," she whispers a moment later.

I've missed Gregor's first half of his response, but the words I hear next make me want to take Wane and run.

"You've come to your last day as Summit leader, Alamea Virgili," he says.

It could be just the two of them out there, or it could be more. The whole Summit could be crowded into the lobby, but I don't think that's the case.

I don't know what to do, but I do know this cannot happen. Gregor can't oust Alamea. He needs to pay for what he's done.

"Stay here."

"I can help," Wane says, and a golden light glows in her eyes.

"Pick your moment," is all I say to her. Then I walk out of the elevator bank and into the corridor.

The lobby of the Summit is not full of people.

The only people in it are Alamea, Gregor, the Mitten at the front desk, and Jaryn.

Only Jaryn sees me at first, and he gives me a look that is pure relief. He towers above Gregor and even Alamea in her heels. When he meets my eyes, I know he knew I was there all along. I mouth *thank you.*

He gives me a well-what-do-you-know sort of smile that tells me those were the last two words he ever expected to hear from me. I can't say I blame him.

I can be a real dick.

I stride into the lobby, back itching and head held as high as I can. "I know what you did."

My voice rings out through the cavernous space, and every pair of eyes finds me.

Gregor smirks and turns to Alamea as if he's just won a bet.

He doesn't realize I was talking to him.

"Gregor Gaskin," I say. "I'm speaking to you."

Gregor turns, his face incredulous. "What are you talking about, Storme? Wheedle told me he told you what happened, what Alamea's trying to do."

"Yeah, well, Wheedle's so full of shit he's overflowing." Even from across the lobby, my voice carries clearly, and the Mitten at the front desk looks positively terrified. He's the same MIT I saw a few weeks ago. Connor. No, Conroy.

"Storme," Gregor says. He takes a step in my direction, but stops when he sees my hand go to my hilt.

He may have the years of experience on me, but he's outnumbered and he knows it.

"Don't *Storme* me," I say. To my surprise, my voice falls an octave. Now, face to face with the man who set up to blackmail me, who's lied to me for month, who's used me, used the people I love, who's violated every single gods damned thing I stand for—I can't speak further. I feel as though words like *fury* and *rage* fall away when I look at this man. I have no words for what he's done, or for how I feel when I look at him.

My hand finds the hilt of my sword, and with it, my tongue finds my words.

"You lied to Carrick." I start with the easy thing. "You told him Miles was dead, with his head ripped off by a jeeling."

"Miles is dead," Gregor insists. "I saw him die. Storme, listen to me. Whatever Alamea's told you is wrong."

Alamea herself is strangely silent.

"Alamea?" I say. "Alamea hasn't told me shit. And sure, Miles is dead as a doornail. I'll be sure to tell him that when I see him again today."

Gregor's face goes white.

"You sold my friends to some rich sonofabitch and made them murder for you. You manipulated them into doing the one thing I worked with them so hard to teach them that they could live without. They know it is wrong, and you pulled their strings because you knew their guilt. You, Gregor Gaskin, are responsible for the murder of at least twenty norms who you told me we were charged to protect. Hells-worshippers or not, we were meant to protect them. And you took money to kill them."

I can see Jaryn's face, see in his eyes that he's looking into my memories and that he knows it's true. Gregor puts his hand in his pocket, nonchalantly leaning to the side.

"Is that what Miles told you?"

"I saw their bodies with my own eyes!"

Gregor chuckles.

For a moment, I doubt myself. I look behind him at Alamea, and fear snakes through me. What if I'm wrong? What if he's laughing at the absurdity of it? What if it really is Alamea behind this?

"You weren't supposed to see that, Ayala. For that, I'm sorry."

Jaryn's eyes widen, and his mouth drops open.

Too late.

A momentous crash shakes the air.

It takes a heartbeat for me to process what it was.

"Everybody take cover!" I yell the warning as loud as I can, diving back into the hallway just before the skylight from seven stories above us sends a rain of deadly glass shards plummeting down at us.

The glass hits the marble floor of the lobby with the sound of ten thousand champagne flutes crashing to the ground. Pieces hit and ricochet, some of them the size of my forearm even after they shatter.

Frantic, I look for Alamea and Jaryn. They were at the foot of the stairs, and somehow seem to have somersaulted over the railing to take cover beneath it. Gregor, it seems, knew exactly where to stand where the glass wouldn't reach him.

"Conroy, are you okay?" I can't see the Mitten, but I hear a thump from under the desk.

"I'm fine!"

"Stay the fuck down!"

Another sound reaches my ears, and I look up.

Three shades are swinging down story by story. Each of them is wearing a hat.

It's the shades who have been murdering people around the city. The shades who killed Grace's favorite regular. The ones who murdered the late night workers at Walden's Puddle. They've left bodies all over my city, my home, threatened people I care about.

Gregor did this. Gregor. The man who trained me since I was a child. Carrick and the others couldn't catch them because they were following Gregor's information, and Gregor didn't want his shades caught.

My breath hisses out between my teeth.

None of them are wearing shoes, but they ignore the glass on the floor when the first two hit. I recognize one of them, but he doesn't look at me.

I unsheathe my sword.

"Now, now, Ayala. Is that any way to greet your brother?"

My world becomes a tunnel.

Brother.

The third of the shades touches down in the center of the floor, just past the yin yang symbol. Everything around him blurs, but he is in perfect focus. He pulls off his hat.

Underneath it, his hair is bright yellow-orange.

Just like mine.

I look at his face, and I see my face. My nose. My ears, with their strange little cartilaginous nub at the top of the conch. His chin isn't quite the same, but the shape of his eyes is just like mine. Same pale skin. Same stance, even.

My breath is a shudder and a sob in one.

"Hello, Ayala," my shade half-brother says. "I'm Evis. I think I'll kill you now."

39

"MIGS, KELBY," GREGOR MOTIONS to Alamea and Jaryn under the stairs, and I lurch forward.

Evis clucks at me and wags his finger. "No, no."

Somewhere behind me, I hear another crash, but it doesn't register.

Under the stairs, I can see Alamea's grey slacks are stained with blood. A shard of glass protrudes from her leg. One of the shades—Migs or Kelby, I don't know—kicks her once in the head. Her eyes roll back, and she slumps over. They grab Jaryn by the arms.

I know psychics. They are empaths as much as they are telescopes into the minds of others. When the shades touch him, Jaryn screams.

Somehow his scream is louder than the sound of the breaking glass from the domed skylight above.

“Jaryn!” I scream his name and throw myself forward, but Evis intercepts me, his arms snapping into place around me, pinning mine to my side.

Every kill, every look of fear, every final, terrified release of bowels—I can almost see it flicker across Jaryn’s face as if it’s in my own mind. My entire body is shaking. Evis holds me against his chest, facing forward so I can’t look anywhere else.

They rip Jaryn’s arms off.

I can’t help the primordial sound that reverberates through me. Tears and snot and spit meld on my face as I feel a cool splatter of blood across my cheeks.

They take his legs next.

All I can see is blood and broken glass.

When Migs and Kelby cradle Jaryn’s head in their hands, Evis presses his cheek against my hair. “You can’t kill me now. I win. This is what I’m going to do to you.”

The heat of his body pinning me to him cannot stop the freezing chill that cascades over me.

Jaryn’s head leaves his body.

Something hits me hard from behind.

A snarl cuts through the sound of distant screaming—Conroy—and I get one glimpse of Gregor’s self-satisfied smirk vanishing before I hit the ground sideways.

I slide away on a bed of glass shards, released from the straitjacket of Evis’s grip. My hand is still clenched so tightly around my sword that I don’t think I could drop it if I wanted to. The back of my hand is bleeding from a dozen cuts, but I scramble to my feet.

Wane is a lion, and her jaws are clamped tight on Evis’s hip.

“I told you,” Gregor bellows from the stairs. “I told you she would never love you. I told you she would want you dead!”

Gregor looks at me, and I see him clearly for the first time. He is more hideous than a golgoth demon, more putrid than anything that has ever climbed out of the holes of hells. He meets my eyes as hatred and rage burn out every nerve ending in my body. I am going to kill him. He will feel the bite of my blade against his throat before I take off his head, and I will hold it by the hair and make him look me in the eyes with the last flutter of his eyelids.

Gregor looks at me and flinches.

Just for a moment. Just the tiniest flicker of movement. But he knows.

Dimly, I'm aware that the others are here. Saturn, Miles, and Carrick fall on Migs and Kelby, and I don't watch.

Mira pulls Alamea out from under the stairs.

"Wane, stop!" I come back to myself. Evis is fighting her back, but weakly. He's already lost a lot of blood.

Wane isn't listening to me.

"Wane!" I shriek her name and throw myself at her, kicking her off of Evis's body.

His fist catches me in the face. I drop my sword, but I don't care.

"Evis," I say. "I don't want you dead."

He punches me again, and my head shudders with the pain.

"I don't want you dead! I never wanted you dead!" I yell it at him. His face is anger, but I know what Gregor did.

I know how Gregor made him kill.

I know why he targeted places and people who mattered to me. Because they mattered to me, and Gregor told him he didn't.

I know what I need to do.

"Evis." I reach out and touch his shoulder with the tips of my fingers. "Gregor lied. I never wanted you dead."

"Ayala," Mira says, her voice troubled.

Evis and I are surrounded.

I can't see Gregor, and right now I don't care. Mira, Saturn, Ripper, Devon, Wane, Carrick—they form a ring around me and my brother.

My brother.

I reach out again, and I touch his shoulders one by one.

He watches me, his eyes assessing my every move. Again I feel myself held immobile against his chest, feel the heat of his body and the warmth of his breath as he tells me he's going to kill me before I can kill him.

Fear still crawls under my skin, seeps through our joined gaze.

But I don't care.

"You're safe with me," I tell him.

Evis is staring at me now, his own eyes full of fear, the anger vanishing into terror.

"I don't hate you. I don't want you dead. I didn't know you were here and wasn't even sure you existed. I should have looked for you. I should have tried harder. You shouldn't have had to meet me this way." I can't stop the tears from rolling down my cheeks now. "I never would have asked you to kill like that. I never would have lied to you like he did."

My own anger tries to boil back up, but I force it back to a simmer. I can't let Evis see it.

I toss my other sword away. It skates between Carrick and Ripper's legs.

"I don't hate you, Evis. Give me a chance to love you." I'm aware of Wane and Mira side by side, of the bond they have. They are family. I've never had one. A yearning comes over me, and I don't know what to do. All I know is that this is my brother, and if he can be saved, I will save him.

My cheek throbs, and I can feel it swelling even now. My lip is puffy and fat.

"Please," I say. I don't even know what words are about to come out. "Please don't let him take our family away from us."

Looking into Evis's eyes, I have no way of knowing what he sees. I never knew our mother, but he has her memories.

Looking into Evis's eyes, I feel him like a buzz of a horsefly next to my skin. I will him to see that I mean it.

"She wanted me," he says, as if he can tell what I'm thinking.

"I'm sure she did," I say, because for whatever the fuck reason hells-zealots sign up for this, that's for sure.

"She wanted me to find you," says Evis.

"What did you say?"

Did my mother want him to kill me? Confusion swirls in my head, and I can't think. Could she have been so ashamed of birthing a Mediator that she volunteered to die to give a shade life just to find me and end mine?

But Evis is shaking his head, again as if he knows what's in mine. "She missed you."

He reaches out a hand, tentative and slow.

His fingers touch my shoulder.

THERE ARE TOO MANY people in my apartment, and half of them have bare butts.

Evis is in my room, asleep on my bed. He shook for a long time, holding my hand. I lost track of how many times I tell him that I want him alive, that I don't hate him. Nana curled up right next to him, and I don't know which of us was more surprised.

I try to push what he's done out of my mind. He killed norms purely because Gregor told him to. But then again, almost all the shades I know did the very same. Maybe even for less reason.

The tension in my living room is like a newly stretched guitar string.

I close the door, leaving Evis and Nana to rest.

Alamea limps past me and coats the cracks in my bedroom door with dust. By now, I'm familiar with the ear-popping that accompanies the spell, but everyone else jumps.

Except Carrick, whose face looks like a thundercloud that swallowed Eeyore.

"We can speak freely," Alamea says. "But we don't have much time. I have to return to the Summit."

Mira, Devon, and Ripper are all on the couch. Wane—back in human form and dressed—is perched on the end of the sofa next to Mira, and the shades all hover by the balcony door as if they have to have an escape route pinned down.

“Gregor is gone,” Alamea says. “He was last seen heading west outside of town. I’ve communicated to the local police departments and sheriff departments outside the city that he is to be apprehended at all costs, and I’ve put out a bulletin to all other Summit leaders as well.”

The last part is a little strange to me, since he can’t go far.

“This is going to destroy the Summit,” says Devon. His face is chiseled deeply with worry, and Ripper nods.

Alamea shakes her head. “I don’t quite think so.” A small smile appears on her lips, though the skin around her eyes stays smooth and unwrinkled. “I think anyone who supported Gregor will shortly be very chagrined.”

It dawns on me what she’s talking about only half a second before Mira, and we say in unison, “Cameras.”

Understanding ripples out, and the tension in the room relaxes minutely.

I dance a mental jig at the thought of Ben Wheedle finding out.

The cameras in the Summit lobby will show everything that happened. Every last second.

“What about Evis?” Ripper says.

“What about him?” I ask, even though I already know.

He pauses, and all eyes in the room look anywhere but me. “Please take what I have to say with some…grace, Storme.”

I nod, nervous.

“The cameras. While they definitely incriminate Gregor, he’s not the only one they will damn.”

Oh.

Migs and Kelby won’t be enough. Knowing that they are dead will put people’s minds at ease, but Evis still lives.

The weight of Ripper’s words grows heavier with each tick of the clock on the wall.

“No,” I say.

“Ayala, you need to consider it.”

“I won’t.”

"Everyone's going to be calling for his head. You know that." This time it's Alamea talking.

"No," I say again.

"He murdered innocent people."

"I won't become what Gregor promised him I would be!" I yell it, and in the seconds that follow, silence reigns.

I try to collect myself, try to think of words of reason.

"They'll see what Gregor did to him," I say, and Mira nods. That nod means more to me than just about anything in the world right now. I give her a grateful look.

The shades look uncomfortable, and I meet Miles's eyes. I know he killed norms before we found him. Most of them did. They didn't know what else to do. They were hungry and alone in a strange world.

"A reason is not an excuse," Alamea says softly.

"I never said it was." My words sound hollow in my ears. "I won't kill him."

"We would never make you do it."

Tears burn at my eyes. "I can't let you kill him. He deserves a chance."

Alamea's eyes search me, and I can tell she knows I mean it. "Remember what I told you before."

I know exactly what she's referring to, and I nod without thinking.

That's all anyone else says on the subject.

I have a brother, and he will know what it means to have a sister who loves him. If he dies, it will not be at my hands or at the hands of any of my friends if there is anything in my power that can prevent it.

Friends.

It's strange, how just days ago, Alamea thought I had none.

Now I have friends. And family. And a bunny.

I'm downright domesticated.

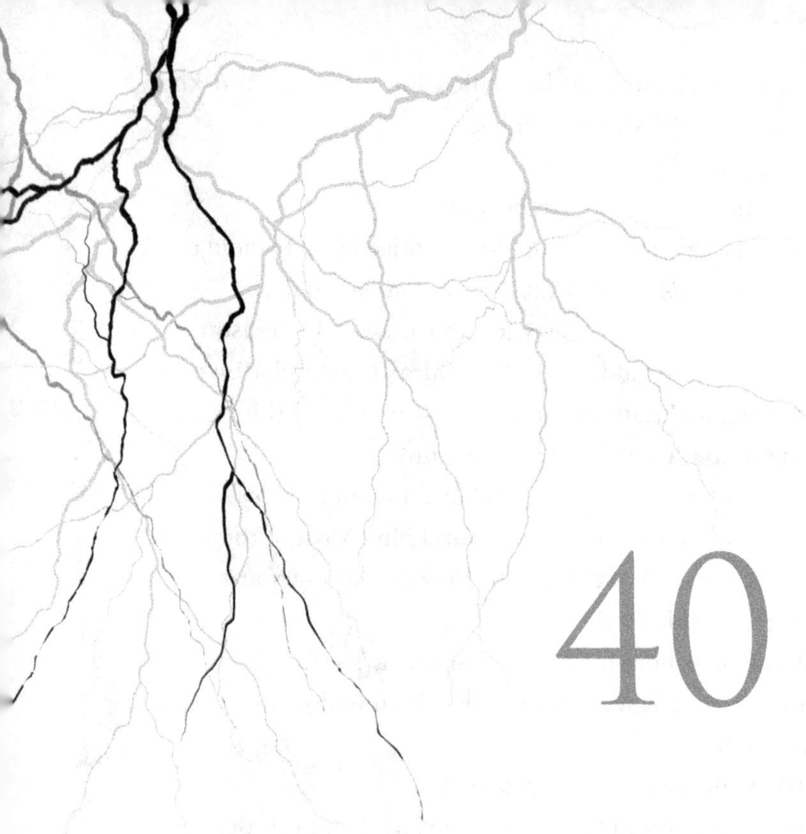

40

ALAMEA LEAVES FIRST, HEADING back to the Summit to prepare for the inevitable fallout.

Ripper and Devon leave after that, both with hugs for me and handshakes for my shade friends. Wane goes with them. I think she's not sure how to take me kicking her off of Evis.

The shades vanish after that. I know without asking that they need to find the others and tell them what happened—and what Gregor did.

Soon it's just me and Mira in the apartment. I crack the door to check on Evis and to break the spell Alamea cast. I don't want more secrets from him right now. I sit down in the corner of the couch at the opposite end from Mira, and we clink glasses of sake.

"So," she says. "You have a shade for a brother."

I nod, not knowing what else to do.

"I get the feeling you're not entirely surprised."

That makes me shift uncomfortably in my seat. "No," I say carefully. "I'm not. Back when this all started, when Gregor asked me to look into the disappearances of those men and women and Lena Saturn and all that, it was because he found out I'd been looking for my mother."

Mira's eyes go wide, and she sets down her glass. "You went looking for your mother?"

Heat effuses my cheeks. "I was curious. When I found her name, it was in the papers. She'd disappeared six months before."

"Gregor knew."

I nod. "Gregor knew. I think he planned to blackmail me if I didn't cooperate, but I played right into his fucking plot, so he didn't have to."

Disgust wrinkles Mira's face. I can see a few pink spots on her left cheek where the markat spit scarred. The entire left side of her neck is pink as well, and I know the line continues down her chest and beneath her breast, just as I'll bear the scars on my back for a long time. Maybe forever. It takes a lot to scar a Mediator, but markat venom'll do it. I'm going to start carrying the anti-venom in my belt.

"So you know," she says. "What it's like to find them."

"Yes." I pause, then lift my glass to her. "Thank you."

"For what?"

"For sticking up for him. I don't know what I'd do if everyone had tried to take him away." The thought makes me swallow hard enough that the sake burns my tonsil. "He didn't come into this world a murderer. He didn't ask for this. None of them did."

"You don't have to explain yourself to me," says Mira.

"I know," I say. And I mean it.

MIRA LEAVES AFTER A while, and I sit on the couch, quietly reading one of Carrick's favorite books.

My face is stiff and sore where Evis punched me, but it'll heal.

I take a short break to call and make sure Alice and Laura and the others are aware they can go home and return to work, then I go back to the book. Carrick's right. It's a good book.

Carrick comes home not long after dark, and he comes right to the sofa and sits beside me, not at the other end.

To his credit, he doesn't ask if I'm okay.

He just picks up a different book, and we read in silence.

Forty-five minutes later, my phone starts blowing up, and I find out exactly what Alamea meant by consequences.

She's sent out a video bulletin to all Mediators in the Summit territory. I grab my tablet and pull it up.

The first part is the video footage of what happened in the lobby. I skip that, feeling green. I can't watch Jaryn die again. Conroy got moved directly to debriefing and trauma care, which is actually something we have, and I always forget about it.

The second part is a message directly from Alamea herself.

"It is with extreme sadness that I inform you that our friend and loyal employee, Jaryn Trident, was killed today. He was a long term friend and someone I admired deeply. He will be missed, even more for who he was as a friend and person than for the services he provided to our Summit and our cause.

"Today I must also tell you, that from this moment forward, Gregor Gaskin is a traitor to the Summit of Nashville and the world Summit at large. He is charged with conspiracy to murder; willful, malicious, and intentional murder in the first degree; fraud; conspiracy to accept monetary compensation for murder in the first degree; wrongful death; conspiracy to manipulate vulnerable persons with complete disregard for human life; kidnapping; wrongful imprisonment of a civilian; obfuscation of Summit imperatives while acting as a representative thereof; exploitation of vulnerable persons; and finally, defaming in action the imperatives, mission, dignity, and good standing of this Summit."

The charges used by the Summit sound similar to those used in criminal and civil legal proceedings in the norm world, though for us, the last weighs much heavier than it might to anyone else. Alamea pauses and looks right into the camera.

"Finally, it is with great sadness that I inform you that from this day forth, Mediator Ayala Storme is hereby stripped of any and all honors bestowed upon her. She is henceforth censured by this Summit. She did knowingly and willingly harbor a person who was a danger to herself and her community. No direct punishment outside of this censure will be enacted. Ayala Storme is henceforth unknown to this Summit."

My heart stops.

Carrick reaches out and snags the tablet before it falls from my hands. My phone's still blowing up, buzzing relentlessly next to my leg.

She actually did it.

Ben was right.

I pick up my phone, more because I don't know what else to do. Mira. Ripper. Devon. Even Jax and Saturn.

And a surprise.

Alamea.

I open it, my fingers shaking.

Delete this immediately. Check your bank balance—you're still on the clock. Stay out of sight. Get out of town. This is not over, and you will be needed. You will always have a friend in me.

I delete the text, but not until after I take a screenshot.

If I don't, I won't believe it later.

I ignore the other texts and open my banking app.

And nearly drop my phone.

I'm not poor, and I have investments and hefty savings. But I'm not rich, either.

Or at least I wasn't.

She's put a quarter million dollars in my account.

I SPEND THE REST of the evening trying to get a mover who will agree to help me put all my stuff in storage.

No one will take me.

I try begging. I try pretty-pleasing. And considering what Alamea gave me, I try outright bribery. Not a single mover will agree to help me.

Even though the Summit announcement only went out to Mediators, word travels quickly, and my name is apparently on the evening news.

I can't call Mira. I can't endanger her by letting her be seen with me. Not her, or Ripper, or Devon.

I'm shaking and about to cry when Carrick takes my phone from me and points to the balcony.

It's full of shades, crowded onto the small space shoulder to shoulder.

When Evis wakes up, they all greet him, and though they were all hunting him not long ago, they somehow manage to reassure him that they don't mean him harm.

I sit with him again for a while in my room while everyone bustles around, and after a time, he speaks.

"I'm sorry," he says. "I don't want you to hate me even though I was going to kill you. I only wanted to because Gregor said you hated me and that you were going to find me and kill me if you could. He said you had all the other shades for brothers, and you didn't need me. He said I had to kill you first."

I decide in that moment that I'm going to kill Gregor just a little bit deader for that.

"He lied," I say. "These shades are my friends, and they might be kind of like my family, but they're not my brother. You are."

It's weird, seeing my face on someone else. We're not exactly the same, but we could be fraternal twins easily.

"I'm the one who's sorry," I say to Evis quietly. "I should have searched for you. I think I was afraid I would find you dead."

I think I was afraid I'd find him as I did, murdering the populace. But right now I don't care how I found him, even though the memory of him telling me he was going to kill me like Migs and Kelby killed Jaryn will probably haunt me forever. That's what trust is, I suppose. Knowing someone can hurt you and giving them the chance to.

We're both taking a chance on each other.

Saturn and Udo go out and return with heaps of boxes from liquor stores, and they start packing up my things.

"Go," Miles tells me. He pushes my suitcases in front of him instead of pulling them. "You and Evis and Carrick, go. We'll take care of everything."

"I don't know where to go," I say dumbly.

Saturn presses a paper into my hand. It's covered with his precise handwriting. There's an address on it. Southern Kentucky. "Jax is there. He found a place to live. You can stay with him."

Jax found a place to live.

"Nana," I say. She's in her cage, wuffling at the bars and pawing at the latch. I reach through and scratch between her ears.

"Mira will take her," he says. "You'll see her again."

I don't know if it's because Nana was a gift from Mason or because I'm used to her little red furry body hopping around everywhere or because I feel like everything I know has been severed, but the tears spill over, and I cry, dropping tears onto Nana's fur.

I feel about three years old, like I'm just entering training for the first time and they just handed me my first sword, too heavy to lift.

It's Evis who makes the tears stop. He puts his hand on my shoulder, his other turning my face to look at him.

"You did this for me." The wonder is written across his features, and it stops my tears like turning off a faucet. "You don't hate me."

I shake my head. "I don't hate you. Not at all."

I wonder how many times I'll have to say it before he really believes me.

I make Carrick drive us to Kentucky. He doesn't have a license, but he learned almost a hundred years ago, so he's had plenty of practice.

We arrive at two in the morning, and Jax greets us. It's a small double wide, and he says he met a nice old woman who wanted to go to Hawaii and asked him to house sit. He shows us the note she left him, her three aquariums of fish, and the goat out back Jax says hates him.

"The goat's mean," he says. "But I can't eat it."

Jax puts Evis in the bedroom with him and shows him where to find the chest freezer full of venison. He's been hunting, and it's full to the brim.

There's only canned fruit cocktail, ramen, and instant rice in terms of Ayala food, and I'm going to have to go to the store unless I want to share with the shades.

I guess if I cook it, it's not that bad an idea, though I don't want to take their food supply. They get cranky when they're peckish.

Jax has Carrick and I in the master bedroom, which is weird to me until Carrick rolls out a sleeping bag on the floor at the foot of the bed.

He pulls out the giant book I've seen him reading.

"What is that?" I ask.

"Old magic." He holds it out to me, and I take it. "I brought it with me from England. A witch coven there gave it to me long ago."

I can't make out the writing. It must be Middle English or older. I hand it back to him. "Anything useful in there?"

"Many useful things."

"Like what?" Asking him about this gives me a chance to not think about Nashville or the panic that threatens to leap onto my back at any given moment.

"Curing illnesses, finding lost things, making monsters, gaining strength."

"Gaining strength?" I ignore the making monsters bit. I don't want to know.

"You certainly don't need more of that," he says.

"I feel weak," I say. Even the words feel weak coming out of my mouth.

"You are anything but that," he says.

"The entire world Summit will be against me now. And even though Alamea said no further punishment, I will have to avoid Mediators. Some will try and kill me on sight and call it an accident. Like Gregor did with Miles." I take a shaky breath in, trying to wrap my mind around this being not a dream or a nightmare and just being real. "If there is anything you think might help, please tell me. Even if it's just a lark."

Carrick is silent for a long moment.

"There is a spell. It's a variation on the one that created the original Mediators."

I start at that. I knew we came from magical origins, that our genes were altered to make us our own species, *homo sapiens libra*, but I've never given it much thought. "What is it?"

He hesitates, then flips through the book. It takes him several minutes to find it. Some of the pages are dogeared, but not this one. The facing page is taken up by a large design. At it's center is a stylized yin yang. It spirals out in lines like the branches of a tree—or its roots.

"It's a tattoo," he says.

"What does it do?" The lines of the design capture my eye, make me follow them. I go over to Carrick and reach out, tracing them with a finger.

"It increases strength, speed, stamina."

"Just a tattoo can do that? Some ink on the skin?" My skin tingles at the thought; I've never gotten any tattoos.

"Not ink," he says. "Blood."

My finger halts on the page, and I pull it back. "Whose blood?"

"A demon," he says.

I flinch.

"Or a shade."

I meet his eyes. A tattoo of shade blood that could make me stronger, faster, give me more endurance.

I remember Alamea's text. *This is not over, and you will be needed.*

And the reason for her depositing the equivalent of two years' salary into my account.I'm on the clock.

Double-0 Ayala, reporting for duty.

"Let's do it," I say.

Carrick looks at me, shock written across his face. "You mean it."

"The demons aren't going away. Gregor is out there somewhere, and we'd be foolish to think he won't be back and bring hell on wheels with him. So yes, I mean it." I point at the design. "Where does it go?"

He winces. "Your back. Over your spine, which gives you strength to stand and connects your nerves to your whole body."

My back. Which is covered in still-healing scars.

"Do it."

Evis volunteers his blood, and Carrick goes into town in my car and breaks into the single tattoo parlor there. He brings back a machine, and I don't question him. He's lived four hundred years and says he knows how to do this, so I'll trust him.

I'll buy the tattooist a new gods damn set of machines if she wants.

I lie facedown on the bed, Evis at my side, watching his blood drip into a little sterile pot on the nightstand.

He squeezes my hand.

The needle touches down.

Some hours later, it's finished.

Carrick gently cleans it with soap he stole, covers it with a thin layer of ointment, snaps a picture with my phone, and bandages the tattoo. It takes a lot of bandages. My back is alight from the nape of my neck to my tailbone.

Evis and Jax retreat, each of them gently touching my shoulder—a safe distance from where the needle traveled.

Carrick shows me the picture. The design is meticulous, and he worked quickly. It's deep red, almost seeming to glow. It's going to clash with my hair and eyes. I guess nobody's aesthetics are perfect.

"You'll heal fast," Carrick says. "Probably faster than normal."

Now that he mentions it, the swelling from the bruiser Evis gave me has already gone down, and my lip is normal size.

I look up at him, and he jumps.

"What?"

He shakes his head. "It's probably just the light."

"Bullshit. You can see in the dark." I get up painfully, shuffling to the large antebellum vanity that's out of place in this modular home. I flip on the lamp and look in the mirror.

I immediately turn the light back off, swallowing hard.

I feel different. It's hard to put my finger on, but it's there, like a traveling itch.

I've just made a choice that will change everything for the rest of my life, and everyone will know.

Not because they'll see the tattoo.

Because of my eyes.

They're indigo.

ACKNOWLEDGMENTS

In the dedication for the first book in Ayala's series, I wrote, "To Kristin and Jes, who always keep fighting." This was for two of my dear friends who, like me, had a very-very-very hard year in 2014 and early 2015. Two months after *Storm in a Teacup* came out, the two stars of my favorite television show *Supernatural,* launched a t-shirt campaign called Always Keep Fighting to benefit those who suffer and survive every day with invisible illnesses like depression, bipolar disorder, anxiety, and more.

This book is very much a product of an ongoing fight, as is Ayala's life.

As someone who lives with invisible illness, it was important to me to include this note. That little synchronicity between my last book's dedication and Jared Padalecki and Jensen Ackles' campaign fits very well with one of the major themes in Ayala's story as well as the show *Supernatural.* When I first wrote *Storm in a Teacup*, I had never seen a single episode of *Supernatural.* (Yes, yes, I know. I lived under a rock from 2005-2012.) Though I am unaffiliated with the show, I believe deeply in the message shared by Jared and Jensen to keep fighting.

It's hard. Life likes to kick us in the ass, and unlike Ayala, we can't physically kill our demons. We have to live with them, keep them at bay, and sometimes fight them off without swords.

Sometimes it can feel like we have our own personal hellshole that follows us around, spewing out demons faster than we can kill them.

This book is for you. Bravery isn't about not being scared—it's about keeping on when you are. It's about looking the monsters in the eye sometimes, crying sometimes, and yes, sometimes making butt jokes and swearing until you laugh.

I urge you, if you're reading this and your personal fight feels like it's too much to bear, to reach out to someone. There are people who want nothing more than to talk to you when you are hurting and to fight beside you.

You can find international suicide hotlines at *www.suicide.org*, including specific lines for LGBTQIA youth, military veterans, and more. Reach out. There are people ready to reach back.

ABOUT THE AUTHOR

EMMIE MEARS WRITES THE books they always needed to read about characters they wish they could be. Emmie is multilingual, autistic, agender, and a bad pescetarian.

Emmie makes their home on planet Earth, and (soon) more specifically in Glasgow, Scotland. They live with their partner and two rescued kitties who call Emmie and John a forever home.

However you felt about the book, please consider leaving a review on Goodreads or the site of your favorite retailer (or if you're feeling extra angelic, both). Reviews are golden to author-folk. Thank you for reading and for supporting!

Visit the author's website at:
www.emmiemears.com

CPSIA information can be obtained
at www.ICGtesting.com
Printed in the USA
LVHW041159300920
667477LV00002BA/65

9 781946 006882